ST. JOHN'S FOLLY

Kathryn R. Wall's Bay Tanner Mysteries

In For a Penny
And Not a Penny More
Perdition House
Judas Island
Resurrection Road
Bishop's Reach
Sanctuary Hill
The Mercy Oak
Covenant Hall
Canaan's Gate
Jericho Cay
St. John's Folly

ST. JOHN'S FOLLY

A BAY TANNER MYSTERY

KATHRYN R. WALL

BellaRosaBooks

ST. JOHN'S FOLLY

ISBN 978-1-62268-041-2

Printed in the United States of America on acid-free paper.

Also available as e-book: ISBN 978-1-62268-042-9.

Cover artwork courtesy of James Hartley Smith.
Gazebo image copyright: Darryl Brooks 2013, used under license from Shutterstock.com.

Book design by Bella Rosa Books.

10   9   8   7   6   5   4   3   2   1

In loving memory of my husband, Norman
Always in my heart

AUTHOR'S NOTE

In 2011, my beloved husband Norman lost his battle with Alzheimer's disease. It was a long, painful journey for both of us, and I felt for a long while as if I'd be unable to write again. When I finally decided to plunge into another Bay Tanner mystery, I knew I'd need to honor our struggle and perhaps use the novel format to impart some hard-won insight into this terrible disease. I hope I've been able to do that without sounding as if I'm standing in the pulpit. As I and my fellow baby boomers age, dementia in all its forms could well turn into an epidemic. It's said that knowledge is power, and I've tried, in my own small way, to bring additional awareness to the problem through my fictional characters.

Memory Matters is a real organization here on Hilton Head. It began in a local church as a respite care program for those dealing with the issue, allowing exhausted caregivers to have a few hours of relief each week. From there, it has grown into a nationally recognized program of support, care, and resources that should be the model for other communities to follow. You can learn about their history and the wonderful work they do at *www.memory-matters.org.*

I am especially indebted to Sharon and Marshall Miller and to Sheila and Chuck Mahony for their donations to Mem-ory Matters in a recent auction fundraiser. Their generosity will help fund this vital program and allow it to reach even more dementia sufferers and their families. I hope Marshall and Sheila enjoy the characters named for them.

I would also like to thank two local people who have con-tributed their time and expertise. Natalie Hefter of the Coastal Discovery Museum allowed me to use her name in *St. John's Folly.* She is a wonderful resource for information about Hilton

Head Island before it turned into a world-class resort and was very helpful in my research into the hunt club era. For a fascinating look at this time period in our island's history, check out *Hilton Head Island (Images of America: South Carolina)*, which Natalie edited.

My friend Jim Smith is an accomplished photographer whose work appears in local galleries and publications. His generosity in providing my publisher with wonderful images for the covers of my later books, including this one, has been a special gift. I hope you're enjoying his work as much as I am.

To all of my readers who have blessed me with their condolences and special words of comfort and kindness, a simple *Thank you* seems inadequate. Without your encouragement, I would never have had the confidence to begin writing again. I can't tell you how much I appreciate your taking the time to share your thoughts with me.

A special nod to my sister Lynne for the title, proving that beach walks can be very productive.

And thank you, Barry, for giving me the courage to start again, in so many ways.

CHAPTER
ONE

"'It was the best of times, it was the worst of times.'"

I tried valiantly to control a snort, but a hint of it must have risen above the soft *shushing* of the waves.

Dr. Nedra Halloran jerked herself upright on the chaise. "Lydia Baynard Simpson Tanner! Don't you dare mock me!"

That made me laugh out loud. "Oh, for God's sake, Neddie. Just because you had one required English lit course sprinkled in with all that psych stuff doesn't mean you get to be offended on behalf of Charles Dickens. *A Tale of Two Cities.* It's just so . . . predictable."

My old college roommate grunted and flopped herself back down. I noticed a couple of pimply teenagers, boogie boards tucked under their arms, slowing down to admire the view. Red-haired, thoroughly Irish, and even in her forties sporting a voluptuous figure, Neddie often turned heads during our infrequent sojourns on the beach. The fact that the straps of her green bikini top dangled alongside a generous spill of bosom didn't seem to faze her in the least, but it certainly could draw a crowd.

"Okay, smartass," she said, pulling her wide-brimmed straw hat down lower to shelter the delicate skin of her snub nose, "what's yours?"

We'd been fiddling away a glorious late October afternoon, sipping on warm iced tea and edging back away from the incoming tide at regular intervals. By all rights, I should have been at work, overseeing my staff of three at Simpson & Tanner, Inquiry Agents. But being the boss had its perks, including screwing off on a Thursday if the spirit moved me. I felt guilty about it, of course, because I tend to feel guilty about pretty much everything, sooner or later. The truth was I had an ulterior motive, one I knew Neddie had probably seen through about thirty seconds into my call inviting myself over to the Sea Cloisters off Folly Field

Road. As Savannah's leading child psychologist—and one of my oldest friends—she was pretty quick to spot bullshit, especially mine.

"'Last night I dreamt I went to Manderley again.' It's an easy one," I said, just to goad her a little more. From that first encounter at Northwestern, more years ago than I wanted to count, our relationship had relied on jabs and taunts to cover our embarrassingly deep feelings for each other. Neither one of us was very good at feelings. At least not our own.

Neddie hummed when she was thinking, an annoying habit she'd retained from our early years on campus.

"If you ever got your nose out of medical journals," I said, stretching my long frame out to its full five feet ten, "you'd recognize that in a heartbeat."

I rose up on my elbows and checked the gently rolling Atlantic. Hilton Head Island sits sheltered in the wide curve at the bottom of South Carolina's meandering coastline. It's a lousy place for surfing, but hurricanes tend to slide on by us and slam the poor folks on the Outer Banks to our north. Even Kitty, which had come way too close for comfort the previous month, had done us relatively minor damage.

"Give up?" I asked around a swallow of tepid tea.

"No, I don't give up." Neddie's hand fumbled in her beach bag, and I swung my legs over the side of the chaise.

"Oh, no you don't! Put that phone down. Googling is not allowed. The Judge would have a cow."

My father, Judge Talbot Simpson, and I had played a similar game with quotations, points being awarded for a correct citation of both author and source. His recent death had left a void in my life that had surprised me with its depth. Our old antebellum mansion on St. Helena Island just off Beaufort had become the repository of both my late mother's horde of antiques and generations of family junk as well as a hollow place of both terrible and wonderful memories. Only the comforting presence of our longtime housekeeper, Lavinia Smalls, made my visits home bearable.

And the reason for my need of Neddie's professional advice.

"*Rebecca*. Daphne du Maurier. It's a classic gothic mystery," I said, mostly to move things along.

"Trust you to come up with something gory. Next time I get to pick the category. Famous first lines is too obscure."

I let it go and turned to face her. "Listen, I need to ask you something."

Without even glancing my way, she said, "I know. You hardly ever call me unless you're in trouble."

That stopped me, mostly because she had a point. I wiped a drop of sweat from the end of my nose and stared over her shoulder at a flock of pelicans riding the soft breeze in loose formation.

Neddie let the silence linger a moment before she said, "Julia?"

The mention of my half-sister sent shivers dancing along my spine, in spite of the warmth of the autumn sun. "Yes," I said softly. "What do you think?"

"About what?"

"Damn it, Neddie, you know about what."

I had hoped she wouldn't make me spell it out. My poor sister, her intellectual development stunted by a horrifying trauma that touched too close to home, seemed not to have progressed much beyond that of a ten-year-old. She had been cared for by her late mother's best friend for decades in an old rice plantation outside Jacksonboro on the Charleston road. But time and financial worries had worn down the aging Elizabeth Shelly, and a few weeks after our brush with Hurricane Kitty, she and Julia had come to live at Presqu'isle, my old family home.

Where, just a few days later, Elizabeth had tumbled down the grand staircase. To her death.

"You're going to make me say it, aren't you?"

"Look at me." She pulled her sunglasses down to the end of her nose and studied my face. "If I seriously thought Julia had anything to do with Miss Lizzie's accident, don't you think I would have said something already?" When I didn't immediately respond, she added, "Don't you?" with a flash of anger in her dark green eyes.

"She's changed." I squirmed a little and dropped my gaze. "Julia, I mean. Haven't you noticed?"

The sigh was a combination of indulgence and annoyance.

"Of course I've noticed. She's much more relaxed. She and Lavinia seem to be getting on well, and I'm hopeful she's going to continue to make progress with her PTSD. Give it some time, Bay. She's undoubtedly, in her own way, still mourning her loss."

I resisted the urge to fire back. *Sorrow* was not the look I'd seen on my sister's face as she spied on me from the doorway into the attics. Self-satisfied would have been more accurate, at least in my estimation. But Neddie was the expert. And I trusted her. Mostly.

"I worry about Lavinia," I whispered, startled to hear myself actually put it into words.

"Bay, listen to me. This is crazy, and that's not a word I throw around lightly. Julia loved her Miss Lizzie. She may not have been able to articulate her feelings properly, but that doesn't mean they aren't there. You've seen her with Lavinia the past few weeks. I'd say those two have bonded pretty well, under the circumstances."

She paused, and I knew she expected me to *validate* what she'd just said. Hell, I hadn't spent all those dorm years cooped up with a psych major without picking up some of the jargon, even though I had a difficult time buying into a lot of it.

Neddie's voice dropped. "Are you sure there's not a little jealousy thing going on here? After all, you've had Lavinia to yourself for a long time now."

I could feel my anger boiling, a hard knot in the center of my chest, and it took considerable effort to speak calmly. "I'm not even going to dignify that with an answer."

"Okay, okay. Maybe I'm out of line there. Occupational hazard. Look, honey, I don't know how you got fixated on this notion that Julia is somehow responsible for Miss Lizzie's death, but you need to put it out of your head. Your sister needs you. You're the only living relative she has left."

That stung. In a strange twist of karma or fate or whatever, *my* mother had been at least marginally responsible for the death of Julia's and the trauma that had trapped my half-sister's childish personality in a middle-aged woman's body. Not to mention our mutual straight-arrow father who had slipped off his charger big time all those years ago. When I laid it out like that, it sounded like some tacky Southern soap opera, and I was in it up to my eyeballs, like it or not.

Without making a conscious decision, I jumped up and slid my feet into my beach sandals. "I have to go."

"Oh, come on, Bay, don't get pissy on me. You wanted my professional opinion, and I'm giving it to you. Lighten up and try to establish a good relationship with Julia. I'll keep seeing her, and I think you'll be amazed at how much progress she makes over the next few months. At least give her a chance."

Put like that, I didn't seem to have much choice. But my misgivings and suspicions were going to be a long time receding. Neddie hadn't seen Julia's face in the half-light of the attic or that cat-that-ate-the-canary smile. I'd back off, but I would keep my eyes open.

"I'll try," I said, stuffing the towel into my bag and hefting it onto my shoulder. "Thanks for listening. Your new condo is fabulous, by the way. I'll call you."

Without waiting for a reply, I slogged through the small strip of loose sand back toward the tall building that housed Neddie's fourth-floor hideaway with the spectacular view of the Atlantic. Originally, she had planned it as an occasional weekend pied-à-terre, but her stays had gotten longer and longer. Good for me, as it made it easy for her to drive over to Presqu'isle, mooch a meal from Lavinia, and spend her allotted hour with Julia. Driving into Savannah wasn't my favorite outdoor sport, especially with my phobia about suspension bridges.

I tossed my bag into the back of the Jaguar and changed into un-sandy shoes. As I slipped behind the wheel, I spotted the envelope, the same pale blue as the previous ones. I flung open the door, reached out, and snatched it from beneath the windshield wiper.

I'd shown the first one to Neddie, expecting her to laugh and come out with something like, "Oooooo, a secret admirer!" Instead, she'd looked at it for a long while, chewing on her bottom lip before handing it back to me.

"Creepy," she'd said. "Any idea who it's from?"

"Not a clue."

"Has Red seen it?"

"No."

My husband, employee, and former sheriff's deputy has a great sense of humor but a low tolerance for anything that remotely threatens our sometimes shaky relationship. I was pretty certain I didn't want to open that particular can of worms with him.

Neddie had seen my point, cautioning me to be careful.

"You don't think this is anything to be concerned about, do

you? I mean, really, it's just some goofball playing games, right?"

"Maybe," she'd said, "but don't make assumptions. There are some serious weirdoes out there. You of all people should know that. Just keep your eyes open."

I'd sloughed it off, only marginally more aggravated when the second one appeared just a week later. I'd been trying to track down a deadbeat father, and the search had led me to an office building just off New Orleans Road. It wasn't one of my usual destinations, so it occurred to me that this creep had to have followed me. I'd checked the parking lot, looking for a familiar vehicle, but nothing clicked.

Now he'd found me at Neddie's condo. I looked over the top of the Jag to survey my surroundings, mostly high-end imports and SUVs scattered among the palms and lush landscaping. If anyone sat waiting to observe my reaction, I couldn't spot him. I slid back into the car and tossed the envelope on the seat beside me. If he was out there somewhere, watching, I wouldn't give him the satisfaction of seeing me read his latest drivel.

As I moved sedately out of the parking lot, my phone beeped.

"Bay Tanner."

"Hey, it's me, which you'd know if you bothered to check Caller ID."

Erik Whiteside, my partner in the inquiry agency, was a confirmed and unrepentant geek. Lucky for me, as anything more complicated than a microwave tended to tax my extremely limited techno-skills.

"Yeah, yeah, yeah. What's up?"

"New client. From Atlanta. Stephanie took the call. He's going to be in town for a couple of days. Are you and Red still on sabbatical, or do you want in?"

My husband and I had planned to take a few days off, maybe head up toward the mountains to do some gawking at the fall foliage. Our last case had put a bullet through his arm. Maybe it wasn't exactly the right time, what with Miss Lizzie's death and all, but I felt an overwhelming need to escape, just for a while. I had confidence Erik and his fiancée Stephanie Wyler could handle things while we were gone.

"Anything interesting?"

With me it was always the puzzle, the challenge. I left the more routine and mundane to the others, including my husband.

Red had recently joined us after retiring from the Beaufort County Sheriff's department, and he regularly rode me about my penchant for danger and mayhem.

"I'm not completely sure. Steph said it's about his uncle and some beach property."

"Sounds as if he needs an attorney."

"Strangely enough, he is one. Hubbard—'Call me Hub'—Danforth. I'm not sure exactly what he wants us to do, but it will involve surveillance and reporting. I think we can handle it."

The name, in light of Neddie's and my recent battle of the opening lines, made me smile. Not exactly *Danvers*, but close enough. Maybe it was an omen. Or not. Sometimes life is just strange that way.

"Okay. I'll let you know where we'll be. Call if you need us."

I hung up and pulled out onto the narrow pavement. I turned right at the light onto William Hilton Parkway, known to locals simply as 278, and headed for home. I spared a moment to feel bad about how abruptly I'd bailed on Neddie, but I knew what I knew. Maybe being out of town for a few days wasn't such a good idea.

Lavinia Smalls was my last connection to my childhood.

I didn't intend to lose her, too.

CHAPTER TWO

It took me only five minutes to roll through the gate of Port Royal Plantation and wind back to my house nestled just behind the dunes. If I'd felt like it, I could easily have walked down the beach to meet Neddie. God knows I could have used the exercise. Maybe it was middle age creeping up on me, but my energy level didn't seem to be as high as it used to be. I was firmly in the camp of if it ain't broke, don't fix it, but menopause loomed, and I knew that sooner or later I would have to surrender to the inevitable and get a checkup.

I nosed the Jag in alongside Red's restored Ford Bronco. My husband had obviously decided to play hooky today, too, although he had a much better excuse. He still had his arm in a soft sling, which made doing much of anything difficult.

Except catnapping on the chaise on the deck that wrapped around three sides of the weathered house. His raucous snores rattled the tendrils of Spanish moss hanging from the live oaks that shaded the property and had probably sent all the gulls and squirrels streaking for cover.

I tiptoed into the house for a fresh glass of iced tea and carried it back outside. I eased into the other chaise, lowering myself as quietly as I could. In spite of my precautions, my husband stirred, and his eyes fluttered open.

"I see your Spidey sense is still operational," I said with a smile.

He grinned back. "I got shot in the shoulder, not the head." He stretched, as much as he could with only one functional arm, and yawned widely. "What time is it?"

"A little after four thirty. Did you go in at all?"

"For a couple of hours. Not much happening, at least that the kids couldn't handle."

I smiled at his euphemism for Erik and Stephanie. Both of

them hated it, but they liked Red too much to call him on it.

I took a sip of tea and lay back. "Erik called. He's interviewing a new client. Some lawyer from Atlanta."

Red turned toward me. "Nothing interesting, I assume, since you didn't immediately jump on it."

"Probably not. You hungry?"

"Absolutely. How about we hit Bubba's for some shrimp and oysters?"

"Sounds like a plan." I paused, my conversation with Neddie scratching at the back of my mind. "You still want to head up to the mountains this weekend? It could be crazy up there, especially around Asheville. The leaf gawkers will be out in full force."

He took a moment to respond. "I thought that's what you wanted to do. If we leave early tomorrow morning, we can be settled in before the madness starts. We can park the car and just walk wherever we need to go." Again he hesitated. "Unless you've changed your mind. Is it the new client?"

"No."

I debated whether or not to put my fears for Lavinia into words. I'd hinted at my concerns a couple of times, but Red hadn't picked up on it.

"I'm a little uncomfortable with being so far out of touch. In case they need us for something at Presqu'isle."

"Like what?" my husband asked.

"I don't know . . . Something." I waited another beat. *Oh, what the hell*, I thought. *In for a penny*. "Lavinia's not getting any younger, you know. And Julia isn't the most trustworthy person on the planet."

"You worry too much." Red reached across the gap between the chaises and ran his fingers along my bare arm. "They'll be fine."

I opened my mouth to give vent to all the fear sloshing around in my stomach, then changed my mind. What good would it do? Even Neddie thought I was crazy. "I need a shower," I said, swinging my legs over the edge.

"Do you require assistance, madam?"

I laughed out loud at Red's exaggerated, leering grin. He wiggled his eyebrows like Groucho Marx.

"Think you're up for it?" I grabbed his good hand and hauled him to his feet.

"We'll just have to see, won't we? I'll certainly give it my best shot."

He followed me inside. As I moved down the hallway toward our bedroom, I heard the *snick* of the lock on the French doors.

An hour later, I cursed myself under my breath as I slid into the Jaguar.

Red dangled the blue envelope from two fingers. "What's this?"

"Nothing," I said, even as my husband settled himself in the passenger seat. Driving was manageable but difficult for him with only one functioning arm, so I had become his chauffeur whenever we went out together. Funny, though. His disability hadn't hampered him at all in the shower.

"Then why are you trying to snatch it out of my hands?" Red made a show of sniffing loudly. "No telltale aftershave. Must not be a mash note." He turned it over. "Hmmm. No stamp or address. Just 'Bay'. Now I am curious."

I backed out and hit the button to roll down the garage door, then aimed us toward the security gate. I didn't look at my husband, hoping he'd lose interest in taunting me. I knew for certain he wouldn't open the envelope without an invitation. One thing Red had in spades was integrity.

The silence became uncomfortable as I merged with the off-island traffic onto 278. "Somebody left it under my wiper while I was at Neddie's. I don't even know what's in it."

"Wait a minute. You're trying to tell me you haven't even looked at it? The woman whose curiosity could have killed a couple of hundred cats? You're joking, right?"

I accelerated through the yellow light at Mathews Drive, but even that cardinal sin couldn't deflect Red's attention. I let it ride until we came to a stop at the intersection giving access to Hilton Head Plantation on one side and Indigo Run on the other. Without speaking, I extended my hand, palm up, and he dropped the envelope into it. I ripped it open and extracted the single sheet covered, as before, with neat, precise block printing. Quickly, I scanned the lines, laid out like poetry, but having neither rhyme nor meter.

With a sigh, I handed it back just as the light changed. I accelerated a little faster than necessary, but Red never flinched. I darted an occasional glance to gauge my husband's reaction. He read it twice.

"How long has this been going on?"

I knew he was seriously angry by the soft tone and slow cadence of the question.

So I was busted. No point in trying to hedge my way out of it. "That's the third. They're all pretty much variations on a theme."

He let me hang for a moment or two. "And you were going to tell me about this when?"

"Come on, honey, it's just some kook having a little fun at my expense. No big deal."

"If a client came to you with this—with three of these, actually—what would you advise her to do?"

I concentrated on merging into the traffic pouring down off the Cross Island Parkway, but I could feel his steady gaze boring into my right cheek. I opened my mouth to surrender, but he cut me off.

"I'll tell you what you'd say. You'd advise her to take them to the sheriff. This is harassment, not to mention stalking and menacing." He whipped his head forward, and I knew he was seriously ticked off when he snapped, "And where the hell are you going? You just blew by Squire Pope Road."

"Oh, crap," I muttered and muscled my way across two lanes, whipping into the parking lot of the Crazy Crab restaurant. I backed around and lucked into a gap in traffic, again cutting across until I was in the left-turn lane at the light. I glanced at Red, who was just releasing his one-handed death grip on the armrest. "Sorry. You distracted me."

To my intense relief, he laughed. "Okay. How about we wait to discuss this until you're no longer in control of a very expensive and potentially lethal weapon?"

"Deal," I said and turned sedately when the left arrow flipped to green.

"So tell me about these other notes." Red slurped down an oyster and looked across the high, round table before dropping the shell into the bucket filling the hole in its center. "Did you save them?"

I considered lying but decided it was probably pointless. "They're at the office. In my desk."

"Good. I want to take a look at them. Maybe something will jump out at me."

It wasn't that I didn't have faith in my husband's abilities, but the implication that I might have missed a clue rankled. Just a little. I peeled the translucent shell from the last shrimp and dropped it in the bucket.

"Look, Red, let's not get all bent out of shape about this, okay? There's nothing threatening about these notes. In a way, they're kind of flattering." I could see his hackles rising, and I reached over to lay my hand gently on his sling. "It's very eighth-grade when you come right down to it. I'm not worried. Really. And you shouldn't be, either. Let's just enjoy the evening."

Red had tucked the small envelope into the pocket created by the canvas sling, and he slipped it out. He opened the single sheet, his frown deepening as he once again scanned the contents.

"'The sun rises and you glow. Your brilliance lites the day. In agony I watch you slip thru my life craveing the warmth of your skin beneath my fingers.'"

There was more, but he didn't finish. I was glad he'd at least had the good sense to keep his voice down.

"See? It's just drivel. Middle school stuff. And his spelling sucks."

When I reached out to take the letter back, he folded it neatly and stashed it back inside his sling.

"Someone talks about feeling your skin underneath his fingers, and you don't think that's seriously threatening? I can't believe you don't see how wacked this guy is."

The appearance of Dwight "Bubba" Mitchell towering over us cut off what could have escalated into a first-class row.

"Everything okay, y'all? Get enough to eat?"

"It was great, Bubba, thanks." I smiled up into his wide, black face. At well over six feet and built like a brick outhouse, as the Judge used to say, the ex-football lineman could have blocked out the sun. "And thanks for shucking Red's oysters."

"One-armed man's at a serious disadvantage when it comes to shuckin'," he boomed. "No problem. Y'all enjoy."

He moved away to greet the other locals who had crowded into this hole-in-the-wall on Skull Creek. Knowing about Bubba's was kind of like belonging to the Masons. In an undeclared pact, we did our best to keep its existence from the tourists.

It was my turn to buy, and I left the cash on the table. It was considered bad form to ask Bubba to take credit cards. Outside, it was full dark, the stars exploding over Skull Creek beyond the reach of the single arc light in the parking lot.

"Let's go sit by the water for a while," I suggested, ambling in that direction. I knew there was a bench under one of the oaks overhanging the shore. "We may not have too many of these evenings left."

Although winter was often only a whisper in our subtropical paradise, nights would be decidedly cooler as we moved toward November and December. I flashed on a memory: Neddie and I slogging our way through thigh-deep snow on the campus of Northwestern, her Boston upbringing making her much more adaptable to the bitter wind biting through my six or seven layers of clothing. No doubt about it—Chicago knew how to do winter.

Red's voice brought me to a halt, and I realized he hadn't followed me. I swiveled around to find him standing alongside the Jaguar. This time, the envelope he held in his hand was white.

And addressed to him.

CHAPTER THREE

As it turned out, we didn't make that trip up to Asheville. By the time we'd stopped at the office to pick up the other notes, driven home, and growled and grumbled at each other until well after midnight, neither of us was in much of a mood to think about being stuck together in a car for half a day. Or even half an hour. Besides, I was still worried about Lavinia.

I woke on Friday with the alarm at seven thirty and slipped out of bed. I needn't have bothered to be careful. Red had ended up on the sofa in the great room. His choice, not mine. I padded barefoot down the hallway and risked a peek around the corner. He lay on his back, his good arm flung over his head, his hair standing straight up as if he'd run his hand through it a few dozen times during the night. I retreated to the shower.

By the time I emerged into the kitchen, he was sitting at the glass-topped table in the bay of the window, gazing at the driveway and nursing a mug of coffee. I pulled a tea bag from the canister on the counter, filled a cup with tap water, and shoved it into the microwave. I sliced an English muffin, popped it into the toaster, and opened a new jar of extra-crunchy peanut butter.

"You're going in to work?" My husband's tone held a note of challenge, although he spoke softly.

"Yes. And so are you. We have a business to run." I turned to face him and suddenly realized what was different. "Where's the sling?"

He shrugged. "I'm sick of the damn thing." He straightened his arm and flexed his fingers a few times. "See? Good as new."

"And when did you get the medical degree?"

I smiled, actually pleased that he might be almost back to normal. A moment later, my husband's face lost its belligerent look as well. One of the best things about our marriage is that neither one of us can hold onto a grudge for long. Okay, he's a lot better at that than I am, but I'm working on it.

Red slurped down the last of his coffee. "Give me fifteen minutes."

He brushed my shoulder with his fingers on his way by, and I knew that most—if not all—had been forgiven.

I carried my breakfast to the table, glancing at the headlines in the *Island Packet* as I settled into the chair. Local politics usually dominated the news on the island. Much of it had to do with development, redevelopment, dredging, permitting, zoning, rezoning—in short, anything that impacted our reputation as a first-class tourist destination as well as a paradise for a growing number of retirees who wanted something different from Florida. Of course, we have pristine beaches, award-winning restaurants, and five-star resorts, making Hilton Head a mecca for visitors. But what I always thought might be our biggest attraction, especially for those looking for a more permanent place to settle, is that we're really just a small town. Except for those three crazy months in the summer when it seems as if the whole world has descended on us. Other than that, we enjoy a pretty laid-back lifestyle most of the year.

I was just finishing an article about a hassle between a local landowner and a real estate conglomerate out of Charlotte, when Red appeared at the bottom of the three steps leading up into the kitchen. His light brown hair lay slicked against his head, and I could make out wet comb tracks. I dumped my dishes in the sink and ran a little water over them. Dolores Santiago, my part-time housekeeper, was due later, and I didn't want to give her any reason to think we didn't need her anymore.

Red reached for my hand as I joined him at the foot of the steps. "We're okay, right?"

"Right," I said with a smile and linked my fingers with his. "Come on. Now that you're out of the land of the lame and halt, it's time you actually did some work."

He set the alarm and followed me out to the garage. I felt confident we'd moved beyond the disruption of the silly anonymous letters.

Sometimes I absolutely don't have a clue what the hell I'm talking about.

• • •

We beat Erik and Stephanie by a whisker. I'd called earlier to let them know we were coming in, so neither of them evidenced any surprise.

Red held the door for me, showing off how well his injured arm had recuperated. My partner and his fiancée trooped in behind us.

After a round of good mornings, Stephanie distributed the Starbucks containers. While Erik and I used to take turns, it had somehow morphed into our newest employee's responsibility to make sure we all began the workday with a good jolt of caffeine.

"What's on the agenda for this morning?" I asked, entering my office and dropping my bag onto my desk. Old and dinged up a little bit, its warm mahogany surface still glowed. It had been my father's, first in his law offices and later in his study before his illness had necessitated its removal. Retrieving it from the attics of Presqu'isle had required a solid game plan and several hefty men, but I knew it belonged here the moment they set it in place.

I sipped chai latte and settled into my chair.

"Hub Danforth, the lawyer from Atlanta, wants us to get started today, if possible." Erik leaned against the doorway. "Steph and I were working out a schedule for surveillance, but if you two are going to be around . . ." He let his voice trail off and swiveled his head between Red and me.

"We're in," my husband said. "Got details?"

"I'll bring in the file." Stephanie turned toward the reception desk and unlocked a drawer. A moment later she laid the slim folder on my desk. "There's not too much in there yet," she said. "He came in late yesterday afternoon, so I haven't had a chance to check him out completely."

"Well, how about everybody pull up a chair and let's take a look."

Amid the confusion of everyone's getting settled, Red spoke. "Before we get into that, I have something else to bring to your attention." He didn't even glance my way as he produced a long envelope from the pocket of his jacket and dumped the contents out in front of me. "Bay's got herself a stalker."

"Red—" I began, but he cut me off.

"We're going to talk about this, Bay. If you have someone skulking around your car at all hours of the day and night, the kids have a right to be aware. It could impact them, too."

It sounded like an instant replay of the night before, but I had neither the inclination nor the energy to start our argument all over again.

Erik reached for one of the blue envelopes, then jerked his hand back. "Are we worried about prints?"

"No," I said emphatically. "We're not going to involve the sheriff or anyone else outside this office. Clear?"

Despite my stern delivery, Erik smiled. "Aye, aye, Captain." His boyish grin faded. "Are they threats?"

"More like lovesick teenage angst," I said. "Take a look." I reached over and shuffled them into order. "This was the first."

Stephanie sat demurely in her chair, hands folded in her lap. No one spoke as he scanned the three addressed to me. Erik frowned up at me when he'd finished the fourth. "This one doesn't worry you?"

The note Red had found on the windshield of the Jaguar the night before had a decidedly different tone, one I was forced to admit gave me pause.

"'Mine.'" Erik read aloud, then looked up. "Just the one word. Now that's pretty creepy. You were at the Shack last night?"

I nodded.

"So he followed you from home."

"Either that or he has a tracker on the Jaguar." I smiled to let them know I was just kidding, but no one smiled back. "Oh, come on. Seriously?"

"Stranger things have happened," my husband said. "I'll take a look when we're done here." He rightly interpreted my single raised eyebrow. "Yes, I know what to look for, in a general sort of way. We got into all that stuff after nine-eleven. The Feds paid for a lot of training for local law enforcement. Homeland Security held seminars."

"Fine," I said, dismissing the whole idea with a blithe wave of one hand.

"The rest of us will keep our eyes open for any strangers hanging around out front during the day." Red paused and got two affirmative nods. "You, of course," he added, turning to me with a scowl, "will have your head firmly planted up your—uh, in the sand."

I had to laugh. "Nice save. Now, can we get back to the paying customers? Steph, what have you got?"

I smiled at my former partner's daughter. It never ceased to amaze me that she could smile back with such apparent sincerity at the woman who had gotten her father killed. Everyone except me said I couldn't have done anything to change the outcome at that dinky marina south of Amelia Island. Ben Wyler had saved Erik's life at the expense of his own, and he'd gone into the whole situation almost blind because I was too proud, too stubborn, to tell him what I knew. That Erik and Stephanie had connected at all, let alone fallen in love, was a measure of their characters and a capacity for forgiveness that was way outside of my understanding.

"Hubbard Danforth," she said, referring to the few sheets in the folder. "He's a criminal defense attorney in Atlanta. His uncle—his mother's brother—lives in a little house on the beach. It's been in the family since sometime after the Civil War. Although the uncle owns the majority interest in the property, Danforth and his sister are on the deed. They inherited quarter shares from their late mother."

"Are we talking slave descendants? Was this one of the original 'forty acres and a mule' grants?"

Fortunately, I didn't have to explain that my question had nothing to do with the color of Mr. Danforth's skin. The tangled web of fractional shareholders in much of the property once deeded to the freed slaves on Hilton Head had caused no end of headaches when the time came to sell. Oftentimes no one could produce a clear title, and the county had had to devise a special plan for dealing with them. It was called heirs property, and it had to be handled in a specific manner in order for any sale to take place.

Erik spoke up. "No, there's just the three of them, but this may be just as bad. It seems the uncle is an older gentleman, lives alone, and he's, uh, apparently not got all his marbles. Danforth has been trying to get the old man to deed him his interest in the property so he and his sister can dispose of it and get him into some kind of assisted living. He's worried about the old guy out there all by himself."

I flashed on the article I'd read in the *Packet* that morning. "Are we sure he's concerned about his uncle and not the property? You said it's on the beach. Where, exactly?"

"Somewhere around the folly," Stephanie said. "He showed

us on the map." She pulled a photocopy out of the file and handed it to me.

The area had been enlarged so that the small side streets running from 278 down to the beach stood out sharply. The small *x* nestled almost right at water's edge, although I assumed there were the same sheltering dunes as those separating my home from the ocean and maybe a stretch of marsh. Still, it looked perilously close, not to mention vulnerable, to the vagaries of tide and storm.

I handed the sheet to Red. "Aren't there a lot of super expensive places in that area?" The towering, five- and six-story *homes* I remembered looked more like boutique hotels than actual residences, but zoning wouldn't have allowed anything that smacked of a commercial structure that close to the water. At least I didn't think so. When my beach runs took me in that direction, I recalled marveling that people were willing to sink a few million bucks into something that could have gotten blown into the middle of next week if the path of Hurricane Kitty had ticked a few degrees to the west.

My husband studied the printout. "It's just before you get to the folly, down at the end of Burkes Beach Road. Near the Chaplin Park complex."

Stephanie handed over another piece of paper. "The owner is Malcolm St. John, eighty-two, widower. No children, at least not that I could find. He served in the Army in the fifties, Korea, but no combat, and he was honorably discharged. That's about all I could find in the few minutes I had to look last night. I'll get more background on him today. And on Mr. Danforth." She smiled. "At least his retainer check is good. I checked that first thing."

Erik's fiancée had been a quick study. After only a few weeks on the job, she had become almost as adept as Erik at teasing information out of the databases to which we subscribed.

"Any way to find out if anyone's been nosing around to buy the place? You have to figure it's worth a small fortune to a developer, even in this economy."

"I guess a little downturn probably doesn't affect the kind of people who can afford those things in the first place," Erik offered.

"It's all relative," I said. "So. Anyone have any qualms about taking Mr. Danforth on?"

"I'm not crazy about the guy," Stephanie said softly. At least

I'd broken her of the habit of raising her hand when she had something to contribute.

"Why?"

She shrugged. "I don't know. He was way too smooth for my taste, but maybe that comes with him being a criminal lawyer. He says he only wants what's best for his uncle, but he didn't strike me as the kind and loving sort, you know?" She tilted her head to one side. "Or maybe it's just me. Dad was never very fond of the lawyers who got the scumbags off on obscure technicalities."

"Never discount a gut reaction," I said. "Erik? Did Hub give you the creeps, too?"

"No, not exactly. But you've always said that we don't have to like the client. We just have to be sure we're okay with what he's asking us to do. If the old man is really off his rocker, he could be a danger to himself, especially if he lives alone. It's probably a good thing to get him into some kind of home where he can be looked after." He paused. "Danforth said he thought the sheriff or the fire department had been called out there a couple of times, but he's not positive. He wants us to look into that as well as keep an eye on Mr. St. John for a couple of days. Document any erratic or dangerous behavior."

"To what purpose?" I asked. "Is he gathering evidence for a competency hearing?"

With a start, my mind flashed back to my arguments with Lavinia when my father lay dying in the hospital. Heart surgery might have prolonged his life, but he had made it clear in no uncertain terms that he wasn't willing to go through another bout of incapacity and recuperation. He was tired. Lavinia, who had loved the Judge for longer than I had been aware of it, wanted me to have him declared incompetent so I could exercise my medical power of attorney and authorize the surgery. I had flatly refused to countermand my father's wishes. That difficult decision had caused a breach between Lavinia and me that had been a long time healing.

His death had been as crushing a blow to me as it had been to her, although I knew in my heart it was what the Judge had wanted.

"He didn't say," Erik replied, jerking me back from the well of painful memories. "But it's a pretty good bet. You have a problem with that?"

I thought again of that last conversation I'd ever had with my father, of his stern gray eyes softened with the knowledge that he was signing his own death warrant. I'd known then that it was his decision to make, and I didn't like the idea that someone might be trying to railroad Mr. St. John into doing something he didn't want to do with the remaining years or months of his life. Still . . .

"Okay. Then if no one has any serious objections, let's get cracking. Red, will you check out the sheriff and fire department reports? Let's see what actually happened. Erik, you said you two had worked out a schedule for surveillance. Can you cover the weekend, or do you need Red and me as well?"

"We weren't counting on you, so we're all set. Unless you want in."

I shook my head. "No, we'll just be standbys in case you run into anything."

Stephanie and Erik rose in unison. They fit so well together, almost always seeming to be on the same wavelength. I envied them that.

"What about you?" my husband asked.

I smiled. "I think I'll take a walk on the beach."

CHAPTER FOUR

My husband and I left together. I knew without looking at him that his eyes had jumped immediately to the windshield of the Jaguar, which lay sparkling and pristine in the soft autumn sunshine.

"Let's head home so I can change. I think I'll turn this into a good excuse to get some exercise and take a run. I'll look less conspicuous, too."

"Fine. I'll take the opportunity to check under the Jag as well. For any kind of tracker."

He sounded angry again, but I didn't want to get into it. This was the hard part about working together. Even though both of us considered ourselves professionals, our private lives often leaked out into our business relationship.

A few minutes later we rolled into the garage. Dolores Santiago's venerable blue Hyundai was pulled up onto the pine straw at the side of the drive. I called out to her as I pushed open the door into the house.

"Ah, Señora. *Buenos Dias*! I no expect to see you today."

She squirmed a little as I bent to hug her. Dolores disliked displays of emotion, especially from me. Though I counted her my friend, she always tried to maintain the decorum befitting an employee-employer relationship. But she had saved my life after my first husband's plane had exploded in front of my eyes, leaving me with deep and lasting scars, both emotional and physical, and I loved her for the unwavering care and concern she had showed me during my long months of recovery.

"I won't be in your way," I said, stepping back. "I just have to change."

"You no work today?"

"This is work," I said, smiling at the frown that wrinkled her coffee-colored brow. "It's for a client."

"Sí, Señora," she remarked and resumed the dusting my unexpected appearance had interrupted. "If you say so."

It took me under five minutes to pull on my shorts, T-shirt, and running shoes. By the time I emerged from the bedroom, Red was sitting at the table in the kitchen, a fresh cup of coffee in front of him.

"I tell Mr. Red he no should work," Dolores huffed, eyeing me with suspicion. "He no have good arm yet."

Red shrugged, his smile suggesting he was enjoying Dolores's pampering way too much.

"You find anything on the car?" I asked, securing my long hair into a high ponytail which I pulled through the opening in the back of my Braves baseball cap.

"No." The monosyllable spoke volumes about the likely duration of our current disagreement.

"See you later," I said and did a quick exit through the French doors onto the deck.

Behind me, I heard my husband's voice call, "Be careful."

I ignored him. It was another glorious fall day, although there was a chill bite to the wind off the ocean, and I had no intention of spoiling it with any more harsh words. Call me a coward, but there it was.

I trotted down the steps and took the wooden boardwalk across the dunes. I hadn't bothered to check the tides, but it appeared to be about halfway in between high and low. The sand stretched out in both directions, packed hard and relatively deserted. Most of our autumn visitors preferred the green of the golf course to the dun-colored beach. I warmed up for a few minutes, feeling a mild protest from some of the larger muscle groups I had woefully neglected over the past few weeks, then set off to my right, past the Westin and the Sea Cloisters where I had lounged with Neddie the day before. The issue of Julia and Lavinia snaked its way into my mind, but I banished it almost immediately. Running was my escape, my refuge. No problems were allowed to intrude.

It took me a while to recapture my usual rhythm, but I soon found myself pounding along at a decent pace, my breathing only a little labored. I blew by a few dog walkers near Hilton Head Beach and Tennis, and the first of the mansions rose out of the sand. Two of them looked Italianate, with stone balustrades and

Mediterranean touches. I couldn't quite decide on the architectural style of the next few, but they all had one thing in common: at least three stories above a garage and tons of balconies canted to maximize the view of the Atlantic rolling away toward Africa. And a price tag with a lot of zeroes. Even so, they were built so closely together, I wondered if there weren't also some excellent views into their neighbors' bedrooms.

I slackened my pace a little as I came abreast of the entrance to Burkes Beach Road. Although it wasn't marked, I remembered it was the next one after the mansions. For the time being I simply glanced up the path and kept on running. A couple of hundred yards later I came to the folly and slowed to a stop. To my right, a wide marsh extended back toward the highway, the seemingly endless boardwalk to Hilton Head Resort snaking its way through the cordgrass and hummocks of vegetation. I stood and stared into the deep channel that at one time nearly cut the island in half.

It soon became apparent that the tide was on the ebb as a fairly steady flow of brackish water coursed through on its way back to the ocean. At the point where the two bodies of water met, the surf roiled and eddied, reminding me that this was no place to be wading or swimming. We'd had a couple of drownings over the past few years, mostly kids who just wouldn't listen to the warnings about the fierce rip currents that were sometimes created where the underground river met the sea.

I'm not sure how long I stood there, mesmerized by the quiet display of the forces of nature at work before I turned and headed back toward home. I detoured near the packed sand marked with a trash barrel and walked up toward Burkes Beach Road. There was a small paved parking area with meters on the left where I remembered just a sandy turnout, but such is progress. It had probably gone in when the town bought the acreage that later became the Chaplin Community Park and adjacent sports complex.

Just across from the parking area, a narrow street formed a T. The corner lot was empty, with a venerable live oak spreading its twisting branches to cover nearly the entire space. I smiled when I noticed the remains of a tree house nestled in a wide crook. I took out my cell phone and fumbled with a couple of buttons before I found the right one and snapped a picture. A little farther along stood a small cottage, flat-roofed and obviously having withstood decades of attack by the salty sea air. The peeling stucco, once painted a pastel green, had become weathered and pockmarked over the years. It sported a rusting set of wrought-iron scrollwork on the windows. The old place crouched forlornly, its front porch sagging into the tiny, barren patch of yard.

All of which made the place on the left appear like something out of another world. The pristine, towering house rose majestically into the late autumn sun, three stories above a pair of double garages separated by the graceful curves of a split staircase. Its white paintwork gleamed against the sandy beige of its exterior, and wide balconies extended across the top two floors. I was pretty certain there would be a spectacular view across the marsh to the ocean, unsullied by the dilapidated beachfront house across the street.

Another one of the island's dichotomies, I thought, as I retraced my steps. I'd be willing to bet I'd found our Mr. St. John's home, although I had seen no signs of life at all on the short, nearly hidden street. If he really was as frail and confused as our new client claimed, where was he? I wondered if he still drove, or if he had to rely on the kindness of friends or neighbors to take him to the grocery store, post office, church. My father had had the luxury of a loving companion, a sometimes dutiful daughter, and enough money to keep most of the wolves of old age and infirmity away from his door.

Judging by the condition of the cottage I'd just examined, I had a feeling Mr. St. John hadn't been so fortunate.

Red was gone by the time I jogged back up the steps to the deck. I bypassed the main entrance and let myself directly into the bedroom through the French doors. After a quick shower, I once again emerged into the kitchen looking at least semi-professional.

I could hear Dolores humming from the laundry room, so I poured myself a glass of iced tea, grabbed my phone, and settled onto the white sofa that faced the fireplace in the great room.

"Hey, Erik, it's me." I gave him a quick rundown on my reconnaissance. "But I didn't see anyone around. The place looks almost as if it had been abandoned."

"Yeah, I know. That's what Steph said. She saw you checking things out."

"Where was she?"

My voice had a little more snap to it than I'd intended, but Erik's words had triggered a bad feeling in my gut. If I couldn't even detect when I was under surveillance by my own team, what did that say about my ability to nail the fruitcake who had been leaving mash notes on my windshield?

My partner laughed. "She'll be thrilled you didn't spot her. I think she's found herself a little hidey-hole in some of the vegetation by the parking area. She's all set up to keep an eye on the house for the next few hours."

"Is St. John there? Has she seen him?"

"He went out about ten minutes before you got there. Someone picked him up. I was just running the plate when you called."

"I'm sorry, I didn't quite catch that." Strictly speaking, checking out vehicle ownership was against the law, even for licensed investigators. Actually, *especially* for licensed investigators. But Erik never met a firewall he couldn't scale, as much for the joy of the challenge as for the information. Our agreement on such breaches was that I operated on a what-you-don't-know-can't-hurt-you basis. *Don't ask, don't* tell should have been engraved over the door to my office.

"Sorry," he said, although I could tell from his tone that he really wasn't. "Turns out it's registered to a Fanny Williams on Spanish Wells Road. Steph said she's an older black woman with a van. She helped Mr. St. John in, and they drove off. Steph said he looked pretty spry for his age, just needed a little help with the step up. I didn't think it was important to follow them at this stage. You have a different take?"

"No. Obviously he has someone to help him run errands. I didn't see a vehicle anywhere near the place. If he's voluntarily given up driving, it would seem he has a pretty good grasp of his limitations."

"Makes sense. But we don't know for certain it was voluntary. It's early times yet, right?"

"Good point," I said. "Is Stephanie taking photos?"

"Yup. Her new phone has zoom capabilities, so she can stay back and get some good close-ups if necessary. Anything else?"

"Sounds as if you two have it under control. I'm going to grab some lunch, then I'll head back your way. Can I bring you anything?"

"No thanks. We brought sandwiches from home this morning since we figured one or both of us would be tied up with the surveillance. I'll see you later."

I hung up just as Dolores carried the vacuum cleaner into the room.

"Sorry, Señora. I come back."

"No, that's okay. I'm on my way out."

"I make the tortillas, for tomorrow. The *niños*, they like, no?"

Red's two kids from his marriage to Sarah spent most weekends with us. Since Scotty was heavily into soccer, we sometimes made the drive to Beaufort to watch his games. Eventually, though, he and Elinor ended up here until Sunday afternoon. It wasn't difficult to get them to agree when we had the beach and ocean right outside the back door. Strangely enough, I'd been their aunt before becoming their less-than-wicked stepmother. My first husband, Red's brother Rob, had been murdered by a gang of drug scum he was investigating for the state attorney general's office. I knew a lot of people found it strange, my marriage to my former brother-in-law. Being proper Southerners, however, they mostly confined their expressions of disapproval to the occasional raised eyebrow and knowing look.

I rose and tucked my phone into the pocket of my slacks. "The kids love all your food. Thanks."

"*Nada*," she said, smiling as I passed her on my way to the garage.

I carried my burger and fries into the office a little after one. I pulled a Diet Coke from the mini-fridge and settled behind my desk. A moment later, Erik wandered in, the remnants of a ham and cheese sandwich in his right hand, and took one of the client chairs.

"Want some fries?" I asked, shoving the cardboard container in his direction.

"Sure. Thanks." He helped himself and leaned back. "So what did you think of Mr. St. John's place?"

I shook my head. "It's been neglected for a long time. Looked to me as if it could come crashing down with the first big wind, but it's obviously withstood a lot over the years." I chewed and swallowed. "It's really hard to believe there are places like that still left on the island, but I know his isn't the only one by a long shot."

"I always felt like the rest of us sort of swooped in and changed everything. The development and all that. I mean, I'm guessing these folks like Mr. St. John were probably doing just fine on their own before the McMansions went up next door."

I sighed and took a couple of fries. "I know what you mean. Hilton Head and the Sea Islands were almost completely isolated after the War Between the States. The Gullah and Geechee people managed to feed their families from the land and what they could catch in the creeks and the ocean. Still, it must have been a pretty difficult life."

We both looked up as the outer door opened, and Red strode into the office. I suffered a momentary pang that I hadn't been in touch with him about lunch.

"Did you eat?" I asked, prepared to share the remainder of my burger if the answer was no.

"Yeah, I grabbed something. Actually, I took one of the deputies out to Aunt Chilada's. Got quite a good bit of information for my trouble, too."

"About Mr. St. John?" Erik asked.

Red nodded. "Seems Hub Danforth wasn't too far off. Billy told me they've had to go out there a couple of times. Once for an attempted break-in, and once when the old guy locked himself out." He shook his head. "Poor fella sat outside on the stoop all night long until someone came along and notified the sheriff. One of those cold nights in January, too. The deputies called in the paramedics. Billy said the old man was only in a T-shirt and thin pants. Bedroom slippers with no socks. They were afraid he might have caught pneumonia or something."

"Was he hospitalized?"

Red swiped a couple of fries before answering me. "They checked him out and sent him home. Apparently he wasn't the worse for it."

"Did he—Mr. St. John, I mean—have any explanation?"

"He said he thought he heard someone sneaking around on his porch. Didn't think he locked the door behind him, but he must have. Billy said they had to dismantle the doorknob to get in."

Erik and I exchanged a look. "So maybe Danforth wasn't exaggerating," he said, polishing off the last bite of his sandwich.

"Let's not jump to any conclusions," I cautioned. "All of us have locked ourselves out at one time or another, either from the house or the car."

"I never did," my husband offered, and I rolled my eyes. "No, seriously," he went on, "I don't ever remember getting locked out."

"Do you remember teaching Rob and me how to jimmy our way in with a credit card?" I asked with a snarky smile. "Did you learn that so you could circumvent having to wait for a search warrant?"

Red laughed. "Touché. Let's just leave my burglary skills out of this. I understand what you're saying, though. What Billy told me wasn't really enough to prove anything. The old man doesn't seem to have caused any more trouble than your average citizen."

"How about the fire department?"

"Billy talked to a friend of his, and he only remembers one time. Mr. St. John fell asleep with the tea kettle on the stove. More smoke than anything else. Someone walking up from the beach called it in. By the time the trucks got there, he already had it under control."

"Probably not what our client wants to hear," Erik remarked just as his phone chirped. He reached into his pocket and checked the screen. "Steph," he said. Then, "Hey, what's up?"

Red and I watched the smile fade from his face.

"When? . . . Okay . . . Okay . . . Got it. I'll call you back."

"Problems?" I asked.

"I don't know. Mr. St. John is still gone, but Steph said there's a big black Lexus parked in front of his house. She thought at first maybe it was someone just scoping out the mansions down the street, but it hasn't moved in about half an hour."

"Can she see who's inside?" Red asked.

"A man got out—she called him 'a suit'—and walked around the place a couple of times. She took a stroll herself, like she was just going for a walk, and got a quick look inside the car. She says there's a woman in there too, in a business suit, hair all done up, lots of makeup. She wants to know if she should try to get back to her hiding place or just come on back, now that they've seen her."

"What do you think?" I turned to Red.

"Did she get any photos?"

"A few. She didn't want to be too obvious."

"Why don't you go relieve her? And have her get back here with the pictures. I can't think of too many reasons that people of that description should be hanging around waiting for our subject, can you?" I didn't wait for an answer. "Have her check the plates when you call her back, okay?"

Erik smiled. "Already done. North Carolina. And there's a dealer bracket around the plate, so probably not a rental. Why?"

Again I flashed back to the article in the newspaper that morning, and a slow knot began to form in my gut. Maybe a coincidence that developers from Charlotte had been trying to buy up land on the island.

Or maybe not.

CHAPTER FIVE

Red typed up his notes on his meeting with the deputy sheriff so they could be added to the file while we waited for Stephanie to return. I logged on to the county real estate site and did a title search for the property off Burkes Beach Road. I'd made a mental note of the house number, but it seemed as if something had changed in the years since the deed had been recorded, because I couldn't find any record of it. My frustration level had risen incrementally until I was ready to take a hammer to my terminal when Erik's fiancée slipped through the outside door.

Stephanie's pretty face was flushed, and a few strands of her sun-streaked dark hair had escaped the ponytail riding high on the back of her head.

"Hey!" she said, slipping her phone from the pocket of her jeans and laying it on the reception desk. "Did Erik fill you in?"

"Yes," I replied and smiled at the eagerness in her voice, softened from its New York harshness over her months in the South Carolina Lowcountry. "Anything new to report?"

"No. Just that the car was still there when I left. The woman finally got out, probably to stretch her legs, and I got some good shots of her. Give me a minute to upload my phone to my laptop, and we can all take a look at them together."

Red and I exchanged smiles that spoke volumes about how far behind we were in the technology game. I wondered if the next generation after Steph and Erik would be born with miniature iPads tucked in their chubby little hands.

"There," she said just a couple of minutes later. She swiveled the screen, and Red and I crowded around behind her to look over her shoulder. "I set it up in a slideshow format so they'll automatically click over after a few seconds. I can stop it, though, if there's one you want to study."

As advertised, the images of Malcolm St. John and his friend slipped by first, the old man looking quite dapper in a red polo shirt, khaki trousers, and a navy blue windbreaker. It was difficult to judge with only stills to go by, but he seemed fairly upright, his back bent only a little by age and probably arthritis. Next came the Lexus, black and gleaming in the dappled sunshine that filtered through the swaying limbs of the huge live oak on the corner.

The man looked tall, maybe six feet or a little more, and his impeccable gray suit had obviously been tailored to fit his lean body perfectly. His crisp white shirt offset a decent tan, one that looked as if it had been acquired naturally and not from a tube or artificial sunlight. I guessed his age at late thirties, maybe forty, his dark hair showing no signs of any distinguished graying at the temples. He paced back and forth beside the car, or at least that's what it looked like in the photos, first his face—blurry and indistinct—then the back of his head showing up.

"Hold that a sec," Red said, and the image of the North Carolina license plate stilled. He grabbed a pen and notepad from Stephanie's desk and copied down the number. "Okay, go ahead."

The next few images were of the woman, first as just an outline through the tinted glass of the car, then in full face and figure once she'd emerged out onto the dusty roadway.

"Great suit," Stephanie said. "I'm guessing designer or a decent knockoff. Too bad she can't really carry it off."

I smiled at the quasi-catty remark. The woman certainly wasn't the skinny little thing that Stephanie was, but she had a figure very much like Neddie's: voluptuous, with curves in all the places men expected to find them. If the skirt strained a little over rounded hips, the jacket had a difficult time containing a more than ample chest. Since she wore no blouse underneath, I'd have been willing to bet that some serious cleavage could distract any male within a ten-yard radius. Her sleek red hair glistened in the afternoon sunlight and fell in soft curves to bracket her chin.

"She looks like she's all business," I said, observing the stern look that kept her face from any prettiness.

"I think she's probably the one in charge," Stephanie said as the slideshow came to an end. She put it on hold as it began a rerun of the first photos. "Just an impression, but he seemed to be listening pretty intently when she spoke."

"You didn't get a chance to hear any of it?"

She shook her head. "They clammed up when I came strolling down the path. He had already knocked on Mr. St. John's door, then when she got out, they stood at the back of the car talking. I didn't want to seem too conspicuous, so I didn't get real close. Sorry if I should have gotten—"

"No, you handled it just right," Red offered, patting her shoulder. "Nice job."

In spite of my husband's atta-girl, Stephanie looked at me.

"Red's right. No need to spook them. The job now is to figure out who they are and what they want with Mr. St. John." I paused. "Steph, can you bring up the *Island Packet* online? There's an article about some developer from Charlotte who's been nosing around. I think there was a corporate name. If so, see if you can get a directory. Sometimes they have photos of their officers and directors, even employees once in a while. Maybe we'll get lucky, and you can spot these two."

"I'm on it. I'll just save these to the Danforth file."

I left her to it and motioned for Red to join me in my office. When he had flopped into one of the client chairs, I stretched out in my own and slid off my shoes.

"What do you make of the big-shots nosing around Mr. St. John's place?" I asked, flexing my ankle to work out a kink in my right calf muscle. The older I got, the longer it took to recover from the infrequent battering I gave my body. Maybe it was time either to get back into running on a regular basis or just hang up my Nikes.

"Nothing at the moment," my husband replied. "But I'm not ruling out that someone other than his loving nephew might be interested in his property. It has to be worth a ton of money, situated where it is."

"We should check and see if anything in the area has been sold to someone from out of state. Maybe his is the last one they need to complete some big deal."

"Jumping a bit fast to conclusions, aren't you? We haven't even been on the case for twenty-four hours."

"I know. I just don't believe in coincidences."

"Alert the media." Red smiled, a crooked, sardonic grin that reminded me so much of his dead brother. "I think that's been pretty well established over the decades."

I jerked myself upright in my chair and slid my feet back into my shoes. "I wonder if Billy Dumars would be willing to check that out for me."

"Is that the real estate guy who was suspected of killing his wife?"

I saw the cloud pass over Red's face as he no doubt recalled that scorching Sunday afternoon when he'd discovered Tracy's body in the trunk of her Mercedes out in the marshes of Okatie. I knew it had been horrific for him, in spite of his macho deputy sheriff façade that day. I remembered that the haunted look hadn't left his eyes for quite some time.

"Yeah. That's the one."

I let the memory simmer for a moment before I jerked him away from it.

"But he didn't do it, if you recall. And, despite the best efforts of your former associates to tag him with it, he walked away. Rightly or wrongly, he thinks he owes me for that." I paused and scribbled myself a note on the desk pad. "I'll ask him to nose around and see if he's hearing any hot rumors."

Red sighed and seemed to shake himself. "He should have access to the sales in the past few months, too, right?"

"Right. I'll give him a shout." I reached for the phone, then drew back my hand. "You know, I want to meet him. Mr. St. John, I mean. I really don't like that I'm getting all my information about Danforth second-hand, either. I trust Erik and Stephanie, but there's nothing like being able to size up someone firsthand."

"I know what you mean. But for now you're going to have to go with what the kids have to say."

I looked up as Stephanie stuck her head around the door. "Sorry, but I found some info you might be interested in."

"What've you got?"

She carried a single sheet of paper in with her and sat down next to Red. "I checked out that company from Charlotte, the one you mentioned from the *Packet*? It's a pretty big outfit. Midsouth Asset Development, Limited. They do condo projects, malls, and resort communities all over the Southeast. I found their Web site. It's got a lot of stuff about what they build, but not much about their staff. I printed out what there was." She handed the paper across the desk to me. "The board is there because it's a publicly traded company, and the officers, but nothing on employees." She paused to let me begin scanning down through the list of names, before she interrupted. "Check out the CFO."

My eyebrows shot up, and I whistled softly.

"What?" Red asked, reaching for the printout. It took him a moment to zero in on what had caught Stephanie's and my attention. "This is way beyond coincidence, don't you think?"

"You bet." I looked across at Stephanie. "Did you run a background?"

"Not yet. I wanted to see how deep you wanted me to dig."

"To China, if you have to," I said. "I want to know why someone named Cynthia Danforth Merrill, chief financial officer of Midsouth Asset Development, is nosing around Mr. St. John's property."

"I'm on it," Stephanie said as she jumped from the chair and headed back to her own desk.

"And I want to know what the relationship is to Hub, first thing," I called after her.

"Yes, ma'am," she said, making me smile.

I had told her a million times not call me *ma'am*, but her upbringing apparently trumped my wishes on the subject.

"So now what?" Red asked, handing the printout back to me.

"Now I'm going to see if I can round up Billy Dumars. We've got a lot of lines in the water—we'll just have to wait and see who bites first."

CHAPTER SIX

I left a voicemail for Dumars, and Red wandered back to his own office. Though I had plenty to keep me occupied with the case, I decided to carve out a few minutes to check on things at Presqu'isle. While Neddie had assured me that I had nothing to worry about, that persistent, nagging knot in the pit of my stomach refused to go away. I really did have faith in my former roommate—at least that's what I kept telling myself. But I'd also learned, over many years of trial and error, to trust my own gut instinct. Sometimes it led me into impossible situations and near-disastrous mistakes that made me feel as if I had the insight of a turnip. But I was right more often than not, and my errors of judgment had almost always been made in trying to protect those I loved.

For some reason, as I listened to the phone ring on the hall table in the old antebellum mansion, a flash of memory, so vivid it made me gasp, exploded in my head: *A steamy, August afternoon, the sun so blindingly brilliant it hurt my eyes. Rob waving at the top of the short run of steps leading up to the small jet that would have him at the state capital in half an hour. The roar of the engines—the graceful liftoff—the life-shattering explosion—*

"Hello, Bay."

I jumped about six inches off my chair. "Hey," I squeaked, then recovered my equanimity and my voice. "Hey, Lavinia. How did you know it was me?"

"I decided it was high time I joined the twenty-first century. I got three of these high-tech new phones. Had the fellow put one in the kitchen and another in my room upstairs. It has this little picture window thingy on it that tells who's callin'. Never thought I'd see the day."

"Me either. Now I feel really bad."

"Why, honey?"

"Because, even as techno-phobic as I am, I always knew there was at least one person more terrified of it than I am. I guess I've just moved to the bottom of the heap."

She laughed, that rich, rolling sound that came straight from her heart. I felt myself smiling back, pleased more than I could say to hear such genuine joy. She'd been a long time recovering from my father's death, and then the sudden, appalling incident that had taken Miss Lizzie from us. It made me want to forget everything negative I'd been thinking about my half-sister. Maybe I should just make polite conversation and hang the hell up.

Lavinia's next words made that a non-starter.

"Actually, it was Julia's idea. She saw an ad in the Sunday paper about how the phone company was having this special thing for senior citizens. Of which I am one," she added with another laugh, "in case you hadn't noticed. We got such a good deal, both on the phones and the installation and all, that I just couldn't pass it up. And the nicest young man came to put everything in for us. Harold, his name was, and he's related some way to Miss Hammond, on her mama's side, I think."

"I didn't know Julia paid that much attention to the paper," I said without thinking.

The slight pause before she answered let me know exactly how that statement had come across. "There's a lot you don't know about Julia, Bay. You should come visit more often. Your sister has made a lot of progress. Nedra has been a great help to her."

"I'm sure she has," I said, lightening my tone. "She's the best." I waited, but there was no response. "How's the canning coming along?"

The end of the summer growing season usually ushered in a mad dash to get the okra, butter beans, snap peas, and all the other wonderful products of Lavinia's extensive vegetable garden processed and put up before anything had a chance to spoil. I well remembered the steamy kitchen on a shining fall afternoon, jars boiling in kettles on the stove, chopped and cleaned vegetables waiting to be processed spread out on every available surface. Lavinia with a kerchief tied around her hair and sweat pooling in the crooks of her arms and running down the back of her neck.

"If that was an effort to change the subject, it isn't going to wash, honey. I don't know why you've taken this dislike to your

sister, but it needs to stop. She's had more than her share of
misery in her life, and you of all people should understand that."
She paused for a moment. "I expected better of you."

The ultimate condemnation. I bit the inside of my cheek.

"I don't mean to sound harsh, Bay, but I think you're being
very unfair to Julia. She asks about you all the time, wondering
when you're going to come home. It's really not so much to ask, is
it? She's been without family for so many—"

"I get it, Lavinia, okay? I'm a miserable, worthless human
being."

"You're no such thing, and you know it. All I'm sayin' is that
you were raised up to do your duty, even if for some reason you
don't find it to your liking."

Not much I could say to that.

"Why don't you and Redmond come to dinner?" she asked in
a softer tone.

I swallowed my anger. "You're right. I'm sorry. But we're tied
up on a case at the moment. I promise we'll stop by on Sunday
after we take the kids back to Beaufort. Around two thirty, three.
Is that okay?"

"I'll make sure I have somethin' chocolate for you," Lavinia
said, and I had to smile.

"See you then."

As usual, the rock and harbor of my childhood didn't say
goodbye.

I sat for a moment after replacing the handset in its cradle,
my chin resting on my steepled fingers. I was used to tongue-lash-
ings from Lavinia. They'd been a staple of my growing-up at
Presqu'isle. And generally, like the one I'd just received, the lec-
tures had their foundation in her insistence on honesty, integrity,
and character. A deeply spiritual woman, she lived her faith without doubt or waver. Family—and its place in the hierarchy of life's
important responsibilities—was almost a second religion to Lavinia, and violating this tenet fell pretty much at the top of her
personal list of mortal sins.

I tried really hard not to be found wanting in her eyes, but
sometimes there was no way I could live up to her expectations.
Or my own.

"Bay?"

I looked up to see Stephanie framed in the doorway.

"Sorry to interrupt."

"It's welcome," I said, letting go of a long exhale and a small portion of the tension. "What have you got?"

"Cynthia Merrill is Hubbard Danforth's ex-wife. They were divorced ten years ago, but for some reason she still uses his name as part of hers."

"That's strange. We multi-name Southern women usually have our mother's maiden one stuck in there somewhere. It's pretty unusual to retain an ex's as part of the package. Anything interesting about their split?"

"I didn't try to access their settlement, but nothing jumped right out. Do you think it's a coincidence that both Hub and his ex-wife are sniffing around Mr. St. John's property?"

I smiled. That word again. "No way the two things aren't connected. I wonder if they're still in touch—Mr. and ex-Mrs. Hub."

"We could just ask him."

"That would certainly be the quickest route to an answer. When are we due to report to him?"

"Monday. He's going to be out of touch for the weekend. He didn't say why."

I thought for a moment. "So let's just table that for now. There are a lot of conclusions we could jump to, but it can wait a couple of days. Let's just concentrate on doing what we've been hired for—keeping an eye on Mr. St. John. And speaking of that, how are you guys set up for the weekend? Do you want Red or me to take a shift?"

"We've got it covered. You have the kids tomorrow, right?"

"Yes. I don't know if Red has anything special planned, but don't hesitate to call if you find yourselves in need of backup."

"No problem. I'm going to update the files and head over to relieve Erik, if that's okay."

I smiled at the eager anticipation on her pretty face. "No problem. Do what you have to do. And Stephanie?"

She turned back. "Yes, ma'am?"

"Nice work today."

She beamed. "Thanks. We'll keep you informed if anything unusual goes down."

I tidied up my own desk, glancing frequently at the phone, but Billy Dumars didn't return my call. At four I buzzed Red and asked if he was ready to hit the road.

"Any time you are, honey. Got any thoughts about dinner?"

"Let's see what we can scrounge up at home, okay with you? Maybe we'll get lucky, and Dolores will have left something for us. She mentioned tortillas for the kids this weekend."

"If not, we can always order in."

"Let's hit it then," I said and hung up. I'd just retrieved my bag from the bottom desk drawer when the phone rang. "Got it!" I hollered and picked up.

"Bay, darlin'!" Billy Dumars' voice reverberated down the line. "Good to hear from you."

"Where are you, Billy?" I asked. "You sound like you're down a well."

"Just headin' out into the Calibogue. Supposed to be a great weekend for fishing, though in my case the fish usually end up winnin' most of the rounds." He chuckled. "You said you needed some information on land deals?"

"Yes, for a case. But I'm guessing you didn't bring your files along on your fishing trip."

He laughed, a hearty bellow that made me hold the handset away from my ear. "When you gonna make it into the new millennium, girl? Got my iPad and my phone right here. Never leave home without 'em. What do you need?"

"I'm wondering if you've ever heard of an outfit called Mid-south Asset Development. There was an article in the *Packet* this morning about their being in some sort of hassle about acquiring property on the island. Do you know anything more that maybe didn't make it into the paper? Any scuttlebutt in the real estate community? Have they been buying up land around here for some kind of project?" I laughed. "I'll even settle for outright rumor or gossip."

"Nothing off the top of my head. I know who they are, of course. Got a pretty good reputation, far as I recall. What's your interest?"

I heard the change in the tenor of his voice, from his usual good-ol'-boy bluster to the highly successful real estate professional. Billy was smelling an opportunity.

"Confidentiality, Billy, remember?"

"Yeah, I do. Helped keep me out of the slammer. Point taken." He paused. "I can do some nosing around if you like. No extra charge."

That made me smile. "Just keep an ear to the ground and let me know if there are any rumblings. I'd appreciate it."

"Will do, darlin'. How's that husband of yours? I heard he left the sheriff's."

"He's working with me at the agency."

"No hanky-panky in the office now, hear? Bad for business."

"Thanks, Billy, I'll keep that in mind. And I won't ask if those words of wisdom come from personal experience. Have a good trip."

"Talk to you," he said and hung up.

I looked up at Red standing in the doorway. "Anything?" he asked.

"Nope," I said, hefting my bag onto my shoulder. "But he'll let me know if he comes across something."

I moved around the desk, and Red draped an arm across my shoulder as we made our way outside. I set the alarm and locked the door behind us.

"Son of a bitch."

I turned at the sound of my husband's voice, his anger a dark presence in the warm afternoon light.

And saw the heart-shaped balloon tied to the driver's door of the Jaguar.

CHAPTER
SEVEN

No envelope, but the word *love* was stenciled in all caps across the face of the silly thing.

Silently, I worked at the red and white ribbons holding it to my car, but Red had other ideas. In a flash he had retrieved a stick from the bushes in front of the office and jabbed its pointy end into the balloon. With only a pitiful little *pop* it settled into an innocuous puddle on the ground.

"Son of a bitch," my husband said again, this time more softly. "This guy is seriously pissing me off."

I finished disentangling the ribbons and reached to pick up the deflated balloon. "Are we saving this, too?" I asked and earned myself a formidable scowl. I shook my head. "Come on, Red. Why are you getting so angry with *me*? To hear you tell the tale, I'm the victim here. You want to keep this ridiculous thing or not?"

He took it from my hands. "I'll follow you," he said, climbing into the Bronco.

As I cranked the Jaguar's powerful engine and drove sedately out of the parking lot, I realized I couldn't ignore the harassment any longer. It was all well and good for me to slough it off as some sort of prank. But now the whole thing was seriously interfering with my relationship with my husband, and we were more often than not on shaky ground as it was. Maybe it was time to consider things as I would a case, just as Red had suggested. I slid into the left-hand lane toward the Port Royal entrance and tried to conjure up where I might have encountered my stalker. I'd seen enough cop shows and read enough mystery novels to know that some kinds of perverts didn't need even the tiniest bit of encouragement. They invented connections in their own minds, convincing themselves that the object of their obsession was only waiting for the right moment to declare his or her devotion. I might have passed him on one of my infrequent forays into Publix or sat across the room from him at lunch. I might even have glanced at him as we passed on the street or in a parking lot.

I smiled at the young man at the gatehouse as he waved me through into the plantation.

Just like that, I told myself. If that guy were some sort of sexual stalker, he could misinterpret that simple act of courtesy as confirmation that I was his for the taking. Now that I really thought about it, the whole idea made me slightly nauseous.

I pulled the Jag into the garage, and Red eased the Bronco in beside it. We met at the foot of the steps.

"You're right," I said before he had a chance to get his anger cranked up again. "This is getting past an annoying joke. Let's eat, then put our heads together. Maybe we can figure out who the hell is messing with me."

His answer was to pull me to him in a crushing embrace. "Now you're talking," he said, leaning back so I could catch the full benefit of his satisfied grin.

"Good idea, bad execution," I said later that evening as we lounged on the sofa in the great room.

I'd almost suggested a fire, but it wasn't cool enough for one yet. We'd had Chinese delivered, and the empty cartons still littered the coffee table. I'd grabbed a legal pad from the bedroom Rob and I had converted to an office all those years ago, something I was going to have to deal with in the near future. With Scotty approaching puberty and Elinor becoming increasingly self-conscious about sharing a room with her brother, we'd need to shift our priorities. Even though we only had them for weekends and alternate holidays, both Red and I felt it was important that they feel as comfortable with us as they did with their mother during the week.

My husband's voice jerked me back to the problem of the moment.

"Well, you must have run into this asshole somewhere or other. Think."

"I *am* thinking, for God's sake. Didn't you get any training in dealing with creeps like this? It may have been the most casual contact. Maybe I should rent you a couple of seasons of *Criminal*

Minds. Those FBI profilers deal with this kind of thing all the time."

I thought it might make him smile, but he wasn't having any of that.

"Earth to Bay—please return immediately to the real world. This isn't one of those damn TV shows that gets everything wrapped up in an hour."

I watched him visibly take himself in hand, and his next words came out more slowly and much more softly.

"These kinds of people are dangerous. I've come close to losing you more times than I want to count." He reached out a hand and laid it tenderly against my cheek. "In more ways than one. Don't ask me to take this lightly, okay?"

I smiled and covered his hand with my own. "Okay."

"So." He straightened his shoulders and picked up the legal pad with my scribbled thoughts. "Try to remember what you were up to just before you got the first note. I don't recall any cases at the office that might have put you in this guy's crosshairs, do you?"

I sighed, reluctantly remembering Winston Wolfe and Morgan Tyler Bell. The series of tragedies at Jericho Cay. Red lying bleeding on this very floor. I shuddered and hugged myself.

"Cold?" my husband asked. "Want me to make a fire?"

"No, I'm good. Just bad memories." I shook my head to clear it. "We haven't had an individual client since Wolfe. Until Hubbard Danforth, that is. Just the usual background grunt work. You've been there, too, remember?"

He ran his hand through his hair, leaving a few strands standing straight up. "Yeah, I know. I guess I want this to be somebody we can put a face to. And a name. If it's really just some deviant who happened to rub shoulders with you at the post office, we're never going to find him."

Until he finds me, I thought and looked up to see the same fear staring back at me from my husband's troubled eyes.

In the end, we accomplished precisely nothing, tidying up the food cartons and the kitchen before heading off to bed. I slept fitfully, waking every hour or so to stare at the red numerals on the clock before rearranging the pillows and flipping back over. As often happened, Red let me sleep in and made the trek to Beaufort on his own. I'd had just enough time to shower and get things organized in the kids' room when they came trooping into the house.

I couldn't remember if there'd been a soccer game that morning, but if so they must have lost. There was no whooping and hollering and high-fiving as they plodded up the steps from the garage.

"Hey, gang," I said. "What's up?"

Elinor, who usually made a beeline for a hug, hung back, her father's hand clutched in both of hers. Scotty dropped his backpack on the counter and went immediately to investigate the refrigerator without a word of greeting.

I looked quizzically at Red, who mouthed *Later* at me.

Aloud, he said, "So what's on the agenda for today, troops? Homework all done?"

Scotty spoke from the interior of the refrigerator. "Yes, sir."

"Yes, Daddy," Elinor nodded. "Is it too cold to go swimming?"

Red glanced at me.

"I think so," I said, although Neddie and I had stuck our toes in on Thursday afternoon. Though the sun was warm, the water had been decidedly chilly, not the bath-water temperature we came to expect in the height of summer. "We could go play out there, though, if we bundle up a little. Build a sand castle, maybe toss the ball around. How does that sound?"

The response was underwhelming, except from Red, who seemed as much at a loss as I was by the strange, subdued behavior of his usually exuberant children.

"That sounds like fun. How about it? We'll have some lunch—"

"I'm not hungry." Red's son finally emerged with a bottle of lemonade clutched in one hand. "I'd like to go read in my room, if that's okay."

"Me, too," Elinor piped up.

"Why do you have to follow me around all the time? Go find something to do on your own for once."

Elinor's wail and Red's, "Scott Michael Tanner!" burst into the room simultaneously.

"Sorry," his son mumbled before scooping his backpack off

the counter and stomping down the hallway.

Red knelt and folded Elinor into his arms. "It's okay, honey, don't cry."

I laid a hand on her silky, dark blond hair. "Sometimes boys are just yucky," I said and was rewarded with a watery smile. "They can't help it. It's just their nature."

"But what am *I* gonna do?" she managed between hiccups of tears.

Inspiration struck, meshing nicely with my thoughts of the evening before. Scotty needed his privacy. So did this sweet little thing. I could shift the desk into the master bedroom and get rid of a lot of the other stuff that was just taking up space. We could move in one of the twin beds and fix the room up fit for a princess. I'd never had occasion to decorate a bedroom for a little girl, but I was sure I could pull it off. I knelt down next to Red and put my arm around the sniffling child.

"You and I are going shopping," I said, and my husband smiled at me over his daughter's head. "Why don't you go blow your nose and use the bathroom. We've got a lot of territory to cover."

"Is it okay, Daddy?" she asked, running her bare arm under her dripping nose.

"Absolutely, sweetheart," Red answered. "Now go get ready."

"Yes, Daddy." She scampered toward the hallway. "And no yucky boys get to come, right, Aunt Bay?"

"Right you are, kiddo," I said, and she turned and darted off.

"Good save." Red gave me a hand up. He looked toward where his children had disappeared. "Something's going on with Sarah."

Red's ex-wife had helped me out of a scrape a few years back, and I'd thought she had come to terms with our marriage. "About us?" I asked.

He shook his head. "No. I'm not sure, but the kids have been on edge ever since I picked them up. I've tried to pry it out of them, but I'm not having any luck. See if you can get El to clue you in."

I allowed myself a furtive glance over my shoulder to make sure we were still alone. "But why do you think it's about their mother? Does she have a boyfriend or something?"

"I don't think so. For one thing, she looked like hell when

she came to the door, almost like she'd dragged herself out of bed. And they told me they fixed themselves cereal for breakfast because mommy wasn't feeling good. It might be a flu bug or maybe a cold, but she looked really rough. Either she's sworn them to secrecy or they really don't know, because I'm getting stonewalled with every question. See what you can do, okay?"

That sinking sensation that I tried very hard to pay attention to was gnawing at my stomach, but I forced a smile. "I'm going to redo the office for Elinor. It's time she had her own room."

Red pulled me to him and hugged me. "That's a great idea. I'll try to keep the sulking tweener occupied. You girls go have fun."

I smiled back, but the niggling worry had already taken firm control. Sarah Tanner was a first-class mother. Nothing mattered to her as much as her children. If she wasn't able to haul herself out of bed to fix them breakfast, something was seriously wrong.

"Ready!" the little voice announced from just behind us. Elinor raised her arm to show her little change purse dangling from her fragile wrist. "I brought money. Just in case you run out, Aunt Bay."

I scooped her up in my arms, surprising us both with the ferocity of my hug. "That's great, honey. We're going to shop 'til we drop."

"Shop 'til we drop!" she echoed, her sweet smile lighting her elfin face.

And in that moment, I knew I'd do whatever it took to keep it there.

Whatever it took.

Miss Elinor proved to be less trouble and more fun than I'd anticipated as I dragged her from Home Goods to Stein Mart to Belk's with a final sweep of Walmart and a brief break for lunch. It took us three trips to empty the backseat and trunk of the Jaguar. We dumped everything on the floor in the office and retreated to the kitchen.

"How about some iced tea?" I asked, scanning the refrigerator. Sarah forbade the consumption of soft drinks except on special occasions. "Or there's lemonade."

"Lemonade, please." Elinor settled herself at the round table in the alcove of the bay window. "And may I have a glass?"

Her formality made me smile as I filled tumblers for us both. Sarah—and Red—had done a wonderful job of instilling manners in their two kids. The *sirs* and *ma'ams* flowed as easily from their lips as mindless profanities did from some of their contemporaries.

I joined my little niece/step-daughter at the table. We sipped quietly for a moment, the rigors of shopping washed away in a tinkle of ice. Though I'd made a couple of feeble attempts to draw her out, this seemed like a perfect moment for a little girl talk. I didn't know where the menfolk had gotten to, but I decided to take advantage of their absence.

"Your dad said your mom wasn't feeling well this morning."

"Unh-uh. I mean, no, ma'am."

"Does she have a cold?"

A shrug of the narrow, bony shoulders.

"The flu?"

Another shrug.

"Has she been sick long?"

The silence was punctuated by the soft banging of the heels of the girl's pink sneakers against the rung of the chair.

"Elinor?"

She mumbled into her glass. "I'm not s'posed to talk about it."

I gave her a moment. "Why not? Your dad and I are worried." Her head snapped up. "Just a little bit. Maybe we could help her if we knew what was wrong."

Again her words were garbled, but I managed to get the gist.

"So she's been throwing up?" The child nodded. "All the time?"

"Lots of the time, but mostly in the morning."

Oh, God, I thought. *Pregnant?* I did some quick math. Sarah was several years younger than I, so it wasn't impossible. Hell, it wouldn't be impossible for *me*. I gave that thought a vicious kick toward the back of my head.

"That's too bad. Does your mom have any special friends who come to visit? Maybe stay overnight?"

Jousting with IRS agents and recalcitrant clients in my old CPA days certainly hadn't prepared me for interrogating a nine year old, as evidenced by her sudden descent into tears. Quickly I moved around the table and gathered her into my arms, wondering where in the hell her father had disappeared to. I felt completely incompetent to handle this kind of situation. "Don't cry, sweetheart. I didn't mean to make you upset. If you don't want to talk about it, that's fine." I left her long enough to grab some tissues from the box on the counter. "Here, blow your nose and let's go unpack our treasures, okay?" She sniffled and blew. "Better?"

"Mommy doesn't want anybody to know," she whispered against my shoulder.

"Know about what?" I asked softly.

"She said all her hair is going to fall out, but then she'll be better real soon."

I pressed her quivering body to mine as the horrible truth finally penetrated.

CHAPTER EIGHT

We took two cars, the kids riding with Red in the Bronco.

I trailed behind them, the horror of their mother's situation sitting front and center in my thoughts. Why she hadn't confided in Red was beyond my understanding, but I was sure she had her reasons. If something terrible . . . if the worst . . . It didn't bear thinking about.

But we'd have to think about it, I realized as I made the turn from 278 onto 170. Sarah incapacitated—or Sarah *dead* I forced myself to acknowledge—would mean an instant and constant family for their father and me. I tried to picture what that would look like in terms of my life, my job, my business, but nothing came. I had never before seriously contemplated being a mother to anybody, let alone children who would be lost and grieving. And resenting the hell out of someone trying to take their mother's place.

I shook myself literally, like a dog, trying to banish the pointless speculation. Red would sort it out with his ex-wife. And together they'd decide what was best for their children. I really had no role to play in those decisions, except to be standing by, ready to pick up the pieces.

Just across the Broad River bridge, Red veered off with a honk of his horn. I waved desultorily and carried on toward Presqu'isle. And some more family issues that had landed squarely in the middle of my plate. I remembered a day, not so long ago, standing alone in my office, when I had declared myself an orphan. I was beginning to see the lure of that situation right at the moment.

It was a glorious fall Sunday in the Lowcountry, and I tried to distract myself from the mud wallow of self-pity. Sunlight bounced off the calm waters of the Beaufort River as I made my way across the high arch of the bridge onto Lady's Island. There were a lot of things I didn't miss about my college days up North, but I did find myself yearning at this time of year for the riot of color in the turning leaves, the nip in the air as football season got into full swing. Even though poets often referred to autumn as the dying of the year, it always seemed to me to be a lovely respite, a gathering of strength to face the coming winter. I wished now that Red and I had taken the opportunity to spend a couple of days in the mountains. It might have prepared me better for what looked to be a long and challenging season of change.

Presqu'isle sparkled in the mid-afternoon sun as I pulled up into the semi-circular drive. As always, an explosion of flowers greeted me as I approached the split staircase. Lavinia seemed able to rotate things so that no season of the year left the front of the house devoid of color. In fairness, I thought, trudging up the steps, she probably followed a pattern laid down by my late mother, who prided herself on the excellence of her gardens. In that, as in so many other things, I had proved a sore disappointment to her. I couldn't grow grass.

"It's me," I called, dropping my bag next to the console table.

"In here." Lavinia's voice drifted down the hallway from the kitchen.

I found the two of them, my friend and my sister, hunched over the scarred oak table, a bowl of deep chocolate icing between them. Cupcakes, just as richly brown, cooled on racks. About half of them had already been frosted.

"Just in time," Lavinia said, rewarding me with a radiant smile for keeping my promise.

Before I had a chance to respond, Julia had bounded around the table and smothered me in a choking embrace.

"Oh, Bay, you came! Miss Lavinia said you would, but I wasn't sure!"

I patted her shoulder, doing my damnedest to hide a shudder of unease, and gently pried her arms from around my neck.

"Hello, Julia." I studied her beaming face for a moment before it dawned on me why she looked so different. "You cut your hair!"

She stepped back and twirled around, letting the short pageboy that just hugged her chin fly out around her. "Do you like it? I asked Dr. Nedra, and she said it was a good idea. Miss Lavinia took me into Beaufort. And I got my fingernails painted, too."

She held her hands out for my inspection. "It's called *Raspberry Crunch*."

"Very nice," I said, stepping back out of range. "What are you making?"

Lavinia held my gaze, her own slightly disapproving. "That should be obvious. I did promise you something chocolate."

"So you did." I slid into the chair I had been occupying since I'd been old enough to sit at the table with the grownups. "They smell heavenly."

Julia bounced back beside Lavinia and took up her narrow spatula. "We're going to sprinkle the top with chopped pecans because that's how you like them best."

Her exuberance reminded me so much of Elinor's. Neddie had said she was making progress, and maybe this was it. Maybe being able to interact with us, even on a childish level, was the beginning of her stunted mind's finally catching up to her adult body. I made a silent pledge to get my act together and give my sister whatever help and support I could muster. Nothing would be accomplished by holding onto my fears and suspicions.

"What can I do?" I asked and found that my smile this time was genuine rather than forced.

"You can chop the nuts," Lavinia said, the warmth back in her regard of me. "You know where everything is."

"Yes, ma'am," I answered and went to retrieve the cutting board.

If it hadn't been for my worry about Sarah—and the presence of my half-sister—it might almost have been like old times.

Almost.

I headed back to Hilton Head with a plastic container of cupcakes and a sense of confidence that things were going to work out, on a number of fronts. That calm lasted until just past Moss Creek and the first of the two bridges that would take me onto the island.

I fumbled around in my bag on the front seat beside me and finally pulled out my cell phone. Red and I had already agreed to meet at Jump & Phil's for a sandwich before going home, and I wondered if something had happened to change his mind. But it was Erik, sounding slightly breathless.

"Bay, it's me. Where are you?"

"Just coming on-island from Presqu'isle. What's up?"

"It's Mr. St. John. Steph and I have been taking turns keeping an eye on his place. Nothing much happened since we saw you last. He got home from his outing on Friday, and the Williams lady helped him carry in some groceries. We knocked off about ten, since we figured he'd be in for the night."

I wanted him to move it along, to explain the undercurrent of concern in his voice, but I knew my partner well enough to realize that he'd get to it in his own way.

"Okay," I said by way of encouragement.

"Yesterday—Saturday—he pretty much stayed put. He came out in the morning to get his paper and then sat on the porch to read it. He was in and out a couple of times, to sweep up some leaves and take a short walk down to the beach and back. I was here this morning early, in case he went to church, but I haven't seen him at all."

I glanced at the dashboard clock which showed a few minutes shy of four. "Not at all?"

"Nope. His Sunday paper is still out there. Then, a little after noon, the black Lexus was back. This time the Merrill woman went right up and knocked on the door, but he didn't answer. She tried a couple of times, then went back and sat in the car for about half an hour before she tried again. Altogether, she made three attempts before she finally gave up and drove away."

I could feel the fear gathering in my gut again. So much for mellowing out. "And you still haven't seen him?"

"No. I just went up and knocked myself. I figured it was worth blowing our cover to find out if he was okay in there."

"Nothing?"

"No response at all. I looked in the front windows. With that iron scrollwork on them—and the dirt and dried salt spray—it's almost impossible to see in, but I couldn't detect any movement or hear any noise, like a TV or radio. What do you want me to do?"

The decision seemed simple. "Call Red and ask him to meet us there. I'm on my way."

Long shadows fell from the massive live oak at the corner of Malcolm St. John's property and shrouded the tiny bungalow in

darkness. I swung the Jaguar into one of the metered parking slots
at the end of the street. As I slid out, Erik stepped out of the
tangle of stunted trees and foliage.

"Anything?" I asked, and he shook his head.

"Red was a little farther out, so he'll be a couple of minutes."

I could read the question in his eyes: Why had my husband
and I driven separate cars to Beaufort? I pushed those issues to
the back of my mind.

The narrow street that T-ed into the one we were on couldn't
have been more peaceful. Some of the usual onshore breeze ruffled through the limbs of the oak, but the silence was profound. I
looked out toward the ocean where the deep blue of the October
sky had begun to fade a little in anticipation of sunset. A few more
weeks and daylight savings time would be a thing of the past,
bringing full night earlier and earlier. I shifted my weight from
foot to foot, checking repeatedly over my shoulder for any sign of
Red's Bronco.

"I don't like this," I said aloud. "I can see an old man not
venturing out all day, even one as gorgeous as this has been. But
not picking up the Sunday paper? And not answering the door
several times makes me nervous." I paused. "Any chance you
could have missed him? I mean, maybe someone came and picked
him up last night."

Erik shrugged. "I suppose it's possible. But I stayed until his
lights were out and he'd presumably gone to bed. Why would he
get up again and leave in the middle of the night?"

"I grant you it doesn't make a lot of sense, but I like it a
whole lot better than the other possibilities."

"That he's sick or injured in there? Or—"

"Dead."

I turned at the sound of an engine and watched Red pull in
beside me. Before he'd had a chance to get out of the car, I
reached into my pocket and retrieved the American Express card
I'd fished from my wallet. When he'd slammed the door behind
him, I handed him the card.

"Okay, James Bond," I said with a lightness I didn't feel, "do
your thing."

In the end, we didn't require Red's breaking-and-entering skills.

The door, though latched, yielded to a slight push. I held my breath when my husband eased it open, fearful of the rush of a sickeningly sweet odor that would have confirmed my worst fears. Instead we were met with complete silence and a slightly musty smell that spoke of closed windows and the need for a long over-due cleaning.

I let the men take the lead, slipping in behind them into a small but neat living area. A sagging recliner took pride of place, its green velvet worn to thin patches on the arms and footrest. A round oak table stood next to the chair, and a discolored metal floor lamp hovered behind it, like a nosy neighbor peering over its shoulder. The inevitable television, one of the old bulky ones, hunkered on a rickety stand beneath the window.

I stepped onto the wood floor and felt the grit of sand under my shoes. It might have been the original heart pine, but years of wear and exposure to the elements of the beach had turned its finish nearly black.

"Turn on the lamp," I said, squinting in the meager, waning sunlight filtered through the iron scrollwork on the windows.

Red complied, but it did little to banish the gloom of the tiny space. The three of us seemed to overwhelm the narrow room.

"Mr. St. John?" I called, not too loudly. I didn't want to ter-rify the old man into a heart attack. "Sir? Are you all right?"

Behind Erik I could see what looked to be the kitchen, and another doorway led off to the right.

"I'll check around." Red moved down the short hallway and disappeared.

"I've got the kitchen," Erik said and turned in that direction.

With the tiny cottage covered, I wandered the confines of the main living area. There was a stack of newspapers beside the re-cliner. I lifted the top one and checked the date. Saturday. Mr. St. John must have been a recycler, because the pile looked a couple of feet high. Or maybe he just hadn't gotten around to throwing them in the trash. There was a copy of *Hilton Head Monthly*, our local glossy magazine, but it was from July. I couldn't spot any-thing that might hold letters or correspondence. No computer, which didn't surprise me, but a fairly up-to-date portable tele-phone, which did. Or maybe Mr. St. John had taken advantage of the same special offer that enticed Lavinia into the twenty-first century. I turned as Red strode back into the room.

"Small bedroom, one bath. Neither especially clean, but neat. Like the rest of the place. Nothing that could tell us where the old guy has gotten to."

Erik joined us. "Same in there. The groceries he came home with seem to be about all there is in the cupboards and refrigerator. The usual staples and some pre-packaged stuff. Nice microwave, which is probably what he uses to cook with most of the time." He shrugged. "Oh, and one cup, rinsed and on the drain board next to the sink."

"No coffee pot or tea kettle?" I wondered if that had been his last cup the night before or the first one this morning.

"Nope. The coffee in the cupboard is instant, so he probably just nukes water in the microwave."

"Maybe he learned his lesson about boiling things on the stove," Red offered, "after he fell asleep and let it catch fire."

"Maybe." I turned full circle in the tight confines of the cottage's front room, my mind trying to avoid the obvious conclusion. "So where in the hell is he?"

"Time to call it in?" Red asked.

"And who's going to pay any attention if we do? Isn't there a forty-eight-hour rule for adults?"

"Technically. But with the elderly, especially since they have a little history with Mr. St. John, we might be able to get something going sooner. I can try."

"We haven't looked around outside," Erik said into the stillness.

"Good point." I took two steps and reached for the door handle. "Let's do that first."

Back out in the clear evening air, the stifling closeness of the little bungalow dissipated quickly. In tandem, we walked around the far side of the house.

"I wonder if there's any point in asking the neighbors," I murmured, gesturing toward the towering mansion across the street. No lights showed in its windows, and the driveway was devoid of vehicles.

"Probably not," Red answered.

We stopped together as if the move had been choreographed and scanned the back yard, mostly overgrown with scrub palmetto. The only clear areas lay beneath the live oak and its crumbling tree house and the swath of dead grass that bordered the bungalow. The sky out over the ocean had melted into a pale aqua with tinges of rose and orange as the placid surface of the water reflected the last rays of the sun sinking over the mainland. Somewhere off to our left, a squirrel chattered and was answered by the high-pitched screech of an owl.

"We could walk down to the beach, take a quick reconnoiter." Red's voice sounded unnaturally loud in the shimmering stillness of the Lowcountry dusk.

"We'd need flashlights by the time we got down there," I said. "You have one in the car?"

"Small Maglite," Red answered. "It might do the job."

"I'm game," Erik said as we moved toward the end of the house facing the parking area. "I feel sort of responsible, since we were supposed to be keeping an eye on him."

"That's ridiculous. We didn't sign on for twenty-four/seven, did we? Besides, there could be a perfectly logical—"

My left foot encountered the obstruction a moment before I tumbled headlong into the dirt.

CHAPTER NINE

Our first instinct was to carry the old man into the house, but that was quickly vetoed.

"We should call the paramedics," I said, once I'd managed to get my breath back. "We have no idea how seriously he might be injured."

No one argued the point, and Red stepped away to use his cell.

"I'll get a blanket from the house," Erik offered and moved off before I could reply.

I'd immediately checked for a pulse, finding it steady when I finally managed to locate a vein in his frail wrist. His skin felt clammy, but his breathing seemed regular and even. He could almost have been asleep except for the fact that my tripping over him, landing with one knee in the middle of his back, hadn't caused the slightest reaction.

"On their way," my husband said. "How is he?"

"His vitals seem good, near as I can tell, but I'm no expert."

"Any apparent injuries you can see?"

In the failing light, I hadn't detected any blood, but that didn't mean there wasn't any. I ran my scraped hand gently over his skull and gasped when I encountered a nasty lump just behind his left ear.

"What?" Red asked just as Erik came around the corner of the house.

"He's got a big knot on the side of his head."

I took the blanket from my partner and laid it gently over the wizened old man.

"He might have fallen, maybe even inside, and dragged himself out in search of help," Erik offered, but I didn't think so.

Even before the rescue squad came screaming down the street, with a Beaufort County Sheriff's cruiser hot on its heels, I felt certain someone had attacked Malcolm St. John.

And whether or not it was our responsibility, I was going to make the son of a bitch pay.

Red and I stopped at home to consolidate into one car while Erik headed for the office to notify our client. It was a call I had been prepared to make, but my partner had insisted. If it would help wipe the flush of guilt from his face, I figured I should leave him to it.

At the hospital, they, of course, told us nothing. Not just because that's the way they usually operate, but mostly because we had absolutely no standing in regard to Mr. St. John. In the past, I'd been somewhat successful in cajoling or browbeating information out of poor receptionists and clerical workers, but none of my usual bag of tricks did me any good.

I'd hoped that perhaps Red would be able to tease at least some basic intel out of one of the deputies who had accompanied the old man to the hospital, but he, too, struck out. Finally, at a little past nine o'clock, we decided to pack it in.

My stomach grumbled all the way out into the emergency room parking lot, but I also felt slightly nauseous. Red solved the problem by taking a short detour to Wendy's, which stayed open later than most of the other fast food restaurants. I put up a token protest that was quickly overridden in favor of fresh, hot fries and a burger that had been cooked just a few minutes before. It tasted heavenly.

We sat at a table in the chill air of the restaurant with only the staff behind the counter for company. When I'd satisfied my deeper cravings, I leaned back in the plastic chair.

"What do you think?"

Red swallowed and stared back at me. "I think we know what happened, don't we?"

"Someone bashed that poor old man's head in. I'd be shocked to hear they considered it an accident. But why? And *who*?"

"It could have nothing to do with us, with our client, I mean. Muggings happen here in paradise, like it or not."

"But that doesn't make any sense. No one could seriously consider that he had anything worth stealing. He could have wandered outside after Erik left him and encountered trouble, or he let someone in. I can't wrap my head around either scenario. The only thing he seems to have of value is his property. Can you seriously envision Hub Danforth or his ex-wife beating up the old man for that? I mean, what good would it do them?"

Red slurped down the last of his Coke and wiped his mouth with a handful of paper napkins. "It makes more sense for it to have been a random attack. Maybe he got confused and thought it was morning. He could have run into somebody up to no good, and they just whacked him to get him out of the way."

"That's just as hard to believe as a deliberate attack. I wonder if he'll be able to remember?"

Red shrugged. "Given his age and condition before, I can't think a blow to the head would help any. We'll just have to wait and see."

My phone rang, and I dug it out of my bag. Erik's voice sounded way beyond tired.

"I just talked to Mr. Danforth. It took a while to track him down."

"And?" I mouthed *Erik* across the table to Red.

"He was shocked. And angry. I guess he figured nothing like this could happen while we had Mr. St. John under surveillance."

"Totally unfair. If he had any inkling that his uncle was in some kind of danger, he should have revealed that to you and Stephanie during the interview. We would certainly have handled things differently." I paused. "Did he give any indication to you tonight that he wasn't surprised? I mean, did he imply that he knew Mr. St. John might be at risk?"

"No. Like I said, he seemed totally shocked. He's on his way down, but he won't get here until the middle of the night. He said he'd notify his sister. She must live somewhere up that way."

There wasn't much else to say. "Go home to Stephanie," I said. "We'll hash this all out in the morning. And Erik?"

"Yeah?"

"None of this is your fault, got it?" When he didn't immediately reply, I said more tersely, "Got it?"

"Sure. Let me know if you hear anything about how Mr. St. John is doing. See you tomorrow."

I flipped the phone closed and dropped it back in my bag. I gave Red the gist of the conversation.

"You can't order him not to feel guilty," my husband said as he rose and followed me out to the empty parking lot. "God knows it doesn't work with you."

That made me smile for the first time in what seemed like days. Then another sobering thought hit me right between the eyes. "What happened at Sarah's?"

"Nothing."

"What do you mean, nothing? Did you talk to her? Ask her about the . . . her illness?"

"She wouldn't come to the door. I followed the kids in, but she was in her bedroom. I didn't feel right making a scene, barging in or anything. I made grilled cheese sandwiches for them and kind of waited around, but she never even acknowledged that I was there."

I thought about Sarah Jane Tanner as we turned into the plantation and made our way home. Such behavior was so unlike the woman I'd known as my sister-in-law during the years I'd been married to Rob. We'd never been close—sister-close—but we'd spent an awful lot of time in each other's company, on holidays and out to dinner, parties at each other's homes. Her divorce from Red hadn't been exactly amicable, but they'd both seemed to have moved beyond it, their shared love for their children making them civil at least. At one time, I'd thought Red might be making a move to reconcile, but that idea had apparently died on the vine. It was beyond my comprehension that she could keep something this important from him, especially as it would have a profound effect on the kids. I wondered if there was something else going on, although it was hard to imagine anything more devastating than a diagnosis of cancer. Maybe she'd talk to me, though that seemed a stretch.

"Don't borrow trouble," I murmured as we pulled into the garage.

"What, honey?" Red asked.

"Nothing. Just thinking out loud."

We climbed the stairs together, our arms around each other. I felt so sad—for Red and his children and for Mr. St. John. Maybe it was time to find another profession, one that didn't bring me into contact with so many people's miseries. It seemed I had enough on my own doorstep to keep me occupied for a long time to come.

Sometime during the night, a front had moved through, leaving us with a light, drizzling rain. The weather did nothing to improve anyone's temper. As we gathered in my office with our caffeine delivery systems of choice, the mood pretty much matched the lowering gray skies.

I'd made a call to the hospital the moment I'd stashed my bag in my lower desk drawer. Pretending to be Mr. St. John's cousin had gotten me precisely nowhere, other than to hear the standard put-offs. I hung up and found three expectant faces framed in my doorway.

"Doing as well as can be expected. Spent a comfortable night. Blah, blah, blah," I said. "Have we heard anything from Hub Danforth?"

Stephanie shook her head. "No messages. Would you like me to see if I can reach him?"

I waffled, not entirely sure whether or not to kick that sleeping dog awake. "Let's give him a couple of hours," I finally decided. "If he didn't get in until the wee hours, he may be catching some sleep." I glanced at my watch. "If we don't hear from him by eleven, you can give it a try."

"So what now?" Erik still sounded depressed, and the usual upbeat smile was missing from his face.

"I think we need to track down Danforth's ex-wife. Let's see what Cynthia Merrill can contribute to any of this. Erik, can you handle that? Stephanie has some info on the company—" I had to stretch for the name. "Midsouth Asset Development. If she's down here on some sort of assignment, they should be able to tell us how to reach her. Lie if you have to. Say we have some property we're thinking about selling. That should at least get you through their first line of defense."

That did bring a little light into his eyes. "Right." He turned back toward his own desk.

"Stephanie, let's get into the county real estate records. I had a quick look on Friday, but nothing popped right up. There must be something funny about Mr. St. John's address. I seem to remember the post office is fond of screwing with the mailing addresses of places on the island to accommodate some new delivery plan or whatever. I'd like to know what his place has been appraised for, tax-wise. Also, see if any other property in the area has recently changed hands."

"I thought your real estate guy—Dumars—was going to check on that for you." Like the rest of us, Red sounded more subdued than usual.

"I know, but that was before there was any urgency to the matter. I don't want to wait around until he finds a few spare minutes."

"You think what happened to Mr. St. John has cranked things up a notch?" Red asked.

"Don't you?"

"Maybe. But we still don't know exactly what happened. One thing could have absolutely nothing to do with the other."

I cocked an eyebrow at him. "You've been involved with this stuff a lot longer than I have. Do you really think it's all some innocent convergence of circumstances?"

"Probably not. But there's no evidence to support either assumption."

"So go get some. Pump your old pals for some solid information. If the old man is conscious, they've no doubt talked to him by now, right?"

"I live to serve." My husband managed a passable grin, and I felt some of the gloom lifting. We all needed to snap out of it and take care of business.

Which proved extremely difficult for me. I'd parceled out the tasks that needed handled to everyone else, leaving myself way too much time to sit and brood. A couple of times I reached for the phone to call the hospital but forced my hand back onto the desk at the last moment. Experience had proved it to be an exercise in futility.

I downed the last of my chai tea latte, grown lukewarm over the past hour but still drinkable. I found myself staring at my diploma from Northwestern, one of several documents I'd arranged on the wall across from my desk. The inevitable progression of thoughts led me to Neddie Halloran and my half-sister Julia. I wondered if my assessment of her progress would prove to be enough to rid myself of those nagging feelings of suspicion and distrust that had plagued me for the past few weeks. Her sudden appearance in the doorway of the attic that night had startled me, as much for her stealthy approach as for the enigmatic smile that had sent shivers of apprehension shooting down my spine.

I remembered I'd been reading through the journals I'd stumbled upon in an old trunk while trying to assess the damage to the attics from the glancing blow struck us by Hurricane Kitty. After Julia had turned and retreated that night, I'd gathered them up and carried them downstairs. Rooting in the hall closet where my father used to store his hunting jackets and old boots, I'd pulled out a musty duffel bag and stacked the leather-bound books inside. I'd stashed them in the back of my closet and hadn't looked at them in the intervening month or so, but I remembered clearly the opening line of the first entry: *I was fourteen when Papa and Boy were taken by the fever, and Mama began to lose her mind.*

Madeleine Henriette Baynard. I'd been meaning to do some digging into my mother's genealogical records to determine just how we might be related, but the days had slipped into weeks, my time filled with work and family obligations. I made a mental note to ask Lavinia where all those papers had gotten to. Perhaps pursuing a little family history might prove a welcome distraction from the present and its mounting complications. Or not. It sounded from that opening line, dated April 23, 1860, that my distant something-or-other relative may have had more than her own share of trouble to contend with. Still, it might be good to—

The phone jerked me back to reality. A moment later, Stephanie buzzed me on the intercom.

"Mr. Danforth is on one," she said.

"How does he sound?"

"Tired, but not angry or anything like that."

"Okay, I'll take it." I let out a long, calming breath, and punched the blinking button. "Good morning, Mr. Danforth. This is Bay Tanner."

"Good morning. Thanks for taking my call."

"Not a problem. Do you have news about your uncle? We've all been tremendously concerned about him."

"That's very kind of you. He's been conscious since about five this morning, but I'm afraid he's not making a lot of sense. He doesn't remember much about what happened."

Which was precisely what I'd been afraid of. "Has anyone from the sheriff's office been in to question him?"

I looked up as Red came into the office, and I held up one finger. He nodded and dropped into one of the client chairs.

"Yes, one of the deputies stopped by about an hour ago, but Uncle Malcolm wouldn't talk to him. I thought maybe it was the uniform, but I didn't do any better once the officer left. He just keeps rambling on about . . . Well, it's sort of complicated to explain."

I glanced at Red, a little discomfited by the edgy tone of Hub Danforth's voice. It was almost as if the man didn't want to share whatever his uncle had told him for fear of upsetting me. Which made absolutely no sense whatsoever.

Before I could formulate a coherent question that might get us back on track, Danforth spoke again. "I know this is going to sound a little strange, but did you by any chance smell . . . whiskey? I mean when you found Uncle Malcolm?"

"Do you mean you think he was drunk? No, absolutely not. And there was no evidence that he kept anything like that in the house." I hurriedly continued. "I'm sorry, but we did make a fairly thorough search of the premises. Just to be certain Mr. St. John hadn't been taken ill or fallen inside the house."

"Oh, no, that's not what I mean. My uncle doesn't imbibe. At least not any more. There've been stories in the family that he might have been something of a hell-raiser back in the day, but he's been a solid, church-going man for decades now."

He paused, and I wondered what turn this strange conversation was going to take next, when Hub Danforth added more fuel to the fires of confusion.

"No," he said. "This would have been outside, maybe sprinkled around the area where you found him?"

"No," I replied, "nothing like that." Again there was silence. "What exactly are you getting at, sir?"

Red raised his eyebrows at me, and I shrugged. If he thought my end of the exchange sounded weird, we were both in for a shock.

"I believe my uncle was out there trying to ward off a plateye."

For a moment, I flashed back to my own encounter with the root magic and ancient beliefs of the native black population of the Lowcountry. And the disastrous results that followed.

"A plateye?" I asked, dredging up the arcane vocabulary I'd shoved into the back of my mind. "Is that anything like a hag?"

"Worse," the sophisticated Atlanta lawyer said without a trace of embarrassment. "And they love whiskey."

CHAPTER TEN

I think Danforth was surprised at my reaction and maybe more than a little pleased that I hadn't intimated I thought he, too, had lost his marbles. He asked if I'd like to come up and talk to his uncle and suggested we have a more detailed discussion of the various spirits that might have been plaguing the old man. At least in his mind.

I told him I'd be there in fifteen minutes and hung up the phone.

Red shook his head. "Don't tell me. The old guy believes in the root and all that other nonsense. I thought we were done with all that after the business out at Sanctuary Hill."

I shrugged. "What can I say? I suppose it's not surprising that someone his age would have been exposed to the old beliefs even though he's been a practicing Christian for most of his adult life. We learned that the two aren't mutually exclusive, right? I mean, look at Lavinia."

He nodded. "Still. Once that stuff gets mixed up in a case, logic pretty much goes right out the window."

"Did you have any luck?" I figured we were due a change of subject since trading words about the ancient African beliefs of the descendants of freed slaves would get us exactly nowhere.

"The old man wouldn't talk. He just stared at the deputy sent to take his statement."

"That's pretty much what Danforth said. Maybe I'll have better luck." I pulled my bag out of the drawer. "Hold down the fort, okay? Let me know if either Steph or Erik comes up with anything."

"What about lunch?"

"I'll take Hub out, if he's willing. Do a little brain-picking over shrimp salad or whatever. I think there are a few important things he hasn't been quite forthcoming about."

As I walked around the desk, my husband rose to give me a quick hug.

"Don't get sucked into this root magic stuff, okay? Last time things didn't turn out so well, if you recall."

I thought about the two kids whose lives had taken such a tragic turn, the contents of the Styrofoam cooler washing up on the pluff mud of Presqu'isle that had set the whole thing in motion, and nodded. "Unfortunately, I do," I answered and headed out the door.

Hilton Head's hospital has grown over the years into a sprawling, modern facility surrounded by low buildings housing doctors' offices and other health care related services. The interior is bright and welcoming, but I never entered it without a sinking feeling akin to foreboding, though maybe not so strong. My brain knew that the whole purpose of the enterprise was to heal, but somehow I always managed to associate this and places like it with death and dying.

Hub Danforth had agreed to meet me in the lobby, although neither of us had ever laid eyes on the other. Still, I didn't have any trouble recognizing the tall, imposing man who rose from one of the overstuffed chairs as I stepped inside and shook off the thin layer of droplets that had collected on my hair during my walk from the parking lot. He just somehow looked like a criminal defense attorney. A certain arrogance in his carriage, even though he was dressed in a white polo shirt and wrinkled khakis. Maybe arrogance wasn't a fair assessment, I decided as I smiled in his direction. *Confidence* would be kinder and more accurate. He wasn't exactly handsome, but his narrow face had a certain elegance about it, aristocratic cheekbones and wide-set brown eyes. His skin had the creamy latte color that made many mixed-race people look so striking.

I crossed the distance between us and clasped his outstretched hand. "Bay Tanner, Mr. Danforth. Thanks so much for meeting me."

His grip was firm and lasted just exactly the right amount of time. I made and held eye contact with him, waiting for the *give-me-the-creeps* vibe Stephanie had voiced, but I didn't get even a slight buzz of it.

"It's I who should thank you, Mrs. Tanner. You can't know how much I appreciate the care you've taken with my uncle."

"Please, call me Bay. Shall we sit for a moment?" I indicated the cluster of chairs.

"Certainly." He waited until I'd seated myself, another indication of his Southern upbringing. His mama had taught him well.

"How is Mr. St. John doing?" I asked as I set my bag on the floor beside my chair. "Any change?"

"They'll be releasing him, maybe as early as this afternoon, so I guess he didn't suffer any permanent damage," Danforth said. "It's hard to tell in his condition."

"Which is what?" I asked. "Specifically."

"They've diagnosed moderate to severe Alzheimer's disease, although I'm somewhat skeptical."

"Why is that?"

"Because it's so . . . I don't know, subjective, I guess? They just ask him some questions, like the date and who's president and his address. Depending on how many he gets right, that's how they rate his dementia. I suppose it's not fair to attack their methods. They certainly know much more about the elderly than I do." He sighed, and a rueful smile lit his eyes. "It's just I'm used to dealing in hard facts and evidence."

I didn't know the first thing about Alzheimer's or any other form of senile dementia. I had been blessed in that my father's impressive intellect had stayed with him right up until the end. As for Lavinia, she seemed not to have changed for the past forty years.

"So there's no blood test or MRI or anything like that?"

Hub Danforth shook his head. "Only to rule out other things, like a tumor or a stroke. They want to start him on some medication, but my research tells me it isn't very effective, especially for someone Uncle Malcolm's age."

"Is he okay to be alone?"

"That's the trouble. He outright refuses to have anyone care for him at home. I was hoping that your agency might be able to document some erratic behavior that I could use to get myself appointed his guardian."

Again the suggestion of forcibly altering the old man's life stabbed at my conscience. "You want to put him into some sort of care facility?"

Apparently my tone of voice had communicated exactly how

I felt about that, because Danforth's smile vanished.

"What's the alternative, Mrs. Tanner? Wait until he sets the house on fire? Or goes chasing after ghosts and ghoulies and gets himself lost? Should I let him wander out to the ocean and drown?"

His voice had risen, and I noticed the white-haired lady at the reception desk glance worriedly in our direction.

"Look, you're right. That's really none of my business." I forced myself to speak softly. "But what you seem to be forgetting is that someone hit your uncle over the head. Deliberately. I assume that must be what the doctors concluded."

"It's possible. They wouldn't commit either way. It could have been a fall."

"Do you believe that?"

He stared for a long moment into my eyes. "Apparently you don't."

I decided to try another tack. "Who else might be interested in your uncle's place?" It wouldn't hurt to learn if he was aware of his ex-wife's visits on behalf of her employer.

"You think someone attacked him because of that rundown old shanty? That's ludicrous."

"Really? You seem like a smart man, Hub, so let's not play games. The house isn't worth the taxes he's paying on it. But oceanfront property on Hilton Head Island? What do *you* plan to do with it if you gain control of your uncle's assets? Let it sit there and rot into the scrub palmetto?"

I watched him visibly control his anger, a talent he must have perfected over lots of run-ins with prosecutors and unfriendly judges. I'd goaded him deliberately, not only to find out his intentions, but to see if I could provoke a reaction. But he had himself well under control, as I would have expected from someone in his profession.

"Of course not. My sister and I are not wealthy people, Mrs. Tanner, although we do all right. I've looked into the cost of dementia care facilities. Do you have any idea how much they run?"

"Not a clue," I said, leaning back in the chair.

"Even the most basic facilities, with no bells and whistles, can be as much as three to four thousand dollars a month. A month! Some of them run as high as nine or ten thousand. And that kind

of care isn't covered by Medicare or any other kind of insurance
Uncle Malcolm has. Sissy—my sister, that is—is divorced and . . .
unable to contribute anything. And I'm pretty much in the same
boat, what with two kids in college. The only alternative would be
to let him go on some kind of welfare, and that's not going to
happen." He paused and lowered his voice. "That land could take
care of my uncle for the rest of his life. That's all we're concerned
with here. I know my profession has a bad rep, but I'm not an evil
person, Mrs. Tanner. I just want to do what's right. For everybody."

I believed him. I'm not sure why, but I did.

"So what do you think happened to him last night?" I asked.

"He's been talking about this plateye thing for the past few
months. He told me it comes into the house—just floats through
the walls—and sits on the end of his bed. He may have been
trying to lure it outside with a trail of whiskey. I'm told that sometimes works. He could have fallen and struck his head."

"And you don't think that kind of behavior would be enough
to get you appointed his guardian?"

Hub Danforth smiled. "Maybe in Atlanta. But here? I'm not
so sure. I seem to remember a lot of his contemporaries, especially
the ones over on St. Helena's, who believe in the root as strongly
as we believe in the existence of gravity."

He had a point. I recalled how astounded I'd been to hear my
own died-in-the-wool Baptist Lavinia lecturing me on the power
and mystery of the root and its magic.

"Do you think your uncle would be up to talking to me?" I
asked. "Maybe we can get a definitive answer straight from the
horse's mouth."

"I don't know. He's been pretty tight-lipped about it, but we
can give it a try."

He stood and offered me his hand. I let him help me from
the chair.

"One thing, though," Hub Danforth said as we walked together toward the reception desk.

"What's that?"

"Just be prepared. Uncle Malcolm always had an eye for a
beautiful woman."

I wasn't sure whether or not to thank him for the implied
compliment, so I let the remark pass. He'd said it matter-of-factly,

the way he might have commented on the weather, but I had to admit it gave me just a little pause about what the next few minutes might bring.

Malcolm St. John looked like a wrinkled little boy lost in the vastness of his parents' bed. He lay on his side, one hand tucked under his cheek, one bony hip thrust against the thin sheet pulled up around his chin.

But as we walked into the room, his eyes popped open, and he followed our progress toward where he lay. He sported a thick wad of gauze taped just behind his left ear and an IV drip stuck on his hand.

"How are you feeling, Uncle Malcolm?" Hub Danforth asked, approaching the rail at the side of the bed.

The old man stared back, unblinking and silent.

"I brought someone to see you," he went on, as if it were a normal conversation. He motioned me forward. "This is Mrs. Tanner. She's the lady who found you and called the paramedics."

No response. Not even an eyelash twitched for what seemed like forever before he finally turned his head slightly in my direction.

"I hope you're doing better, Mr. St. John," I said.

Something about my voice must have struck a chord, because he suddenly seemed to come back to life. I watched as a sad, sweet smile lit the deep lines in his brown face.

"Oh, Lord have mercy. I can't believe it's you. After all these years."

Hub and I exchanged a look, and he shrugged.

"My name is Bay Tanner," I said softly. "I don't believe we've ever met before, sir."

Malcolm St. John laughed, a throaty chuckle that finally brought life to his faded eyes. "Oh, there's no need to be callin' me sir," he said, making an effort to ease himself upright.

His nephew hurried to help him, cranking the bed up so that he could have support for his back and head. I had no idea who he thought I was, but I felt pretty certain I wasn't going to get any answers to my questions about who might have attacked him. I smiled back as Hub settled an extra pillow behind him. I decided I'd just have to wait and see how things played out.

"How you been keepin'?" His voice, initially rough with sleep and disuse, had mellowed, making him sound somehow younger. "I swear it must be what—? Thirty years or more? You haven't changed, though. Still a fine-looking woman."

I looked to Hub for guidance, but he seemed as bewildered as I was.

"I'm afraid I don't remember, sir. Why don't you tell me about how we know each other?"

"Now, if I was a touchy kind of man, I might take offense at that, Miss Lily, you not rememberin' and all. Course I was just a young'un then. Used to help my daddy out at the retreat when you and your family come for the huntin'. I'se Little Mal. Used to carry your bags up from the landing, bring in the wood." Suddenly his eyes filled with tears, and a few dripped down his worn cheeks. "It right hurts my heart that you don't remember me."

I couldn't recall too many times when I'd felt so helpless. This poor, sick old man wanted something from me I had no idea how to give him.

"Little Mal," I said, just to fill the empty silence. "That was a long time ago."

He brightened, and the tears dried where they lay. "Thass right, Miss Lily. You was just about the prettiest white woman I ever did see. Daddy threatened to take a switch to me if I didn't quit starin' and get on with my chores. But you always had a kind word to share, and you always said thanks. I remember that 'specially." He paused, and his eyes drifted closed for just a moment. "You could ride like the wind, that red hair of your'n flyin' out behind you. Daddy said you was a wild one, but you was always kind to me. Yass, ma'am, always kind to Little Mal."

A moment later Hub Danforth and I watched the steady rise and fall of his uncle's chest, the sad smile still creasing his face as we slipped quietly from the room.

CHAPTER ELEVEN

Out in the hallway, Hub Danforth and I paused and stared at each other.

"I have no idea what that was about," he said, shaking his head. "That's the first time I've seen him so confused that he mistakes someone. I feel as if I should apologize for him."

That last sentence cemented my feeling that this was a man who had no ulterior motives, Stephanie's vibes be damned. He looked genuinely bewildered and deeply sad.

"It doesn't matter. If it gives him pleasure to think I'm this Miss Lily, what does it hurt? I just wish I'd had some information to go on so I could have held up my end of the conversation. Do you know anything about this woman or the retreat he was talking about? It sounds as if it must have been more than thirty years ago, especially if he was just a kid at the time."

"Let's sit down."

Hub Danforth took my arm and guided me toward a waiting area with several comfortable chairs arranged in a semicircle. When we were seated, he leaned his elbows on his knees, his hands dangling, in a pose that looked very much like defeat, although I had no idea what the contest had been. The silence, punctuated occasionally by the muted tread of nurses' feet, gathered around us.

"I seem to remember that my grandfather, Malcolm Senior, worked for a couple of the hunt clubs that used to operate on the island. Before all the development, of course. That would have been back in the thirties maybe. I really don't know all that much. Both Papa and Nonnie died when I was quite young." He sighed. "And, like most kids, I didn't have much interest in all that ancient history stuff." He looked up at me and smiled.

"I know what you mean. It seems to happen so often—by the time we're old enough to be curious about those times, the only people who can tell us about them are gone."

"I heard someone say once that everyone over the age of sixty should write—or dictate—their histories. He said that every time an old person dies, it's like a private library burned down."

"What a lovely—and sad—sentiment," I answered, my mind flicking to the journals in the duffel bag pushed to the back of my closet.

I forced my thoughts back to the issue at hand.

"I don't think you need us any longer," I said. "Any judge with half a brain is going to see that your uncle needs a guardian. And fulltime care once he gets out of here."

Hub Danforth shook his head. "But that's the problem. He isn't always like this. At least he wasn't before. Maybe the shock and the blow to the head have made things worse. I'll have to get a complete evaluation from his doctors and see where to go from here." He lifted his head and held my gaze. "I don't know how to thank you for all you've done. He might have died out there if you and your employees hadn't gone above and beyond. I'm really grateful."

His praise made me uncomfortable. "Just doing what you hired us to do, Hub. Is there any other way we can be of assistance?"

"Would you be willing to testify if I can arrange a guardianship hearing? Just to relate what happened here today? I think it might go a long way toward getting my uncle the care he needs."

"Of course, if you think it will help."

Hub Danforth rose then and extended his hand. "Send me a bill at the office, and I'll see that you're paid immediately. I'll be in touch if we need your testimony."

I let him help me to my feet, a feeling of loss suddenly overwhelming me. I wanted to know who had struck down the confused old man. I wanted to know why Hub's ex-wife was skulking around Mr. St. John's property. I wanted to make sure he was well looked after and safe. None of which was going to be any of my business once I tallied the final bill and sent it on to Atlanta. I sighed and forced a smile.

"I intended to invite you to lunch, but I suppose you have a lot to take care of."

Hub smiled back. "Rain check? I feel as if I should get going on what needs done here. I have a trial starting on Wednesday, and I need to get back. Thanks again for everything. I'll let you know how it goes."

"Please do," I said and allowed myself to be guided toward the bank of elevators.

I nodded once at Hub Danforth as the door slid closed.

I found I didn't have much of an appetite. I needed gas, so I filled the Jaguar and grabbed a Snickers bar from the counter of the convenience store attached to the station. I'd just finished it when I wheeled into the parking lot in front of the office. A quick scan told me everyone's vehicles were present and accounted for. That would make delivering the news of the questionable conclusion of our relationship with Hub Danforth and Malcolm St. John a little easier.

As I gripped the doorknob, I wondered why I felt such a heavy sadness at the thought of letting the case go. I'd always been the one to lecture the *kids* about not getting emotionally involved with the client or the reason that had brought him or her to us. It was always easier said than done, though, I had to admit. We saw people at their most vulnerable—afraid, angry, confused—so it was difficult not to identify and, in some cases, sympathize with them as human beings. No one had ever accused me of being particularly empathetic, but it seemed, especially as I aged, that I found myself more often than not putting myself in the shoes of those whose troubles had led them to our door. I wasn't sure if that was a good thing or not. It just *was*.

I pushed the door open and stepped into chaos.

Red and Erik huddled around the reception desk, talking animatedly, while Stephanie stared at the screen of her laptop. The voice of an announcer blared out from the speaker, and everyone's eyes seemed glued to the image. No one heard me come in, and I stopped for a moment, confused by the looks of shock and consternation on their faces.

Finally, when no one acknowledged my presence, I let the door bang shut behind me. That got their attention.

"What's going on?" I asked, crossing to Stephanie's desk.

"Why's your phone turned off?" Red's voice was both excited

and accusatory. "We've been trying to get you for the last half hour."

I patted the pocket of my slacks. "I turned it off in the hospital."

"You don't turn it off," my husband said, his eyes once again drawn back to the screen. "You put it on vibrate."

"So sue me," I said, anger rising to replace the sharp sadness I'd been feeling a couple of minutes before. "What's going on?" I repeated.

"A ship blew up in the Savannah harbor," Erik said.

"My God! Terrorists?" I felt that terrible, sinking sensation I always associated with the beautiful autumn morning of September 11.

"They don't know yet, but they think it was more likely an accident. But they're shutting everything down. The National Guard is on its way. Some damage to Hutchinson Island, some on River Street. One of those giant container ships."

I joined them behind Stephanie, drawn, in spite of my fear and anxiety, to the images scrolling across the screen. Sirens screamed, nearly drowning out the announcer, who hadn't been able to get much closer than the park that ran above the edge of the harbor. As he rehashed the same skimpy details over and over, we stood mesmerized by the unfolding drama. Occasionally one of us would make a comment, but mostly we held our peace as the frightening images rolled by in a continuous loop. Finally, I forced myself to step back, take a long, trembling breath, and get us back to our own reality.

"Nothing we can do about this," I said firmly. "I need to talk about Hub Danforth and Malcolm St. John." I picked up my bag from where I'd dropped it on the floor. "Guys?" I cocked my head toward my office. "Stephanie, keep an eye on developments."

Reluctantly, Red and Erik tore themselves away. I marveled again at how prone we are to a fascination with tragedy. Maybe it was seeing others facing dire circumstances and being able to congratulate ourselves on having escaped. Or maybe it was some atavistic survival instinct that sent us rubbernecking at traffic accidents and devouring newspaper accounts of earthquakes and famines. Whatever the cause, it struck me that the personal devastation of Malcolm St. John, the loss of his mind and memory, was more deserving of our time and pity. I found out quickly that I was alone in that assumption.

Both my husband and my partner refused to sit, fidgeting from foot to foot as I related the details of my visit to the hospital. They seemed to take turns casting looks over their shoulders at where Stephanie sat, manning the computer.

"So, we're out of it as of today," I said. "Erik, I need you to get an invoice generated and sent off to Hub's office in Atlanta. Don't bill him for the time we all spent yesterday at the bungalow."

"Right," he said absently, and I knew his attention was anywhere but on what I was saying.

"I feel bad about leaving this hanging," I said, but neither one of them replied.

I gave up then and waved them away. It took less than two seconds for both of them to scuttle back to the computer on the reception desk. I leaned back in my chair and closed my eyes. Of course I hoped the explosion had been an accident and not the opening salvo in another war on terror. The last one hadn't turned out so well, even though our troops had fought valiantly against our unknown and often unknowable enemies in Iraq and Afghanistan. Saddam and Osama were both rotting in hell, and that was a good thing, but the hatred and bloodshed never seemed to abate.

I thought back to one of the Judge's favorite aphorisms: Save your energy for worrying about the things you can do something about. I couldn't help the poor people caught up in the mess unfolding in Savannah, and it seemed now that I couldn't help poor Mr. St. John, either. I glanced at my watch. Three twenty. Maybe a good time to hang it up and head for home. It was obvious from the huddle in the outer office that nothing much else was going to get done. I had just reached for my bag when I heard Red's voice drown out the TV announcer.

"Jesus!"

I called out from my chair. "What's the matter?"

My husband took only a second to stride to my doorway. "There was just a blurb scrolled across the bottom of the screen, other news they've been keeping up on."

"And?" I couldn't imagine what could have shocked him more than the events playing out in the beautiful city just a few miles to our south.

"They've found a body in a room at the Sea Oats." He swallowed. "Tentatively identified as the chief financial officer of a Charlotte development company. Name withheld pending notifycation of next of kin."

We stared at each other for a long moment. Neither of us needed to voice what we both already knew.

I'd bet everything I had that Cynthia Danforth Merrill was dead.

CHAPTER TWELVE

Though we stuck around until nearly five o'clock, no other details emerged about the single death on Hilton Head Island. All eyes and attention were on Savannah, although it was beginning to seem as if it might have been just a tragic accident. Initial reports pointed that way. Still, the whole country was on heightened terror alert, and the Savannah airport had been locked down, just as a precaution.

We finally broke up and went our respective ways. I reminded Erik on our way out the door about the invoice for Hub Danforth, and he promised to get to it first thing in the morning. As Red and I walked toward our cars, I spotted the blue envelope stuck beneath the wiper blade of the Jaguar. I bit back the string of expletives rising from the back of my throat and wondered if I could snatch it out of there before my husband caught on. Of course, I had no such luck. Apparently it wasn't a day for things to go right, anywhere.

His reaction, though, was a bit calmer than on the two previous occasions. Red stopped dead in his tracks and stared at it a moment before his gaze swiveled toward me.

"Got any kind of plastic bag on you?" he asked in a measured tone that scared me more than his ranting and raving.

"I don't think so. Why?"

"This one's going to the sheriff for analysis. If they can raise any prints, maybe we can track this miserable son of a bitch down."

"Honey, really—"

"Don't 'honey' me, okay? I've had about all I can take of this crap!"

I could see there was no sense arguing with him. I opened the Jag and rummaged around in the glove compartment, coming up with a plastic sleeve that held my registration and insurance cards.

It looked about the right size for the small envelope. I emptied its contents on the passenger seat and held it out to Red.

"This do?"

"Fine," he snapped, jerking it out of my hand.

He took his folded white handkerchief from his back pocket and worked the envelope loose by one corner. He eased it into the sleeve and wrapped the hanky around it.

"You go on home," he said. "I'm delivering this in person."

"Don't I need to make a complaint or something?"

"That can wait. I'll get Malik or someone to get on this right away. Don't wait dinner for me."

I watched my husband climb into the Bronco without a backward glance. No goodbye, no kiss, no nothing. I had rarely seen him this angry, and it frightened me a little. I was usually the one who flew off in a rage, and Red the calm, collected voice of reason. It had to be a combination of all the upsets of the past few days: Sarah's illness, the attack on Mr. St. John, the tragedy in Savannah, the possible death of someone involved—even if only peripherally—with our office. I turned for home thinking that if *I* was going to have to assume the role of the reasonable one in our relationship, we were in big trouble.

I flipped on the TV in the great room so I could keep up on developments and scanned the contents of the freezer. I pulled out a pound of shrimp that would quickly solve the dinner dilemma, emptied them into a colander, and set cold water running over them before getting a pot of water boiling for pasta. As I assembled the herbs and garlic and began chopping, I kept an ear open for anything relating to the body found in the elegant boutique hotel tucked against the marsh at the south end of the island, but every resource of the local stations seemed to be trained on the explosion in Savannah.

I wondered what sort of luck Red was having in badgering his friend Malik or someone else at the sheriff's office into running prints from my latest mash note. *No guarantee there even are any*, I thought, as I melted butter in the large sauté pan and tossed in the garlic. Although if there weren't, that would tell us something, too. A slightly nutty admirer wouldn't be concerned with things like that. But someone with more sinister intentions—

Red's steps on the stairs leading up from the garage reverberated through the house. It sounded as if he were stomping bugs. I had a sinking feeling that didn't bode well for the success of his mission. I inhaled the pungent aroma of the sizzling garlic and waited.

"Idiots!" my husband snapped. He tossed his keys on the dining room table and thumped up the three steps into the kitchen.

"I'm glad you're back," I said, ignoring his outburst. "I'll have shrimp and pasta ready in about ten minutes. Do you want a salad or garlic bread? Or we can do both. I'm starving. All that business at the hospital put me right off any idea of lunch, and—"

"Bay, for God's sake quit babbling."

I swallowed the snappy comeback that sprang to my lips and took a deep breath. "I take it you didn't have any luck? What did Malik have to say?"

"He was gone by the time I got there. I tried to see Mike Raleigh, but he was out. I'm thinking he probably caught the unattended at the Sea Oats."

I sensed some of the anger seeping out of his voice, so I kept my tone as level as I could manage. "The one we think might be Cynthia Merrill?"

"It's her. I got at least that much out of my former colleagues." He snorted, an effort that would have done my late father proud. "You know, I wonder if they're being such a pain in the ass because I'm just a lowly civilian now, or if it's because I'm working for you. You're not exactly at the top of their hit parade, you know."

If I hadn't been concerned about ruining a perfectly good tarragon butter sauce, I would have flung the pan at him. Instead, I slid it off the burner and counted to ten under my breath in English, French, and Spanish, my one ability in the two foreign languages. Then inspiration dawned.

"Let me guess. You ran into Lisa Pedrovsky."

"Bitch," he muttered, a rare use of a word my husband usually found very offensive, even though it was the perfect description of the detective with whom we had crossed swords on any number of occasions. I often thought that if you looked up the word in the dictionary, you'd probably find her picture attached.

"Look," I said, easing the pan back onto the heat, "let's just forget about it for now, okay? We've got enough on our plates without worrying about this lovesick kook." I broke the vermicelli in half and dropped it into the boiling water. "So what'll it be? Salad, bread, or both?"

"I don't give a damn about food! I want to lay my hands on this moron and wring his miserable neck! And quit trying to humor me, okay? I'm pissed off, and I think I have a damn good right to be!" He flung himself into one of the chairs pulled up at the round table in the bay window on the other side of the kitchen. "And you acting like it's no big deal isn't helping any."

That last one did it. I whirled from the stove, guns raised and ready to blaze away. Until I saw his face. I didn't often detect fear in my husband's deep-set eyes, and it frightened me. I clamped my mouth closed and crossed to where he sat with his head resting in his hand. I stroked the back of his head and gently pulled him into a loose embrace.

"I'm sorry," I said and felt the tension drain from his rigid shoulders. "I know you're worried about this, and I don't mean to disparage your concerns. It's just that we have so many more important things to worry about right now." His arms went around my waist then, and he tightened his hold. "I promise I'll be more observant and more careful until we figure out who's playing games with me, okay?"

He raised his head, and I leaned over to kiss him gently on the lips. A moment before I smelled the rank odor of burning garlic.

"Oh, hell and damnation!" I jerked myself free and ran for the stove, but I knew I would be too late.

I flipped on the water in the sink and dumped the whole thing into the garbage disposal, but it would take forever before the sickly smell dissipated. I turned to find my husband smiling for the first time in a long while.

"Bubba's," he asked, "or Jump and Phil's?"

I dumped the partially cooked pasta, put the thawed shrimp in a plastic bag with the hope that they might be salvaged for the following evening, and joined Red in the Jaguar. He seemed to have lost the chip on his shoulder, and we managed to make our way to our favorite watering hole without ticking each other off. Mostly we listened to the news on the radio, the tension in the beautiful antebellum city to our south easing as it became apparent there had been no sabotage involved in the explosion aboard the container ship. The worst part of it would be the disruption to river and harbor traffic and the cleanup along the shore. It appeared that the only loss of life had occurred on the ship itself, with injuries to those on land relatively minor.

We walked into Jump & Phil's to find the usually quiet local hangout buzzing with talk about events in Savannah. The moose table was open, and we settled ourselves beneath the massive head of Waldo, his antlers decorated with twinkling yellow and green lights. It took me a moment to place their significance. Football season was in full swing, and the bar was the local gathering place for Green Bay Packer fans. They must not have been playing on *Monday Night Football*, otherwise there wouldn't have been a table or barstool not occupied by emigrant cheeseheads.

We ordered burgers and fries, our usual fare, and Red opted for a Fat Tire, an excessively weird name for a beer, at least to my mind. He usually didn't drink in public, a throwback to his deputy days when he felt it didn't look good for a member of the sheriff's office to be tossing them back, even if he was off duty. We mostly listened, our fellow islanders' shock at the possibility of terrorism in their own backyard making for lively conversation.

We'd finished about half our dinners when I looked up to see Detective Mike Raleigh striding through the side door. He paused, scanning the room in the same way I'd seen Red do back in the day, before he spotted us. I was facing his way and raised a hand briefly, which he apparently took as an invitation to join us.

"Raleigh's here," I said softly, and Red turned in his chair.

"Hey, Mike. Have a seat."

"Sergeant. Mrs. Tanner. Don't want to interrupt anything."

"Don't be silly," I said, pushing back the chair next to me. "You on your own?"

"Yeah," he said. "Thought I'd grab something before I head back to the office. Probably going to be a long night."

It was the perfect opening, and I didn't intend to let it slip past.

"You catch the body at the Sea Oats?" I asked around a mouthful of burger, just to let him know I was only making idle conversation. It might become necessary to disclose our tenuous connection to the dead woman at some point down the road, but until then I'd just play nosy civilian and see where it got us.

"You heard about that?" He paused to order a pulled pork sandwich and an iced tea before resuming. "I didn't know it was out on the wire yet." He gestured toward the six or seven televisions mounted around the restaurant, all of them tuned to some news channel, both local and national. "I thought everybody'd be too involved with that to pay much attention to a death on Hilton Head."

"The locals are running it on the crawl, but they don't have any details."

It wasn't a question, but I let my voice rise a little at the end of the sentence, inviting confidences, if any were to be had. Mike Raleigh smiled at me.

"Nothing much to tell at the moment. The coroner has to rule on cause of death, but it wasn't anything violent. At least not at first glance."

"Was she an elderly woman? Natural causes, you think?"

I caught Red's annoyed stare out of the corner of my eye, but I ignored him. When fate presented you with opportunities, it seemed ungrateful not to take advantage of them.

"No, I'd say not. Elderly, I mean. We've IDed her from her driver's license. She was forty-seven." He laughed, a brief chuckle. "From where I'm sitting, that's not looking very old."

"I hear that. The TV said she worked for a developer in Charlotte."

Raleigh sat back as Heather, our usual waitress, slid his plate in front of him. He smiled his thanks.

"You know," he said, sprinkling his fries liberally with salt before hefting the gooey barbeque sandwich in his hands, "it never ceases to amaze me how the media manage to get information almost before we do."

Sources, I thought to myself, either in the sheriff's office or the coroner's. Or maybe both. In this day of instant communication, it wouldn't take more than a twitter or a tweet or whatever the hell you called it to keep a cooperative civil servant in beer money.

Mike Raleigh occupied himself then with demolishing his dinner, his gaze flicking occasionally to one of the television sets across the room. Red and I finished and let the detective do the same in relative quiet. I didn't want to tip our hand about being peripherally interested in the fate of Cynthia Danforth Merrill, so I took Red's unspoken advice and backed off. As we sat, the bar began slowly filling up as the hour for kickoff approached. Apparently these were just avid football fans, not concerned with who was playing. The noise level grew with each opening of the door until it had become impossible to discern individual conversations.

"Well, we should be getting home," my husband said, waving at Heather for the check. "It was good to see you, Mike."

"Don't rush off on my account," the detective said, wiping his mouth and hands on the blue cloth napkin. "I have to be heading out, too. I don't think this thing in Savannah will spill over into our territory, but everyone is on alert. Hell of a thing, isn't it?"

"Too bad every accident like this kicks us all into panic mode, but I guess it's understandable," I offered.

"Sign of the times," Raleigh said.

We all settled up and walked outside together. The night air held a little bite to it, a welcome relief from the unrelenting heat and humidity of the summer. I always loved October in the Lowcountry, both for the perfect weather as well as for the absence of the bulk of our two-point-five million tourists. Grateful as we were for their patronage, there was something to be said for having the island mostly back to ourselves come autumn.

We stopped by the Jaguar, and Red finally made his move. I'd been waiting for him to bring up the subject ever since Raleigh had walked through the door, and I'd wondered what had been holding him back. Timing, I guessed, and his own sense of protocol.

"Listen, Mike, I need to ask you about something."

The detective glanced at his watch in the faint light from the streetlamp. "Sure, Red. What's up?"

In a few succinct sentences, my husband related the exploits of my phantom admirer. "So I was wondering if someone would do me a favor and check the latest envelope for prints. I know it's asking a lot, but I'm concerned about Bay's safety."

"No problem," Mike Raleigh said. "Professional courtesy. Drop it off at my desk, and I'll see what I can do."

Red reached inside his jacket and extracted the plastic sleeve still wrapped in his handkerchief. "Just happen to have it with me," he said with one of his patented boyish grins.

Raleigh laughed. "Always prepared. Can't take the Marine out of the man, I guess." He took the strange package and tucked it into his own pocket. "Might take a while. Lots going on right now."

"Whatever you can do. I really appreciate it."

The two men shook hands, and Mike Raleigh moved to the far end of the parking lot where he'd left his unmarked. Red and I pulled out onto Greenwood Drive and negotiated the Sea Pines traffic circle, exiting on 278. We rode in silence for a few minutes before my husband spoke.

"Now maybe we'll get some answers."

"Maybe," I said, recalling my thoughts about the likelihood that my stalker had left his prints on his ridiculous love letters. "But what are you going to do if he comes up in the system? And assuming Raleigh will tell you if he does."

"He damn well better."

"And then what?"

He looked over at me for a long moment. "You don't need to know," he said in a voice that didn't exactly scare me, but that sent a little shiver of apprehension skittering down my spine.

CHAPTER THIRTEEN

By Tuesday morning, the excitement to our south had pretty much died down.

We'd spent a quiet evening at home, the football game running on the massive TV Red had mounted over the fireplace while I tried to read, and my husband dozed. Normally it would have taken a Savannah-type explosion in the middle of the great room to drag my attention away from the latest John Sandford novel, but I found my mind drifting to the craziness of the past few days. It seemed nearly impossible to me that there wouldn't be some connection between the attack on Mr. St. John and the yet unexplained death of Hub Danforth's ex-wife. The property was the obvious link, especially as it seemed Cynthia Merrill's company might have an interest in it. But again I couldn't see what anyone would gain by either of the two events.

We'd finally trooped off to bed a little short of midnight with the outcome of the game still in doubt and neither of us caring too much how it eventually played out. I'd slept fitfully, waking just about every hour on the hour until the alarm went off at seven thirty. So I wasn't in the best of humors to begin with when we pulled into the parking lot a little before nine to find Hub Danforth standing in front of the office door. I stuffed my sour mood and forced a smile as I climbed out of the Jaguar.

"Good morning," I called, and Danforth gave me a half-hearted wave.

As I approached him, I noticed that his eyes were bloodshot, and he'd done a slapdash job of shaving. He looked about as bad as I felt. I was fairly certain I knew the cause.

"I'm so sorry about your former wife," I said, extending my hand.

He took it briefly and nodded. "I wasn't sure you'd heard about it yet."

"We happened to have dinner with the investigating detective last night." I unlocked the door and held it for him.

"Thanks. Then maybe you know more than they've been willing to tell me."

Red followed us inside after parking the Bronco. He and Danforth exchanged a few mumbled words, the male equivalent of expressing and accepting sympathy, I guessed. I moved into my office, and the men followed. I hoped Erik and Stephanie wouldn't be far behind us because I suddenly felt as if I was going to need my hit of chai latte caffeine. Soon.

"Did you know Ms. Merrill was here on the island?" I asked, taking the chair behind my desk.

"No," Danforth answered, "I had no idea. I'm aware she travels quite often in her job, but we don't have a lot of contact." He paused. "Still, it does seem strange. That we were both here, I mean, and neither of us knew it."

I wondered if that was entirely true. We had no way of verifying whether or not Cynthia Merrill had known of her ex-husband's presence.

We fell silent for a few moments, perhaps each of us contemplating how serendipitous life can sometimes be.

"How's Mr. St. John?" I finally asked.

"Better. At least he's making sense. Well, as much as he can, I guess. They're going to keep him for observation for a couple more days so I can get some home care set up for him."

"How's he going to take that?"

Danforth shrugged. "I can't worry about that now. I've already contacted a few providers, and I have interviews scheduled for later today. I'm going to have to make clear to them that Uncle Malcolm isn't going to be the easiest client they've ever worked with." He sighed, and the sound struck me as about as forlorn as any I'd heard in a long time. "I've postponed my trial for tomorrow, but they've only given me until the first of the week to take care of things down here. I was surprised the judge even agreed to that." A ghost of a smile flitted briefly across his face. "She's not noted for her leniency, either with defendants or their attorneys."

The arrival of the other half of our staff halted conversation for a few minutes, during which I apologized for not having anything hot to offer our client—or was it former client? I wasn't so sure. Hub Danforth waved away bottled water or a soft drink. I sipped gratefully after inhaling the exotic aroma of the tea and waited for him to get to the point. The day before, he'd dismissed us with thanks, and now here he sat in my office. I'd have bet my next dividend check that it had to do with his ex-wife's death, and it took only a few more minutes for me to be proven right.

"I don't know quite what to do about Cyn," he said finally. "I've called the kids, of course. They wanted to come, but I've convinced them there's no reason at this point. Nothing we can do until . . ." He sighed deeply. "I'm just feeling a bit over-whelmed by it all. We've kept in touch, mostly about the children, although they hardly qualify as that now." Again the hint of a smile twitched at the corners of his mouth. "Justin is a senior at Georgia, and Jillian just started her sophomore year at South Carolina."

"Must make for interesting Saturdays during football season," Red offered, and that broke Hub Danforth's face into a wide grin.

"You have no idea," he said with the first glint of warmth in his voice. "And when they play each other, I try to be out of town. It can get pretty intense."

"I'm sure they're devastated," I said, and the mood swung back to somber. I needed to find out just what Danforth wanted from me—from *us*—and I couldn't help hoping it had to do with his former wife's death. The day before, I'd been lamenting the loss of any legitimate reason for us to stay involved in the saga of the St. Johns and Danforths. I trusted I didn't look too eager as I waited for Hub to get to the point. He didn't keep me hanging for long.

"Look, the thing is I'm kind of conflicted about how to handle things. Cyn's other ex-husband will have some say in the arrangements, I suppose, but I'm guessing it will mostly fall to me. The kids are going to want an explanation, and right now I don't have anything to tell them." He paused, and I saw genuine sadness in his eyes, maybe even a touch of regret.

"Do you want us to act as a liaison with the sheriff's office?" I asked softly and heard my husband's sharp intake of breath. "We do have some connections there, and we might have a better chance of getting information."

"It isn't something they're going to want to do," Red offered, struggling to keep his annoyance with me out of his voice. "It's true I still have some friends in the department, but there's no

guarantee they're going to want anyone running interference for
you. I mean, you're an attorney. You must have had lots of contact with law enforcement. I'm not sure we'd do any better than
you would at dealing with them."

It was one of the many times my husband and I had come
down on opposite sides of an issue, usually one relating to his
former employer. And it wasn't as if he didn't have a point. Still,
something about the whole scenario—maybe Malcolm St. John's
poignant dialogue with this Lily person, the woman he mistook
me for—or his total helplessness in the face of his waning
faculties . . . I didn't know exactly what it was that was drawing me
into the muddle of this disjointed family. I only felt certain that I
could help in some way. And that I needed to.

"Of course I can deal with them," Hub Danforth replied, a
little asperity in his tone. "That's not the point. I have to figure
out how to make sure Uncle Malcolm is taken care of, comfort my
kids, arrange for Cyn's body to be taken back to Atlanta . . ." His
voice trailed off. "Or maybe Charlotte. I don't really know if she'd
made any arrangements for her funeral. Hell, she was only in her
forties. And she wasn't the kind of woman who wanted to think
too much about that sort of thing. She was fighting middle age
pretty hard the last time we saw each other. I'm pretty sure she'd
had some work done. You know, a lift or something."

His face had softened as he spoke of his ex-wife, and I wondered whose idea the breakup had been. It seemed to me as if
there might be some feelings left over.

"Sounds as if you have a full plate," I said softly and directed
a quelling gaze toward my husband. "Just tell us what we can do
to help."

"I appreciate that, Bay, I really do."

It was the first time he'd used my first name.

He drew in a long breath and let it out slowly. "Okay. I'm
prepared to authorize you—your firm—to act as liaison between
my family and the authorities—sheriff, coroner, whatever. I need
to know the cause of death, when the body will be released, and
so forth. If you can have something typed up, I'll sign it right now.
Just push whoever you have to and get me some answers. I have
interviews with the caregivers set up, starting in about half an
hour. You can reach me on my cell."

After that, things progressed quickly. Stephanie had the letter of authorization ready in a matter of minutes. Hub Danforth scratched out a few changes, whipped his signature on the document, and made a hasty exit. For a few moments after he left, we sat in silence. Red was the first to break it.

"Why do you want to get involved in this thing? I don't understand your reasoning."

I took a little time before answering. Erik and Stephanie, who had been listening to the entire exchange with Danforth from the front office, now stood in the doorway. Apparently they shared my husband's confusion.

"I think it's all connected," I finally said.

"What?" Erik asked from across the room. "Mr. St. John and Cynthia Merrill?"

"Exactly. And the line that ties them together is the property."

"Reaching." Red dropped the one word into the silence.

"Maybe," Erik replied. "It all depends on how Merrill died, doesn't it?"

"Yes. And Mike Raleigh told us last night that there was no evidence of violence. She probably had a heart attack or something. As usual, Bay, you're seeing murder behind every tree, and there's just no evidence to support that. None."

"Yet," I said, and that effectively ended the conversation.

Red grumbled and complained, but he set off shortly after Hub Danforth to see what he could squeeze out of his old cronies. Erik and Stephanie had background checks to run for both the county and for the Town of Hilton Head, and the office was soon filled with the muted click of their keyboards. I spent about half an hour arranging files and generally clearing my desk, taking care of a couple of housekeeping emails and answering some other correspondence. Around ten thirty, I leaned back in my chair with an uncluttered desk in front of me and nothing else that required my immediate attention. Just as I had planned.

I took out a clean legal pad from the top right-hand drawer and stared at its pristine page for a minute or two before beginning a reconstruction of Malcolm St. John's strange conversation in his hospital room. I tried to recall the details of his reminiscences about Miss Lily and the *retreat*, I thought he'd called it. I

had a vague recollection of stories I'd heard—I had no idea where
—about the hunting camps and clubs that used to exist on Hilton
Head before the development began. I wondered who would have
information about that time. My father would have been the obvious first source. His knowledge of the Lowcountry had been
expansive, and he had been of an age that might even have given
him firsthand experience. He and his contemporaries had been
avid hunters in their youth, so I would have expected him to be
able to fill me in.

I missed him on so many levels it sometimes took my breath
away.

The next best thing would be Google, and I pulled my keyboard toward me and began searching. I had no idea what the outcome of all this sleuthing would be, what I hoped to accomplish. I
just knew that something I couldn't put a name to was driving me
to make a connection, however tenuous, with Malcolm St. John.
And if taking on the role of his well-remembered Miss Lily was
what it took, I was up for the challenge.

CHAPTER
FOURTEEN

An hour later, I had a lot of questions and not many answers.

Google had provided me with its usual overwhelming number of hits to my query about Hilton Head and hunt clubs. Most interesting were the articles and references to Honey Horn, the sole remaining plantation building on the island dating back to the War Between the States. It had been purchased, along with about 9,000 acres—nearly the entire island—back in the thirties by a couple of banking and investment types from New York. They had refurbished the house and invited their wealthy friends to join them for hunting expeditions that took down countless game birds and deer over the next couple of decades. Arriving on one of the two steamboat ferries that plied their trade between Beaufort, Daufuskie Island, Hilton Head, and Savannah, these scions of Depression-era privilege spent long days on horseback, led by native Gullah trackers, whose ancestors had farmed the land, both as slaves and as free men. At night, they dressed for dinners prepared by the wives of the trackers and held elegant parties replete with candlelight and champagne.

Not bad, I thought, when the rest of the country was struggling just to put a meal on the table. But then I, too, was a daughter of privilege, if not exactly on their level, so I decided I might want to refrain from tossing stones at glass houses.

As is usual when you embark on one of these searches, I wandered all over the Internet, learning more than I really wanted to know about all kinds of peripheral and basically unrelated stuff. The nugget was that Honey Horn, which now housed our wonderful Coastal Discovery Museum, could well have been where Malcolm St. John encountered the elusive Miss Lily. I jotted down the titles of a couple of books that might prove helpful and logged off.

I looked down at the notes I'd scribbled. The bulk of the

information I'd gathered seemed to indicate that the thirties were probably the time period in which most of the hunting activity would have taken place. I did a little math, based on the information Stephanie had first gathered on Mr. St. John, and figured it was just possible. He would have been a kid, maybe nine or ten by the end of that decade, just about the right age to form a crush on an older woman, I supposed. Or the encounters could have taken place in the early forties, during the war. Either way, the timeline was feasible. And even though I hadn't found any reference to anyone named Lily connected with Honey Horn, I felt as if I had made at least a small inroad into understanding the old man's somewhat shaky memories of his childhood.

Which got me exactly nowhere, if I were being honest with myself. It didn't tell me who might have struck the poor man down just outside his home. Or why Cynthia Danforth Merrill had met her fate. If her cause of death turned out to be completely natural, I had no idea where to go from there. Or why the hell it mattered so much to me.

I leaned back in my chair and closed my eyes, and the image of Romey Gadsden popped into my head. The old gentlemen had become entangled—through no fault of his own—in one of our cases a couple of years back. He, too, had been sliding into that twilight of confusion that seemed to be affecting Malcolm St. John. And he, too, had been subjected to rough handling by some creeps who had a lot to lose if his memory suddenly became more lucid. I'd formed an affection for the withered black man, who continued to cling tenaciously to life in spite of myriad illnesses and setbacks. Lavinia kept me informed, and I promised myself that I'd make the time to drop in on him one day soon. I thought about Hub Danforth's remark the day before in the hospital, the one about how the death of an octogenarian was like the burning of a personal library. Maybe Mr. Gadsden would provide me with some insight into the old days of the hunt clubs or perhaps steer me in the direction of someone who could. Lavinia might be a good source as well. There wasn't much that happened in the black community that she didn't at least have a passing knowledge of.

The outer door closed quietly, and I sat up just as Red walked into my office. I couldn't get a read from his face as to how his fishing expedition had gone, so I waited for him to get the ball rolling. He took his time, shedding his jacket and draping it over the back of one of the client chairs before settling himself.

I've never been known for my patience. "So?" I asked with just a touch of annoyance.

"I need a drink," my husband said, rising and crossing to the small refrigerator in the corner and extracting a bottle.

I chewed on my lower lip to keep from saying things that wouldn't help the situation any.

"There seems to be some question about how Cynthia Merrill died," he said, avoiding my eyes as he chugged back some water.

Again I waited.

"The coroner discovered a lump behind her left ear. He won't know until they get into the actual autopsy, but it could have been a hard enough blow to kill her, even if that wasn't the intention."

I did my best to quell the feeling of vindication, but I was pretty sure it showed on my face. Then I sobered, appalled that I should take pleasure from the violent death of another human being, even one I'd never laid eyes on. Sometimes I don't understand myself at all. Or maybe I do, and I don't much like what I find.

"How long before they know for sure?" I kept my voice low and businesslike.

"It could take a few days. I talked with Mike Raleigh, showed him Danforth's letter of authorization. He wasn't thrilled about it, but he said it looked as if everything was in order. They've begun an investigation into what visitors she might have had, her contacts here on the island, her movements on the day she died. The usual stuff. Just in case."

"And he's willing to share that with us?"

Red paused and finally looked directly at me. "It depends. Mike knows that Danforth is a criminal defense attorney, so he's being overly cautious about jumping to any conclusions. He doesn't want to do anything that could lay the department open to a lawsuit or some sort of complaint being filed."

"CYA time?" I asked, not bothering to disguise my anger.

"Yes, they're covering their butts, but you can't blame them. Danforth and his cronies aren't their favorite people on the planet."

"Gee, I'm glad to hear I'm not the only one on their hit list."

That made him smile. "Oh, you're still right up there, but I think you might have slipped a few notches. Mike Raleigh actually likes you."

"Go figure," I said with a smile. Then the seriousness of the situation overwhelmed me again. "So what are we telling Hub?"

"Just what Mike told me. Wait and see."

"He won't be making any funeral arrangements for a while."

"Nope."

I drew in a deep breath and let it out slowly. "Okay. I'm going to take another run at Mr. St. John. Will you hold down the fort?"

"Sure." Red glanced at his watch. "Want to grab some lunch first?"

"See what Erik and Stephanie have planned, and we'll go from there."

My husband nodded and stepped out into the reception area. I consciously relaxed my shoulders, glad that our always shaky equanimity had been restored, at least for the time being.

We ended up ordering pizza for everyone and ate it gathered around my desk. When the greasy box and empty soda bottles had been deposited in the Dumpster, I headed for the hospital. I stopped along the way and picked up a small bouquet of wildflowers, heavy with oranges and yellows as befitted the fall season. I didn't have any idea if Malcolm St. John had any interest in flowers, but at least they would brighten the white sterility of his hospital room.

I found the old man sitting up in bed, staring at the muted television swiveled on its wall mount so that he could see it without having to move around too much. His gaze didn't waver when I walked in, the bouquet held out in front of me like an offering. I glanced up to see some sort of sports show, probably ESPN, and scores running in the crawl across the bottom.

"Hello, Mr. St. John," I said softly, afraid of startling him, but he didn't acknowledge my presence.

I took a couple more steps into the room and laid the flowers on the tray table next to the bed. Still the old man ignored me. If I hadn't seen for myself that his eyes were wide open, I might have thought he'd dozed off. I cleared my throat, but that didn't elicit any response, either.

"I thought some fall color might brighten the room a little," I said, raising my voice slightly but still afraid of startling him. Maybe his hearing had taken as much of a hit as his memory.

Finally, as I stood shifting from foot to foot, unsure whether to stay or go, he turned to look at me.

"It's Bay Tanner, Mr. St. John. I came to see you yesterday. With your nephew Hub?"

"I thought you were Miss Lily."

I smiled. "Yes, I remember. You seemed very fond of her. I'm sorry to disappoint you."

He took a long time answering, his eyes roaming over me as if trying to recall something just out of reach. "But you're not her, are you?"

"No, sir, I'm afraid not." I hated to interrogate the poor man, but I needed to take advantage of his apparent lucidity. "I'm the one who found you. Outside your house. Remember?"

His gaze never left my face, and his intense scrutiny was beginning to make me uncomfortable. It was strange, but I recognized the moment when his grip on the present slid away. Something about his eyes. They didn't exactly lose focus, but it was almost as if a veil had been dropped over them, a haze almost . . . I couldn't come up with an adequate word to describe it, but I watched as the old man slipped back into the past, both of us powerless to do anything about it.

"Mr. St. John?" No reaction. I thought a moment, then said, "Little Mal?"

A frisson of unease rippled down my back. What the hell did I think I was doing? My mind flashed to an episode of *Law & Order*, my all-time favorite cop show. They were interrogating a young woman about her missing child when they suddenly realized they weren't talking to her any more, but to another side of her, with a different name and entirely different persona. Although multiple personality disorder is extremely rare—and, according to the writers of the script, some psychiatrists claim it doesn't even exist—the premise made for an interesting legal conundrum for the fictional cops and prosecutors.

That's how I felt, as if I were attempting to summon an alternate Malcolm St. John, one who lived only in his muddled brain. I had no business meddling with this man's mind. I took a step back and bumped into the table, sending a plastic drinking glass tumbling to the floor. When I straightened up from retrieving it, I turned to say my goodbyes to find him staring intently at me again.

"Mr. St. John?" I said softly.

"Who are you?" His voice was strong and querulous, his eyes wary and alert.

"I'm Bay Tanner. We met yesterday. I'm a friend of your nephew, Hub."

"I don't recall meetin' you. What do you want? I'm a sick old man. I ain't got time for any nonsense." He paused and pulled the sheet up to just under his chin. "I ain't buying nothin'. I ain't got no money." He snorted and surveyed the hospital room. "These damn fools like to take everything I got, anyway." He turned over on his side, showing me the gap in the hospital gown where his knobby spine lay exposed. "And I ain't selling nothin', either. Go away."

I took a deep breath and walked slowly around to the other side of the bed. He immediately snapped his eyes closed, the lids scrunched up like a child who wants to pretend that the bogeyman he can't see isn't there.

"Mr. St. John, I'm Bay Tanner. I'm the one who found you on Sunday evening. You were lying in the dirt outside your house down by the beach. Do you remember?"

He made no reply, and his eyes remained tightly shut.

I pulled up a chair and sat down, hoping the scraping of its legs on the linoleum would startle some response out of him. To no avail.

"Sir, I believe someone struck you on the head while you were outside. Either they lured you out there, or you let them in for some reason. Can you think back to Sunday? Do you remember what you were doing?"

"Go away." The words were spoken softly, but there was no mistaking his meaning.

It's hard to read someone's emotions without being able to see their eyes, but I had the distinct impression the old man was afraid. Maybe it was the way his hands clutched at the hem of the sheet bunched underneath his chin. Or maybe it was the slight tremor I thought I detected in his voice. Or maybe I had no idea what the hell I was talking about, but I gave it one last try.

"If someone hurt you, sir, I'd like to find out who it was. No one should be allowed to go around attacking senior citizens and getting away with it. Can you help me at all in figuring out exactly what happened to you?"

I waited for what seemed like a long time, but might have been only a minute or so, for some response. In the silence I could hear the low murmur of voices passing down the hallway and the *ding* of the elevator as the doors opened. Finally, I rose, admitting defeat. At least for the time being. I moved back around the bed and found a battered plastic vase on the top shelf of the clothes cupboard. I ran water from the sink and did my best to arrange the wildflowers. I smiled, thinking how disappointed my late mother would have been with my effort. I set the vase on the table and picked up my bag. I had an overwhelming urge to brush a farewell kiss against Mr. St. John's forehead, but I realized that it would have been an incredible intrusion. The man didn't know me from Adam. And, although I felt a kinship with him for some strange reason, it seemed way too presumptuous of me.

I had turned for the door when he spoke.

"Miss Lily? Don't leave me here alone, Miss Lily. The plat-eye'll get me, sure as anything."

I debated with myself, certain my impersonating the woman he remembered from his childhood was neither right nor fair, but needing desperately to make some connection with this confused old man. For a long moment I stood, poised between going and staying, before I expelled a breath and slipped quietly out of the room.

I sat outside in the waning October sunshine on a bench beneath overhanging branches that dappled the light against the sidewalk in front of me. The shifting patterns were mesmerizing, and I found myself lulled almost into a meditative trance. It took the squawking of a pair of mockingbirds, arguing over something high in one of the pines, to jerk me back to reality.

I squared my shoulders and ended my own interior argument. I'd arrived prepared to impersonate the mythical Miss Lily if that's what it took to gain the old man's confidence. I supposed I should have given myself a pat on the back for resisting the impulse, but I found I was ashamed of even having considered it. I've never

been a person who believed in ends' justifying means, but sometimes my curiosity, my tenacity, my unbridled *need* to find answers
overwhelmed my innate good sense.

The breeze that ruffled the leaves had turned chilly, and I
forced myself to my feet. A snippet of a quotation, some remnant
of the game my father and I had played almost up until the day of
his death, popped into my head. I muttered it out loud.

"Something about manhood, then '. . . from none but self
expect applause; He noblest lives and noblest dies who makes and
keeps his self-made laws.'"

I thought it might have been Sir Richard Burton—the explor-
er, not the actor—but I wasn't certain. I gave myself half a point
and headed for the car.

CHAPTER
FIFTEEN

I called the office and told Stephanie I was knocking off for the day. She reported nothing much happening. She and Erik were finishing the background checks and would spend Wednesday collating and printing reports for the various agencies. We had been contacted by a woman hoping to locate her birth mother, and Steph had explained to her that we didn't get involved in that kind of investigation. I felt bad for those who had been adopted and longed for the connection with their biological parents, but that whole scene was a minefield. I could never reconcile myself to coming down on one side or the other. It seemed to me that both had legitimate arguments, and it was a large can of worms I didn't want to open.

She told me that Red had gone out about an hour earlier, and they hadn't heard anything from him since. I thanked her and disconnected.

One of the things I love about living on what is essentially a small island is that things are never too far apart. Within ten minutes, I was pulling into my garage in Port Royal Plantation and shutting off the Jaguar. Red's Bronco was missing, so I let myself in, checked for messages, and peeled off my work clothes. On impulse, I dragged out my running gear and was on the beach in no time at all. I breathed in the heady salt air, marveling at how soothing just the repetitive *shush* of the rollers could be to a troubled soul.

Okay, maybe that was a little over the top, I told myself. I had accepted responsibility for my baser intentions back at the hospital. Time to forgive myself. Or punish myself might be a more accurate description of my decision to run it off. I finished my warm-up stretches and set out toward the folly.

I'd tied a sweatshirt around my waist, thinking that the return trip, into the wind, might prove too much for my bare arms

pumping away as I gathered speed. The beach lay relatively deserted at this time of day, and I pounded along the packed sand without interruption. A few hardy souls huddled outside the Westin,
one of them tossing a Frisbee to a gorgeous golden retriever. Un-
daunted by the falling temperature of the ocean, he splashed
gamely into the shallow water to snatch the bright orange disc out
of midair before trotting triumphantly back to his owner.

I honestly had no intention of veering off the sand onto the
boardwalk that led up to Burkes Beach Road, but I found my
Nikes slapping against the wooden bridge almost before I realized
I had made the decision. Out of the sun, I felt a chill as the brisk
breeze dried the perspiration on my arms. I untied the sweatshirt
and slipped it on as I slowed to a walk. I stopped for a moment to
survey the back of Mr. St. John's property, the wisps of Spanish
moss dripping from the heavy limbs of the live oak swaying in the
cooling air. I wondered who he had built the tree house for.

Up on the paved road, I paused again. There was no activity,
no cars or even pedestrians. I wondered if the owners of the beautiful home across the street were permanent residents or only occasional visitors to the island. Now was the time when a lot of
Northerners and Canadians planned their escapes south before
the real tentacles of winter began to wrap themselves around the
colder climates.

I waited another couple of minutes and set off through the
scrub to the back of Malcolm St. John's bungalow.

The patch of dirt where his body had lain for all that time was
easy to spot. The ground had been pretty thoroughly trampled by
the EMS and sheriff's people. The wound on his head hadn't bled
much, but I could still discern the faint outline his body had made
in the loose soil beside his house. I shivered a little, and it had
nothing to do with the falling temperature.

I realized for the first time that there wasn't a back door. For
some reason, I found that strange. He'd had to walk all the way
around from the front, although it wasn't really that far. It was a
very small house. Still, I tried to trace what path he might have
taken, keeping in mind Hub Danforth's suggestion that he might
have been laying a trail of whiskey to lure the plateye out of his
home.

That made me smile. *Really?* I asked myself. I had no doubt,
especially after the incidents at Sanctuary Hill, that many of the

native islanders all along the South Carolina and Georgia coasts believed in these strange, other-worldly spirits, as well as the power of the root and its magic. Just because I understood their adherence to the ways of their ancestors, though, didn't mean I bought any of it myself. Well, not most of it, anyway.

At the far corner of the house, I thought I detected a slight darkening of the dirt, a wavy line, and I dropped to my knees for a closer look. I bent over and stuck my nose practically onto the ground, but I couldn't discern any odor. The Judge had favored bourbon and lemon, so I wasn't unfamiliar with the smell of liquor. In fact, I had mixed more than my share of drinks for him, especially after his series of small strokes had confined him to a wheelchair.

I had just sat back on my haunches when I heard the car door slam.

I scrambled to my feet and edged around the back corner of the house. Working my way quietly, I gained the front and risked a quick peek. The black Lexus so prominent in the photos Stephanie had shot during her surveillance sat pulled up in Mr. St. John's yard. I leaned against the side of the house and tried to decide what to do. The last time this car had been parked on the old man's lawn, Cynthia Merrill had been a passenger.

And it suddenly occurred to me that we'd never looked very hard at her driver. It had been Stephanie's impression that Cynthia had been the one in charge, so I supposed we could be forgiven—a little—for having pretty much ignored him. And to be fair, we hadn't had much in the way of info to go on. He'd done a pretty good job of concealing his face most of the time, as I recalled. Still, in light of the coroner's suspicion about the cause of her death, we should have pursued it.

Time to remedy that oversight.

Erik and Red had both finally badgered me into the habit of snatching my cell whenever I left the house or the office, so I had it tucked securely into a pocket of my running shorts designed for that very purpose. I slid it out, made sure the ringer was on vibrate, and clicked to the photo option. Even in the fading light, I thought I just might be able to get a decent shot of him.

And, if all else failed, I'd just jump out and ask him who he was and what the hell he thought he was doing harassing a sick old man.

For some perverse reason, the mere idea of it made me smile.

The decision was taken out of my hands when the intruder suddenly pivoted and headed straight toward where I huddled against the side of the house. I stepped out into the deepening twilight and snapped off a few quick pictures before dropping the phone into my pocket. It took him a few seconds before he looked up and spotted me.

"Who the hell are you?" he barked, taking a quick step backward.

"My question exactly," I said, standing my ground.

"This is private property."

I could have come back with something equally inane, but I decided to stop playing games. "My name is Bay Tanner. I'm a private investigator here on the island. Who are you and what do you want here?"

We stood staring at each other, the situation rapidly deteriorating into something of a Mexican standoff, before he reached into the breast pocket of his well-tailored suit. I felt my body tense, and a part of me cursed myself for not having tucked the Seecamp into one of the other pockets of my running shorts. His hand came out with a business card, and I ordered my muscles to relax as I reached to take it from him. That put us a lot closer to each other, and this time I did back off, squinting to make out the embossed letters on the heavy cardstock.

"Bradley B. Winter," I read, "Associate Director of Acquisitions, Midsouth Asset Development." I looked up to find him regarding me warily. "You were here last weekend with Cynthia Merrill. I assume you know she's dead."

I'd done it deliberately, but it was still something of a jolt to see the sharp sting of shock on his face. I softened my tone. "I'm sorry for your loss."

He gathered himself before speaking. "Cyn and I have—*had* —worked together for almost three years. We were friends as well as colleagues." He paused and set aside his apparent grief. "What business is all this of yours, if I may ask?"

His voice had a nice Southern roll to it, not exactly a drawl, but it was evident he hadn't spent much time up in Yankee territory. I shoved my hands in my pockets to demonstrate the end of the confrontation and leaned against the side of Mr. St. John's bungalow.

"My business interests and my client's name are confidential, but I can tell you my concerns are personal as well as professional. Was your firm looking to purchase the property for development?"

His smile changed his whole demeanor. Bradley B. Winter had a boyish charm, not conventionally handsome, but I could understand how he might be good at his job. He mimicked me by pushing back the sides of his jacket and sticking his hands in his own pockets. We regarded each other for a moment before he shrugged.

"I'm also under confidentiality constraints, Ms. Tanner. And how do I know you're who you say you are?"

I smiled back. "I don't usually carry business cards in my running shorts," I said, "but you can check me out. We have a Web site, and my picture's on there. I was just taking a quick look around before heading back up the beach."

He nodded. "You must live close by."

"Are you staying at the Sea Oats as well?"

Again we let the quiet of the Lowcountry evening settle between us.

"I guess we can declare this one a draw," he said without rancor. "It was nice to meet you."

Before I could reply, he turned and made his way back to the Lexus. I watched him maneuver the car out of Mr. St. John's yard and back onto the pavement, then tracked the distinctive taillights as they disappeared into the night.

CHAPTER SIXTEEN

Red was standing on the deck, gazing out toward the ocean, when I jogged back down the boardwalk and into the yard. As I mounted the steps, he held out a towel and a glistening glass of iced tea.

"How was the run?"

"Enlightening," I answered, wiping the sweat from my face and draping the towel across my shoulders. I took a long swallow of tea and filled him in on my encounter with Bradley B. Winter.

"Interesting."

We stretched out on the chaises set side by side on the deck. The breeze off the ocean had died to a whisper, but I still felt the chill on my overheated skin. Unconsciously, I shivered.

"Want to go in?" my husband asked, and I shook my head.

"I'm fine. What do you want to do about dinner?"

"I resurrected the shrimp we didn't eat last night. Everything's all laid out. I made a salad, and the water's boiling for pasta."

"I knew I married you for more than just your boyish good looks," I said. "Let me get cleaned up. Shouldn't take more than a few minutes to get things on the table."

Red's hand on my arm held me gently in place. "What do you make of this Winter guy? Any thoughts?"

I settled back on the chaise. "I don't think he knows about Mr. St. John. About his injury. At least that's the impression I got. I think he expected to find him at home."

"Or he's a damn good actor. But didn't you say he was heading for the back of the house? If he came to call, wouldn't he have gone straight for the front door?"

"Good point," I said, sipping tea. "It was getting dark, and there weren't any lights on, so maybe he was checking to see if the old man was in the backyard." I shrugged. "I don't know. He did seem genuinely upset about Merrill's death."

"Doesn't mean he isn't involved somehow. With both of them."

I couldn't suppress a brief smile. "I have the distinct feeling I've been a bad influence on you, my dear. Your cynicism quotient has risen dramatically since we've gotten together."

I could hear the amusement in his voice. "You can take credit for it if you want, but I didn't just fall off the back of the cabbage truck. We've both encountered plenty of pretty nasty characters who exuded charm and innocence, haven't we?"

"*Exuded?* Your vocabulary has improved, too."

Red stood and jerked me to my feet. In a second I was locked in his warm embrace. "You're not Henry Higgins, and I'm not Eliza Doolittle, sweetheart, much as you'd like to think so." He leaned back to gauge my reaction. "And yes, I do watch something besides sports once in a while."

I laughed and nestled my head against his cheek. "Right you are, Sergeant."

The kiss lasted a long time before we both eased back.

"I need a shower," I murmured as I turned toward the French doors.

"Yes, you do," my husband replied, swatting me soundly on the butt before I could move out of reach. "And then I want dinner, woman."

I flicked the towel at him as I scooted out of range and headed for the bedroom.

And suddenly found my throat tight with unshed tears. The scene had reminded me so poignantly of exchanges I'd often had with Rob that I had to choke back a sob. As I turned on the shower to just short of boiling, I wondered if I'd ever get the unfair comparisons out of my head.

The shrimp had indeed survived my burned garlic fiasco, and we both ate way too much before settling in the great room with tea and coffee. We'd spent much of the meal hashing over the possibilities of Bradley B. Winter's involvement in recent events. I'd toyed with the idea of setting Erik on his trail, but we both decided it could wait until morning.

"Where'd you disappear to this afternoon?" I asked, tucking

my legs up under me on the white sofa that faced the fireplace.

Beside me, Red held the remote, running through the on-screen guide. With over 200 cable channels and the special sports package he'd subscribed to, there wasn't an evening when he couldn't locate some form of game, be it baseball, basketball, football, or hockey. This was the time of year he loved best, when all his favorite sports were running simultaneously.

An embarrassment of riches, I thought and smiled. Molière? Maybe Voltaire? I was sure it was from one of those seventeenth- or eighteenth-century French writers, but I couldn't place it exactly. I had gotten woefully out of practice without the stimulus of the Judge's critical eye when I failed to deliver on a quotation.

My husband settled on a baseball playoff game—the Yankees, of course, and Texas—then answered my question. "I dropped back by the sheriff's office. It's a lot handier now that they've moved up to our end of the island."

The satellite station had recently taken space in an out-of-business wellness center not far from the mall, which was also getting ready to face major changes. I wondered how it would affect the island when the only enclosed shopping area fell under the wrecking ball to make way for a new grocery store, outdoor retail shops with condos above, and a controversial gas station. I took it as a sign of my advancing age that I hated the very idea of such drastic changes to our beautiful landscape, regardless of how enticing the architects' drawings looked in the *Island Packet*.

"Anything new?" I asked.

"Nope. Raleigh was out, and I didn't want to put Malik on the spot. I'll check back with them tomorrow."

I stretched out my legs to prop them on the coffee table and reached for my book, eager to resume my Lucas Davenport fix. I tuned out the frenzied voice of the announcer on the baseball game and let myself sink into the joy of a well-written mystery. I'm not sure how long we sat, both of us lost in our respective pursuits, when the doorbell rang. The sound was so unusual that we jumped simultaneously. After a quick exchange of startled looks, Red hauled himself up and walked toward the foyer. A few moments later I heard the series of beeps that signaled the alarm had been disconnected, followed almost immediately by Red's shout.

"God damn it!"

His profanity shot me off the sofa in a flash.

"What's the matter?"

Before I could reach the door, he was out onto the porch and streaking away into the night.

"Red, wait! Where the hell are you going?"

As I moved to follow him, I nearly tripped over a huge basket of fall flowers placed smack in the middle of the doorway. Yellow mums and other orange and cream blooms registered on my vision as I stepped over the bouquet and squinted out into the dark.

"Red! Where are you?"

Barefoot, as I usually was inside the house, I hesitated to chase him down, especially since I didn't know which direction he'd taken. I stood, half in and half out of the house, my head swiveling in a vain attempt to locate my husband in the gloom. A moment later I heard his heavy breathing, and he appeared at the foot of the steps.

"What the hell are you doing?" I asked in a voice I knew had gone shrill and accusatory. I took a deep breath. "What's wrong?"

He walked up the steps and stood gazing down at the basket. "I'm laying serious money that's from your stalker. I thought maybe I could run him down, but he got away up the beach."

"You saw him?"

"Yeah, the son of a bitch." Red aimed a kick at the bouquet, but I countered by sliding it away with my foot, out of his reach.

"Settle down. Did you ever stop to think you might just have scared the daylights out of some poor delivery guy?"

The mental image made both of us smile, and the tension level subsided.

"Not possible. Don't they have to call for a pass?"

He had a point, although I reminded him that some businesses paid for commercial decals so their delivery people could avoid the hassle.

"Did you get a decent look at him? Height, weight, anything?"

"Too dark. I'm guessing pretty young, though, or in really good shape."

"Why, because he outran you?"

"No, my dear, because of *how* he ran. Loose, easy." He managed another smile. "Like you do."

I nodded in acceptance of the compliment. "So maybe a woman?"

His frown was almost comical. "I hadn't thought of that. Why would a woman be sending you those ridiculous letters?"

"Come on, Red, join the twenty-first century."

"That's just wrong," my husband said, ending that particular discussion by reaching for the basket. "Might as well see what illuminating message we've got here. Let's try to preserve any prints. Get a towel, will you?"

I thought of about three dozen snappy comebacks, but I let them all wither unspoken. In a minute, I was back with a dish towel, and Red used it to pick up the basket by its sides and carry it into the house. In the middle of the glass-topped table in the bay window of the kitchen, it looked quite lovely. Some perverse part of my mind hoped we didn't have to tear it apart.

"You know," I said, studying the arrangement from all sides, "this looks a lot like the bouquet I took up to Mr. St. John's room this afternoon. A lot bigger, of course, and mine were just loose stems, but they're the same kind of flowers. Even the colors."

I'd been thinking out loud, not giving much thought to how my statements might affect my husband.

"So he—or *she*," he added with a grimace, "was following you today? I thought you were going to be more careful, keep an eye out."

I refused to be baited. No way was I going down that path again. "I am being careful. If someone's tagging along after me, he's good. I've been trying to keep track of cars around me, looking for the same one showing up in different places. I honestly didn't spot anyone."

Most of the anger faded from Red's eyes. "I know. Sorry. It's just that this is driving me crazy."

I laid my palm softly against the stubble on his cheek. "It's understandable. Let's take a look at the card. I'll get a bag for it."

My name didn't appear on the envelope, but the same printing and expressions of undying devotion left little doubt who the delivery . . . *person* had been. Red had used a pair of tongs to ease the note out and into the plastic baggie I'd retrieved from the pantry. We stood for a long moment just staring at it, and for the first time I felt a shiver of *something* skitter down my spine.

I finally convinced my husband not to pitch the entire thing into the garbage can in the garage. It had to have cost a small fortune, and there was no sense in not enjoying the flowers, if not the sender or the sentiment.

Back in the great room, we resettled ourselves on the sofa. I didn't register how much time had passed when the house phone rang, interrupting a Yankees' bases-loaded-nobody-out situation with the caller ID box.

"Lavinia," I said. "I'll get it."

"Thanks, honey."

I carried the book with me into the kitchen. I glanced at the clock, noting that it was a little after nine. My first thought was that it couldn't be good news. Lavinia had usually retired to her room by now, either to read or to knit. Or maybe she'd changed her routine since Julia had come to live at Presqu'isle. Maybe the two of them watched television together or played Scrabble at the old oak table in the kitchen. I snatched up the receiver, remembering many an evening when Lavinia and I had sat there, the board spread out before us, the tea kettle whistling and the smells of something yummy and decadent emanating from the oven across the room.

"Hey, Lavinia."

"Bay."

I waited, confused as to why she wasn't responding.

"Is something wrong?" I finally asked.

"Why should you think something's wrong? Can't I just call you up to chat?"

As if, I thought. Talking on the phone was one of Lavinia's least favorite pastimes.

"Of course." I floundered around for a suitable topic of conversation. I didn't think it would be a good idea to get into our recent activities in pursuit of my flower-delivering stalker. "How's everything there?"

"Fine. How about you?"

I noted the page number and closed my book. The Judge hadn't believed in bookmarks. "Just a quiet evening at home." I felt no guilt whatsoever at the blatant lie. "Red's watching a ballgame, and I'm reading. What are you and Julia up to?"

I knew she would hear the unasked questions in my voice. This was so un-Lavinia-like.

"I'm just taking a pie out of the oven. Pumpkin."

It had been the Judge's favorite, and I breathed a little easier, certain now I had the real reason for her call nailed down.

"I miss him, too," I said softly. "Are you going to whip real cream or use the packaged stuff?"

I could almost hear her bristle. "Of course I'm going to use real cream. When have you ever known me to skimp when it comes to pumpkin pie?"

"Never," I said with a light laugh. "I wish I was there."

Her sigh wiped the smile from my face. "So do I, child, so do I."

"It'll get easier. At least that's what they tell me."

"The good Lord only sends us the trials He knows we can handle."

I wasn't so sure about that, but her faith had sustained Lavinia through many troubles, and who was I to question it? A change of subject was in order.

"How's my sister?"

It had taken me a long time to come to terms with having a half sibling so close to me in age and to have discovered her in the middle of my life. Still, there she was, and dealing with the situation was becoming easier. If only I didn't have those niggling doubts, shoved by intent to the back of my mind, but lurking there nonetheless. It took me a moment to realize there hadn't been an immediate response.

"Lavinia?"

"Oh, we're doin' just fine, honey. Don't you worry about us." She paused. "Would you and Redmond be planning on a visit any time soon?"

I cringed at the underlying pleading tone in her voice.

"We can. Is there something specific you need us for?"

"No, honey, not really. I just miss seeing you, that's all." Again a pause. "It's awful quiet sometimes."

The woman had been run off her feet when my father was alive, caring for the huge antebellum mansion and catering to the man she loved in his old age and infirmity. I supposed it did seem lonely with only my damaged sister for companionship.

"How about we run over for dinner later this week? I haven't had a decent pot roast since the last time we were there. Seems like the weather for it."

"Sakes alive, child, didn't I give you specific instructions on how to fix that?"

That's better, I thought. I could deal with the feisty Lavinia much better than with the sad one.

"You know nothing turns out exactly right unless you have your hands in it," I said. It was nothing less than the truth.

"Thursday. I'll get all the fixings tomorrow. Six suit you?"

"Sure, that'll be great. We'll see you then. Say hey to Julia for me."

As usual, she hung up without saying goodbye.

I picked up the book and carried it back to the sofa, but I found I'd lost my concentration. Something about the call had set up faint alarm bells, and they refused to be silenced.

"Everything okay?" Red asked, muting the TV.

"Uh huh," I said without conviction, my rampant imagination conjuring up scenarios I didn't even want to contemplate let alone explore. I shook my head. "So who's winning?" I asked and reached for my husband's hand.

CHAPTER SEVENTEEN

I slept badly and woke up with a crashing headache, then snapped at Red when he reminded me for the third time that I needed to haul my butt out of bed. I rolled over and pulled the duvet over my head. He finally got the message and grumbled his way to the shower. When he was safely singing away, off-key, to some obscure Beatles' tune, I forced myself into the bathroom, downed three aspirin, and crawled back under the covers.

I could tell from the grayish light that seeped around the edges of the drapes that the weather had changed sometime overnight. That would account for the pounding in my sinuses that kept rhythm with my heartbeat. I burrowed a little deeper under the covers, thinking how absolutely lovely it would be just to fall back to sleep, maybe to the accompaniment of a soft rain on the roof . . .

"Bay, honey, come on."

I jerked awake to Red's hand stroking my bare shoulder, his breath just inches from my ear.

"Go away," I said, attempting to flip onto my other side, but he gathered me into his arms before I could execute the maneuver.

"You know you're gonna hate yourself if you don't get up and go into the office. You'll be bitching all day about wasting time, and none of us will be able to do anything to your satisfaction. Think of the kids."

For a moment, the images of Scotty and Elinor popped into my head before I realized he was talking about Erik and Stephanie. A little frisson of fear made me shiver, and Red pulled me closer.

"Cold?"

"No. I was just thinking about Sarah. You have to find out what's going on with her."

Red leaned over and kissed me on the forehead. "I'm doing the best I can, honey, but I can't tie her down and make her talk to me."

I eased out of his embrace and doubled up one of the pillows behind my head. "But if she's got . . . you know, something seriously wrong with her, we have a right to be told. Well, maybe not me, but you certainly need to be able to plan how to deal with . . . whatever's going on. It's only fair to your kids."

"You're preaching to the converted. If you've got any ideas on how to get her to level with me, I'm all ears."

Of course I didn't. The truth was, I could hardly bear to think about the devastation that would be visited on all our lives if something happened to Red's ex-wife. I had been an adult when both my parents died, although the two events had been decades apart. Still, I couldn't imagine how Scotty and little Elinor would be able to go on if . . .

"I'll think about it," I finally said, banishing the unthinkable to the back of my mind. "Okay, let me up. I suppose it'll be better to deal with this headache than to have you bugging me for the rest of the day."

I said it with a faint smile, and Red leaned over to kiss me again. "Good girl. I'll go get some tea going for you. Dress warm. Must have been a cold front that moved through last night. It's only in the fifties."

I shivered at the very thought and reconsidered my decision, but only for a brief moment. Duty called, and I was, after all, my father's daughter. With a sigh, I forced myself out of bed and shuffled toward the bathroom.

In dark brown slacks and creamy cashmere sweater, I shoved my feet into my Bass penny loafers and gave my hair a final brush. I looked almost as bad as I felt, the dark circles under my eyes refusing to yield to my limited makeup skills. In the kitchen, Red had moved the basket of flowers onto the floor to make room for my morning mug of Earl Grey and his usual coffee. Ever since he'd successfully petitioned for one of those single-cup gizmo machines, I never knew what obscure blend of flavors he'd be trying next, but his day never began without a mug of something caffeinated. These small offerings held us until we could make it to the office and our *Venti* cups from Starbucks.

"English muffin coming up," he said, his back to me as he hovered over the toaster.

"I really don't want anything to eat."

"I know you took aspirin on an empty stomach, and that's not—"

He stopped at the buzzing of his cell phone lying on the built-in desk. He always hooked it up to the charger before going to bed, a habit I needed to acquire as mine was always running out of juice.

"Tanner," he said, balancing the small square between his cheek and shoulder while he dropped the muffin halves onto a plate. He set it in front of me, then went back for the jar of peanut butter and a knife.

I busied myself with my breakfast, my mind centered on the dilemma of Malcolm St. John, Hub Danforth, and the late Cynthia Merrill. My ears pricked up when I heard Red's sharp indrawn breath. I waited, but he was listening intently, his gaze focused on the French doors leading out onto the deck from the great room. I followed his line of sight, noting the writhing of the limbs on the live oaks in the freshening breeze off the ocean and the spattering of raindrops on the windows. Farther out, a flock of gulls hung suspended, almost motionless, their efforts to buck the headwind proving futile. I watched them wheel and swoop in the opposite direction just as Red found his voice.

"Well, I guess that's pretty conclusive. Any leads?"

I waited for him to turn in my direction, but he seemed mesmerized by whatever it was that had caught his attention outside. I could guess, though, that he was talking to Mike Raleigh and learning that Hub Danforth's ex-wife had not died of natural causes. I ordered myself not to jump to conclusions, but I rarely listen to those kinds of admonition. I bet myself a hundred bucks that I was right and waited impatiently for Red to end the call.

"Okay, Mike, thanks for the heads-up. We'll stop in and give you what we've got on the players . . . Oh, sure, that's fine." He finally pulled his attention back into the kitchen and looked over his shoulder at the clock on the microwave. "Ten should be good . . . Right. See you then."

"Cynthia Merrill was murdered," I mumbled around a mouthful of muffin, and it came out sounding like gibberish.

"If you just said that Cynthia Merrill was murdered, you'd be right. The blow to her head caused intracranial bleeding, which was the cause of death."

I swallowed. "That came down pretty fast. I thought it was going to take a couple of days."

Red shrugged. "I guess they weren't as backed up as Mike thought they'd be. Anyway," he continued, joining me at the table, "he's coming by the office around ten." He glanced at me over the rim of his coffee cup. "I told him we'd cooperate in any way we can."

If he was looking for an argument, he wasn't going to get one from me. "Fine, although I don't know how much we have to contribute. She was only on the periphery of our investigation, if you can even call it that. We really never got the thing off the ground."

My husband cast a quick glance over his shoulder, out toward the French doors. "You want to notify Danforth, or should I do it?"

"Let's wait until after we talk to Raleigh. We might have more information to pass along."

Red rose and carried his mug to the sink, but again I could see his attention drawn toward the deck as he said, "You about ready?"

I gulped down the last two bites of muffin and stood, accidentally kicking the basket of flowers a few inches across the floor. I had to admit the stalking thing was getting a little out of hand. My efforts to dismiss the notes as the work of some prankster had pretty much blown up with the balloons, the nasty message left for Red, and now this invasion of our space by leaving this damned thing on our doorstep. Maybe I'd run it by Mike, see what he had to say, I thought as I dumped my dishes alongside Red's and lifted my bag from the desk.

He spoke without looking at me. "You go ahead. I have to grab a jacket from the bedroom."

I looked at my husband and knew immediately that something was up. "Your jackets are in the guest closet in the foyer, as you well know. What's going on?"

"Just go get in the car, will you, honey? I'll be right there."

In answer, I marched down the three steps and across the floor toward the French doors that led to the deck.

"Bay, for God's sake will you just this once do what I ask you?"

I stopped, surprised by the vehemence in his voice. But he should have known me better than that. "I don't know what you're trying to hide, but you're really lousy at deception." I softened my voice. "That was a compliment, in case you're wondering."

He moved quickly to block me, and we stood for a moment staring into each other's eyes.

"I'm just trying to spare you, that's all," he said quietly.

"Spare me from what? I'm a big girl, Red."

I skirted around him and pulled open one of the doors. Rain spattered my face as I scanned the length of the damp wooden planks, finally coming to rest on the scraggly wet mound of fur beside the chaise I habitually used. It took me a moment to identify the pitiful body as that of a squirrel, its poor head smashed beyond recognition.

But, sickening as that sight was, it was something else that sent the blood draining from my face.

Propped up against the tiny creature's remains was a sheet of paper, encased in plastic as protection from the rain, its single word completely legible:

Mine.

Of course we were late to the office. I took a sip of the nearly cold chai latte and dropped the cardboard cup into the trash. I felt at that moment as if I'd never be able to swallow again.

Red had used his phone to take photos of the carcass and the note as we'd found them, then retrieved the message and secured it in another baggie. I felt the nausea rise in my throat as I remembered the smell of blood and wet fur as Red covered the tiny corpse with a towel, just in case Mike Raleigh wanted to see it for himself.

There was no longer any question of involving the sheriff. Even if Red hadn't insisted on it, I would have spilled the whole story on my own. But first we needed to take care of business.

Mike shifted a little in the client chair, his long legs stretched out in front of him. "So you never met or spoke to Ms. Merrill?"

"That's right," I said. "We photographed her as part of our

surveillance of Mr. St. John's cottage, and Stephanie and Erik tracked down her identity. I'm not sure if it was a coincidence that she should be hanging around that part of the island at the exact time her ex-husband was trying to get his uncle declared incompetent. It's a question I would have liked to ask her."

"We'll be talking to her associate—" He glanced down at the notepad balanced on one thigh. "Winter. How did he strike you?"

I shrugged. "I only talked to him for a couple of minutes, but I didn't get any bad vibes from him. My impression was that he had no idea Mr. St. John had been injured. He seemed genuinely upset about Merrill, too."

"And what about the ex? This Danforth guy."

"You've talked to him yourself, right? I know there's no love lost between law enforcement and criminal defense attorneys, but he seemed pretty straight-arrow to me. I had a chance to see him interact with his uncle at the hospital. If he's involved in some way with the attack on the old man, I'd be very surprised. I think his motives may not be as altruistic as he'd like us to think, but I can't see him doing violence to Mr. St. John. He seems to care about him, at least as far as I could tell."

Detective Mike Raleigh tapped his pen twice against the notepad and flipped it closed. "Okay, I guess that's it. I really appreciate all the information."

I leaned back in my chair, glad to have that part of the interview out of the way.

Red shifted in his chair and rested his elbows on his knees. "Anything you can share with us about Merrill's death? We need to let Danforth know about the ruling of homicide."

Raleigh tucked both the pad and his pen back into the inside pocket of his suit coat. "She probably died between eight and midnight on Sunday," he said. "Single blow just behind the left ear, delivered with considerable force. Death wouldn't have been instantaneous, but she probably wouldn't have regained consciousness before she bled to death internally."

The details, recounted in Raleigh's soft monotone, seemed all the more horrific for his bland recitation.

"Left ear. Wouldn't that make the killer left-handed?"

"Maybe," Raleigh said, "although it's not a sure bet. The coroner said it could have been either, depending on the height of the person wielding . . . whatever the weapon was, and on Merrill's position when the blow landed."

"No clue about that? The weapon?" Red asked.

"Unfortunately, no. A blunt object. There wasn't any blood on the skin, just the knot."

"Mr. St. John's injury was to the left side of his head. Behind the ear."

I don't know if I expected Mike Raleigh to jump up and shout *Eureka!* or something equally dramatic. Instead, he nodded.

"Duly noted, Bay. I'm not sure how that factors in, but be sure we'll be looking at that incident as well." He slapped his hands on his thighs. "So, anything else I can tell you?"

As he rose, Red held out a hand. "If you could give us just a few more minutes, Mike, there's another issue I need to run by you."

"Sure," the detective said, resuming his seat. "Fire away."

I opened my mouth, but Red quelled me with a look. He focused his attention on Mike Raleigh and leaned in a little closer.

"This wacko who's stalking my wife is escalating big-time, and I need you guys to find him before I do." His voice deepened. "Otherwise, it'll be me you're investigating for homicide."

CHAPTER
EIGHTEEN

I spent the rest of the morning fuming, both at Red's hyperbole and my own feelings, a mixture of anger, frustration, and . . . I didn't want to put a name to it, but I had to be honest, at least with myself: *Fear.* It had been easy to be flip about my secret admirer, to joke with Neddie and everyone else about the silly love letters.

The dead squirrel on my deck changed the game.

That and my husband's ridiculous threats. Thank God Mike Raleigh had taken them as some sort of macabre joke, although he seemed genuinely concerned about the stalking. He asked me to come down to the substation and fill out a formal complaint. That way he wouldn't have to work off the grid when it came to running the various notes for prints.

I understood his decision not to confiscate either the basket of flowers or the murdered squirrel remains.

I let Red deal with Hub Danforth, a cowardly act on my part that didn't improve my generally crappy mood. I shut myself in my office, confident no one would be foolhardy enough to come knocking on my door unless the place was on fire. I needed space. Too many problems were elbowing around in my head, vying for attention. A serious bout of prioritizing was in order.

Because I always seem to think better with a pen in my hand —a throwback to my accounting days, no doubt—I pulled a legal pad out of my desk and spent several minutes just doodling. I'd found that if I let my mind roam free, with no predetermined destination or outcome, I often arrived at clearer conclusions. At least it used to work that way when I was stumped by a knotty accounting problem.

After a while, I looked down at my scribbling to find that I'd pretty much summarized the situation: The stalker. Julia. Cynthia Merrill. Malcolm St. John. Sarah. Under the last name, I'd scrawled *instant family?????* That might have been the most frightening scenario of them all.

And beneath the word *stalker* I'd sketched the stick figure from the hangman game, complete with gibbet and noose.

Maybe Red and I weren't on entirely different pages after all.

I emerged from my self-imposed exile free of the headache and much of my bad humor. Three pair of eyes followed my progress as I made my way to our unisex bathroom, and I even managed a couple of smiles that could pass for pleasant.

Red was waiting when I stepped back into the reception area.

"Back among the living?" he asked, his hand resting lightly on the small of my back as he guided me toward my office.

"I'm still pissed off at you for all that posturing in front of Mike Raleigh," I said, but in a much less belligerent tone than I'd used earlier in the morning.

Red flopped into one of the client chairs as I made my way behind the desk. "I meant what I said."

I waved a hand. "Okay, let's not get into it again. Did you talk to Hub?"

He nodded. "Yeah. Not the most pleasant conversation I've ever had."

"He didn't take it well?"

"I don't think he was completely surprised, but it was a shock anyway. He wants to keep us on the payroll to make sure the sheriff does everything possible to find out who did it."

"Any reason he thinks they wouldn't?"

"Because of the way high-powered attorneys like him always view the cops. They all think they're smarter than we are. That we look for the easy way out to close a case."

I thought about that for a moment. "He could be right sometimes, but it's a pretty broad generalization. Maybe he realizes that he could be at the top of their suspect list, and he's trying to stay ahead of the game by getting us to feed him information."

Red stared at me for a moment. "Boy, and you talked about me being cynical. I'm not even in your league, honey. What put that idea into your head?"

I didn't have an answer for that. "I don't know. Maybe because the spouse—or ex—is always the first one to be looked at.

Isn't that right?"

"Yeah, but there's nothing here to suggest he even knew she was in town."

"That's an assumption. All we have is his word for it." I paused for a moment. "Stephanie?" I called over Red's shoulder.

A moment later she stood in the doorway. "Yes, ma'am?"

I cringed. "Will you check your notes in the Danforth file and see if I ever mention talking to Hub about his wife sniffing around Mr. St. John's property?"

"Sure," she said and disappeared.

"I think I'd remember that," Red offered, and I shrugged.

"Maybe, but a lot has happened in the meantime."

"You seriously think Danforth might have killed his ex?" Red studied me across the expanse of mahogany desk. "Wasn't that you defending him to Mike Raleigh just a couple of hours ago? Now all of a sudden you're looking at him as a murder suspect?"

I shrugged. "You said it yourself, Red. There are some really gifted actors out there. And a criminal defense attorney has to be something of a showman, doesn't he? If Hub didn't know about Cynthia's being in town until after Sunday night, that's one mark in his favor." I sighed. "Still, I have a hard time thinking of him as being capable of that kind of violence."

"Most people are capable of just about anything if they're pushed hard enough."

I thought about his earlier outburst. Did I really think Red could be goaded into some crazy act of vengeance against my stalker? He'd certainly changed since his retirement from the sheriff's office, but to that extent? Or maybe I wasn't nearly as good a judge of character as I liked to give myself credit for.

"Good point. Let's wait and see what Steph comes up with." I sighed again and consciously relaxed my shoulders as my gaze traveled to the scribbles on my legal pad.

"Now," I said, "let's talk about Sarah."

We had lunch at the Skull Creek Boathouse, even though the weather precluded our sitting outside by the water. Rain still spluttered in little bursts as we made our way back to the Jaguar. My shoulders hunched in anticipation of finding another message tucked under the wiper blade, but the windshield was blessedly clear of small blue or white envelopes.

We'd spent most of the time when we weren't downing shrimp salad sandwiches and seafood chowder trying to come up with a game plan for getting the truth about Sarah Jane Tanner's condition. The kids were out, mostly because neither of us felt right about making them choose between loyalty to their mother and a direct order from their father. No doctor who valued his malpractice insurance would talk to us, although I did have a couple of connections in Beaufort that I might be able to tap if it came right down to it. That left family and friends, all of whom would be guarding Sarah's privacy, especially against her ex-husband and his former sister-in-law turned second wife.

I slid into the passenger seat and leaned back. "The only viable solution is for one of us to get Sarah to talk to us."

Red backed the car around and eased over the speed bump on his way to Squire Pope Road. "Well, she's already made it pretty clear she's not going to confide in me."

"That's so unlike her. She has to know you'll be the one taking on the kids if something happens to her. Why would she want to keep you in the dark?"

Another shower dropped out of the leaden sky, and Red flipped on the wipers. They made a single smooth pass before the one on my side suddenly flew off in a clatter of metal on glass.

Red hit the brakes. "What in the hell was that?"

"The whole wiper blade just disappeared," I said, my heart thudding unnaturally loud in my chest. "Scared the hell out of me."

My husband reached for the door handle. "Good thing it didn't happen when we were out on the road."

And then we looked at each other, knowledge heavy between us.

"Next stop is the sheriff's office," he said between clenched teeth as he darted out into the rain to retrieve the broken wiper.

"Damn straight," I said. And added, to my nameless, faceless tormentor, "Okay, you slimy bastard. Game on."

We were back in the office by a little after three. I'd made my complaint and turned over all the notes in their protective baggies along with printouts of Red's photos of the dead squirrel. With the rain, there was no point in wasting time looking for footprints or any other evidence the creep might have left behind during both his forays onto my property, but Mike promised to stop over and have a quick look just to cover all the bases.

I knew it wouldn't be much of a priority, what with Cynthia Merrill's murder on the front burner, but I felt better for having dumped it all in someone else's lap. I took the detective's admonitions to be careful and observant with as much good grace as I could muster and promised myself that the Seecamp pistol would never be far from my hand going forward. I might descry Red's wild threats, but I didn't think I'd have any trouble putting one in whatever part of my tormentor's body came to hand.

Maybe I should be packing something bigger, something more accurate at long range. I'd see what Red thought about my appropriating his Glock, the same kind of gun he'd used when he'd first taught me how to shoot. I'd need some time on the practice range, but that shouldn't be a problem. I had a license to carry, even though it had been obtained under the table by my late father. I wondered if there was enough ammo. Or maybe I should just get myself a new weapon, maybe a Smith & Wesson or—

"Earth to Bay, come in please." Red's voice jerked me out of my retribution fantasies.

"Sorry. What did you say?"

"I asked you where you want us to go on the Malcolm St. John thing. Erik asked me about it. Are we still surveilling him or what?"

I hadn't given that part of our investigation much thought. "Do we know if he's home from the hospital yet? Hub Danforth talked about having to make arrangements for someone to stay with him before they turned him loose."

"I don't know. Didn't Danforth say he had to be back in Atlanta today for a trial?"

I glanced at the calendar. "I think he said he'd gotten a postponement. Ask Stephanie to check with the hospital and see if Mr. St. John's been released. I'll try to contact Hub."

As I reached for the phone, it rang under my hand. A moment later, Stephanie buzzed me on the intercom.

"Mr. Danforth for you, Bay."

"Thanks," I said and picked up.

"Hello, Bay. I'm just wondering if you have any news for

me." Danforth still sounded exhausted.

"I'm sorry, Hub, nothing. You talked to Red about the homicide ruling, right?"

He took his time answering. "My kids are devastated. It's bad enough losing their mother, but to think that someone . . ." His voice trailed off.

"I understand. Right now, the detectives are checking her whereabouts on Sunday, who she might have interacted with in the hours leading up to her death. The investigation is still in its early stages, as I'm sure you can appreciate."

Hub Danforth defended criminals. Or at least those the cops believed to be criminals. Surely he knew how the system worked. Again, I wondered about his motives in retaining us to erect a wall between himself and the authorities charged with solving his ex-wife's murder.

As if sensing my unspoken words, he said, "It's a whole lot different ballgame when you're personally involved in it."

"I can appreciate that. How are your children holding up?"

He sighed. "Not well. I don't think Jillian's stopped crying. From what I can gather, she and her mother had some sort of row a few days ago, and she's blaming herself. I can't seem to console her."

I again thanked providence for the fact that I'd had the opportunity to say a proper goodbye to my father. I don't know how I might have reacted if we'd parted for the last time amid harsh words and anger. I'd been similarly fortunate that Rob and I had spent an idyllic weekend together at the beach before he'd suddenly vanished in front of my eyes in a hideous fireball of destruction and death.

"I'm so sorry," I said, meaning it. I swallowed and put my sympathy on hold. "You said you didn't know Cynthia was on the island?"

He didn't respond for so long I thought he might have hung up on me. "Yes, that's what I said." Another long pause, and this time his voice had lost its defensiveness. "But I'm not surprised she was here."

That was new. "Really? Why do you say that?"

"I'm not unmindful of the value of Uncle Malcolm's property, Bay. As I told you, Sissy and I were sure it could be the source of enough proceeds to keep him in comfort for the rest of his life." He spoke even more softly, almost as if he were ashamed of his next words. "I did some investigation before I hired you, into what kind of selling price we might expect. The name of Cyn's firm came up a couple of times as a potential buyer. Apparently, they're looking to expand onto Hilton Head."

I knew that was true. I'd read about it just a few days before in the *Packet*.

"So you think she might have been on the island to look into buying your uncle's property for her firm?"

"I'd lay money on it," Hub Danforth said with conviction.

"Why?"

His answer and the vehemence with which he delivered it made my head snap up.

"Because she's lusted after that lot ever since the first time I brought her down for a visit. And Cynthia was nothing if not tenacious. She hated to lose, and she especially hated losing to me. If there was a way for her to cut me off at the knees and steal the property out from under me, believe me she would have done it without a single thought to the consequences."

Consequences, I thought as we said our goodbyes. An interesting choice of words. Had Hub Danforth just provided himself with an excellent motive for murder?

CHAPTER
NINETEEN

I spent a few minutes writing out verbatim as much of the conversation as I could remember. I wished, not for the first time, that we didn't have a law against taping phone calls without the corresponding party's permission.

I'd just finished when Stephanie stepped into my office. I looked up in acknowledgement.

"Two things," she said, glancing at a note pad in her hand. "There's nothing in the file that indicates any one of us talked to Mr. Danforth about his ex-wife being in town. And Mr. St. John will be released tomorrow sometime, probably around noon."

"How on earth did you manage to get information out of the hospital?"

"I got to know a lot of the people there when I did an article for the *Monthly* about the new administrator. I just called in a couple of favors."

Stephanie's first job on the island had been as a freelance writer for the local magazine. Because she'd become such an integral part of Simpson & Tanner, I often forgot that she'd only been with us for a matter of weeks. Our interactions before that had been sporadic, mostly in regard to her issues with her father's messing in her personal life. I felt the familiar sadness tinged with guilt at the memory of my late partner and marveled again that his daughter could have become so comfortable working for me.

"Thanks. I've got some notes to be added to the Danforth file. Would you mind entering them?"

"No problem," she said, taking the single sheet of legal paper from my hand. "Anything else before we head out?"

I glanced at my watch, surprised to find it was already after five. "Leave that until tomorrow. We'll need to put our heads together and figure out where we're going on the surveillance for Mr. St. John.

"Okay," she said, and I picked up on her hesitation.

"What? You disagree?"

"Oh, no, it's not that. I mean, Erik said he thought there wouldn't be any point to it since he'll have a caregiver. And he probably won't be going out much."

"Both valid points. That's part of what we need to discuss. I'm thinking whoever Hub hires to stay with him will be a better source of information than we could be just watching the house." I paused. "But I'm more concerned about his safety than in documenting any aberrant behavior."

"Understood."

I smiled. "At any rate, we can hash all that out tomorrow. You and Erik have a good evening."

"Thanks, you, too."

I tidied my desk and dug my bag out of the lower desk drawer, surprised that Red wasn't already fidgeting in my doorway. Ever since he'd given up the crazy schedule he'd had to keep as a sheriff's deputy, my husband had become a regular nine-to-fiver, always eager to be on our way once the workday had officially ended. Not that some of our investigations didn't have us running around at all hours, but we tried to keep business in its proper place. Whenever we could.

I crossed the empty reception area and stuck my head around the door to his tiny space. With just enough room to accommodate a small desk and chair, Red's office couldn't really be classified as such, but it seemed to work for him. He spent a lot of time out on the road, and his computer skills, while adequate, weren't even in the same ballpark as Erik's and Stephanie's.

I opened my mouth to remind him of the time when I realized he was on his cell phone. He'd swiveled around in his chair so that his back was to the door. I stepped back, not wanting him to think I was eavesdropping, although, if it was business, I had every right to listen in. But something about the set of his shoulders and his low, even tone told me it might be personal. I edged back another few feet and cleared my throat.

He spun around so quickly he nearly lost his balance. It might have been comical except for the stricken look on his face. He motioned me in with a quick wave of his free hand. I stood in front of his desk, my heart pounding, waiting for him to finish up.

"Okay," my husband said, "I understand . . . No, really, it's all right . . . Yes, of course, my main concern is for my kids, that's why— Sure, Rebecca, whatever she needs. You know I'll be there for her . . . Right . . . Okay, talk to you soon."

Rebecca. Sarah Jane Tanner's sister. She lived somewhere out West, Colorado or maybe Arizona, I couldn't remember. Maybe we had finally found an ally. And a source of information.

"Let's talk at home." Red stood and took my elbow, guiding me out toward the front door before I could formulate a single question. "You stay here and let me scope things out first."

I was too stunned to speak, and in those few seconds of hesitation Red had pulled the door closed behind him. I finally found my voice.

"Oh, no you don't!" I yelled, yanking at the knob and scurrying outside.

I'd hoped to cool down by the time Red followed me into the garage, but I was still angry enough to spit when I stomped up the stairs and into the house.

"What was that all about?" he asked, reaching for the charger cord and plugging in his phone. "I was afraid a few of our neighbors were going to organize a lynch mob if they had to wait too much longer."

I'd roared up to the gate of Port Royal Plantation way too fast and had been forced to endure a mild tongue-lashing from the guard on duty. As a consequence, a line of impatient residents, including Red, had snaked out behind us.

"Nothing," I said and poured myself a glass of iced tea. "You want a beer?"

"Not yet. What are we doing for food?"

"I haven't thought about it. Besides, we need to talk, don't we?"

"Yeah, we do."

I carried my glass down into the great room where my husband had kicked off his shoes and sprawled on the sofa, his feet propped on the coffee table.

I sat down beside him, ordered myself to get over my anger at his highhandedness back at the office, and tucked my legs up under me. "What did Rebecca have to say? Did you call her or vice-versa?"

Red sighed and reached for my free hand. "She called me. Apparently she'd had a conversation with Elinor last night. You must have gotten through to her over the weekend. She asked Becky if it was okay to talk about things with her Aunt Bay, and then she started crying. Becky said it nearly broke her heart."

I swallowed and set my glass on the table. "So Rebecca called you?"

"Yeah. I think El really shook her up. Even though she'd promised Sarah that she wouldn't talk to me about it."

I waited. When he didn't go on, I said, "And what exactly is 'it'?"

"You were right. Sarah has breast cancer," my husband said and burst into tears.

I had never seen any of the Tanner men—either of my husbands or their father—shed a tear. Even as Red had stood over the gravestone in Newberry when he'd driven me on my first and only pilgrimage to the final resting place of Rob's pitifully few remains, he'd been stoic. The uncontrolled bout of weeping made my heart hurt in a way it hadn't since my father's death.

I tried to think of something comforting to say and found nothing that would ease his pain, so I simply pulled his head onto my chest and held him. Darkness descended over the ocean, the room growing dim as we sat huddled together, each of us locked in his own private misery. I smoothed his unruly hair and murmured soft shushing sounds, and eventually he raised his face to mine. I kissed him gently on the forehead, and he pushed himself upright.

"Wow, sorry about that, honey. It just all of a sudden seemed more than I could handle."

I kissed him again, softly. "You're entitled. Even though we sort of had it figured out, it's another thing entirely to have someone say the word out loud."

I rose and returned from the kitchen with a handful of tissues which I divided equally between us. "Did Rebecca give you any details?"

"Not many. Sarah's been on chemo for the past month. She seems to be tolerating it pretty well, although she was really nauseous the first couple of times. And it leaves her weak and exhausted. She sleeps almost all the time the kids are in school. I guess I caught her on an especially bad day. Mostly she drags herself up to feed them."

I could see the tears pooling in his eyes again.

"She's the best mother I've ever encountered. I know she'll do whatever it takes to make sure Scott and Elinor are well cared for." I paused and forced a smile. "And you know that, too, right?"

He swallowed hard. "I thought I did."

"What do you mean?"

"The best thing would be for them to come to us while she's going through all this. And if it all . . ." He let his voice trail off, and it took a moment for him to get himself back together. "If it all goes bad, they'll be here anyway. Permanently."

I shook off the sudden wave of panic that washed over me. "It isn't practical for them to be here right now, Red. They go to school in Beaufort. We're gone all day and sometimes half the night. We just aren't set up to handle them fulltime." I saw the brief flash of anger in his eyes and forged ahead. "If it comes down to something permanent, then we'll figure it out. But right now Sarah needs them by her. At least I assume that's how a mother would feel, not that I have any right to an opinion."

Red's face softened, and he reached out to cup my cheek in his hand. "You have as good a heart as anyone I've ever known. I wish you'd quit putting yourself down about this motherhood thing. If it comes down to it, you'll be a wonderful stepmother to my kids. I know that as sure as I'm sitting here blubbering like an idiot."

I smiled through my own effort to keep from breaking down completely. "I think that's the nicest thing you've ever said to me."

My husband straightened his shoulders and tossed the wad of sodden tissue onto the coffee table. "Right now we have to do what we can to help. Any ideas?"

I took a moment to blow my nose. "Yes. We can hire someone to go in and take care of the housework and the meals so Sarah can concentrate on beating this damn thing. I'll call Lavinia and get some recommendations."

I pushed myself up and headed for the kitchen.

"You think she'll buy that? Sarah, I mean?" Red asked, trailing behind me.

"We won't give her a chance. Once she has some help, I think she won't care where it came from." I picked up the receiver of the house phone. "Why doesn't Rebecca come down and lend a hand? That would be the ideal solution."

Red opened the refrigerator and took out a beer. He popped the top on the can and took a long swallow before answering.

"Because she has her own problems. Her husband has a heart condition and needs bypass surgery. She doesn't feel she can leave him alone for more than a couple days at a time."

I punched in the number for Presqu'isle and turned to my husband. "So it's up to us to take care of things, and that's exactly what we're going to do."

Red smiled tentatively and shook his head. "I guess the cancer better get the hell out of the way. Bay Tanner is on a mission."

I smiled back, a weak one, but the best I could do. I didn't like all this talk of compassion and caring. God knows it always made me uncomfortable, but in this instance I felt as if it was totally undeserved. Yes, I cared about Sarah. And yes, I worried about Scotty and Elinor. But deep down, in the place I tried not to look at too closely unless forced to by circumstances, I knew it was, at least in large part, absolute terror that drove my decision.

I wasn't ready to be a parent.

I wasn't sure I ever would be.

CHAPTER
TWENTY

Lavinia came through, as I knew she would, and by the time we'd wandered off to bed, I had three names of caregivers who met my old friend's exacting standards. She'd even offered to speak with each of them first, sort of feel them out to see who was available and amenable to taking on the care of a sick woman and her two kids. Lavinia promised me that, by the time Red and I showed up for dinner the next night, she'd have something nailed down.

I'd smiled as I hung up the phone and relayed the gist of the conversation to Red.

"Between your father's genes and Lavinia's upbringing, it's no wonder you turned out the way you did."

I took that as a compliment and pushed the problem to the back of my head as I pulled the covers up to my neck and settled into my husband's arms. I'd expected to toss and turn and was completely astounded to wake to sun streaming in the window and the smell of coffee wafting in from the kitchen.

I arrived in record time to find a steaming mug of tea and an English muffin already sitting at my place at the table. I feared it might mean Red had had a bad night, but he turned from the toaster with clear eyes and a genuine smile on his boyish face.

"Good morning, sweetheart. I let you sleep in a little, so we'll need to hustle to make it to the office on time."

"Umm," I murmured, my mouth full of Earl Grey and peanut butter. "You sound good," I said after swallowing. "Sleep okay?"

"Unexpectedly good. You, too, I noticed." He smiled as he joined me at the table.

"We need to get organized about Mr. St. John," I said. "What're your thoughts on keeping up the surveillance?"

"Does Danforth want to keep paying for that?"

I shrugged. "He left it up to us, I guess. I wonder if he'd be willing to spring for a perimeter alarm system of some kind. It could alert us if anyone came sneaking around, and it might be a good failsafe if the old guy goes wandering around in the middle of the night."

Red eyed me over his coffee cup. "Might not be a bad idea. It might turn out to be less expensive than paying us by the hour to keep an eye on the place. Do you think the caregiver would live in? I mean, after dark could be the most vulnerable time for Mr. St. John."

"I have no idea, although I don't know where she'd sleep in that tiny place. We'll have to check with Hub and see what arrangements he's made."

"You could float the idea of the alarm with him, too."

I washed down the last bite of muffin and carried my dishes to the sink. "We need to be at Presqu'isle a little early tonight. Lavinia said she'd see if any of the ladies she has in mind were free to stop over and meet with us. That okay with you?"

Red joined me at the sink and slid his arms around my waist. I could feel his warm breath against the side of my neck.

"You're pretty damn wonderful, do you know that?"

I could feel an uncomfortable flush heat my cheeks. "Don't go getting all mushy on me, Tanner. It doesn't suit you."

He laughed and stepped away. "You mean it doesn't suit *you*. I never knew a woman so determined to reject a compliment."

"You should be used to it by now." I kissed him chastely on the cheek. "Come on, Romeo, we've got work to do."

We piled into our respective vehicles. Red backed out first, pulling into the turnaround and waiting for me at the end of the driveway. I told myself it was just our regular routine, that he wasn't hanging around to make sure some crazed, lovesick stalker didn't jump out from behind one of the live oaks that overhung the pad in front of the garage. I clicked on the button to lower the door, waiting as I always did for it to slide closed completely when I saw the first inkling of trouble.

In a haze of anger and a sinking sense of déjà vu, I watched the letters form as the garage door finally seated itself to the concrete with a soft thump. The last time someone had seen fit to decorate my house, it had been kids, upset by my investigation into an embezzling scam engineered by one of their relatives. I'd been at a loss at first back then, completely ignorant of who might hate me enough to decorate my house with filthy words and threats.

This time I didn't have to wonder who the culprit was. At least in a general way. The message consisted of only one word:

MINE.

This time Detective Mike Raleigh did come to the house, arriving in a matter of a few minutes after Red's call. I spent the time explaining the situation to Erik so that he and Stephanie could get things rolling at the office. I floated the idea of the alarm system and asked my partner to run it by Hub Danforth. I also asked him to get specifics about the caregiver, both so we knew when she could be expected to be there and also so we could run a background on her. As long as we had the capability, I thought it would be stupid not to make sure Mr. St. John was in good hands.

I almost asked him to check out Lavinia's candidates for caregiver to Sarah and her kids, but I stopped myself. I trusted my old friend, and I didn't want it to seem to her that I didn't, just in case word somehow got back to her that I'd been perusing databases instead of relying on her judgment.

Raleigh came alone, for which I was grateful, took some photos with a digital camera that had apparently become standard equipment for sheriff's officers, and scribbled notes in the little book that seemed to be a permanent part of his wardrobe. When he'd tucked it into the breast pocket of his sport coat, he leaned back in the wing chair next to the fireplace and crossed one long leg over his knee.

"It's hard to figure that you've got no idea who this wacko is," he said. His smile took any implied criticism out of his words, but I bristled nonetheless.

"Believe me, I've been wracking my brain trying to come up with someone. If it was just a revenge thing, there might be a couple of candidates, although I think most of them are still in the slammer. But it's the notes that get me. If I have a demented secret admirer, I have no idea who the hell he—or she—might be."

The detective leaned forward. "You think it might be a woman? Any reason for that?"

"Not particularly, although Red mentioned that the person he was chasing—after the flowers showed up—ran like I do."

My husband chimed in for the first time in several minutes. His silence had been making me nervous, as if he were spending the time plotting. Of course, he might have been. I had no way of knowing.

"I just said that the . . . *person* ran like Bay does, as if they do it on a regular basis. I have no idea whether it was a man or a woman. Too dark, no moon, and the sucker was fast."

Raleigh sat back. "Okay, I guess I was just assuming it was a guy. Because of the notes. I get that it doesn't necessarily follow, things being what they are today."

I wasn't so sure the more liberal times had anything to do with it, but it didn't seem worth calling him on. "Regardless of the gender of this nutcase, I still don't have any clue as to who it might be. I've been going back over our cases, back as far as when I first got involved with the Grayton's Race project, but I'm still coming up empty."

"What about that kid, Anderson? Is he still doing time?" Red looked at me with sympathy, and I bristled.

"He got a relative slap on the wrist because of his age," I snapped, "but he's locked up. I have a little arrangement with the county solicitor to let me know if and when he's released. Even then, he'll probably be extradited to Florida. He got way too involved in his grandfather's drug empire, although he did testify against him. And he seriously hates my guts. I can't see him remotely involved in this."

The events that had come to a head out at Fort Fremont on St. Helena still had the power to chill me to the bone. My father's life had hung in the balance that night, and it had been touch-and-go. At least I had been able to buy him more time, though as it turned out, not much.

"Anyone else?" Raleigh asked.

I shook my head. "I told you, Mike, I've given this a lot of thought. It's true that I've pissed off a number of people over the years, but I really don't think this has anything to do with the agency." I chose my words carefully. "This is personal, and getting more so every day. I'm convinced I don't know this person, not in any meaningful way."

"It's not unheard of, Bay, as I'm sure you're aware. I think the FBI profilers call them sexual obsessives, although from the notes you've been receiving, it doesn't sound as if he's, you know, interested in *that*."

I smiled at his discomfort. "Sex, you mean. You're right. I kept calling them teenage angst, and they do sound particularly juvenile, don't you think?"

"There's nothing *juvenile* about bashing in the head of squirrel," Red snapped. "Or messing with your wipers."

I reached over to where he sat next to me on the sofa and patted his knee. "I know, but it's not as if he tampered with the brakes or something that could have caused us real harm. It feels like . . . I don't know, almost like it *is* a kid, wanting my attention." I straightened. "And I'll sure as hell give it to him if I ever get my hands on the little bastard."

"The thing is, Bay," the detective said, leaning forward with his elbows on his knees, "this is sort of familiar."

I jerked upright. "You mean someone else is getting the same treatment? Locally? Why haven't you said anything before?"

Raleigh held up a hand. "Whoa, there. No, nothing local and nothing current. I might be getting a vibe from one of the cases we studied when I was at Quantico a couple of years ago. It was about profiling, and we looked at a number of old files. The names were redacted, but there was one that played out pretty much like yours, if I'm remembering correctly." He stood and shot the cuffs on his pale blue oxford shirt. "Let me do a little digging. I think I still have the notes from that course somewhere in my desk."

The idea that someone might be repeating an old pattern had never occurred to me, and I had to admit the thought was intriguing. Maybe it wasn't personal. Maybe I had just been selected at random, as I'd first hypothesized. In which case, there wasn't a damn thing to be accomplished by my scouring my background and past cases to come up with a suspect.

"I don't like that scenario at all," my husband said, following the detective toward the front door.

"I understand that, Sergeant. Let me do some checking, and I'll get back to you." He turned to face me. "In the meantime—"

"Be vigilant. Be careful. Got it, Detective." I softened the harshness of the words with a smile. "Thanks for coming out."

"Call a painter and get on with your life," he said and trotted down the steps.

Red and I stood in the doorway a long time, neither of us

willing to voice our thoughts. Finally, Red reached out and took my hand. "I'm sorry about all this, sweetheart."

"Can't be helped," I said, reaching for my bag where I'd dropped it on my way in from the garage. I slid my hand inside and felt the chilled metal of the Seecamp. "There is something you can do for me, though."

"What's that?"

"Get the Glock out of the safe and let me carry it."

My husband smiled and reached behind him underneath his jacket. When his hand reemerged it held the solid weight of the semi-automatic pistol. "Sorry, honey. This baby's staying close to me. But I know where I can lay hands on an S and W. That suit you?"

"Perfectly," I replied, happy that I was married to a man who didn't require lengthy explanations when it came to concealed weapons. "Perfectly."

CHAPTER
TWENTY-ONE

We made a detour to see Len, Red's barber and a licensed firearms dealer. He'd been the Judge's contact for the Seecamp a few years back, and he and my husband apparently talked guns whenever Red was getting a trim. He did indeed have access to a Smith & Wesson, which we could pick up as soon as he had it in hand. He didn't blink when I handed over my carry permit, even though I knew my father had obtained it in less than the traditional—and legal—way.

So it was nearly noon when we walked into the office to find Erik and Stephanie huddled over their respective computers.

"Sorry," I said as I passed through into my office. Red peeled off and headed for his.

I checked the message slips on my desk and found nothing pressing except a note to call Billy Dumars. I tapped in his number and swore when I was almost immediately flipped into his voice mail.

"Billy," I said, "sorry I missed your call. Do you have some scuttlebutt for me? Give me a ring, either at the office or on my cell. I could be in and out this afternoon. Thanks." I left the numbers and hung up.

A moment later Erik stood in my doorway. "Want us to bring you guys some lunch? We're going out for Chinese unless there's something we need to handle first."

"No, that's fine. Bring me back a General Tso's chicken, will you? And—"

"White rice. Got it."

I smiled. "I'm pretty damned predictable, aren't I?"

"In some ways. Are we still going to talk about Mr. St. John?"

I glanced at my watch. "He should be getting home about now, if they released him on time. Yes, let's convene after lunch. Then I think I'll make a trip over there, chat with the caregiver.

Did you get a name from Hub?"

He stepped farther into the office. "I talked to him a little bit ago. He's intrigued by your suggestion of the perimeter alarm, said he's going to check out a couple of companies for prices and lead time for installation. I floated the idea of saving money by not having us sitting outside the house all day, and I think he'll go for it. Steph is working on backgrounding the lady who's going to look after Mr. St. John. So far, she looks good."

"Nice work. Okay, you two take a break. See if Red wants anything, okay?"

The phone rang just as he turned away.

"Got it," I called and picked up. "Simpson and Tanner, Inquiry Agents. This is Bay Tanner."

"Bay, darlin', Billy Dumars. Glad I caught you."

I leaned back in the chair. "Me, too. What's happening in the wonderful world of real estate?"

He laughed, a loud guffaw that had me holding the handset away from my ear. "Not as much as there should be. I swear, this recession is gonna be the death of me."

"I hear you. Still, you've been the top salesperson in the county for the last fifty years or something like that, right?"

Again his hoot of laughter sent ice picks piercing into my brain. "From your lips to God's ear, darlin'. Listen, I was at the club last night having dinner, and I ran into a couple of the boys that mostly do commercial, you know? Don't work for me, but they're good guys. Randy said he heard that Midsouth outfit you were askin' about has been putting out feelers all over the place. Seems they need beachfront, and a lot of it, quick."

I straightened and reached for a pen. "Really? Anything more specific?"

"Word is they got themselves in something of a bind. Had an option on some land that fell through when the sellers couldn't clear the title. Brett, that's Randy's buddy, said *he* heard they had a boutique hotel chain all primed and ready to go, some bunch out of Atlanta that's lookin' to get a toehold on the island. If Midsouth can't deliver, they stand to lose a bundle in upfront and guarantee money."

I had no idea how the whole development thing worked, but Billy sounded impressed with the information, so I needed to take serious note. "Any idea how much?"

"Money? Not specifically, but you know it's got to be a boatload. And you can bet some heads are gonna roll if the whole thing falls through."

I thought about Cynthia Merrill, dead on the floor of her own boutique hotel room. Her head hadn't exactly *rolled*, but she'd certainly paid the price for . . . what? I had no clue how Billy's information might impact the investigation into the murder of Hub Danforth's ex-wife, but it certainly had implications—for Mr. St. John, as well.

"Thanks, Billy, I really appreciate the heads-up. If you hear anything else, please pass it along."

"No problem, sugar. You doin' okay?"

"Fine, Billy. Take care now."

"You, too," he said and hung up.

I set the phone in its cradle and leaned back in my chair. A lot of money at stake, a deal circling the drain, and Cynthia Merrill with an inside track—or so she thought—into a nice piece of beachfront property that could maybe be had quickly if she could leverage her connections to the Danforth/St. John family. It went a ways toward explaining her willingness to hang around the old man's cottage all afternoon, and also why her subordinate, Winter, had made another trip back. I needed to know more about this development deal and how the whole process worked.

I had actually reached for the phone to call my father before reality kicked in. I let my hand drop onto the desk and willed the sadness and loss to the back of my head. Who else did I know who might shed some light? I'd have to think about that, I decided, just as Erik and Stephanie came through the outer door, white Styrofoam boxes balanced on their arms.

"We decided to bring everything back here," my partner said. "We can talk and eat at the same time."

"Multitasking. Good thought," I said, sliding papers out of the way as he set the containers on my desk. I reached into my bag and pulled out two twenties. "My treat."

Erik knew better than to argue with me about money. He took the bills with a nod of thanks while Stephanie began handing out utensils. Once we'd called Red and everyone had a drink, we got down to business.

"So what's the consensus on surveillance?" I wiped my mouth and took a long swallow of Diet Coke to counteract the spicy Chinese food.

"I think Mr. Danforth will go for the alarm idea," Erik offered. "In the meantime, we can keep a loose eye on the place."

"I'm going over for a visit as soon as we're done here. If he's not settled in yet, I'll wait."

Red pushed his empty container a few inches away and leaned back. "You still think he can tell you what happened to him? It doesn't sound as if he's hooked up to reality too much of the time. And even if he was, his memory isn't reliable." He rightly interpreted my look of annoyance. "Hey, don't shoot the messenger. I'm just saying what everyone, including his nephew, already knows."

"I think you're right to try to talk to him."

Stephanie's voice held a note of assertiveness I hadn't heard from her in the short time she'd been with us. It brought a quick smile to my face, and I saw her redden immediately.

"I mean," she stammered, "I just think it isn't fair to write off Mr. St. John just because he's old and sick."

Red, who had a soft spot for Ben Wyler's lovely child, held up a hand. "Okay, ladies, don't gang up on me. A man knows when he's outnumbered."

That eased the mood a little. "He does have some moments of lucidity, Red."

"Fine. What do you want the rest of us to do?"

"Erik can finish the background on the nurse. What's her name, by the way?"

I'd asked the question earlier and gotten sidetracked.

Stephanie answered. "Sheila Mahony. She works for a big homecare company out of Savannah."

"So they would have vetted her before hiring her, right?" I asked.

"I'll still do some digging," Erik said, and I smiled. I knew he'd be convinced that no one could ferret out the stuff people wanted kept hidden better than he could.

"Okay. I guess, other than that, we're back to business as usual."

I closed the lid on half the rice and chicken, apparently not nearly as hungry as I'd thought I was.

"What about your situation?" Erik's voice held just a note of challenge, as if he half expected me to jump down his throat.

"What about it?"

He and Stephanie exchanged a glance. "Well, isn't there something we could be doing to help? Do you have any clue who's stalking you?"

I shook my head, but Red jumped in before I could reply.

"Mike Raleigh's on it. He's looking into some old cases he studied when he took a profiling course at Quantico. He thinks there might be some similarity—"

He was interrupted by an explosion of coughing that had Stephanie's face contorted into a look of pain and panic. She gasped for breath, obviously choking. Erik immediately pounded her on the back. I nearly leaped across the desk to grab her bottle of water and try to shove it into her hand. But in a moment she had regained herself, breathing heavily, a fine line of sweat glistening along her top lip.

"I'm . . . okay," she managed to gasp out. She took the bottled water and downed a long swallow.

"You sure?" Erik hovered, his arm around her shoulder.

"I said I'm fine." Her voice had an edge to it I'd rarely heard her use with her fiancé. Or anyone else, for that matter.

"Good," I said, settling back in my chair.

She brushed her hand across her face with a crumpled paper napkin and turned to Red. "You were saying?"

"Just that Raleigh thinks he might remember a similar case when he was at an FBI training session. He'll let us know. But as for who might be doing it?" My husband glanced at me. "We're still pretty much in the dark."

Erik helped Stephanie stack the Styrofoam containers. "Well, anything we can do to help."

"Thanks. Let's all just get back to work."

I studied Stephanie as she walked slowly behind my partner, her gait a little unsteady. I'd come to care about the girl in a way that surprised me, and her sudden attack had seriously alarmed me. I hoped it wasn't anything more than one of those killer Asian spices.

When Red and I were alone, I reached in the desk for my bag. "I'm heading over to Mr. St. John's. What about you? Don't forget we have to be at Presqu'isle around four thirty so we can interview whoever Lavinia has coming over. I want to make sure you're happy with her choice since the woman will be spending a lot of time with the kids."

"I'll be ready. Are we leaving from here, or do you want to go home first?"

I glanced down at my black pants and sensible flats. "I think I'm good. Why don't we meet back here shortly after three. That should give us time to battle the traffic over to St. Helena."

"You better get a hustle on, then. It won't give you much time."

I shrugged. "I don't hold out a lot of hope for getting anything useful out of Malcolm St. John, but I just want to satisfy myself that he's being well looked after."

Red smiled. "You really are an old softie, aren't you? You collect strays the way other women collect cookbooks."

I thought that was probably meant as a compliment, so I let it go. Still, I bristled at his characterization of Mr. St. John as a *stray*. I thought about it as I headed down 278. I did have a penchant for taking up the causes of people who didn't have anyone else to stand for them. I hated injustice, especially when it was visited on those who had done nothing to warrant being jerked around by the system or by unscrupulous people who made a business out of preying on the weak. But, in spite of being a lapsed Episcopalian, I tended more toward the Old Testament view of the world. *Vengeance is mine* resonated more with me than *Turn the other cheek*.

Joan of Arc in a Jag, I thought, and smiled.

I pulled up in front of Mr. St. John's crumbling cottage behind a sparkling white Camry with Georgia plates. I took mental note of the license number just in case and made my way to the front porch. Before I could raise my hand to knock, the door flew open. The woman who stood as if she were guarding the gates to Fort Knox fixed me with a glare.

"Ms. Mahony?" I asked.

"And who might you be?" The drawl was genuine, but the sharpness of the words belied any hint of Southern hospitality.

"I'm Bay Tanner. Mr. St. John's nephew, Hub Danforth, engaged my inquiry agency to keep an eye on his uncle."

"Do you have any identification?"

Rather than taking offense, I wanted to applaud Sheila Mahony's dedication. I pulled my wallet from my bag and allowed her to study my license. A moment later she handed it back and stepped away from the door.

"That's all right, then," she said, her arm gesturing me inside.

She was rail-thin and almost as tall as I, but she radiated strength. I had no doubt she could handle feisty patients if the need arose. She wore one of those printed smocks in a rather hideous green over black slacks and black running shoes. Her salt-and-pepper hair was cut short, but not severely so. She could have been a first-grade teacher or someone's favorite aunt.

But her next words shattered those images in a hurry.

"Malcolm is resting now, and I won't allow him to be disturbed. And if you came to check up on me, you don't have to worry. Anyone who wants to harm that wonderful old gentleman will have to get past me first. And it won't be easy."

I studied her stern face for a moment. "I have no doubt about that."

"Good. Now that's settled, I'll make some tea. Sit in the rocker."

"Yes, ma'am," I said as I lowered myself into the old wooden chair.

I wondered if Sheila Mahony was committed to caregiving or if she might consider taking up a new career. I was giving serious thought to offering her a job on the spot.

CHAPTER TWENTY-TWO

I learned pretty much everything there was to know about Sheila Mahony in the half hour I spent over perfectly brewed Earl Grey served in thick china mugs, mine with the logo of the state flag with its quarter moon and palmetto tree on a blue ground.

"I'm good with the elderly, especially dementia patients. I don't know why, exactly," she said and paused to sip her tea. "I did have a dotty old aunt, but that was when I was a kid. Still, there's an art to dealing with these kinds of people. Too many family members want to argue when their husband or grand-mother or whoever starts talking nonsense. There's no point, but a lot of folks think they can sort of 'logic' their loved ones out of it, if you know what I mean."

I didn't, not really, but I nodded anyway.

"But their brains just aren't operating like other people's. And no amount of talking or shouting or explaining will make a whit of difference. No, you just have to go along with whatever it is they've got in their heads and try to redirect them."

"It sounds as if you're the perfect person for Mr. St. John."

I thought back to our conversation in the hospital, the first time he mistook me for his Miss Lily. Maybe, by dumb luck or providence, I'd done the right thing by playing along with his re-membrances of his childhood.

"Has he said anything about what happened to him?" I asked,

"Not a word. But it's early times yet." She paused to set her mug on a folded paper towel she'd fashioned into a makeshift coaster, although the scarred old table already had its share of rings and gouges. "He does sometimes touch the bandage behind his ear, and he gets this kind of *wondering* look on his face, as if he can't quite remember why it's there." She shrugged. "Head trauma on top of his other problems sure didn't do the poor old thing any good."

I sipped tea, and we lapsed into silence. I'd pretty much satisfied myself that Malcolm was in competent hands, and it didn't look as if he was going to make an appearance any time soon. There was nothing to keep me from being on my way. Except for the fact that I felt relaxed and comfortable for the first time in a number of days, sitting in the dim light of the old beach cottage with a woman who seemed as content as I with the quiet air of peace that had settled over us.

In a way, Sheila Mahony reminded me of Lavinia. Even as a child, I had marveled at how still she could become, hands resting in her lap, her eyes partially closed as if in meditation. I used to think she was praying, and maybe she was. In the madness that had sometimes pervaded Presqu'isle, Lavinia Smalls had been the one constant, unmovable presence in my life, always there, always ready with a hug or a rebuke, whichever one was warranted. From her, more than from anyone else, I'd learned to be silent and let my thoughts wash over me, just being in the present and listening to my inner self. It was a wonderful gift, one I appreciated and practiced far too seldom.

I don't know how long we sat like that before the shrilling of my cell phone broke the reverie like an alarm bell. I heaved a sigh and fished it out of my pocket.

Red's voice sounded worried. "Honey, where are you? It's almost three, and you wanted to get on the road to Beaufort, didn't you?"

I glanced at my watch, startled to find that so much time had elapsed. "I'm just leaving. I'll be with you in a few minutes."

I shoved the phone back into my jacket and rose. "Sorry to have taken up so much of your time, Ms. Mahony."

She stood with me. "It was nice of you to stop by. I enjoyed it."

"What arrangements have been made for Mr. St. John overnight?"

"Mr. Danforth didn't say. I'm on from eight to eight, or I will be starting tomorrow. I'll get Malcolm his dinner and get him settled for the night. After that . . ." A shrug accompanied the trailing off of her voice.

I hoped to hell Hub was planning on someone's being with his uncle after Sheila Mahony clocked out. Maybe I should volunteer—

A sharp rapping made us both jump. Sheila and I exchanged a look before she crossed the short distance to the door.

The man who stood there looked to be in his early sixties, trim, and with a smile that lit a pair of the bluest eyes I'd ever seen this side of a movie screen. He wore wrinkled khaki shorts and a white polo shirt. His gray hair was cut short, and a pair of sunglasses dangled from tanned fingers.

"Yes?" Sheila Mahony blocked the door as effectively as she'd done when I'd come knocking.

"I'm sorry." The man tried to peer around her. "I'm looking for Malcolm."

"Why?"

Even I was startled by the snap of the single word.

"Who are you? Has something happened to Malcolm?"

Before the caregiver had an opportunity to slam the door in his face, I stepped up next to her. "Mr. St. John has been ill. We're looking after him. And you are . . . ?"

"I'm Marshall. Miller. Malcolm and I are friends."

"Bay Tanner." I held out my hand. "And this is Sheila Mahony. Won't you come in?"

I hoped Sheila wouldn't want to frisk him on the way by, and the smile that idea brought seemed to ease some of the tension.

"Nothing serious, I hope," Marshall Miller said as he edged his way into the tiny room.

I thought of offering him a seat, but there weren't enough to go around.

"He had a little mishap a couple of days ago and just got out of the hospital," I said.

"And doesn't need to be disturbed." Sheila hadn't moved far from the door.

"Oh, I wouldn't want to do that. But I'm only in town for a day or so. Flew in this morning, and I have to be airborne by tomorrow noon. Just wanted to touch base with Malcolm." He smiled. "You sure he's okay?"

"How do you know Mr. St. John?" I asked, making it as conversational as I could. This was the first person I'd encountered who might be able to get Malcolm to talk about what had happened.

Marshall Miller smiled. "Ran into him on the beach one day, oh about six months ago." His face and those lovely eyes faded.

"We got to talking about the old days on the island, how things have changed. Malcolm shared my concern about all the development going on in his neighborhood. It's a fragile ecosystem, the dunes and the marsh over there. And the folly, of course."

I glanced at my watch, wishing I had more time to spend with Marshall Miller. I reached in my bag for a card. "I'd love to chat with you about Malcolm," I said, extending my hand. "Why don't you give me a call?"

"Wish I could," he said, "but as I say I've got to be getting back. I just flew down to check on some property I own." He paused. "Malcolm isn't in any trouble, is he?"

I shook my head. "It's kind of a long story. I'd really appreciate hearing from you. It shouldn't take too long."

His tanned face creased in concern. "If you think it will help with . . . well, with whatever's going on here."

"It would. I'll be available most of the evening. I look forward to speaking with you."

He took it as dismissal, asked to be remembered to Mr. St. John, and slipped out the door.

Sheila Mahony studied me in the silence that followed Marshall Miller's departure. "I hope you don't think I'm being nosy, but you seem to have more than just a professional interest in all this."

It wasn't a question, but I felt she deserved an answer. I wished I had one that might make more sense, but it was what it was. "I'm not sure I can explain it, Ms. Mahony, but I feel an affinity for Mr. St. John that goes beyond my being hired to look out for him." I shrugged. "He somehow managed to sneak into my heart a little, I guess."

I felt myself coloring. It wasn't an admission I'd normally make, but something about Sheila Mahony invited honesty.

"That's how I feel about all my patients," she said softly. "Maybe you're in the wrong line of work."

An idea that had more than flitted through my own mind lately, I thought and smiled.

"Thank you for being here. Please let me know if there's anything at all I can do to help. All my numbers are on my card." I set one down on the old side table. "And I really need to know if Mr. St. John talks at all about what happened to him on Sunday. The sheriff can't do much toward finding his attacker without something more to go on."

"Then shouldn't I be communicating with them? Or with Mr. Danforth?"

"Of course. But if you'd also keep me informed, I think I might be just a bit more able to do something about it. Unofficially."

I knew she understood me by the smile of satisfaction she turned on me. "I believe you could be right," she said. "I'll be in touch."

Traffic turned out to be less of a hassle than I'd anticipated, and we arrived in plenty of time to sit over more tea with the two women Lavinia had rounded up for interviews. In the end, we settled on the grandmotherly Alathea Burton, who'd raised five children of her own and taken in foster kids as well. She came with excellent references from previous employers and could begin the next day if needed. We agreed on a fee, which was more than reasonable, and ushered her out amid promises to be in touch as soon as arrangements could be made with Sarah.

"There's the big stumbling block," my husband said as he eased the heavy oak door closed behind Mrs. Burton.

"Sarah? I know. Do you have a plan?"

We walked together into the kitchen where Lavinia hovered, as usual, over the stove. Julia had made herself scarce as soon as the doorbell rang, and I wondered if she was outdoors with Rasputin, her ungainly beast of a dog. We'd set him up in the expanded run my father had originally built for his bird dogs, and he seemed content to spend his time lolling in the shade of the oaks.

"No. Not a clue."

I set the tea tray on the counter and began transferring the cake plates and cups and saucers to the dishwasher. Lavinia hadn't felt it incumbent upon her to drag out the best or even the second-best china for our interviews, so no hand washing was required.

"Do you want me to have a stab at it? I've intended right along to try to get Sarah to talk to me. I'm willing to have a go at convincing her this is in everyone's best interests."

"I'll have a word with the child if you like."

Lavinia turned and encompassed both Red and me with a knowing smile.

"Really?" I asked.

"I remember her fondly, and I think she felt the same way about me. I've got a lot less baggage than you, Bay, honey."

If by *baggage* she meant my marriage to Sarah's ex-husband who was also my former brother-in-law, she had a point.

"I think that might be a really good idea." Red smiled at Lavinia. "You really are a remarkable woman, you know that?"

Lavinia whipped back around, concentrating again on her cooking, but not before I caught the flash of embarrassment—and satisfaction—in her eyes.

The back door from the verandah banged shut, and my sister swept into the room, the smell of the outdoors and wet dog not unpleasant mixing with the heady aromas already floating around the kitchen. Without a word, she flung herself at me, her arms wrapped tightly around my neck. I patted her shoulder and did my best not to cringe away. So much for putting my fears behind me. I forced myself to return her hug, and she stepped away. In a moment, Red was similarly engulfed, except he didn't seem to have any hesitation about giving as good as he got.

"Hello, Julia," he said around a genuine smile. "What have you done to your hair?"

"Do you like it? I got it cut. Dr. Nedra said it was okay."

"I like it very much," my husband responded, spinning my sister in a little twirl that had her giggling. "Makes you look very grown up."

"I am." Julia fixed me with a triumphant stare. "I'm as grown up as Bay," she announced before whirling off into the hallway.

A moment later we heard her light tread on the stairs.

Lavinia turned, and our eyes met for just a moment, long enough for me to register the same dismay I knew she found reflected in mine.

"I'm worried about Julia," I said as Red negotiated his way down the Avenue of Oaks a couple of hours later. Full night had fallen, and avoiding the potholes in the old sand road was nearly impossible with just the headlights for guidance. I held my hand against the roof of the Jaguar as we bounced our way finally onto the asphalt.

"I don't get it." Red glanced briefly in my direction. "I think she's doing great. Doesn't Neddie think she's making progress?"

I was glad the dim light from the dashboard made my grimace hard to make out. "Yes, so she says."

"And you're not buying it?"

I sighed. "I don't know, Red. There's just . . . *something*. I can't put it into words. I know Lavinia feels it, too, but she can't bring herself to talk about it. She feels so protective of Julia. And it's not as if I don't understand that. I think she has some twisted-up notion that she's responsible. Because of her relationship with Mother and the things she knew and never talked about." I paused, choosing my words. "And everyone seems to keep forgetting that on my first encounter with Julia, she attacked me. With a knife."

"But that was a while ago, honey, and she's come a long way since then, don't you think?"

I slapped my hand sharply against my knee. "Damn it, I don't know! How is anyone supposed to make a judgment about things like that?" Suddenly, I sighed and lowered my voice. "I just feel like Lavinia is keeping things from me. And if she has reservations about having Julia at Presqu'isle, she should just come right out and say so."

Red let a few seconds of silence go by before he said, "Are you sure you're not projecting your own fears onto Lavinia?"

I snorted so loudly I startled myself. "*Projecting?* Dear God, do I have to listen to psycho-babble from you, too? Isn't getting it from Neddie enough?"

My husband reached across the console and laid his hand gently on my forearm. My first instinct was to jerk away, but I ordered myself to calm down. In a moment, I covered his fingers with my own.

"Sorry. You may be right." I turned and smiled at him. "And you know how I hate that."

"I love you," was all he said, but it was enough. For then.

CHAPTER
TWENTY-THREE

Friday morning began calmly enough. No messages from either Hub Danforth or Sheila Mahony, so I assumed arrangements had been made for Mr. St. John overnight. Mike Raleigh had apparently made little or no progress in the death of Cynthia Merrill, nor had he run across any information on the old case that my stalker had reminded him of. Marshall Miller hadn't called, and I was surprised at how much that disappointed me.

Stephanie came in late, a doctor's appointment she'd forgotten to tell me about. I missed her presence in some unnamed way that eluded me, and I found myself smiling when I heard her call good morning.

The pleasant feeling didn't last long.

I looked up to find her standing in the doorway, her pretty face solemn.

"What is it?" I asked, laying aside the pen I'd been making notes with.

"I really wish I didn't have to say this, Bay. I know it's been a couple of days, and you probably thought it was all over with."

It took me a moment to realize she held something in her hand. Between the folds of a damp Kleenex, she clutched a small blue envelope.

"Where did you find it?"

"Under your wipers. I saw it when I parked."

I wiggled my fingers, and she crossed into my office. The paper felt cool in my hand, but not as if it had been out there for long enough to absorb any of the moisture that threatened to turn into rain at any moment. The skies had been darkening all morning, and a downpour seemed inevitable. I told myself the hell with fingerprints and ripped it open.

I scanned the contents, the familiar block printing and atrocious spelling coiling a knot in the pit of my stomach. What in the hell did this maniac want from me?

"I don't suppose you saw anyone around when you came in?"

Stephanie shook her head. "No. Just Mr. Stafford from next door at the CPA office. He said good morning, but that was all."

"Thanks, Steph," I said, mustering an encouraging smile. "I guess we'll just add this one to the pile."

She nodded and hurried back to her desk. I sat staring after her for a long while, the contents of this new missive bouncing around in my brain. If I thought the dead squirrel and the message scrawled on my garage door had upped the ante, this new one sent a genuine shiver of fear down my spine. I debated for several minutes, my eyes darting toward where my husband sat in his little cubbyhole of an office, before I lifted the receiver and dialed the sheriff's office.

Detective Mike Raleigh was at his desk.

"Good morning, Bay. What can I do for you?"

"I've had another note, Mike. Stephanie found it on the windshield when she came in just a few minutes ago."

"Want to drop it by? Or I could swing around and pick it up."

"No, I'll bring it to you. I opened it up. I figured you had enough fingerprint exemplars."

"Yeah, but so far no joy. Nothing popped on the state database, so I'm expanding it to the national one. Could be your boy hasn't ever been in enough trouble to get printed."

"I understand. It was a long shot, anyway." I let a beat go by before plunging in. "Look, Detective, this one's a bit . . . different. The tone seems to have changed. It's less like some lovesick kid and more like . . . I don't know. More threatening, I guess."

I could almost hear Raleigh straightening his shoulders and sitting up a little taller.

"Read it to me," he said.

"Okay." I picked up the single sheet. "It says, 'Quit ignoring me. I've given you every chance to acknowledge me and my feelings. Instead you've laughed and given my letters to strangers. I won't tolerate any more disrespect. Be warned.'" I paused to clear my throat. "There's the same misspellings, mostly the big words, but no half-assed poetry. This is a flat-out threat."

"What did the sergeant have to say?"

"I haven't shown it to him yet. You know how he'll react."

"Yeah, I'm afraid I do. But he can't really go off on anyone since none of us has a clue who the hell this moron is, right?"

I glanced out my open door to find Stephanie staring in at me. The moment she met my gaze, she dropped her eyes and began pounding away at her keyboard. I kicked myself for not shutting the door before talking with Raleigh. The poor kid didn't need to be any more spooked than she already was.

"You're right," I said to the detective, "but I'd still rather keep this between us."

"Might be tough to do, Bay, but I'll give it a shot." He paused, and I heard the rustle of paper on his desk. "By the way, I ran across those files I was telling you about. You know, the ones about the stalker cases?"

"Anything jump out at you?"

"Yeah, a couple. I'll take the files home tonight and give them a good read-through. Too much commotion around here for any serious concentration. But the one from New York's probably the best bet. It's the sequence I think is interesting, the escalation. I don't know where this last note of yours might fit in, but I'll work up a profile of the case, and we can sit down and run through it." Again he hesitated. "You carrying?" he finally asked.

It almost made me smile. "Yes, and I'm picking up a new S and W this weekend. A little more firepower than the Seecamp."

"Good. Keep it handy. I'll give you a call in the next day or two. In the meantime . . ."

"Got it. Thanks, Mike."

I hung up and motioned Stephanie into the office. She took her time, and I wondered if her pointed eavesdropping had embarrassed her.

"You heard?" I asked before she had a chance to sit down.

"Sorry. It was kind of hard not to."

"No problem. But I need you to keep this to yourself, just for now."

Erik had gone out as soon as he'd finished checking for messages and downing his morning coffee to see how things were at Mr. St. John's. We'd promised Hub Danforth to keep a loose surveillance on the place and to intercept any more of Midsouth Development's point men who might come snooping around, including Brian Winter.

"Why?" Her chin rose a fraction in what might be interpreted as defiance.

"I don't want Red to know. Or Erik."

I could tell she didn't like it, but she also knew who signed her paycheck. She nodded once.

"Thank you, Stephanie. I appreciate your understanding."

She nodded again and scurried back to her desk. I wasn't sure if I did indeed have her understanding or even her loyalty. I had to keep reminding myself it was early times. It would take more than a few weeks to figure out just where my newest employee stood on any number of things. I tucked the note into my bag and forced my concentration back to the data I had been analyzing.

But my mind kept drifting to the tortuous spelling and underlying menace of my admirer's latest effort. Sooner or later my luck had to change. Sooner or later I would catch the little bastard in the act. I let myself imagine for a moment what that encounter might be like before forcing my revenge fantasies into the back of my head.

Gone, for the moment, but certainly not forgotten. Not by a long shot.

The rain finally came a few minutes later, blown by a gusty wind into great horizontal sheets that battered the windows and made concentration nearly impossible. Mesmerized by the ferocity of the storm, I swiveled around in my chair and watched the onslaught. The fury abated as quickly as it had arisen, and it seemed only moments before the sky began to clear out over the ocean. By the time I forced myself back to the work at hand, the sun was making a valiant effort to dissipate the remaining clouds.

"Bay?"

Red's voice in the extended silence made me jump.

"Sorry, honey. Didn't mean to startle you," he said, plopping into a chair. "Some storm, huh?"

"It was a good one. What's up?"

For a moment I panicked, until I remembered that the telltale note sat tucked safely in my bag.

"Bad time?" he asked, his head gesturing to the stack of folders on my desk.

"No, not at all." I waited, but he seemed disinclined to get to whatever was on his mind. "Is something wrong?" I prompted.

"No, nothing like that." A pause, during which he looked everywhere except at me. "Well, not anything earth-shattering."

I rarely saw my husband squirm, but his fidgeting in the chair reminded me of Scotty when he was a toddler, never happy sitting still for longer than a few seconds.

"So spit it out." I had no idea what was making him so uncomfortable. I reached across the desk and ran my fingers lightly over the hand that rested there amid the chaos that littered the surface. "You're leaving me for a Victoria's Secret model?"

That brought a smile. "Cute," he said. "As if one of them would have me."

"Oh, I don't know. You're not bad looking, in a boy-next-door kind of way. And there's always the cachet of being a private eye. I hear that turns the girls on."

Red didn't rise to the bait, and his eyes had lost the little sparkle our exchange had engendered. I tightened my grip on his hand.

"What is it? The kids?"

His head jerked up. "You're pretty damn good at this detecting thing."

My heart rate ratcheted up. "Just tell me."

"It's nothing, not really. I mean, no one's hurt or in trouble or anything like that. I was just thinking . . . Maybe I should go and stay at the house. In Beaufort. Until we can get Mrs. Burton installed. Do you think Lavinia has talked to Sarah about it yet?"

I found I wasn't surprised, although Red's returning to his family, even temporarily, hadn't actually occurred to me as a possible solution.

"I can call and ask. What put this idea into your head?"

He shrugged. "I don't know. I guess I was just thinking about my conversation with Sarah's sister, and the fact that she said Elinor was crying on the phone. I know their mother is doing the best she can, but I just keep picturing my little girl in tears with no one to hold her and tell her it'll be all right."

I could feel a few tears pooling in my own eyes at the picture that suddenly sprang into my head.

"Would Sarah agree to that?"

"Then you don't think I've completely lost my mind?"

I sniffled as quietly as I could and forced a smile. "I didn't say that, but I can see that this is important to you. Let me get on the horn and check with Lavinia. If she's met with some resistance to the idea of a caregiver, maybe you can bulldoze Sarah into accepting the idea more effectively if you're there on the scene." I paused. "Or were you thinking you'd take the place of Mrs. Burton?"

"Oh, no, no, no. Not at all. It'd be more of a stop-gap measure until we can get that part of it sorted out." He flipped his hand over and gripped mine tightly. "I'm just not sure leaving you alone right now is the best idea."

"You mean because of this nut case? Come on, Red. Give me some credit, okay? If it comes down to taking care of your kids or babysitting me, it's no contest."

I could see the struggle going on behind his eyes, and it softened the tone of my voice.

"I'll be fine. I can pick up the Smith and Wesson from Len tomorrow morning, right? I'll take a run over to the range and get in some practice." I squeezed his fingers. "It'll be fine. Let me call Lavinia, okay?"

I disengaged my hand and reached for the phone.

It took a few exchanges, but eventually we got it all worked out. I marveled at Red's persistence in his conversation with his ex-wife after we'd learned how Lavinia had eventually worn her down. But Sarah had insisted that she didn't need anyone over the weekend, since we'd have the kids with us. Both Red and I vetoed that plan, primarily because Lavinia said she had the distinct impression that Sarah would spend the time alone doing major housecleaning in preparation for the woman who was supposed to remove all those burdens from her. If Red was there, he could hold her in check, make her rest, and do what little straightening up made her comfortable. And he could also get his children used to the idea of a stranger, albeit a kindly one, taking over many of the things their mother had been trying so valiantly to keep up with.

All in all, I thought we'd gotten everything ironed out about as well as we could have expected. Red and I grabbed a quick lunch and went home to pack him a few things. At a little before two, he was ready to be on his way. He hoped that would put him in Beaufort before the kids got off the school bus so he could have ample time for explanations.

"I'm going to worry about you," my husband said as we stood in the doorway. One hand gripped his small bag and the other held me tightly against his side.

"Don't," I said and kissed him lightly on the cheek. "Give me a call after you get everyone settled and let me know how it's going."

"What will you do for dinner?"

"Not cook, that's for sure," I said with a smile. "That's why God provided us with so many takeout options. How about you?"

He managed to smile back. "Pizza. I can get them to do just about anything for pizza."

"Better get on the road," I said, disengaging myself from his embrace. "You don't want to miss the bus."

"Are you going back to work?" he asked.

"I don't think so." We'd moved onto the small front porch, and the sun slanted through the twisted boughs of the live oaks. "It's gotten really warm. I think I'll take a run."

"And check up on Mr. St. John while you're at it?"

I answered his questioning smile with one of my own. "Maybe. I've become a big fan of multitasking."

"Be careful," he whispered against my lips, and his kiss held more than a little urgency.

I leaned back and looked him squarely in the eye. "Concentrate on getting things settled over there. I'll be fine."

I gave him a gentle nudge toward the steps and folded my arms over my chest.

"I love you," my husband said.

"You, too," I called and turned back into the house.

Minutes later I was in my running gear and stretching out on the deck. As I jogged across the boardwalk and onto the sand, I turned my face into the slight wind. I felt a lightness that was out of all proportion to the myriad troubles that seemed at times to be overwhelming me. That was the beauty of running, the ability to concentrate on my body, on its rhythms and functions, to the exclusion of just about everything else.

For the next hour or so, I would let the welcome November sun and the rain-washed, cloudless sky sweep my mind clear of all its muddle and worry. Overhead, the gulls wheeled and screeched, their raucous cries a welcome accompaniment to my solitary journey.

CHAPTER
TWENTY-FOUR

I really hadn't intended to stop in at Malcolm St. John's house. I thought I'd just take a quick look around to make sure everything seemed peaceful and continue with my run.

But there was a strange car pulled up across the street, and Sheila Mahony's white Camry was nowhere in evidence. I slowed to a jog as I passed the decrepit Ford Taurus, its once red paint faded to a dull rust color. I glanced back to note the number as I made my way down the street. Georgia plates, so maybe it was a substitute caregiver. Or maybe they alternated patients or something. Either way, I didn't like it. I did a quick U-turn and walked back to the cottage.

The woman who answered my knock looked as nonplussed to see me as I did to encounter her.

"Yes, what is it?" she asked in a haughty voice that immediately set my hackles up.

"I'm Bay Tanner," I said with as much authority as I could muster in my baggy T-shirt and leggings with sweat running down my face and neck. It's hard to stand on your dignity when you look as if you've just gone a couple of rounds with a sparring partner.

"The detective?" She didn't do anything to hide the skepticism in her voice, and I found I couldn't much blame her.

"Yes. And you are?"

For a moment I thought she wasn't going to respond. Then she lifted her chin even higher.

"I'm Clarista Gaines. I'm Hub's sister."

If you'd given me ten chances, I might have eventually gotten around to guessing her identity, but it would certainly have had nothing to do with any resemblance *Sissy* might have had to her brother. She had none of his elegance, his grace, or his good looks. A plain woman, if stated charitably, she stood a head short-

162

KATHRYN R. WALL

er than I, her dumpy polyester pantsuit doing nothing to flatter— or camouflage—her stocky build. Her gray-streaked black hair was pulled back into an unattractive knot at the back of her head, emphasizing the sagging of the skin around her chin and neck. Her only saving grace was her eyes, beautifully shaped but oddly light, a soft hazel, so unlike Hub's penetrating dark gaze.

I stuck out my hand to cover the awkward silence that had fallen while I took in her appearance. I wondered if she was used to the unflattering comparisons with her striking sibling.

"Nice to meet you," I said, mustering a smile. "I was just on my way by and stopped to see how Mr. St. John was doing."

I glanced pointedly over her shoulder, but she made no move to invite me in, although she did manage a limp handshake in return.

"He's resting," she said.

"Are you filling in for Ms. Mahony?"

"The nurse has gone to do some shopping. Groceries," she added in response to my raised eyebrows. "Is there something else?"

Clarista "Sissy" Gaines certainly hadn't inherited any of her brother's charm, either.

"I just wanted to say hello. If Mr. St. John is awake. It'll just take a second."

I could tell by the scowl gathering on her face what the answer was going to be, but suddenly she turned, inadvertently opening the door wide enough for me to see her uncle standing uncertainly in the middle of the tiny living room. He wore a tattered bathrobe of some indeterminate color, and his feet were half in and half out of a pair of worn house slippers.

"Uncle Malcolm," she said, her voice all of a sudden soft and full of concern, "what are you doing up?"

"Sadie? Who's that at the door? Why don't you invite the young lady in?"

The Gaines woman turned back to me, a look of panic on her face. "He thinks I'm his late wife," she whispered.

"Go with it," I said, remembering Sheila Mahony's advice as I stepped around her and inside. I didn't exactly have to push her out of the way, but it was a close thing.

"Hey, Mr. St. John. It's Bay Tanner. I just stopped by to see how you were doing."

He looked pale, and his hair stood straight up as if he'd just gotten out of bed, but other than that he seemed okay—steady on his feet and in control of himself, at least as much as he could be.

"I told you people before to leave me alone."

I recognized the closed look I'd seen in the hospital a moment before he'd pulled the covers up over his head. Again the urge to use my resemblance to his Miss Lily warred with my better judgment.

"How are you feeling?" I asked, keeping my voice low and conversational.

"Can't believe a decent woman would come callin' in a getup like that! Ain't you got no mama to teach you better?"

Under other circumstances I might have laughed, but I could tell Malcolm St. John didn't find anything amusing about finding a sweaty, half-dressed woman confronting him in his own living room. As for having a mama, I thought the question had been largely rhetorical, so I let it go.

Clarista Gaines whirled around. "Thank you for stopping by, Ms. Tanner."

She took a step toward the door and swung it all the way open.

I saw no option but to retreat. "Nice to have met you," I said, lying through a forced smile that probably didn't fool her for a second. "I'll be in touch with Hub."

I hadn't really meant it as any sort of threat, but a look of panic flashed briefly across the woman's doughy face.

"Why? Everything's fine here. You tell him anything different, and I'll make sure he knows you're a damn liar!"

The outburst took me completely off-guard. "I'm sure it is, Mrs. Gaines." The look of venom in her eyes shocked me and set my antennae quivering. Where had that come from? "But I'll be checking back in on a regular basis. As your brother requested."

I didn't have a chance to register her reaction because I was suddenly looking at the door swinging closed in my face.

I spent a long time in the shower, replaying the bizarre encounter with Hub Danforth's sister over in my mind. I pulled on sweats and white socks to counteract some of the chill that had crept into the house with the advent of sunset and debated my dinner choices while curled up on the sofa. Nothing sounded really appealing, and I finally decided to cobble something together from whatever I could scrounge up in the kitchen. I was certainly due for a run to Publix, even though Dolores did her best to keep the larder stocked on the days she came to clean. I hate grocery shopping with a passion and tend to put it off until we're reduced to eating dry cereal out of the box. Red sometimes picked up my slack, but he wasn't any more enamored with the process than I was.

We had two eggs and a couple of slices of bacon whose package announced they were well past the sell-by date, but they smelled okay. I used the next-to-last English muffin and ended up with a fairly creditable breakfast sandwich. I nuked myself a cup of tea and sat at the small table in the bay window of the kitchen, idly watching the shadows cast by the swaying moss in the live oaks surrounding the driveway.

Something was nagging at the back of my mind, one of those vague feelings of unease, of certainty that you've overlooked something you shouldn't have. I had no idea where or when or even what, but the prickling wouldn't go away. I almost welcomed the insistent interruption of the house phone.

"Hey, honey, it's me." Red sounded tired.

"How's it going?"

He didn't answer right away. "Let's just say I'd rather be doing crowd control at a rock concert."

I laughed lightly. "That good, huh?"

"Sarah is being a giant pain in the ass, not that she's not entitled," he added quickly. "But I think I finally have the kids on board. It's amazing what a little pepperoni and Coke can do to put them in the right frame of mind."

I knew he was trying to make it sound easier than it must have been. For my sake, no doubt.

"You knew it was going to be a hard sell, right?"

"Yeah, but I didn't expect quite so much resistance from Scotty. Excuse me, *Scott*. I've been informed by my son that he's far too mature to be saddled with the 'y' at the end of his name anymore."

I stifled a laugh because a part of me dreaded the very idea of having to deal with this kind of teenage nonsense. What in God's name would I do if they ended up having to live with us forever?

"I'm sure you're up to the challenge," I said. "Have you figured out when Mrs. Burton can take over?"

"I'm thinking the first of the week. I've informed the kids that tomorrow is going to be housecleaning day. They're each responsible for getting their own rooms in shape. Sarah is going to direct me from the sofa on the rest of the place." He lowered his voice. "It's really a mess, honey. I can't believe Sarah let things get this bad."

I found myself wanting to defend my former sister-in-law. Keeping house for two kids and working part-time had to be difficult enough without throwing in chemotherapy and its side effects. What I said was, "I'm sure she was doing her best under the circumstances. Do you want me to come over and help?"

"I don't think that's a good idea. I mean, you know, you and Sarah . . ."

He didn't have to elaborate.

"Understood. But let me know if there's anything I can do." I cringed but pressed ahead. "Like maybe grocery shopping or something like that."

"I've got that covered, honey, but thanks. You okay?"

It was an oblique question about my stalker, and I didn't pretend to misunderstand. "Nothing new," I lied, remembering the envelope Stephanie had brought me that morning. "I went for a run before dinner." I took a few moments to fill him in on my strange encounter with Hub Danforth's sister. "She's really kind of weird," I finished. "You can't believe how different she is from her brother. Maybe she got switched at birth, or something."

That made him chuckle. "Unlikely. Well, at least we know the family is keeping an eye on things. I guess that's good."

"Now that I'm back into running, I'll be able to drop in occasionally, too."

"I'm sure you will. But don't be out there by yourself too much, okay?"

"You have enough to worry about, Red. I can take care of myself. I'll stop by Len's tomorrow and pick up the S and W, maybe hit the range. You just deal with things there, okay? I'm covered."

His sigh was less exasperation and more resignation. "Don't you ever have doubts about anything?"

"All the time. I just keep them to myself."

"I'll talk to you tomorrow. Sleep well."

"You, too. Hug the kids for me." I laughed. "Or maybe you'd better just shake hands with Mr. Scott. He may be beyond the hugging stage, at least in his own mind."

My husband laughed, too, a sound that cheered me immensely. "He'll take a hug from his old man, or I'll kick his butt. Good night. I love you."

"Uh-huh," I said and hung up.

I stood for along moment, the phone still clutched in my hand, before I placed it carefully back in its cradle.

CHAPTER TWENTY-FIVE

The weather held long enough on Saturday for me to get in some good target practice with my new weapon, but the skies opened up just as I pulled the Jaguar into the garage. I'd forced myself to make a quick stop for supplies on my way back from the shooting range, so I had dinner covered.

The Smith & Wesson was larger than the Seecamp, and I debated how to keep it handy without actually carrying it around on my hip. Red had a couple of extra holsters, but they felt bulky and way too obvious when I surveyed myself in the full-length mirror, even with a jacket for camouflage. I'd probably have to lug it around in my purse, something the tiny pistol I was used to carrying made relatively simple. Still, I had been impressed with the power and range of the new gun, and I had to admit that having it in my hand made me feel better.

In the end, I left it on the side table next to the sofa while I warmed the small rotisserie chicken I'd picked up and set out the tub of potato salad. Lavinia would have a cow if she could see me eating store-bought stuff like this, but I wasn't in the mood to fiddle around with anything more complicated. My culinary skills had improved markedly over the years, but I had to be in the right frame of mind to spend hours creating a meal. Especially for myself.

I propped the Lucas Davenport novel on the table beside me and cut hunks of warm, juicy chicken as I flipped the pages. Even after I'd eaten way more than I should have, I sat in the glow of the overhead lights, the rain running silently down the bay window behind me, my mind far away in snowy Minneapolis as I followed the exploits of the characters and their prey. Grease had congealed on my plate by the time I forced myself to note the page number at the end of a particularly gruesome chapter and tend to my housewifely duties. With leftovers stashed and the few utensils and dishes safely in the dishwasher, I carried a fresh cup of Earl Grey and my book into the living room and stretched out on the sofa.

Red called at a little past eight without much more to report than he had the night before except that the house was now clean and ready for its new, temporary caretaker. He and the kids had gone out for burgers, Sarah having retreated to her bedroom with no appetite. My husband expressed concern about his ex-wife's weight loss, and I assured him things would probably right themselves when she was finished with her treatment. Besides, I told him with a chuckle, I had a feeling Mrs. Alathea Burton would be creating yummy, tempting things to get her charge back into shape. We promised to talk in the morning after he dropped the kids off at church, and I let out a sigh of relief that we hadn't gotten around to any more conversation about stalkers and the like. Red had enough to worry about.

After hanging up, I glanced briefly at the empty fireplace, the idea of a roaring blaze tempting me to head to the garage for logs and kindling, but lethargy finally won out. Instead, I pulled the afghan over me and settled back in.

I have no idea what time I fell asleep, but I awoke suddenly, disoriented for a moment to find myself on the sofa and not in my own king-size bed. The book lay open on my chest, and my reading glasses had slid down to the end of my nose. I tried to focus on the small clock on the mantel, but everything looked fuzzy. With a sigh, I swung my legs over the side and sat up, dropping the glasses onto the coffee table and rubbing my hands over my face. I had a kink in my neck, and I rotated my head trying to work it out. I glanced out the French doors, but it was too dark to tell if the rain had abated or not.

And then I heard the noise—a faint scratching as if a branch scraped against a window in the wind. For just a moment, it sounded almost like Mr. Bones, the stray cat who had wandered into and out of my life the summer after Rob was killed. Never one to be happy indoors, the battered old tom had loudly demanded to be let out on a regular basis, only to set up an attack on a door or window when cold or wet weather forced him to seek shelter. More often than not, he'd come bearing gifts—a mole or mouse—usually, but not always, dead. Suddenly, I missed the warm presence of . . . anything, even that faithless cat, who had wandered off into the palmettos one night with the same disregard for human feelings as when he'd first appeared.

I stood up and followed the sound, which seemed to be coming from the kids' room. Or maybe the office. Without thinking, I'd picked up the S&W from the table and held it loosely at my side as I made my way down the darkened hallway. I don't know what instinct kept me from turning on any lights.

I paused at the doorway to the office, the pile of bags reminding me that Elinor and I had never gotten around to unpacking everything from our shopping spree of the week before. It flitted through my mind that maybe I'd tackle it on Sunday, have everything all set up by the next time the kids spent the night.

I took in a breath and held it, waiting for the noise to repeat itself, but all lay quiet. In my stocking feet, I crept toward the third bedroom. This time I heard it clearly, a scratching at the window that overlooked the back deck. Cautiously, I moved into the room, keeping my back as close to the wall as the furniture and jumble of Scotty's sports equipment and Elinor's toys would allow. I strained my eyes toward the fainter square, the lights from the front of the house casting a dim illumination on the window.

As I drew nearer, I could see what looked to be a branch, bare of leaves, rubbing against the upper right-hand pane. For a moment I breathed a little easier until I realized that there were no trees close to that side of the house. I felt my hand tighten on the gun, my index finger twitching from where I held it away from the trigger. I stared for a long while at the slender arms moving back and forth against the glass, the rhythm so regular I was almost mesmerized. Too regular for something swaying in the wind, I suddenly realized.

I whirled and sprinted back down the hall, all the anger and frustration of the past few days focused like a laser beam on whoever had concocted this new method of taunting me. I fumbled for a moment with my left hand on the lock then flung open the French doors and stepped out onto the deck. It was soaked, and in only a few seconds my socks were wet through and my feet like ice. I ignored it and moved methodically down the dripping boards, the pistol now up and at the ready. I paused at the corner of the house, took a deep breath, and jumped out.

"I'm armed and prepared to shoot! Stay where you are!"

Nothing moved, and no one responded.

"Show yourself!"

Again silence.

I cursed myself for not having the foresight to grab a flash-light. But the rain and the clouds had moved on, and a thin slice of moon, added to the faint overspill of the front lights, gave me just enough to see, finally, that the deck was deserted.

Dropping the gun again to my side, I sloshed my way to the window. The branch lay forlornly beneath it, right where my tor-mentor had dropped it. I let my shoulders droop, then reached down, and without thinking, flung it far out into the yard.

Back inside, I locked the door behind me and peeled off my dripping socks. I pulled the drapes closed, cocooning me in the safety and warmth of my living room. I picked up the book that had slid onto the carpet and turned out the lamp. In darkness I made my way to the bedroom, crawling in under the duvet with-out bothering to change my clothes. Shivering with both cold and anger, I lay awake, the gun tucked under my pillow.

And into the long hours of the night, I plotted revenge.

I rolled over a little after nine, blinking against the shaft of sun-light streaming into the room through a gap in the drapes. I stretched, surprised to find myself feeling rested and full of pur-pose. Within an hour, I had pulled on clean clothes, wolfed down breakfast, talked to Red, and set out on a run. The sun beamed down from a cloudless sky, and the thermometer on the deck had registered just shy of sixty when I'd left the house. Not bad for the first part of November, and the air held a promise of more warmth to come.

I jogged across the wooden bridge that spanned the dune, considerably undercut by the passage of Hurricane Kitty in Sep-tember, and turned in the opposite direction from Mr. St. John's cottage. I'd promised Red in our brief conversation to let it go for the day and just enjoy myself. I hadn't needed much convincing. I wanted to hold onto my good mood for as long as I could, know-ing from experience that it was unlikely to survive for long.

Back home, I showered and dressed and grabbed the Sunday *Island Packet* from where I'd tossed it on the table. I carried it and a glass of tea out to the open area of the deck. I retrieved the cushions for the chaise and plopped myself down in a pool of warm sunshine.

Cynthia Danforth Merrill's murder had moved from the headlines to a short blurb toward the end of the local news pages. The investigation was continuing, the sheriff had some promising leads, yadda, yadda, yadda. I knew Mike Raleigh would have let us know if anything had broken on the case in order for us to relay the information to Hub Danforth, so I took all that reassuring with a grain of salt. I wondered if this would be one of those crimes that never got solved, like the power couple who had vanished a few years before. While speculation about what might have happened still rippled across our small community, the fact was that their bodies had never been discovered. And despite the questionable suicide of the principal person of interest in the days following their disappearance, the case remained open and un-solved. I loved my mystery novels and crime dramas, but experi-ence had taught me that things seldom worked out that way in real life. I thought of all the intervening years between my first hus-band's brutal murder and the pitiful resolution that I was forced to accept as justice. It would never be enough. Plea bargains and deals for information had reduced the whole process to something that might have been laughable in less tragic circumstances. Some-one caught smoking a joint probably ended up with more time than the monsters—

The doorbell rescued me from totally destroying my good humor all on my own. I hauled myself up and trotted to the front of the house. I took a quick look through the sidelight window and pulled open the door.

"Mike! What are you doing here on a Sunday morning?"

The detective carried a thin manila folder under his arm, and he raised it a fraction. "Got something for you to look at. I hope it was okay to bother you on the weekend, but I can't seem to carve out any down time, what with this murder investigation."

"Come on in." I opened the door wider and stepped aside.

"I tried calling, but there wasn't any answer." He moved into the entryway. "I just took a chance."

"I'm out on the deck," I said. "Would you like some tea?"

"No, thanks. I only have a few minutes."

I led him outside, stopping to scoop up the cushions for the two Adirondack chairs. I pulled them into the sun and got us both settled in.

"Is the sergeant here?" Raleigh asked, crossing his long legs.

I wasn't used to seeing him in jeans and deck shoes. He looked almost relaxed, the short sleeves of his white polo shirt revealing well-muscled arms and the tail-end of a tattoo that trailed out onto his right bicep. It looked like an animal's foot, and I wondered what kind of creature he had thought worthy, in his youth, of adorning his body for the rest of his life. I've never understood the need to pay some hairy stranger to write on your skin with a needle, but that's just me.

"Red? He's in Beaufort with his kids. Some family trouble," I added, not sure my husband would want his wife's illness to become office gossip back at the sheriff's station.

"Sorry to hear that. About the trouble, I mean. And I figured he'd want to be in on this."

He opened the folder which looked to contain no more than a dozen pages.

"I made copies so you could keep this one. I guess you can bring him up to speed when he gets back," the detective said.

"Bring him up to speed on what? Is this about the Merrill murder?"

"No, we're kind of at an impasse with that, although you didn't hear it from me. We're waiting on the forensics, which, despite all the CSI shows, takes a long time. We found a ton of prints, which isn't surprising since the crime scene is a hotel room, and we don't have a murder weapon. The coroner's description of what could have caused the head wound is about as generic as you can get. Could be anything from a whiskey bottle to a baseball bat."

He sighed and shook his head. "And we aren't having much luck with tracking her movements. She apparently didn't know anyone on the island, so we're having to rely on wait staff and hotel people, and it hasn't been very productive, at least so far."

"She knew Malcolm St. John," I said with a touch more sarcasm than I'd intended. I still didn't like the *coincidence* of their both having been bashed in the head in exactly the same place at about the same time. "And what about the Winter guy, her associate? Hasn't he been any help?"

"Not much. They went their separate ways that morning. He says he played a round of golf in Sea Pines, alone. Not many folks on the course this time of year, so no one can verify that. But we checked him out, generally, and he doesn't seem to be a likely candidate. Family man back in Charlotte—two kids, a wife, and a dog." He grinned. "And we can't figure out any reason he might have attacked Merrill. No indications of hanky-panky or anything like that."

I smiled at the anachronistic expression. "Maybe something else in her personal life?"

Mike Raleigh shrugged. "Maybe, but so far we've come up empty." He paused for a moment. "Anyway, that's not why I'm here. This is the stuff from that old case I told you about, the one we studied at Quantico? The stalker?"

He held out the file, and I hesitated. I'm not sure why, but I felt suddenly reluctant.

"Bay?"

I forced my hand out and took it from him, setting it on the table beside my glass of iced tea.

"Don't you want to read it?" he asked, and I could hear the confusion in his voice.

"Later," I said. "Why don't you give me the highlights?"

I could tell he didn't understand, and I wasn't sure I could explain it to him. Or myself. The information he'd brought could lead me to my own stalker, to an end to this craziness I'd been experiencing for the past few weeks. That would be a good thing, right? But somewhere in the back of my mind, I had this nagging feeling that I wasn't going to like the outcome, that in some unspecified, unnamed way, it would change things. And not for the good.

Of course I couldn't say anything so harebrained to Mike Raleigh. I could tell my hesitation had hurt him, as if I'd rejected him on some level. I couldn't have that.

"You're the expert here," I said, forcing a smile. "I'd rather hear your take on it before I get bogged down in details."

He might or might not have bought it, but he nodded. "Okay, I guess I can do that. But maybe I should start at the end instead of the beginning."

I squirmed a little in my chair. "Why is that?"

"Because the woman this guy targeted ending up killing him. He was out on bail, and he just couldn't stay away. She knew his face by then, from the papers, and she just popped him."

I shivered despite the warmth of the sun. "Good for—"

Mike Raleigh spoke over me. "And six months later she popped herself."

CHAPTER
TWENTY-SIX

The pattern of harassment, when Mike related it to me, did sound eerily familiar, right down to the color of the envelopes, the bad poetry, and the minor annoyances that began escalating.

"I can see why you zeroed in on this one," I said, more calmly than I felt. "It does seem as if the progression of events is pretty close."

"It's not just close, Bay. Read the file. It's almost as if someone is following a script."

That brought me straight up in my chair. "But that's impossible! The pervert who did this is dead, right?"

"And buried. But he must have had an accomplice or a friend or something. Somebody out there knows exactly how he stalked and terrorized this Jane Doe. And now he's doing it to you. What other explanation is there?" His rueful smile didn't reach his eyes. "Or do you believe in ghosts?"

"Only the friendly kind," I said, remembering times in the old antebellum mansion in which I'd grown up when I'd felt sure I could hear the slap of slaves' bare feet on the heart pine floor or the swish of crinolines passing through a doorway. I shook myself. "Any other ideas?"

"Not any I'm crazy about." The smile had vanished.

"You're thinking someone in law enforcement, with access to this information?"

"Yeah. And I don't much like where that line of reasoning leads me."

"Me, either." I thought a moment. "Anyone who was there with you at this course you took? Anyone local?"

"Nope. But they run these things year-round, and cops from all over the country take advantage of them. Not from a lot of smaller jurisdictions—no budget. But good-sized cities usually send one or two of their detective-grade people. We were lucky and caught a grant from the state through SLED."

The State Law Enforcement Division was our South Carolina equivalent of the FBI. Rob had had a lot of dealings with them in the course of his drug investigations for the state attorney general's office. I'd had my own run-ins with them, but I'd done my best to put those out of my mind.

"So it could be a former cop, or a retired one. Or someone he told about what he'd learned. Hell, you're sharing the information with me. What's to prevent me from using it to set up my own game plan to harass someone who's ticked me off?"

Again the detective shook his head. "Nothing. That's why I'm not sure how much help it's going to be. But it does tend to narrow the suspect pool, at least a little. I'm still convinced this is someone you know, someone you've had a problem with, either personally or professionally. You really can't come up with anyone who fits that bill?"

"I've tried, Mike, honest to God. Yes, there are people I've pissed off. Some of them are still around." I jerked myself upright. "In fact, two of them are disgraced cops! Jesus, why didn't I think of them before?"

Mike, too, leaned forward, eager. "Who? Are they from around here?"

"Damned right. The Daggett brothers. They worked for you guys. Tommy got bounced out of the department, I don't remember exactly why, and Lonnie blamed me. He actually threatened me, right out in front of the old substation down off Pope Avenue. And he was mixed up in the kidnapping of the Judge."

"Where are they now, do you know?"

"No idea about Tommy." I swallowed, remembering that night at Fort Fremont when Ben Wyler saved my life. "Lonnie is dead. He was shot by one of your predecessors, a former homicide guy from New York."

"Wyler. Yeah, I remember hearing about that. Some connection to that drug cartel out of Florida, right? The ones who—" Raleigh cut himself off, his eyes darting away from mine.

"The ones who murdered Red's brother. Right." I let out a long breath. "Water long over the dam, Mike. At any rate, Tommy's the only former cop I know who might have a grudge against me. Any chance of finding out what happened to him?"

Mike Raleigh stood and smoothed his hands down the thighs

of his jeans. "I gotta run, Bay, but I'll ask around." He found his smile. "I hear your boy Erik is pretty good at tracking down people, at least from the comfort of his desk."

I welcomed the lightening of the mood. "Oh, he's not bad. I'll get him working on it first thing in the morning."

Raleigh followed me into the great room. "I'll ask around at the office. Discreetly, of course."

"I really appreciate this, Mike."

"Read the file," he said. He turned on the first step leading from the narrow porch. "The reason we studied this one was to show that these kinds of things need to be taken seriously, right from the jump, before they escalate into two people being dead. If the local precinct up in New York had given Jane Doe's case a little more effort, they might have prevented a real tragedy." He looked me straight in the eye. "I'd hate to see you end up in the same boat, convinced you or the sergeant had no alternative except to take care of things yourselves."

I nodded, remembering the times he'd inquired about whether or not I was carrying. I'd thought he was concerned for my safety. Maybe I'd been way off on that assessment.

"Message received," I said and meant it.

A moment later I heard the engine of his unmarked fire up and recede down the driveway.

Back on the deck, I fondled the folder he'd left behind before carrying it with me into the office. I felt both drawn and repelled by the idea that the clue to the identity of my stalker might well be revealed in those few pages. I stood for a long time, vacillating, before I finally tossed the file onto the desk. *Later.* Right then I needed to do something physical, something constructive, instead of living inside my head, trying to figure out who hated me enough to go to all this trouble.

Moving furniture, however, could be problematic. I seemed to remember some kind of glide thingies I'd used once before. A few minutes rooting in the storage cabinet in the garage produced them, and I worked up a sweat over the next hour shoving the desk and chaise into the master bedroom. Finding them a permanent home would require some rearranging, plus I had to move one of the dressers and a bed from the room the kids shared.

I worked steadily, feeling the tug on muscles I didn't normally use when running. By the time I had the big pieces situated to my satisfaction, the bed made up and Elinor's clothes transferred, I'd pretty much shot my wad. The pretty stuff would have to wait. Which was probably good, I thought, as I headed for the kitchen and the ice tea pitcher. It would be more fun to do that part with Elinor.

I'd worked up an appetite as well as a thirst, and I stood for a few moments in front of the open refrigerator door, pondering my options. Red had been vague about when he'd be back, probably not until Tuesday, he'd said. He wanted to be there to get the kids off to school on Monday and to act as liaison between Mrs. Burton and Sarah. I didn't envy him either job.

I shut the door of the fridge and decided I'd treat myself to dinner out. Since I'd worked through lunch, I could eat early and be back in before it got full dark. I shook my head at my own timidity, usually quite unlike me, but there was no sense denying the past few days had taken a toll on my self-confidence. Whoever was hell-bent on harassing me was doing a bang-up job and didn't seem inclined to relent any time soon. I glanced down into the great room to where I'd left the S&W on the side table, opting to carry the Seecamp on my run.

"It's a hell of a way to live," I said to the emptiness of the house. "And it needs to stop."

How I was going to accomplish that I didn't know, but the idea of it buoyed me through another shower and out into the garage. The new gun nestled heavily, but reassuringly, in my bag as I backed the Jaguar out into the driveway. With only a little trepidation, I watched the big door roll down, relieved that the quick work of the painters who'd come on such short notice hadn't been disturbed. No doubt my tormentor was right then busy thinking up new ways to drive me crazy.

I made it half way to the street before my phone buzzed. I debated letting it go to voice mail, then stopped the car and reached for my bag. It could be Red, something to do with the kids.

"Bay Tanner."

"Hey, it's Erik."

I pushed the gearshift into Park. "Hey. What's up?"

"Are you home? I tried the house and didn't get any answer."

"I'm in the driveway, on my way out. Why?"

Silence.

"Erik? What's wrong?"

"Can I come over? Or, wait, I guess you've got somewhere to be."

"I'm just going to get myself something to eat. Red's still in Beaufort. Do you want to join me?"

My brow wrinkled in consternation. He sounded almost . . . *afraid*, which made absolutely no sense.

"Could I maybe stop and pick something up? It could be something good, not pizza or Chinese. I mean, I know you get a lot of that kind of stuff at lunch, and you were probably wanting a really good meal instead of—"

"Erik, what in the hell is going on?" I cut him off.

I could hear him swallow. "I need to talk to you."

"Then come over. I'll throw something together."

"No, I don't want to put you—"

Again I didn't give him a chance to finish. "Get your butt over here right now. I'm going back inside and start scrounging up a meal. Where are you?"

His voice suddenly sounded a shade or two brighter. "I just finished taking a quick look around Mr. St. John's place. The caregiver is there, and everything looks quiet."

"Then if you're not here in ten minutes, I'll send the militia out after you. Got it?"

"Aye, aye Captain," he said, some of the usual lightness back in his voice.

I tossed the phone onto the seat, punched the opener, and pulled back into the garage. I sat for a moment, gathering myself to deal with more trouble, before plodding up the steps and into the house.

My partner looked as if he'd been pulled through a knothole backwards, one of Lavinia's favorite expressions that I'd never quite understood, but recognized when I saw it. He flopped himself into one of the chairs at the glass-topped table in the kitchen bay window, his head resting in one hand as he watched me move from stove to refrigerator, cupboards to sink.

"I hate making you go to all this trouble," he said for the second time since arriving on my doorstep eight minutes after we'd spoken.

"Shut up already, will you?" I softened it with a smile over my shoulder as I cranked the heat up under the pot of pasta water. Thank God I always had shrimp in the freezer and vermicelli in the pantry. I'd restocked on butter and garlic bread during my brief stop at Publix on the way back from the range the day before, so I felt perfectly able to throw together my go-to meal in a very short time.

"Sorry," Erik mumbled.

"Tell me what's going on," I said, my back still to him. "Is it something to do with the office?"

"No."

I waited for him to elaborate and finally had to turn to face him. "Damn it, Erik, just spit it out, okay? You look as if the world was coming to an end."

"Maybe mine is."

The whole conversation was so unlike my usually voluble partner—my *friend*—that it was beginning to scare me.

"You know I'll do whatever I can to help. But you have to talk to me."

I busied myself with the dinner preparations for what seemed like forever before I heard his voice, soft and low, from across the room.

"It's Stephanie."

"What about her?"

I turned again so I could study his face, which was as naked with misery as I'd ever seen it. My first thought was that she was ill, something awful and terrifying, like Sarah. That choking spell in the office flashed immediately into my mind, and my heart lurched in my chest.

But Erik banished that horrible possibility almost immediately. He lifted his head and looked me straight in the eyes, the pain in his own almost another presence in the room.

"I think she's having an affair."

CHAPTER
TWENTY-SEVEN

Melting butter dripped down the handle of the wooden spoon and onto my wrist. I shook off the burning sensation and turned back to the stove, my mind a whirl of relief and consternation mixed with anger and disbelief. I bit back my gut reaction and forced myself to think carefully before I spoke.

"Why do you think that?" I purposely avoided looking at him, giving my friend time to get himself under control.

"A lot of things," he finally said.

"Like what?"

I dropped a handful of salt and the pasta into the boiling water. I busied myself with chopping garlic, all the while trying to picture the demure, respectful young woman, who had made herself so essential to the operation of the inquiry agency, as a jezebel. I almost smiled at the anachronism. In this day and age, people cheated on their spouses and lovers all the time. Of course, they'd always done so, I supposed, but it seemed to me that infidelity was much more tolerated, especially among those of the generation that followed mine. Or maybe I wasn't being fair. Maybe we just heard about it more in this era of instant communication—cell phones, Facebook, Twitter, and the like.

Or maybe I didn't know what the hell I was talking about.

When a full minute had passed without a reply, I set down the knife and folded my arms over my chest. The gesture was entirely unconscious, and I wondered what I was protecting myself against.

"Erik? What makes you think Stephanie is cheating on you?"

"Can we eat first?"

I caught the glimmer in his eye, a brief spark of his old, irreverent self, and smiled back. "Just like a man. Food and then conversation."

He didn't answer, and I let it lie. A couple of minutes later, I set a basket of garlic bread and a steaming bowl of shrimp and pasta in front of my friend. We ate in silence, companionable if just a little strained, the quiet interrupted occasionally by a sigh of satisfaction from my dinner partner.

"That was fabulous," he said, swiping the last of the bread around in the small puddle of butter sauce left in his bowl.

"Thanks. I've come a long way from microwaved mac and cheese, haven't I?"

That brought a smile. "I couldn't put together something like this if you gave me a week, let alone half an hour. I'm duly impressed."

"Fiddle-de-de," I said, in a mock, Scarlett-like drawl. "You flatter me, suh."

Erik helped me clear, and a few minutes later we sat across from each other again. He'd turned down coffee, opting instead for a Flat Tire, one of Red's exotic beers. I nursed a cup of Earl Grey.

"Okay, you've been fed and watered. Now spill."

With an effort, he gathered himself. "Okay," he echoed. "She's been lying to me. A lot."

"How do you know?"

"Because she tells me she's going somewhere, and then I find out she didn't."

"Give me an example."

He sighed and took a long swallow of beer. "She said she joined this book club. Someone she knows from the magazine started it. They meet at different restaurants to discuss what they've read, but it isn't one of those where everybody reads the same book, you know? I mean they just talk about what they're reading, exchange books with each other. It's supposed to be every two weeks, and she said they vary the night because a fixed date isn't always convenient for everybody."

He paused to take another swig of beer. I shut up and waited.

"Okay, so last night she says they're getting together, the book club, because it's somebody's birthday, and they want to celebrate. It's the second time this week, but I figured hey, it's a special occasion. She made sure I had dinner before she left. She always does that, because they eat whenever they have one of these things."

He sighed and fell silent.

"So how do you know that's not where she went?" I asked softly.

"Because she said they'd be at Frankie Bones, up on the north end of the island. And about an hour after she left, I noticed that she'd left the book she was supposed to bring lying on the table in the hallway."

"So like a good fiancé you decided to take it to her."

His expression morphed from sadness into anger and back again in the space of a couple of seconds. "Yeah. I'm such a thoughtful guy."

"You are," I said. "And she wasn't there? At the meeting?"

"There wasn't any meeting. No one at the restaurant had any idea what I was talking about. I felt like a complete asshole."

The vulgarity was very unlike Erik, but then so had this whole conversation been.

"Did you ask her about it? When she got home?"

I knew the couple spent the weekends and most other nights at each other's houses.

"I tried. The minute I brought the subject up, she freaked out, shouting at me about spying and trust." He nearly spat the last word. "Pretty ballsy, huh? Yelling at me as if I'd done something wrong."

I wanted to reach out and pat his hand or gather him into my arms. I'd never seen my friend look quite so miserable, but I knew any kind of sympathetic gesture would not be welcomed. Erik was heaving with righteous indignation, and I needed to let him vent it.

"So did she ever offer you any kind of explanation?"

"No. We were supposed to be staying at my place, and she just stormed out, said she'd talk to me when I wasn't acting like a jealous moron. That's a direct quote."

I quelled the urge to leap to my partner's defense and let his words settle a moment. "And from what you said, I take it this isn't the first time?"

"Last night was the most blatant, but she's been out a lot, supposedly running errands or getting together with friends." He sighed, and his shoulders slumped. "I mean, I never thought about checking up on her. I just took her word for it, you know? You have to trust the people you love, don't you?"

It was a rhetorical question, but one I thought deserved an

answer. "Yes, you do, unless and until they prove they don't deserve it."

The silence lengthened, my mind a tangle of disparate thoughts while my eyes focused on a strutting grackle parading back and forth in the driveway.

"What am I supposed to do then?"

I turned my gaze back to Erik, his face sunk in misery, and tried to think of the right thing to say. If there was a right thing. I'd never experienced— Suddenly, an image popped into my head: Geoff Anderson, the object of my teenaged lust and adoration, who had made an unnerving entrance back into my life a few months after Rob's murder. I had been dazzled by my memories of him and the reality of his strong, handsome face. I'd fallen again, not as hard as when I was sixteen, but my hormones had just as eagerly clouded my judgment. My failure to spot his ulterior motives had nearly cost me my life.

"You have to talk about it, Erik. Face to face. Give her a chance to simmer down a little, and then try to have a reasonable discussion about your concerns. It could be something completely innocuous, you know. Maybe she's planning some kind of surprise for you."

I watched the skepticism wash over his face.

"My birthday's not until March."

"It doesn't have to be that. You're jumping to a conclusion here, based on some pretty thin information. Insufficient data," I added with a smile.

"Maybe. But she's changed. I can't put my finger on how, but she's . . . different. Ever since the Wolfe case. That's when I first noticed it, and now I keep thinking that something happened, something . . . Oh, hell, I don't know." He ran his hand through his hair. "I've never been very good at figuring women out. That's why I thought you might have some idea about what's going on."

"I wish I could be more help, but I truly haven't noticed anything at the office. You two need to work this out. I was glad when you got together, really, but this is the one reservation I had. If you can't smooth things over, it's going to spill over into your professional lives, and that can't happen." Again I tried to soften my words with a smile. "I have enough trouble with Red."

Erik didn't respond but nodded. "I thought of that." He pushed back his chair and stood. "I'm going over there right now and see if we can get it back together."

I followed him to the front door. "Don't go in there with guns blazing, okay? A nice, quiet conversation between adults. No accusations. You deserve an explanation, but you won't get it by demanding one."

He turned. "Thanks, Bay. For dinner and the advice. This whole thing is making me feel like I was fifteen and my steady girl was making eyes at the captain of the football team."

I laughed. "I know the feeling. Just be gentle and reasonable." I reached out to pat his arm. "I'm pretty sure you two love each other enough to get through this."

"I hope so," he said.

I stood for a while looking at the door after he'd closed it behind him. I felt drained, the furniture moving weighing on my neck and shoulders. I thought about all the problems whirling around me: Lavinia and Julia, Sarah and the kids, Mr. St. John and Cynthia Merrill's murder. Maybe I was just plain getting too old for all of this. Or maybe I needed a vacation. As our usually mild winter approached, I thought about someplace warmer, the Caribbean or a cruise, perhaps, where I could waste the day sprawled in the sun, with nothing to think about except turning over once in a while . . . fabulous meals I didn't have to cook or drive somewhere to find . . . endless time to read and—

Get serious, reality whispered in my ear, and I turned and walked slowly down the hallway. That wasn't how life worked. At least not mine. I thought my tombstone should probably read, *She always did the right thing.*

I'd already had two showers, but the lure of a long, quiet soak in the tub pulled me toward the bathroom. In a few minutes I was up to my chin in blessedly hot, bubbly water. I lay back, my head resting on a folded towel, and tried to empty my mind of the scurrying little mice of anxiety that seemed always to be nibbling at the edges. I tried to resurrect some of the meditation techniques Neddie had taught me, but thoughts of her morphed inexorably to ones of Julia. And Lavinia. And then to Red and Sarah. I shook my head and sank deeper into the water. I did my best to force down a seed of resentment that Erik had burdened me with yet another set of worries. Not fair. He was my friend, and that's what friends did. They came to each other with their problems, some-times not for solutions, but just for a sympathetic ear, a shoulder to lean on.

I sat up and drained a little of the cooling water, turning the hot tap on full blast. As I settled back, something Erik had said set my mind racing again, something about Stephanie's having changed around the time of the Wolfe case. The tangled web of deceit and murder surrounding the past and present of the secluded island of Jericho Cay had taxed all of us. Red had taken a bullet before it was all resolved. That was when Stephanie had come to work for us, having proved her value as we worked through the old reports of the supposed suicide of missing playboy Morgan Bell's housekeeper.

I let my eyelids slide closed, cocooned in the steamy warmth of the bath, and allowed my thoughts to wander through the twists and turns of the investigation. Stephanie had been involved only on the periphery at first, helping us lay out the facts and trying to make sense of them. She'd proved herself capable and organized, taking a lot of the burden of the computer work off Erik's shoulders. She'd never been in danger—I'd made sure of that. And something else . . .

I knew forcing it wouldn't work, so I readjusted my headrest and began reciting, bits and scraps of things I'd memorized, most without even realizing it: lines from Shakespeare, quotations I'd used to score points against the Judge in our ongoing literary battle, poems I'd been forced to learn in high school English classes . . .

It wouldn't come. But I knew it was there. I stepped out of the tub, dried myself, and wrapped my thick robe around me. This happened to me all the time, this niggling feeling that I'd missed something important, some stray fact or occurrence that would make sense of everything. Almost always it came to me at some completely unrelated moment when my mind was floating free.

This would, too, I told myself as I pulled a pair of flannel pajamas from the bottom drawer. I just had to let it percolate for a while. I crawled into bed, propped all the pillows behind my head, and found my page in the novel I'd laid aside. As I settled in to lose myself in someone else's troubles, I had one overwhelming thought: I would have sold my soul for a cigarette.

CHAPTER
TWENTY-EIGHT

I had no idea what to expect when I walked into the agency Monday morning, but it wasn't what confronted me as I pushed open the door.

Stephanie sat in her usual place at the reception desk. She turned as I entered.

"Good morning," she said in a cheerful voice that took me aback for a moment.

"Good morning," I echoed. I glanced toward where Erik should have been ensconced in front of his computer to find his chair empty. I looked back at Stephanie, my eyebrow raised in question.

"He'll be in shortly. We got a late start this morning, and he's making the coffee run."

Not a hint of any trouble, at least none that I could discern, on her pretty face.

"Good," I said and made a beeline for my office. I'd expected maybe some strain, a remnant of puffy eyes. Some indication that they'd aired their differences. But nothing, except her encouraging use of the plural pronoun. "Good," I repeated to myself as I set down my bag. I retrieved the stalker file Mike Raleigh had brought me on Sunday and placed it squarely in the center of my desk. My first order of business would be to read through it and hope that some detail would jog my subconscious into giving up that amorphous *something* floating around in there.

Almost immediately the phone rang, and I heard Stephanie's standard greeting. Before I could pull out my chair, my line buzzed.

"Bay, it's Hub Danforth."

"I'll take it." I had a moment to chastise myself for my lack of attention to business for almost the entire weekend before I picked up. "Good morning," I said with more cheerfulness than I felt.

"Good morning, Bay." He sounded beyond tired. "I'm just wondering if there's any news."

He didn't voice any criticism, but I could hear it in his voice. Or at least I thought I could. It might have been my own sense of guilt seeping through.

"I spoke with the detective in charge of your ex-wife's case yesterday, but he didn't have any progress to report. I'm sorry."

"And you haven't come up with anything? On your own, I mean?"

I wondered how to admit that delving into Cynthia Danforth Merrill's murder had been pretty much the farthest thing from my mind for the past two days. In fact, I hadn't been feeling any of the adrenaline rush that would normally have sent me haring off in pursuit of her killer. I felt strongly about keeping Malcolm St. John safe, both from his attacker and any other two-legged predators that might be lurking around his valuable property, but somehow the death of a woman I'd never met hadn't sparked that drive to solve the puzzle that usually consumed me.

Whether that was a good or a bad thing, I'd have to analyze later.

"There really isn't much to go on, Hub. No murder weapon, no apparent motive. Nothing was stolen, so it's a good bet it was either a random thing or something in her personal life. It's difficult to get a handle on just who might have wanted her . . . out of the picture."

That was the real crux of the problem, for me at any rate. I knew the police didn't always need to find a motive if they had sufficient forensic or eyewitness evidence to justify an arrest. But it always mattered to me. In fact, it was often finding that connection between victim and perpetrator that cemented things for me. Proof could come later. I sighed. It was probably a good thing I wasn't in official law enforcement.

I realized that Hub hadn't responded.

"I'm sorry," I said again, meaning it.

Hub Danforth cleared his throat and changed gears. "I understand you met my, uh, sister the other day."

It took me a moment. "Yes, she was looking after your uncle while the caregiver was running errands."

I suppose I should have said something pleasant, like how

nice it had been to meet her, or some equally innocuous lie, but I couldn't bring myself to fake it. The truth was, I hadn't liked Clarista Gaines, even before she got bitchy with me.

"She offered to, uh, spell the caregiver," he said, almost defensively. "It'll help keep the cost down."

Again I was surprised at Hub Danforth's poor-mouthing. Maybe things like the O.J. trial and *Law & Order* reruns had given me the wrong impression about the earning capacity of criminal defense attorneys.

"Do you have to get back to Atlanta soon?" I asked.

"I'm already here. I have a trial beginning at ten this morning."

I remembered then the short postponement he'd managed to wheedle out of the judge in his current case.

"Well, good luck."

"You'll let me know if you hear anything?"

"Of course. I have all your numbers in the file."

"Thanks, Bay. And I'd appreciate it if you'd look in on Uncle Malcolm from time to time. I know you're keeping an eye on the house and all, but if you could maybe stop by and just sort of . . . make sure everything's okay?"

So Hub didn't quite trust his sister either, I thought. I could hear it in his voice.

"Sure, no problem. I've taken quite a shine to Mr. St. John."

His laugh was brief. "I noticed. I think the best chance we might have in finding out exactly what happened to him is that crazy notion he has that you're someone from his past."

I wasn't too sure about that, but it did spark an idea that had been floating around in my head.

"We'll see," I said, not yet willing to commit myself to a full-scale deception of the poor old man.

"Thanks, Bay. You don't know how much it relieves my mind to know you and your employees are involved in keeping Uncle Malcolm safe."

"You're welcome. Take care."

I hung up and leaned back in my chair, turning the idea over in my mind. The decision came quickly. I glanced briefly at my desk. Nothing pressing seemed to require my immediate attention, although I promised myself to get into the stalker file as soon as I got back. I picked up my bag just as I heard Erik in the front office. I stepped out to find him juggling a cardboard carrier with three Starbucks' cups. I watched as he set Stephanie's in front of her, noting the brief exchange of smiles between the two of them. Apparently that ship had been righted.

"I'll take mine to go," I said, making them both jump a little.

"Something wrong?" my partner asked, handing me my chai tea latte.

"Just some research. Unless you need me for the next hour or so?"

"Not that I know of," Erik said, retreating to his desk.

"I talked to Hub just a couple of minutes ago," I said, my hand on the doorknob. "Stephanie, just note for the file that he's back in Atlanta, so we'll need to try those numbers if we can't reach him on his cell. He'll be in court this morning."

"Do we have any reason to contact him?" Erik asked. "I mean, is there any news?"

I shook my head. "Nope. I . . . uh, talked to Mike Raleigh yesterday, and they're still waiting for forensics and fingerprints. No murder weapon and no leads."

"Must be hard for the family," Stephanie said softly, and I turned to look at her.

I often forgot how close to home some of our discussions must hit for her. She'd lost her father during one of our investigations, and our sometimes unintentionally callous references to murder and its victims must be hard to listen to. I made a mental note to tread a little more lightly in the future.

"I'm sure. Anyway, I need to check out a couple of things. Give me a shout on the cell if anything comes up. Red should be back tomorrow."

I didn't wait for any questions about where I was headed or why. In what had become an automatic response upon approaching the Jaguar, I checked the windshield. No envelopes. I let out the breath I hadn't been aware of holding and turned my face upward. Yesterday's sunny skies had returned, and I stood for a moment basking in the feeling of warmth and wellbeing.

Not for the first time in the past couple of weeks, I wished it could last.

The Coastal Discovery Museum sits on several acres of land

tucked back behind the Cross Island Parkway on the north end of the island. Turning into its long, winding drive was like stepping back in time. Open fields lined both sides of the narrow road, with outbuildings on the left. One of them was a barn that sheltered several marsh tackies, the small indigenous horses that had provided transportation and farm labor to the Gullah and their descendants for generations before becoming in danger of extinction. Their rescue and resurgence had been a small miracle accomplished by a dedicated group of locals and others.

Since the town of Hilton Head had leased the land to the museum, dozens of community events, from the automotive *Concours d'Elegance* to the AKC dog show and several wine and food celebrations, had made the wonderful resource their home. For a long while, a weekly farmers' market had flourished as well.

I pulled into the parking area in front of the restored main house and followed the short walkway to the front porch. Inside, a few tourists studied the many exhibits of the island's history and culture. I stepped up to the volunteer at the reception desk.

"I wonder if I could speak to someone who could give me some information about the old hunt clubs," I said. "I'm interested in the period of the thirties and forties." I glanced at the shelves to my left. "Or maybe there's a book you could recommend."

"Oh, Natalie, good." The older woman spoke over my shoulder. "Do you have a moment?"

I turned to find a young woman approaching.

"This lady is interested in the hunt clubs. Natalie is our program director, and she's done a lot of research into that time period," she said to me.

"Sure. Natalie Hefter," she said, extending a hand.

"Bay Tanner."

I thought by the brief lifting of her eyebrows that my name wasn't unfamiliar to her, but I let it go.

"Let's step over here," she said, heading for the shelves. "We have several excellent books on that era. Was there something specific?"

I glanced around, aware of several visitors milling in the same area. "It's a little . . . you see, it involves a client. I'm a private investigator."

"I know. I've seen your name in the papers." Natalie smiled

and reached to remove two volumes. "We can chat in my office if you'd like."

"That would be great."

It was a small but well-ordered room. We took chairs across the desk from each other, and I gave her the bare bones of my exchanges with Malcolm St. John, leaving out any mention of the circumstances of our relationship.

Natalie smiled widely at the mention of Mr. St. John's name. "I'm familiar with the family. Well, not personally, but they've cropped up a lot in my research. Many St. Johns worked here when the Thorne and Loomis families owned the property."

"Did that include the thirties and forties time frame?"

"Yes, most of it."

"Mr. St. John has on a couple of occasions mistaken me for someone he knew as a child, a white woman with red hair he calls Miss Lily. That's who I'm interested in finding out about."

"No last name?"

"I'm afraid not. I thought she might be from one of the families you mentioned."

Natalie shook her head. "I don't think so. But they almost always had guests when they were in residence."

"Is there any way to find out if of one of them was called Lily?"

"We do have some old letters from that time period. One day I'd like to get them all scanned and indexed, but it's a monumental job. We rely a lot on volunteers, and finding someone willing to tackle this job hasn't been my easiest sell." She smiled. "But you're welcome to take a look."

The thought of wading through stacks of old correspondence, handwritten and maybe illegible didn't exactly fill me with joy, but I couldn't see any alternative. Maybe I could get Stephanie . . .

"I assume you wouldn't want them to leave the building," I said.

"No, we couldn't do that. But I could maybe find you someplace quiet to go through them."

I wondered if, in one of the Judge's favorite aphorisms, the view would be worth the climb. What would I really gain by spending hours of my own or Stephanie's time poring over the material in the hope of finding something useful? Would it really gain me some entre into Malcolm St. John's deteriorating mind, some way to navigate the murky waters of his memory? I wasn't at all sure that stimulating his recollections of his childhood would move me one inch closer to finding out what had happened to him on that Sunday before we found him unconscious on the bare earth next to his house.

I was just about to decline and head back to work when Natalie said, "Lily? Was that the name?"

"Yes. Apparently I resemble her in some way."

"You know, now that I think about it, that does ring a slight bell with me. They called him Little Mal, didn't they?"

"Yes. The first time he mistook me, he seemed put out that Miss Lily didn't remember Little Mal."

"Hold on a second." Natalie opened one of the books she'd carried in with her and began thumbing through its pages. "I think there was a photo . . ."

I waited, my heartbeat quickening just a little.

"Yes, here it is." She laid the book flat and turned it to face me. She tapped a black and white picture at the top of the left-hand page. "Here he is, holding the reins of the horse."

The little black boy was dressed in bib overalls, his feet bare, a cap a size or so too large for him sitting on his ears. The horse dwarfed him, but he stood as tall as he could, looking proud, one small hand reaching up to rest on its white muzzle.

On the other side, a tall woman beamed at the camera, her formal riding gear a sharp contrast to the little boy's shabby dress. Sun glinted off her high boots, and her tall, rounded cap sat at a jaunty angle atop masses of curling hair. No way to tell its color, but it, too, caught the sunlight. She held the halter of the horse with one hand, a small crop in the other.

"Little Mal St. John, son of one of the plantation's hunting guides, with Blaze and Miss Lily Armstrong, visiting with her family from Newport, Rhode Island."

Across the desk, Natalie Hefter and I beamed at each other.

CHAPTER
TWENTY-NINE

I paid for the book, thanked Natalie for her help, and carried my treasure back to the Jaguar.

Again, I found my windshield pristine. Apparently the gods had decided to smile, in more ways than one. On impulse, I turned away from the car to follow a walkway that led around the restored mansion toward the marsh that bordered the property. Past the butterfly house, I stepped onto a wooden walkout, the sun warm on my head as I meandered out to the sheltered area at the end. A set of those mounted binoculars you find at nature spots all over the country invited closer inspection of the cord-grass and pluff mud, rife with wading birds fishing for lunch.

I settled on a weathered bench and opened the book.

The chatter of children's voices in the distance jerked me back to the present. I wiped a thin sheen of sweat from my forehead and glanced at my watch. I'd been so engrossed in the tales of life on the island eighty years before that I'd completely lost track of the time. I looked across to the other boardwalk, now crowded with youngsters obviously on some outing from school. I smiled at their shrieks of delight when one of the great blue herons lifted off from the marsh, right over their heads, his huge wingspan sending him soaring into the clear blue of the noon sky.

I tucked the book in my bag and made my way back to the Jaguar, which again offered up no additional messages. I began to hope that whoever had begun this reign of annoyance had lost interest in me and had perhaps moved on to other pursuits, like tearing the wings off flies or something equally uplifting.

My stomach rumbled as I turned over the powerful engine, and I thought about the Skull Creek Boathouse. Though Red and I hadn't been able to sit outside on our last visit, this gift of a warm, early November day should be perfect for a leisurely lunch overlooking the small boat dock and placid creek. I headed in that direction, using time provided by the red light at 278 to dial the office.

"Hey, Stephanie, it's me. I'm going to grab something at the Boathouse. Can I bring you two anything?"

"No thanks. Erik headed out to check on Mr. St. John's place, and he'll bring something back."

"Anything cooking?"

"No, ma'am, just the usual routine. I did have a call from a woman who thinks she may be being stalked, but she wouldn't make a commitment to come in. I kind of think she will, though, eventually. She seemed pretty freaked out."

"I know the feeling," I said.

"And Red called. He wants you to get back to him as soon as you can."

"Did he sound upset?" I'd turned off my phone inside the museum, and my absorption in the tales of the old days on the island had made me forget to check for messages. Now, visions of possible disasters involving Sarah or the kids leaped suddenly into my head.

"No, ma'am, not especially. He just said he needs to ask you something."

"I'll give him a call. See you later on this afternoon."

As I pulled into the long driveway of the restaurant, I wondered again what had precipitated my tormentor's sudden loss of interest. It seemed as if Saturday night's little escapade on my deck had somehow been the creep's swan song. I tried to think back to what had been going on that might have spooked him into giving up, but I came up blank.

They seated me at a table right at the edge of the outdoor patio area with an unobstructed view of the water and the activity around the boat dock. As I waited for my shrimp salad sandwich and sweet potato fries, my mind drifted back to the Bell case and Erik's and my frantic efforts to find a boat at this very spot. I smiled, remembering the young man we'd bribed into renting us his dad's, allowing us to witness the explosion just off the coast of Jericho Cay. I wondered what about that case might have prompted Erik to name it as the point in time when he noticed a change in Stephanie. I hadn't given it a whole lot of thought, but maybe just the mayhem surrounding the convoluted chain of events might have triggered memories of her father's death. He had lost his life on a boat, although it had been docked at the time, so perhaps that association had stirred feelings she'd put away over time. She always seemed to be a happy young woman, smiling and pleasant, but who ever knew what was really going on behind the masks we all show the world? Maybe I should make more of an effort to talk with her, to let her vent whatever might be festering below the surface. If there was anything. Sometimes I tend to overdramatize things, as Red was always quick to point out.

Speaking of my husband . . . I pulled my cell phone out of my bag. Red answered on the third ring.

"Hey. How's it going?"

"I'm fine. Stephanie said you needed to talk to me right away. Is there a problem?"

"No, honey. Sorry if I worried you. It's just that I was think-ing you might like to come and have dinner tonight."

I could feel my stomach muscles tighten. "At the house?"

"No, no. I meant just the two of us. I thought maybe I should leave Mrs. Burton to take care of the kids, sort of get them used to having someone else around without me." His voice trailed off. "You know."

"How did it go this morning?"

Red sighed. "Okay, I guess. Mrs. Burton was here before breakfast. She sort of took over with the lunches and everything. The kids were standing outside waiting when the bus arrived, which I remember didn't happen very often when I . . . before."

"Sounds as if things are under control. Why don't you just come home today?"

The pause lasted a couple of beats longer than should have been necessary. "Well, I don't want to just bail out on them. I think if I'm here to get them organized for homework and all that, after Mrs. Burton fixes dinner, that might help them a little with the transition. But we could meet somewhere downtown." Again he hesitated. "I miss you."

I wondered, then banished the disloyal thoughts. "It's a long drive just for an hour or two, especially if you're going to be back tomorrow." I waited for a reply that didn't come. "You are com-ing back tomorrow, right?"

"I, uh, I'm not sure. Sarah isn't doing too well."

I could feel anger rising in my throat, and I swallowed it back down. "I understand that, Red, but I thought the whole idea of Mrs. Burton was to give Sarah the space she needs to deal with the chemo. It can't be easy for her to have you in the house, in case that hadn't occurred to you. It must be awkward for everyone."

"Not as much as you might think," my husband said with an enthusiasm I wasn't sure how to interpret. "Actually, we're all getting along pretty good."

"How cozy." The words slipped out before I even realized they'd formed in my head.

"Come on, Bay, don't be ridiculous. I'm trying to make the best of a bad situation here."

"Sorry, that was bitchy. You stay as long as you need to. Just keep me posted."

"So how about dinner?"

I'd formed a sort of game plan, one that involved a quiet chat with Malcolm St. John, hopefully without the interference of his niece, and I felt itchy to put it into play.

"I have some things to take care of. On the case. Let's see what tomorrow brings, okay? Tell the kids I'm thinking about them."

"Sure, you do what you have to do. Anything breaking?"

I wasn't certain whether to feel relieved or insulted that he'd given in so easily. "Nope. Hub is back in Atlanta, and I told you about the sister. Mike still doesn't have any leads on who killed Merrill."

"No envelopes?"

"No," I answered truthfully, remembering my lie of omission about my Saturday night visitor on the deck. "Nothing."

"Well, you be careful, hear?"

"I'm fine, Red. You have enough to worry about, okay? Talk to you tomorrow."

I hung up without waiting for him to respond.

My lunch arrived, and I concentrated on enjoying the warm breeze off the water and the intermittent parade of boats along the creek while I savored the food. I did my best to let all the concerns, both personal and professional, sink to the back of my mind. At least for a while.

I managed to stretch a lunch hour into closer to two by the simple expedient of dawdling over a second glass of iced tea. When I finally felt able to drag myself away from the serenity of sun and water, I debated whether to return to the office. Instead, I by-passed the turn at Indigo Run and headed down 278. Ten minutes later, I pulled up in front of Malcolm St. John's bungalow.

Sheila Mahony's white Camry was parked out front, and I let out a sigh of relief that I wouldn't have to deal with Hub Dan-forth's nasty-tempered sister. The caregiver stood waiting for me in the open door as I picked my way up the cracked front walk.

"How nice to see, you Mrs. Tanner. Please come in."

She stepped aside, and I eased past her into the dim living room. Even with all the blinds open, the bright sunshine failed to penetrate more than a couple of feet past the windows.

"Please call me Bay," I said as I turned toward her.

"Bay it is. And I'm Sheila." She indicated the same chair I'd occupied on my previous visit. "Have a seat. Should I put the kettle on?"

"A little warm for me, but thanks anyway." I settled as comfortably as I could, my bag on my lap. "Is Mr. St. John sleeping?"

"Probably not. He spends a good bit of time in bed, but I don't think he's actually asleep." Her rich laugh made me smile. "He fakes it a lot, I think because he doesn't want to deal with me."

I smiled back. "How's his memory? Has he said anything about the attack?"

Sheila Mahony was shaking her head before I finished asking the question. "Nope. He rambles on a lot about when he was a child. I just let him go with it, you know? Like I told you before, it's best not to argue with dementia patients. First, it doesn't do any good, and second it just upsets them."

I reached down for my bag and pulled out the book I'd purchased at the museum. "Has he mentioned Miss Lily at all?"

Again she shook her head. "Not to me, but he does tend to mumble a lot to himself in there. I can hear his voice, but I can't always make out what he's saying. I move quietly to the bedroom door, just in case he needs something, but it's usually just a one-sided conversation."

I would have given a lot to be able to eavesdrop on those monologues. During my two visits to the hospital, I'd gotten a vague impression that Malcolm St. John might be using his illness as a cover during his short periods of lucidity to keep from dealing with things he didn't want to talk about. Maybe I was way off base, but I wanted to test my theory. If he did in fact recall more about his injury than he was willing to let on, I was hoping I could somehow wheedle the information out of him, either by direct questioning or subterfuge. Whatever worked.

"Do you mind if I just hang around for a little bit and see how he's feeling?" I tapped the book resting in my lap. "I found this at the Coastal Discovery Museum this morning." I turned to the page number I'd memorized and showed it to Sheila Mahony. "Check this out."

She studied the photo for a moment, and a smile lit her pleasant face. "Isn't he adorable?" Her expression sobered. "So this is the woman he's mistaken you for. I guess there's a resemblance, but it isn't a really good quality picture, is it?"

"Not really, but I'm sort of hoping it will help him to trust me. I really need to get him to open up about what happened to him."

"So you're going to try to trick him?" I didn't imagine the tone of disapproval in her voice.

I thought about apologizing, but there didn't seem any point.

"I guess you could put it like that. It's for his own good, in the long run. I'm not happy about it, but I can't keep him safe if I don't have some of idea of where the threat is coming from."

"I guess I can see that, although it doesn't seem right, you know?"

"Yes, I do. I've tried to come up with another way to approach the issue, but he clams up at any mention of the incident." I paused. "He hasn't said anything at all that might be helpful?"

"Nope. But as I said, he rambles a lot. Sometimes he yells at me that he won't sell his place, so I should just quit bugging him about it. Of course, I've never brought the subject up, but—"

"He thinks you're trying to buy his home?" I could feel the excitement rising in my chest. "Does he ever mention a name? I mean, who he thinks you are?"

"No, not that I recall."

I studied the woman, trying to see who she might resemble. Cynthia Merrill? Hardly. The two women bore no resemblance at all to each other, at least from what I recalled from the photos Stephanie had taken. Clarista Gaines? No way. Both ethnicity and temperament ruled that out. So who did Malcolm St. John think he was talking to? More than ever I needed to speak with him myself, to see if I could guide him into revealing whatever memories were locked away in the parts of his brain that had been scrambled by his disease.

"What if I just sat with him for a while?" I asked. "I promise not to disturb him if he's resting, but maybe being on hand when he wakes up could—"

"Get out of my house, goddammit!"

It seemed impossible that the booming voice from the doorway could have belonged to a wizened old man, but Malcolm St. John stood there glaring at us, his face twisted in anger. Sheila Mahony was on her feet before I could even register the shock that gripped us both.

"Malcolm, it's Sheila." She reached out a hand to steady him, but he slapped it away.

A bony finger quivered in my direction. "You go back and tell that ungrateful little shit that I'll fight him to my last breath. I ain't goin' to no goddamned home, and ain't no one on God's green earth gonna make me!"

The outburst seemed to drain the last of his energy, and Sheila caught him around his pitifully thin chest just as his legs gave way. I jumped from my chair, but she stopped me with a firm shake of the head.

"Just leave me to it, Bay. And you'd best be going. I don't think you're going to get anything out of him any time soon. And I can't have him upset like this. I'd appreciate it if you'd just stay out of his way," she said over her shoulder. Then, "Come on, sweetheart, let's get you back to bed. No one's going to take your house, and no one's gonna make you do anything you don't want to do. I promise."

I watched them shuffle slowly back down the hallway, tears of pity and frustration pooling in my eyes as I turned for the door.

CHAPTER
THIRTY

Stephanie looked up when I walked into the office a half hour later. I'd spent some time in the car getting my emotions under control before I'd felt ready to face anyone.

"Hey," Erik called from his desk in the corner.

He'd moved the privacy screen back so that he and Stephanie had an unobstructed view of each other. I smiled to myself, happy that that particular problem seemed to have resolved itself. It flitted through my mind that I should look for a bigger office, although the prospect of moving again gave me hives.

"I checked on the St. John house. Everything looks calm," my partner said.

"I know." I sat down in the one client chair positioned in front of his desk. "I just came from there."

"Any luck?"

"No." I pulled out the book weighing my bag down. "I found this at the museum. There's a picture of Little Mal and Miss Lily with one of the horses, and I wanted to see if I could use it to get him to open up to me."

"Did he have a bad reaction?"

"Yeah, you could say that. He thought I was trying to buy his house, and he basically threw me out."

"He seems to do that a lot."

I turned at Stephanie's voice from across the room. "What?"

"Well, I was just looking over the file. To make sure I hadn't missed anything. He's mentioned that—about someone trying to steal his house—several times. In different words, but pretty much the same sentiment. I thought it might be important, so I highlighted them."

"Show me." I crossed to her desk and leaned over her shoulder.

"You're right," I said when I'd finished scanning the passages she'd marked. "Sheila Mahony says he's accused her as well. And today, he said something like, 'Tell the little shit he's not putting me in a home.' *He*. It was definitely *he*. But if he thinks his nurse and I are in on it, too, there must be a woman involved."

Erik stood and stretched, then walked over to join us. "So who do we have on the hit list?"

"Hub, for one. And that Winter guy from Charlotte, although he wouldn't have anything to do with a home."

"And Merrill is probably the woman," my partner said, "although it could be Hub's sister."

"If it's them, Mr. Danforth and Ms. Gaines," Stephanie offered, "he's not being delusional, is he? I mean, they *do* want to sell the house and put him in a care facility, right?"

"Absolutely," I said. "So maybe we're reading more into this than it merits. In some part of his mind, he's grasped the basics of the situation. And he doesn't like it."

"You can't blame him, can you?" Stephanie looked and sounded defensive. "It's his house and his life. Other people shouldn't be trying to manage it for him. It's not right."

I thought again of the Judge's insistence on foregoing the surgery that might have prolonged his own life and my decision to acquiesce to his wishes. Had I done the right thing? If I had let them declare him incompetent, given myself the justification to use the medical power of attorney, would my father still be with us? It was the question that often tormented me in the dark hours of the night when all hope of sleep had fled. But did age and infirmity give the rest of us the right to dictate how someone else spent their waning days? Did love and concern override an individual's power over his own destiny? Who could really say whether another's life was still worth living if it wasn't on their own terms? But did Malcolm St. John really have the mental capacity to make those determinations for himself?

"Bay?

Erik's voice startled me.

"You okay?"

I shook my head. "Fine. Just thinking." I cleared my throat. "So does any of this help us figure out who attacked the poor old man? Or who killed Cynthia Merrill? Or why?"

Neither of them responded.

"That's the big issue here, at least for us. If we don't come up with some answers pretty soon, we need to let Hub Danforth off the hook. We're racking up billable hours without any real direction." I squared my shoulders. "Stephanie, I want you to send the complete file to both our computers, including any notes or marks you've made. All of us will take the rest of the day—and this evening, if necessary—to read it carefully and thoroughly. To-morrow morning, we'll turn off the phones and have a brain-storming session." I took a moment to look them both directly in the eye. "If we don't come up with some concrete plan to resolve the problem, I'm sending Hub Danforth a refund check and cut-ting him loose. Agreed?"

They looked first at each other before Erik nodded. "A-greed." He paused. "But what about Red? Shouldn't he be in on this?"

I swallowed the lump that had suddenly formed in my throat. "Red has his own problems," I said evenly. "If he's here, fine. If not, we need to get this settled, one way or the other."

I turned and escaped into my office, closing the door softly behind me.

I had expected to have difficulty concentrating, and I didn't disap-point myself. By the time four o'clock rolled around, I knew I wasn't going to accomplish anything. I saved the file to a flash drive, as Erik had taught me, tossed it into my bag, and aban-doned ship. Neither Erik nor Stephanie seemed surprised when I waved my goodbyes and scuttled out into the waning afternoon sunlight. A few more days and I'd be making the short walk to my car in twilight as daylight savings time came to a screeching halt. I hated getting home in the dark, especially now when I'd just gotten back into my running routine again. There was no way I could pound down the beach, even with a flashlight, without risking a fall or worse.

I stopped dead a few feet from the Jaguar. A blue envelope nestled under my wiper blade.

"God damn it!" I shouted, marching forward and snatching it out.

My hands were shaking with anger, and I ripped part of the notepaper getting it open. I needn't have worried. The message was both short and bizarre:

Sorry.

Just the one word in the same block capitals.

I stood next to the car, my trembling slowly subsiding, as I contemplated the meaning of the terse message. *Sorry* for putting you through this? If that was it, I could truly put the whole strange episode behind me. But why? Why would the jerk go to all this trouble only to sign off and move on? Did he mistake me for someone else?

Don't be ridiculous, I told myself as I slid into the front seat. The notes were addressed to me. And the one to Red. He was at my house, followed me in my car. Unless he was a complete idiot, he had to know he had the right person. So. *Sorry* for making me crazy trying to figure out who the hell he was? *Sorry* for scaring me half to death Saturday night?

I stuffed the envelope in my bag and pulled out my cell phone. My first instinct was to call Red, to run this baffling development by him. I hesitated, suddenly unsure how he'd feel about being interrupted by my problems. Never in our long and stormy relationship had I ever questioned that he would have my back, no matter what. Our conversation earlier in the day had planted a big, fat seed of doubt, and I could almost feel it sprouting in my head. No denying I'd taken Red's devotion for granted. God knows he'd expressed it often enough, and I'd come to expect that he'd always be there, forgiving my occasional bitchiness and preoccupation with my work.

I stared at the phone. Perhaps it was time to do my own reassessment, give the same measure of time and attention to my marriage that I always gave to my clients' cases. Maybe I should—

"Oh, shut the hell up!" I ordered myself.

My fingers fumbled over the tiny keys, and I breathed a sigh of relief when the phone was answered on the second ring.

"Hey, Lavinia."

"What's the matter?"

"Nothing." I forced the tremor out of my voice. "I'm just checking in. How's everything there?"

"Lydia Baynard Simpson Tanner, you are a terrible liar. Something's wrong. You tell me right this minute."

I stammered a little. "Really, nothing's . . . I'm fine. Bad day at the office."

"Where's Redmond?" she asked in the brisk, no-nonsense

tone I remembered so well from my childhood.

"He's still at Sarah's. Mrs. Burton seems to be working out well."

"Then he needs to get home where he belongs. No good is gonna come of him hanging around there. You tell him I said so."

That made me smile. "It's fine, Lavinia, really. He'll probably be back tomorrow." I said it as if I believed it myself.

"Why don't you come to dinner, honey? I've got a roasting chicken in the oven, stuffed and all, and I promise not to make you eat the peas I'm shelling."

"You couldn't. Make me eat peas, I mean." I could feel my whole body relaxing under the familiar banter that had marked all our years together.

"I did, and I can, child. You forget who won most of those battles."

I heard myself laugh. "No, I remember quite well." I sighed. "I really can't tonight, Lavinia, but I'd love to come soon. I'll call you." Almost as an afterthought, I asked, "How's Julia?"

I didn't imagine the moment's hesitation. "Doing fine. Don't you worry about us."

I realized I was almost as attuned to the undercurrents in her voice as she was to mine. "Did something happen? Is everything okay?"

"Don't fuss, child. We're doing just fine. You tell that husband of yours to get himself home, or I'll tell him myself. You take care."

I knew she'd hung up, but I still murmured, "Yes, ma'am," into the silence.

Dinner consisted of microwaved mac and cheese, which I routinely kept on hand for the kids. I ate it standing at the counter in the kitchen before retrieving my laptop from the bedroom. All the furniture and equipment from the spare room office was still stuffed into a corner, and I gave a fleeting thought to spending the evening combing through the mess I'd made when I'd decided to give Elinor her own space.

But duty called, and I hoped to lose myself in the troubles of poor Malcolm St. John and push my own to the back of my mind. I curled up on the sofa, the drapes closed against the darkness out over the ocean and plugged the flash drive into my computer. A cup of Earl Grey steamed at my elbow on the side table as I perched my reading glasses on the end of my nose and set to work. I'd thought about putting on some music to banish the pervading silence of the empty house, but I decided I needed all of my concentration.

As I'd hoped, I soon lost myself in the transcripts of conversations that had begun without me on Hubbard Danforth's first visit to the office while I'd been lolling on the beach with Neddie. A pale window opened in my mind at first, Julia and Lavinia—and Red—seeking my attention, but I pushed those thoughts away.

The cast of characters appeared on stage as the case unfolded: Hub, Mr. St. John, Cynthia Merrill, Brian Winter, Clarista Gaines. I read slowly through the synopses of the various conversations, allowing my impressions of the speakers to give substance to their words. Hub always appeared rational and caring, even though he made his living defending criminals. *Accused* criminals, I admonished myself on behalf of my father, the Judge. Innocent until proven guilty, and all that. I'd been wrong before in my assessment of people, but not that often. Still, the words hurled at me that afternoon by a shouting Malcolm St. John left little doubt, at least in my mind, as to the identity of *the little shit* who was trying to put the old man in a home. But Danforth had admitted as much, apparently without any attempt to hide his intentions. And my own observations and interactions with Hub's uncle had left little doubt that the old gentleman needed looking after. I'd heard we had wonderful facilities on Hilton Head, especially Memory Matters, the adult daycare center that gave respite to harried family members who had responsibility for the care of loved ones stricken with Alzheimer's and other types of dementia. We also had resident facilities that specialized in this type of elderly patient. It would have been wonderful if some way could be found to keep Malcolm in his home, but that would take money that Hub insisted neither he nor his sister could provide.

The sister. Clarista Gaines. I was the only one at the agency who'd met her, and my initial impression had not been good. She seemed overwrought, surely not a good companion for a man who flitted in and out of reality. *Nasty.* That had been the word that jumped immediately into my head after our one and only encounter, but perhaps I had been hasty. It couldn't be easy to

watch someone you cared for—assuming she *did* care about the
old man—slowly losing his grip on sanity. I made a note on the
legal pad I'd set beside me to check out Ms. Gaines a little more
thoroughly. Unless I was completely off base, she seemed to have
the temperament—and temper—to be involved up to her eyebrows in whatever was threatening Mr. St. John.

It was after eleven when I finally tossed my glasses onto the sofa
beside me and rubbed my eyes.

I'd made a few more notes, but nothing had popped right out
at me. Cynthia Merrill had been killed in much the same manner
that Malcolm had been attacked: a blow to the left side of the
head with no apparent weapon found. That couldn't be a coincidence. I didn't believe in them, anyway. She had a connection to
the old man as a result of her previous marriage to Hub and
through her company's interest in acquiring his property. Winter
was just an adjunct, an attractive one, I had to admit, but not likely
to be a major player in the drama.

I stretched, my neck protesting the hours spent bent over the
computer screen, then logged off and closed the laptop. I carried
it and the flash drive into the bedroom and changed into my pajamas. Outside, the wind had risen, whistling through the branches of the live oaks, reminding me of the escapade on the deck on
Saturday night. As I washed my face and brushed the day's tangles
from my hair, I wondered if that had indeed been the end of my
tormentor's attentions, if the latest note was for certain his last.
Time would tell.

I banished the complications of the case from my thoughts
and picked up my John Sandford novel, but again Lavinia intruded. And Julia. There had been something in my old friend's voice,
and I set my mind to reconstructing our conversation. She'd
sounded . . . wary? Was that it? Or perhaps evasive, as if she didn't
want to talk about my half-sister. Had something happened, some
incident she didn't want me to know about? Suddenly all my old
fears resurfaced. Neddie and Lavinia be damned, I knew Julia was
capable of having pushed Miss Lizzie down the stairs. I'd seen it
on her face in the dim light of the attic, that atavistic smile, almost
one of triumph, as if she'd gotten exactly what she wanted with
the death of her caretaker: a permanent place at Presqu'isle with

no one to interfere with her new life as Lavinia's darling.

I tossed the book aside and rolled over, the implications of it too awful to dwell on. No one else had seen it, but I knew what I knew. I would have to be vigilant. Lavinia would have none of it, and Neddie thought I was creating drama where none existed. It was up to me to make certain that nothing else tragic occurred in the old antebellum mansion. Up to me.

I finally fell asleep, repeating those three words over and over, like a mantra.

Up to me.

CHAPTER
THIRTY-ONE

Of course I slept badly, snippets of nightmares chasing me through the night.

I made note of the fact that my husband hadn't called, either.

I was up and ready at a little after seven thirty. I nuked myself another cup of tea and dawdled over my scant notes from the night before. I hoped Erik and Stephanie had done a better job of analyzing Malcolm St. John's case. Unless one of them had ferreted out something more than I had, I'd be recommending that we send Hubbard Danforth on his way. Victory in the battle between my gnawing curiosity and doing the right thing would be granted to the side of the angels.

At eight o'clock I gave up procrastinating and headed for the office. There were other things there to occupy me until Erik and Stephanie showed up at nine. I turned on all the lights against the gloomy morning, rain once again threatening. I sighed, remembering my day on the beach with Neddie just a week or so before, already mourning the coming of even our usually mild winter. I could deal with lower temperatures—for a while—but I'd found over the years that I needed sunshine and lots of it in order to maintain any semblance of well-being.

I settled behind my desk, fleshing out my meager notes of the night before and marshaling my arguments for cutting Danforth loose. I paused after a few minutes, shaking the pen I'd been using, after my scrawl had dwindled to a faint impression on the yellow page. I rummaged in my drawer without success. Stephanie was the keeper of the office supplies, and I rose and crossed to her desk, surprised to find it locked.

True, she kept copies of all the paper files on current cases, with the originals secured in the file cabinet in my office, and backups of the computer stuff stored on various external devices. That was Erik's department, and I trusted him to safeguard our sometimes sensitive information. During our investigation involving the inhabitants of Canaan's Gate, the huge Italian villa in Wexford Plantation, we'd had a break-in in which I'd been struck over the head by whomever had ransacked our office. We'd tightened our security procedures after that, but I didn't remember that they included locking individual desks.

Back at my own, I searched my bag for the ring of keys I'd had to dig out in order to open the door that morning. Two small gold ones looked as if they might fit the desks. I hit pay dirt on the second try, found a supply of pens in the deep drawer on the left, and grabbed a couple from the package. There were also boxes of staples and paper clips along with notepads and legal pads, file folders and stationery. A small box of note cards with an image of the Harbour Town Lighthouse seemed out of place, but maybe they were for Stephanie's personal correspondence. I slid the drawer closed and relocked it.

With a functioning pen in hand, I continued working on what I hoped would be a short presentation. Unless one of the other two had been struck with some startling insight, I couldn't see any way around our bowing out of the case. The sheriff—in particular, Detective Mike Raleigh—would continue to pursue the investigation into Cynthia Merrill's death. Sheila Mahony would guard Malcolm St. John as if he were her own. I had no doubt Hubbard Danforth would prevail in any competency hearing he decided to pursue, and I'd given him my word to testify if he felt my contribution was warranted. I could certainly give evidence of the old man's inability to stay in the present when he seemed to mistake me for someone from his childhood almost every time our paths crossed.

"It's for his own good," I said into the emptiness of the office.

Maybe if I repeated it often enough I'd come to believe it myself.

The *kids* trooped in just before nine.

When everyone had shed jackets, and tea and coffee had been distributed, we gathered around my desk. Erik and Stephanie had their iPads—or minis or whatever they were—plopped securely in their laps. Only I, the dinosaur, had to refer to actual handwriting on actual paper. Sometimes, I thought, they made me feel about a hundred and ten.

"Okay," I began, "I'm ready to close this out. I can give you my reasoning, but that's the bottom line. I'm prepared to entertain any arguments for or against."

I leaned back and waited.

"I don't like it," Stephanie said, her chin stuck out aggressively as if she were ready to take a punch. "We accepted responsibility for Mr. St. John's safety, and we let him get hurt. And we still don't know who or why. What if we just walk away and something—"

She swallowed hard, but I gave her credit for standing her ground.

"If he gets attacked again, how are we going to feel? At least with us keeping an eye on him, we have a chance of preventing that." Her courage seemed to fail her, and she dropped her defiant gaze to her little computer device. With a quick, sideways glance at Erik, she added, in a much softer tone, "At least that's what I think."

"Fair enough." I kept my own voice low and reasonable. "Let's hear what Erik has to say, and then we can each defend his or her position. Partner?"

"I'm not going to be much help," he said, his boyish grin belying the seriousness of the topic of conversation. "I can see it both ways. I'm hoping one of you ladies . . ." He paused to pat his fiancée briefly on the knee. "One of you will be able to persuade me. I mean, I understand your reasoning, Bay, but I also have to admit to some sympathy for Stephanie's concerns."

"I'm not without sympathy for them myself," I said, "but this is a business. People come to us with a problem. If we accept them as clients, we undertake to solve that problem. Mr. St. John has Alzheimer's or senile dementia or whatever label you want to put on it. Bottom line is that he isn't competent to care for himself, and we can't be there twenty-four/seven to make sure he's safe. That wasn't what we were hired to do. Hub Danforth wanted us to document his uncle's erratic behavior so that he could have him declared incompetent. We've more than fulfilled that mission."

"What about Cynthia Merrill?" Again Stephanie's chin was thrust in my direction. "Mr. Danforth also hired us to be his liaison with the sheriff's office on her murder."

"True. But so far the investigation into her death looks as if it's dead in the water, you should pardon the expression." I smiled at Ben Wyler's daughter, but she refused to allow a lightening of the mood. I sobered. "Raleigh tells me they're exactly nowhere on either motive or suspects. We can't continue to take Hub's money when we won't have anything to report that he couldn't get for himself—for free—with a simple phone call to Mike."

"Good point," Erik said, assuming the role of mediator between the two women flanking him. "We should at least let him off the hook for that part of the assignment, don't you think, Steph?"

"What if he doesn't want us to 'let him off the hook'?"

"He's poor-mouthed me enough about the cost of Mr. St. John's care that I can't see him just throwing money away," I said, allowing a little annoyance to creep into my voice.

While I welcomed Stephanie's willingness to engage with me on a subject she obviously felt passionate about, I wondered where all this was coming from. She was involved only peripherally in our cases, her main function to keep the office running smoothly and allow Erik the luxury of not being tied to his computer and desk. Because she had access to all our notes and client information, I valued her opinion. I wouldn't have asked for it otherwise, and it was true that more than once she had offered up suggestions that had proved valuable in our investigations. She'd also, I was forced to admit, proved herself more than competent on the surveillance thing. Still . . .

Maybe it was the old man himself, I thought, studying my young colleagues across the desk. Having lost her own father to violence, maybe she was transferring her protective feelings to Malcolm St. John, even though she'd never exchanged a word with him so far as I knew. It wouldn't be surprising, I guessed. *Transference.* I smiled to myself. Neddie would be proud.

"Well, I think that might not entirely be the case," Stephanie said. "When I was checking him out, he seemed to be doing okay. More than okay, actually. He has a house in Buckhead, and that's not exactly the slums of Atlanta. Plus he has another place in the Caribbean. Roatan. I think it's an island off Honduras. And he belongs to two country clubs. I don't think that comes cheap."

"Hmm," I said. "I didn't know all that."

"Well, it didn't seem important. I mean, it *is*," Stephanie said, her expression a little guarded, "but I was only checking to make sure he could afford the retainer and the fees."

"How's his credit?" I asked.

"Nothing popped right out. The Buckhead place is mortgaged, naturally, but I didn't find anything on the other one, the vacation house."

"So he could own that free and clear. Maybe he's house-rich and cash-poor," Erik offered.

A little niggle of . . . *something* tried to worm its way into my consciousness. "We never checked out the sister, did we?"

"No. I mean, you never asked me to."

"I know. Actually, I meant to look at her a little more closely, but I guess I got sidetracked."

Red. Sarah and the kids. Lavinia. Julia. I knew my own personal issues had intruded more and more into my priorities, but I should never have let Clarista Gaines slip through the cracks.

The stalker and his—hopefully—final note. That was something else I should have shared with the young people. *Later*, I decided.

"Let's correct that oversight. And we'll postpone any decision on Hub until we have more data."

"You think the sister might be involved?" Erik asked. "In what? I mean, the attack or the murder?"

I tossed the question around in my head for a minute before answering. "It seems unlikely. But that one conversation I had with her was decidedly strange. She thought I was checking up on *her*, rather than just stopping in to see Malcolm. And she accused me of being a spy for her brother, more or less."

"I wonder why she's hanging around." Erik's face had grown pensive. "If she's helping pay for the caregiver, you'd think she'd want to spend as much time as possible over there and keep the cost down. But you've only seen her the once, right?"

"Okay, let's do this. Erik, you and Stephanie split up the computer work and do a thorough workup on both Hub and Clarista. Let's do some real digging." Erik opened his mouth to speak, but I cut him off. "Yes, you have my blessing to skirt the rules if you have to. I want to know just how strapped for cash those two really are. It would be helpful to have employment records for the sister, too."

The more I thought about it, the stranger it seemed that Hub would be entrusting the care of his uncle to people he had to pay when he had free labor in the person of his sister already on site. Or did he really not trust her?

"Let's reconvene after lunch," I said, sliding my notes into the center desk drawer. "Will that give you enough time?"

Erik grinned back at me. "Plenty. Come on, Steph." He grabbed her by the hand and literally hauled her out of her chair. "Let's get on it."

I had to smile as they walked together out of my office. When the silence had once again descended, I sat staring at the wall across from my desk, my thoughts a jumble of personal and professional concerns. I mentally prioritized and reached for the phone.

My husband answered his cell almost before the first buzz had faded in my ear.

"Hey, honey. I was just going to call you."

I swallowed down the retort that struggled desperately for voice. "How's it going?" I asked instead, my tone a model of calm and reason.

"Not too bad. Mrs. Burton is a gem, that's for sure. We owe Lavinia big-time for finding her for us."

I let the *us* pass, but not without filing it away for later contemplation. "Good. How's Sarah feeling?"

"Still lousy, although she doesn't have another chemo scheduled until Friday. I guess some people just can't tolerate it at all, but she really doesn't have any choice. She says her doctor is cautiously optimistic that she's going to have a positive result. But she's got to get through all this misery first."

I felt my anger and anxiety softening. "It really sucks, but the alternative is worse. I suppose it won't matter a damn to her, but I'm really holding good thoughts for her."

Some of them were selfish, of course, but I really did like my former sister-in-law, and I sincerely hoped she'd make a full recovery, honestly more for her sake and the kids' than for mine.

"She's okay with you, honey, really. The situation is just awkward, you know?"

"Of course." I drew in a deep breath and dived in. "So are

you coming home today?"

The pause told me all I really needed to know. "I'm not sure that's a good idea."

I waited for a fuller explanation, a few plausible excuses, a little self-justification. None was forthcoming.

"Okay. So what are we looking at? Another day or so?"

"I'm not sure. Do you need me at the office? How's the case shaping up?"

Not *Do you miss me?* Or more importantly, *I miss you.* Not even an expression of concern about the stalker. I would have set his mind at ease with the information that the latest missive seemed to signal the end of that particular problem, but apparently my husband wasn't concerned enough even to ask. I felt a combination of anger and sadness rising in my chest, but I forced myself to speak as offhandedly as he had.

"We're good. I'll fill you in when I see you."

Another perfect opening for him to name a date for his return, but he let it pass.

"I just need to make sure everything is settled here, Bay. I know you understand."

"Absolutely," I said through quivering lips. "Talk to you later. Best to Sarah and the kids."

I swallowed hard as I hung up, ordering myself to suck it up. I always loved the Tom Hanks line from the movie *A League of Their Own*: "There's no crying in baseball." Well, there wasn't any in the private inquiry business, either. I grabbed my purse from my desk, no particular destination in mind as I hurried out the door, calling to Erik and Stephanie that I'd be back shortly.

Outside, I wiped my eyes with the back of my hand. I wasn't sure naming movies and their stars counted as much as written citations, but I awarded myself two points anyway.

Somehow it didn't make me feel any better.

I honestly didn't have any destination in mind as I dodged a few rain drops and slid into the cool leather seat of the Jaguar, but I found myself heading down-island on 278 before I'd had a chance to formulate any coherent plan. Not that coherence had been operating a lot in my thinking processes lately, I told myself with a rueful smile. Off to my left, I could see the sun struggling to break through out over the ocean. I'd dressed for comfort rather than fashion that morning, and I toyed with the idea of a brisk walk on the beach. If I stayed above the tideline, my loafers shouldn't suffer too much, and I'd had the forethought to wear socks as well.

I pulled into the left-hand lane just past the light at Folly Field and Mathews and swung through the sparse traffic onto Burkes Beach Road. A few moments later I eased the Jag into a parking space at the end of Malcolm St. John's street. Just as I stepped out onto the gravel, the sun erupted in a blaze of warmth, its light dancing across the surface of the gently rolling waves.

I took it as an omen.

But when I turned toward the old cottage, the fleeting sense of well-being vanished in a heartbeat. Sheila Mahony's car was nowhere to be seen. And the front door stood wide open.

CHAPTER THIRTY-TWO

She's taken him for a drive or to run an errand, and the door didn't latch completely.

That thought sustained me for about as long as it took to pull the S&W from my bag and dash across the empty road. I had to order myself to slow down. I held the revolver tight against my thigh and approached the open door carefully. I stood completely still and listened, straining for any hint of what might be happening inside the bungalow, although the rising wind rippling through the old live oak and the ever-present *shushing* of the surf made it difficult to discern any other sounds.

I must have stood there for a good two minutes, my senses on full alert for any indication of trouble. I let out a long breath and banged my knuckles against the door frame.

"Sheila? It's Bay Tanner. Is everything okay in there?"

Silence.

"Mr. St. John." I thought a moment. "Little Mal? It's Miss Lily, come to call."

Still nothing.

I didn't give myself time to think about it. I jerked the door all the way open and jumped inside, moving immediately to the right to flatten myself against the near wall and to bring the gun into firing position, just the way Red had taught me.

Nothing stirred except for a few dust motes dancing in the sunlight struggling to penetrate the usual gloom of the tiny room. Slowly I pushed myself away from the wall and walked softly into the kitchen, then the bedroom and bath. The silence held. I could see no signs of a struggle—no overturned furniture or stuff tossed around. It was as neat as the last time I'd sat there with Sheila Mahony less than twenty-four hours before.

I loosened my grip on the revolver and let my shoulders relax. I noticed a mug on the narrow strip of counter. It held the remains of what smelled like coffee when I bent to sniff its contents. I felt the outside. Stone cold. I looked around for further evidence of how long the place had been empty, but nothing else popped right out at me.

I thought of calling Erik—or even the sheriff—but I didn't want to make more trouble for the old man if he and his caregiver were just on some innocent outing, although I'd have something to say to Sheila about the open door. I slipped the gun into my jacket pocket, its weight pulling down the fabric as the tiny Seecamp had never done. Maybe now that my stalker had decided to take a sabbatical I could go back to the less effective but more manageable firearm.

Then the memory of Malcolm St. John, lying in the dirt at the rear of his house, seemed to fill my vision. I retraced my steps and wheeled around the side, almost panting with fear until I found the back yard as empty as the house.

Okay, good, I told myself, although my relief was short-lived. Where in the hell were they? I made my way through the rain-soaked scrub grass back to the car. I stowed the S&W in my bag and pulled out my cell phone.

"Stephanie, it's me. I'm at Mr. St. John's house, and there's no one here. The front door was standing open. Get me the number for Sheila Mahony, the caregiver, will you, please?"

"Oh, no! I mean, sure, just a sec."

I could hear the distress in her voice, and I wondered again about her emotional attachment to someone she'd never met in person. A moment later she rattled off a number with a 912 area code. I repeated the sequence in my head, promised to keep her posted, and immediately dialed again.

"Hello? Is that you, Mrs. Tanner?"

Caller ID.

"Where are you, Sheila?"

She must have heard the anxiety in my voice. "I'm in Hardeeville, with a client." She picked up on the problem immediately. "Has something happened to Malcolm?"

"I'm at his house. The door was open, and he's gone. He's not with you?"

"No. They called and told me they'd made other arrangements."

"When?"

"Yesterday afternoon, not too long after you were there. The sister's supposed to be watching him. You mean, she isn't?"

It took me a moment to digest the implications of what Sheila Mahony had just told me.

"Okay, hold on a minute. You said 'they.' Who actually fired you?"

"I wouldn't call it being fired. Mr. Danforth. He said he'd made arrangements for his sister to stay with the old gentleman, and my services would no longer be required. He was very kind. He even offered me an additional day's wages, under the table, as compensation for cutting me off so abruptly. I said that wasn't—"

"Wait! You talked to Hub Danforth himself?"

"Well, no," she said somewhat hesitantly. "It was Mrs. Gaines, his sister. She said she was just conveying Mr. Danforth's wishes because he was tied up in court and couldn't speak to me directly."

My mind churned with all the ugly possibilities. A tiny part of my reasoning brain tried to insert plausible—and innocent—explanations for the whole scenario, but the suspicion refused to be quieted.

"You said yesterday. So how long has Malcolm been out of your care?"

"I fixed his dinner last night. The Gaines woman showed up around seven, and I left."

"Why didn't you call me?"

I could almost hear her bristling. "I don't work for you, Mrs. Tanner."

I forced myself to speak calmly. "I know, Sheila. It's just that . . . well, you know I've been concerned about him, over and above my company's contract with Danforth."

"You don't think something's happened to him, do you?"

The words came out in a rush, and I knew from the note of dread that Sheila Mahony hadn't just abandoned the old man. But she worked for an agency. She went where she was told.

"I don't know." I took a moment to force some logic into the maelstrom of fear swirling around in my head. "I didn't see that rusted-out Ford the sister was driving, so maybe she took him out."

"But what about the open door?"

"Could be simple carelessness." I paused. "She didn't strike me as the most reliable person on the planet."

"Me, either," Sheila snapped back. "I really didn't like the idea of leaving the poor old gentleman to her . . . *care*, but there really wasn't anything I could do about it."

Her tone begged for absolution, and I felt compelled to offer it. "I know, Sheila. It's certainly not your fault."

"What are you going to do?"

Good question. I gave it a moment of thought. "I'll take a-nother look around first, then see if I can get hold of Gaines." My eyes traveled of their own volition out toward the beach and the dangerous currents of the folly.

"You'll let me know? I won't be able to rest until I know he's okay."

Hub Danforth was an idiot to have let this loving woman go in favor of his nasty-tempered sister. And I'd be happy to tell him so as soon as I took a quick check of the shoreline. I shuddered a little, and not just from the brisk wind that had kicked up while I'd stood talking.

"I will, Sheila. Sorry if I sounded a little curt before, but I'm concerned about Malcolm."

"So am I," she said. "You call me, hear?"

"Will do," I said and disconnected.

I stuffed the phone in my jacket and turned toward the beach.

The wind hit me full in the face the moment I stepped onto the boardwalk.

My eyes teared, and I wished I'd taken the time to retrieve my sunglasses from the Jaguar. It would have been good had I pulled my hair back into some kind of restraint as well. Hanging loose, it whipped around, slim strands slapping me in the face and further blurring my vision.

I expected to find the beach deserted, but the sunshine had apparently lured some of the hardier souls out of hiding. A couple walked hand in hand, hoods from their sweatshirts fastened tightly over their heads. A golden retriever romped ahead of them, al-ternately charging at the waves as they ebbed and barking furi-ously in retreat when they broke against the shore. Another brave man had set up his fishing gear at the edge of the water, two poles stuck firmly in the sand while he cast another, not terribly success-fully, into the wind.

I stepped off the wooden walkway and onto the sand, my head swiveling from side to side. Other than the three adventure-some people I'd already marked, the beach stood empty. I turned right, in the direction of the folly, a feeling of dread pulling me toward the most dangerous stretch of the shoreline. In a short time, I stood gazing at the rushing water as it flowed out of the marsh toward the sea. The cordgrass whipped crazily in the wind, sometimes nearly flattened in the gusts that blew in off the ocean. Deserted as it was, the whole scene seemed somehow primitive, almost as if the towering mansions and resort hotels were merely figments of some futurist's wild imagination.

I turned away, not as reassured as I should have been by the fact that I had not found Malcolm St. John.

CHAPTER THIRTY-THREE

Stephanie and Erik were huddled around her desk in the reception area, the remains of a pizza making the whole office smell like an Italian restaurant. Despite the knot of concern in the center of my chest, my stomach rumbled a little in response.

"We saved you a couple of slices," Erik said, then his voice trailed off. "You didn't find him?"

I shook my head.

Stephanie looked stricken. "What did the caregiver have to say?"

"They canned her. Yesterday."

"What? But why——?"

"Did you get any info on the sister?" I grabbed a slice out of the box and carried it into my office. The other two followed close behind.

"Why?" my partner asked.

"She's supposed to be taking over Malcolm's care," I answered, swallowing noisily. "There's a good chance he's with her right now."

Without being asked, Stephanie had pulled a bottle of Diet Coke out of the mini-fridge and handed it to me. I nodded my thanks and drank some down. She and Erik exchanged a look I couldn't quite interpret, and suddenly neither one of them seemed to want to make eye contact.

"Look, do we have anything on her? If so, bring it in, and I'll give you the whole story. First and foremost, I want a number for her. We need to find out if she has Malcolm or not."

I forced down the slice of pizza and polished off the remains of the Diet Coke. All of it sat in a cold lump in the bottom of my stomach. I ran my hands through my tangled hair, not really giving a damn what I looked like. I was all too familiar with this feeling of dread, and way too often it had proved prophetic. I couldn't think of another time when I would have been happier to be wrong.

When Stephanie stepped into my office a few minutes later, I looked up to see her pretty face white, her lower lip trembling.

"As bad as that?" I asked. My gut dropped another couple of floors. "Let me have her number."

"You probably won't need it," Stephanie said in a low voice I had to strain to hear, but she handed over one of the slips from the pink message pad.

"Why not?"

"Because according to the State of Georgia, Clarista Gaines has been in prison since 2007."

"What? There must be some mistake." I swallowed hard. "Let me see what you've got."

Stephanie laid several pages of printouts in front of me. I scanned the top one, flipped through the rest, and returned to the initial page. Clarista Jewel Danforth Bitterman Gaines had been convicted for trafficking narcotics, specifically cocaine, in a suburb of Atlanta. She had previous convictions for solicitation, possession of a controlled substance, and domestic violence. She'd pretty much skated on most of the raps, getting a couple of months to probation, until she obviously ran up against a hanging judge. She'd been given the max on the possession with intent to sell charge.

"Are you sure she's not out? For good behavior or something?"

Erik spoke from behind his fiancée. "I just checked. She was denied parole last year. Seems she has a hard time not beating the crap out of her fellow inmates."

I shook my head, the information somehow failing to register. "I don't get it." I glanced at the slip of paper I still held in my hand. "Then whose phone number is this?"

"Hub Danforth gave it to us."

"You mean he's in on this?" I let the paper flutter to the desktop. "He has to know his sister is still in jail. This makes absolutely no sense at all."

"I know." Erik shook his head. "We were just talking about it when you came in. I wanted to run some other checks, make sure we had it right before we updated you."

Almost without conscious thought, Erik slid his hand around

Stephanie's.

"We were going to call you as soon as we verified the information," he said in a soft voice. "We . . . I didn't think it was that crucial. We had no idea she has Mr. St. John."

"Get Danforth on the phone."

Stephanie whirled, dragging her fingers reluctantly from Erik's, and headed for her desk.

"What are we going to do?" my partner asked.

"First off, find out who's been impersonating Gaines." I picked up the abandoned note and punched viciously at the phone. "Stephanie!" I yelled.

"Yes, ma'am?" Improbably, her face had gone even whiter than before.

"You make sure you get through to Danforth, do you understand? I don't care if he's in court or having an audience with the Pope. I want his ass on the line within the next five minutes, you got that?"

"Yes, ma'am," she squeaked and scuttled back to her desk.

Predictably, my call went to voice mail, a generic leave-your-number message in that female mechanical whine that drives me up the wall. Whoever decided that it sounded welcoming and friendly needed to have his head examined. I slammed the receiver back in its cradle.

"Stephanie! Where's Danforth?"

I should have felt bad about taking it all out on Erik's poor fiancée, but I needed to vent at someone, and she was handy. Besides, I couldn't believe the two of them had sat on the information about Clarista Gaines. To be fair, they hadn't realized the importance of it until I'd told them about Sheila Mahony's firing, but still . . .

"He's not there."

My head snapped up at Stephanie's words.

"He's not where?"

"Anywhere. He's not answering any of his phones, home or cell, his office says he's in court, but the courthouse doesn't have any record of any hearing he's supposed to be at." Tears choked her voice. "I'm really sorry, Bay. I don't know what else to do."

I drew in a long breath and let it out slowly. "It's okay, Stephanie. Keep trying, especially his cell. Clog his mailbox with messages if you have to." I thought a moment. "Tell him Malcolm is missing. Tell him I need to see him immediately, or I'm going to have to involve the sheriff."

"But what good will that do?" She snuffled, and I could see her resisting the urge to wipe her nose with the back of her hand.

"If he's in collusion with whoever's impersonating his sister, he may already be on his way. Or even on the island as we speak. I want to force him to contact me. Better yet, I want him to come looking for me, if for no other reason than to find out what I know. If the two of them are trying to work some kind of number on the old man, get him to sign papers or something, I want them to know I'm onto their game." I sighed. "Maybe it will keep them from doing anything stupid."

"Like what?"

"Like forcing Malcolm to sign away his rights to the property and dumping him in the Atlantic."

The afternoon crawled by. Every time the phone rang we all jumped, but Hub Danforth remained out there in the ether somewhere, unreachable and unresponsive. I saw no point in leaving my name and number for the phony Clarista Gaines. Hell would be an iceberg before she ever called me back.

At three thirty, I'd had enough.

"I'm going over there," I said, slipping my bag over my shoulder as I walked out into the reception area.

Stephanie looked up from her computer. "To Mr. St. John's?"

"I'll come with you," Erik said, closing the lid on his laptop and rising from his chair.

"I don't need backup," I snapped, one hand on the doorknob.

"You're getting it anyway."

My partner and I stared at each other for a long moment, then I shrugged. "Suit yourself."

I yanked open the door, not waiting to see if he followed.

"I'm driving." Erik stomped around to the passenger side of his huge Expedition and stood silently.

"Fine." I scrambled up inside.

"You know," he said, giving the key a vicious turn, "sometimes you really piss me off."

"Get over it," I mumbled, a little startled by the vehemence in his voice.

"We're partners, supposedly, and you just keep going off half-cocked, almost never asking me what I think or what I want. It's getting old, Bay."

Stung by his words as well as his tone, I clamped my mouth shut. I wasn't in the mood for a confrontation, even if he did probably have a point. We rode in silence down 278, the shift-change traffic clogged in the off-island lanes while we sailed along with little difficulty. The few minutes gave me a chance to cool off, and I resolved to set things right. Soon.

Gaines's rust-bucket Taurus was nowhere in evidence when we turned into the gravel parking area. I'd never taken notice of what Danforth drove, but I'd bet Erik had. Nonetheless, there was no vehicle anywhere in the vicinity. The old bungalow hunkered in the shade of the live oak, already looking as if it had been abandoned for months instead of hours.

I climbed out and had to kick up my speed to catch up with Erik. He knocked once, then wrenched open the door and disappeared inside. I knew what he'd find, so I stayed on the stoop, my eyes scanning the area for any signs of life. All we needed was one nosy or bored neighbor, and we'd have a chance of getting some idea of how long Gaines—or whoever the hell she was—had been gone and whether or not Malcolm had been with her.

Erik slammed the door behind him and stood for a moment staring out over the landscape.

"It doesn't look like he put up any fight, does it?"

I breathed a sigh of relief that his voice was back to normal. "Nope, didn't look like it to me, either. The imposter has taken him somewhere, and it's pretty clear to me that Hub Danforth knows exactly what's going on. Agree?"

He smiled then, and I dared to hope that we were back on steady ground.

"Stephanie had bad vibes about him right from the beginning, remember?"

"I do. It's just so damn hard to believe that someone in his position would stoop to what amounts to fraud, not to mention kidnapping. The man has a lot to lose."

"Maybe that's the problem," Erik said, shoving his hands into the pockets of his khaki pants. "Maybe he needs the money."

I sighed again. "He seemed genuinely concerned about the old man. I would have sworn he wasn't capable of this kind of deception."

"Live and learn." Erik smiled, and I felt the world righting itself again. "Could be he's just gotten himself into some kind of financial mess, and he's desperate. You just never know how someone will react when his back's up against the wall. Remember Nicholas Potter."

Erik's reference to the Washington lobbyist who had killed at least once in order to gain access to his grandparents' vast holdings was a nightmare I didn't want to revisit.

"Now what?" I said, my spirits sinking along with the late afternoon sun. "It'll be dark soon, and I don't have the first idea of where to begin looking for them."

Erik glanced over his shoulder, toward the ocean. "You check the beach?"

I swallowed hard. "First thing after I found the house empty. But the tide was going out, so I . . ."

He saved me from completing the gruesome thought. If they'd already tossed the old man's body, it could be well on its way to the Azores by now.

"Let's not go there just yet. I have a feeling we'll be hearing from Hub before too long."

"Really? Why?"

"I think you played it just right, suggesting that you'd have to report Malcolm's disappearance to the sheriff. I have a feeling that's the last thing those two want."

"I wasn't bluffing. I'm not taking this on alone. I'll give him until five to get back to me, then I'm calling Mike Raleigh."

By unspoken consent, we made our way side by side back to Erik's SUV. He paused, his fingers on the handle of the passenger door when a voice from out of the twilight gloom startled us.

"Mrs. Tanner? Wait up."

We whirled in unison as Marshall Miller, both hands stuffed in the pockets of a dark blue windbreaker, approached from the beach.

"It's okay," I said to Erik, who had tensed beside me. "Friend of Malcolm's." I raised a hand in greeting. "What can I do for you,

Mr. Miller?"

"I just wanted to apologize for not getting back to you over the weekend. Something came up. Business." He nodded toward the cottage. "I was just going to drop in on Malcolm, but the place looks dark. Anything wrong?"

"I'm not sure," I said honestly. "Neither Malcolm or his caregiver is anywhere around. You haven't seen him since we last spoke, have you?"

He was shaking his head before I finished the question. "I had to fly back home. That business I mentioned. But I kept worrying about him, so I hopped in the plane and buzzed down this afternoon. What exactly is going on?"

"I wish I knew." I debated with myself, then plunged ahead. "He's been diagnosed with Alzheimer's."

"I was afraid of something like that. He does tend to sort of wander off, in his head, I mean. That's just a damned shame."

"And he was attacked last week." I tilted my chin toward Erik. "We found him lying in the dirt out behind his house."

"Marshall Miller." He stuck his hand in Erik's direction. "I don't believe we've met."

"Oh, hell, sorry. My partner, Erik Whiteside."

"Pleasure," Miller said. "So you think someone's out to get the old man?"

"It looks that way. Any ideas?"

"This is one hell of a valuable piece of property. I'd say it's the only thing Malcolm has that would be worth coming after him for. But I can't see how hurting him would get anyone closer to inducing him to part with it. He's told me numerous times that he plans to die right here." He gestured toward the darkening sky over the ocean.

"You don't think he'd—?"

"No, no. I didn't mean that. It's just that he loves this place —the tides, the folly, the smell of the sea." Again he looked over his shoulder. "Can't say I blame him. Too much building and not enough care for the things that can't be replaced. Unfortunately, it's not unique to Hilton Head."

I didn't feel up to a discussion of the ongoing battle between the environmentalists and the developers. "Did Malcolm ever say who wants his property?"

"No. Our discussions were pretty general." He paused. "You

think something's happened to him, don't you?"

"We're working on that. And we should get back to it. Thanks for the information, Marshall."

He again offered his hand along with a business card. "Keep me posted, if you can. I've developed a real fondness for that old gentleman."

"A lot of that going around. I'll let you know when we find him."

"Appreciate it." He turned and retraced his steps back to the beach, his hands once again bunched in his pockets against the cold.

"Nice guy," Erik said as he finally pulled open the passenger door. As I slid into the seat, he added, "Maybe we should run all this by Red. What do you think?"

Contacting my husband would be the prudent thing to do, but I'd put it off. Speaking to Red would necessarily entail a discussion of when he might be coming home, and it wasn't a topic I felt prepared to deal with. He had been silent all day: no message, no phone call. Obviously he wasn't coming back to the island as planned, and I hadn't had time to figure out just how I felt about that. My better nature understood his concern for his ex-wife and his kids. The other part of me, the deeper, more visceral side, felt abandoned and discarded. And angry. Probably not a good state of mind in which to have a serious, professional conversation.

I hoped none of my inner conflict showed on my face or crept into my voice. "I'll talk to him from home. Before I decide what to do about the sheriff."

"Your call. Just don't leave it too long, okay? As you say, it's going to be full dark soon. I hate to think about Mr. St. John out there. I mean, even if he's with the imposter woman, it would be better than if he'd just wandered off on his own, you know?"

I nodded as he closed the door, hoping against hope that Malcolm St. John was safe.

"From your lips to God's ear," I murmured as the powerful engine roared to life.

CHAPTER
THIRTY-FOUR

Erik dropped me off about four thirty in the parking lot of the office. I didn't need to check in with Stephanie to see if Danforth had called. I knew she would have been in touch immediately if she'd heard from him. I slid into the Jaguar and turned toward home.

I'd just closed the garage door behind me and started up the steps into the house when my cell phone rang. *Private Number* glowed above a 404 area code which I recognized as Atlanta.

Eager as I was to tear into Hub Danforth, I waited until I was inside the house and had reset the alarm before I picked up.

"Bay Tanner."

"Bay, it's Hub. I got your messages. What the hell is going on down there?"

"I was about to ask you the same thing."

"I don't understand."

I tossed my bag onto the sofa and flopped down beside it. "How's your sister doing?" I asked, unable to keep the sarcasm out of my voice.

The pause before his reply told me a lot. "I don't know what you mean."

"Cut the crap, Danforth. I know all about Gaines and her prison sentence. Do you pop into the women's prison every once in a while to catch up with dear old Sissy?"

This time the silence went on for a long while. "I can explain."

"Oh, I'll just bet you can. Let's start with where you are."

"I'm at home. In Buckhead."

"Really? And where did you spend the day? And don't give me any bullshit about being in court. I already checked."

"Listen, I don't know what your problem is, but I won't be spoken to like that. I had an evidentiary hearing scheduled for this afternoon, but the D.A. asked for a postponement. Since I had some free time, I decided to take a ride in the country, to sort of clear my head. I turned off my cell phone so no one could find a reason to drag me back to the office."

No way to prove that, one way or the other. He could be telling the truth. Or he could be sitting right outside my house.

"You haven't answered my question about your sister. What the hell kind of game are you playing, Danforth?"

"Listen, I'm heading for Hilton Head. I just got in the car." He paused. "I should be there by around nine. We need to talk."

"Damn straight we do. In the meantime, what am I supposed to do about your uncle? Or doesn't it concern you that he's been missing from his house since this morning? Does the imposter have him?"

"I'll explain everything when I see you. Shall we meet at your office or would you prefer somewhere else?"

"You mean somewhere more public? Absolutely." I thought a moment. "Can you find a restaurant called Jump and Phil's? On the south end of the island. It'll be open."

"I'll plug it into my GPS. Let's say nine." Again his silence stretched my nerves. "I can explain everything. Uncle Malcolm is fine."

"So you say. Just so we're clear, I'm giving you until nine fifteen. If you aren't there with a damned good story, my next stop will be the sheriff's office. Got it?"

"Nine o'clock," he said and hung up.

I fiddled around in the kitchen, but nothing appealed. I ate a peach yogurt standing over the sink and followed it up with a few mouthfuls of Vanilla Fudge Brownie ice cream scooped directly from the carton. I rinsed off the spoon and stuck it in the dishwasher.

Back in the great room, I flopped on the sofa, purposefully leaving the lights untouched. As the island twilight softened the lines of the fireplace and the wing chairs that flanked it, I thought about Red. I knew my mind should be focused on my upcoming confrontation with Hub Danforth and the health and well-being of Malcolm St. John, but I just couldn't force my thoughts in that direction. Twice I picked up my cell to call Beaufort, and twice I dropped it back onto the cushions. I felt my eyelids droop and fought hard against falling asleep, exhausted though I was.

I must have dozed, however, because the chiming of the phone jerked me upright. Disoriented, I grabbed it up.

"Bay Tanner."

"Hey there, how's it going?"

Red sounded upbeat, cheerful. It pissed me off.

"Who is this?" I snarled into the phone.

"Very funny. You sound as if I woke you up."

"You did."

"Sorry about that, but it's not even eight o'clock yet. I just wanted to check in." Some of the banter left his voice. "Is everything okay?"

I pushed myself upright. "Let's see. Hub Danforth fired Sheila Mahony and turned Malcolm's care over to his sister. Well, let me amend that, because the real Clarista Gaines has been in a Georgia prison for the past six years, so I'm not really sure who's running all over the county with a man suffering from Alzheimer's disease who also happens to hold the key to property worth a few million bucks and who hasn't been seen for twenty-four hours." I took a short breath so he wouldn't have time to break in. "Oh, and my husband, who was supposed to return home today, seems to be among the missing as well. All in all, it's been a really great day. How about you?"

The silence stretched out, and I did nothing to break it. *The ball's in your court, buster*, I thought, my breath coming in short little gulps.

"I'm sorry, honey." He sounded truly contrite, and I let myself relax a little. "It was thoughtless of me to leave you hanging like that. It's just that I've been running the kids all over creation for their sports and stuff, and the day just got away from me."

Some of the anger eased in the center of my chest. "So I assume you're not coming back tonight?"

"Sarah is really feeling bad, and Mrs. Burton doesn't like to be responsible for driving the kids. It wasn't part of what we asked her to do, so . . ."

"So good old Dad to the rescue, eh?" I hadn't meant it to come out sounding quite so snarky, but it did anyway.

"I thought you understood I have responsibilities," Red snapped.

"Oh, I'm perfectly aware you have responsibilities," I fired back. "And one of them is that you have a job. I know you don't much like it, but you're part of the agency, and all hell is breaking loose around here."

I felt myself trembling on the edge of tears, something that often happens when I get really angry. It drives me crazy, and I fight it every time. But sometimes it gets beyond my ability to control.

"Are you crying? Oh hell, honey, don't do that! Can't you try to understand? I'm really stuck in the middle here."

I drew in a long breath and let it out slowly. "I know. But how long is this going to go on? I have decisions to make, and I . . ." I stumbled over the words, but I knew they were the absolute truth and had to be said. "I need you, too."

"Hang on a sec."

The words, flung so casually after what had been, to me, a major turning point in our relationship, left me gasping for air. I heard my husband yell, "I'm on the phone. I'll be right there."

Then I quietly hung up.

Jump and Phil's was relatively calm on that Tuesday night as I pulled open the door. A couple of heads at the bar swiveled in my direction, and the bartender nodded at me. I took the table in the far corner, nestled up to the fireplace, and slipped off my jacket. I settled into the chair closest to the fire and rubbed my hands to warm them. Winter was nibbling at the edges of our little paradise, and I didn't like it one bit.

I was half an hour early, thanks to Red's unintended wake-up call, and my stomach was rumbling. I ordered a steak sandwich and coleslaw, feeling virtuous for skipping the fries. There was a college football game on most of the television screens, two Mid-America teams I didn't give two damns about, but I let the action pull me away from the depressing thoughts that had threatened to overwhelm me on the drive from home.

I refused to think about my husband.

I glanced up occasionally as I devoured my meal, anxious for Hub Danforth to show himself. I hadn't formulated anything re-sembling a plan for dealing with him. I'd just let him try to explain the bizarre happenings of the past few days and go from there. I had my phone tucked into the front pocket of my jeans and Mike Raleigh's numbers programmed in. If I didn't like what the conniving criminal defense attorney had to say, I'd be on the horn to the sheriff in a heartbeat.

Maybe I should have done that anyway, I thought, not for the first time. Malcolm was out there somewhere, maybe in trouble. These hours I'd wasted might have been precious to his well-being. But something in me, some belief in my own ability to judge character perhaps, refused to see Danforth as a murderer. The imposter, on the other hand—

The door swung open, and I jerked my head up. Hub Danforth, in black jeans and white turtleneck sweater, headed straight for my table. He draped his leather bomber jacket over the back of the chair opposite me, and sat down.

"Sorry I'm late," he said, and I glanced at my watch. *9:02.*

The waitress approached, and he ordered a Fat Tire. I waited until it had been delivered.

"Where's Malcolm?" I asked in as calm a voice as I could muster. "Is he all right?"

"He's fine."

"How do you know?"

I'd stopped at the bungalow on my way down island and found the place as dark and deserted as when I'd left it earlier in the day.

He took a long swallow of the draft beer and rested his elbows on the table.

"I talked to Sis—I talked to the woman who's looking after him." He held up his hand before I could interrupt. "And I talked to Uncle Malcolm, too. He was confused, but he sounded fine."

I hoped he could read the contempt on my face. "Right. Where are they?"

His eyes shifted away from mine, to the television in the corner.

"Where are they, Danforth?" I wiggled my phone out of my pocket. "I have the sheriff's office on speed dial."

"Wait! I don't know for certain. She said they were staying with friends of hers, nearby. Maybe even on the island." He squeezed the glass so tightly I thought it might shatter. "I can't tell you what I don't know."

"What in the hell kind of game are you two playing? This is

kidnapping, you know. You're looking at never seeing the outside of a jail cell for the rest of your life."

"It's not what you think."

"Then tell me what it is. Because from where I'm sitting, it looks like an elaborate scheme to defraud Mr. St. John out of his property. What was the plan? Was this woman supposed to impersonate your sister and get him to sign off on the deed?"

I could tell that at least part of my supposition had hit home. Danforth emptied his glass and banged it down on the table.

"You don't understand."

"Damn right I don't! You've got thirty seconds to start making some sense of this mess, or I'm calling the cops."

I could see the waitress approaching to check on a refill for Danforth, but I waved her away. My eyes bored into his face from across the table, and for a long time he refused to meet my stare. When he finally lifted his gaze to mine, I read fear rather than malice, pain instead of defiance.

He spoke so low it was difficult to make out the words.

"Maybe you'd better do just that."

CHAPTER THIRTY-FIVE

Erik and Red would both undoubtedly have chewed me out six ways from Sunday, but I let Hub Danforth follow me back to the house.

I couldn't help it. I believed him.

I fiddled with Red's new coffeemaker, selecting one of the little tubs at random, and nuked myself a cup of tea. I carried them into the great room where Hub had settled himself on one end of the sofa. He nodded his thanks when I handed him the mug, shaking his head at my offer of milk or sugar. I set my tea on the table next to the wing chair across the room and took a few moments to draw the drapes.

I'd also taken the opportunity while I worked in the kitchen to slip the Seecamp from my bag to my pocket. I'm not a complete idiot.

"Let's have the whole story. Start at the beginning."

Danforth sighed and stalled by blowing across the rim of his mug and taking a tentative sip of coffee.

"I'm in trouble," he said softly, his gaze fastened on the carpet under his feet. "Financially."

"I guessed as much. Go on."

"You don't need to know the details. Bad investments, bad luck, whatever. Let's just say I'm a couple of months away from losing everything. "

"And your uncle's property would solve all your problems."

"It's not like that!" He glared at me for a moment before he ran out of steam. We both knew I'd spoken the truth. "There would have been plenty left over for Uncle Malcolm to live comfortably in a nice facility for the rest of his life. I don't think you realize just how valuable that old shack is."

"Worth a man's life?" I asked softly.

"Jesus, woman, will you listen? No one was supposed to get hurt!"

I sighed. "It's funny how often I hear that in my business. It should sound pretty familiar to you, too. Isn't that the same song you get from a lot of your clients?"

He didn't answer. We sat in silence for several moments, the wind rattling through the palmettoes the only sound to penetrate the closed French doors and drapes.

"So you used me to try to get your uncle declared incompetent. Then you brought in a ringer for your sister to help move things along. What was her role? Was she supposed to be another voice to condemn the old man so you could stick him in a home and steal his property?"

"It's my property, too, damn it! Sissy and I have a legitimate claim. What good is it doing him? Answer me that. I told you before that he could burn the damn shack down around his ears one of these days and himself along with it. You verified that yourself, right? He belongs somewhere he can be taken care of."

I waited a moment for his anger to dissipate. I could tell he was having a hard time maintaining his pose as the caring nephew. He wasn't convincing me. He probably hadn't been able to convince himself.

"You still haven't told me anything I don't already know. Who attacked your uncle? How is your ex-wife involved? Who murdered—?"

"I didn't have anything to do with that! You have to believe me!"

"No, actually, I don't. And neither will the sheriff. You'd better start explaining the whole damn thing, Danforth, and fast. So far all you've done is dig yourself a deeper hole."

I watched his fists clench on his knees, and I suppose I should have been afraid. I wasn't. It might have had something to do with the pistol tucked into my jeans, with the panic button for the alarm system resting on the table beside me. But it was more than that. And maybe it was foolish of me to stake my life on my ability to read a man's eyes. God knew I'd been wrong before. But I wasn't wrong about Hub Danforth. He might have been venal and self-serving, but he wasn't violent. I just knew it.

"It all started with Cyn. Cynthia Merrill, my ex-wife. She called me up a couple of weeks ago, asking if Uncle Malcolm might be persuaded to sell his place. She'd gotten herself into a bind with her company, needed beachfront property fast. It was funny, because I'd been thinking myself about how that might be the solution to my own problems. We talked for a long time, and I told her I'd look into it." He paused for a breath. "The numbers she threw at me were astounding. I had no idea the place was worth that much."

I itched to move him along, but I figured it would be best, now that the floodgates seemed to have opened, to let his story unfold at its own pace.

He sipped more coffee. "I knew about his condition, of course. I told Cyn it would be difficult to get him to sign without a competency hearing, and she suggested I hire someone—an impartial observer—to bolster the case against him. That's why I came to you." He smiled then, a pitiful attempt, and shook his head. "You came highly recommended. I probably should have looked for some firm that didn't have an A-plus reputation. You've surprised me in a number of ways."

Saying thank you seemed out of place, so I let the fulsome compliment go.

"What changed your plans?" I asked, leaning forward a little in my chair. "How did it all get so screwed up?"

"Weezie Lewis."

It took me a moment. "The woman who has Malcolm?"

Hub Danforth nodded, once.

"What does she have to do with the whole thing?"

"It's a long story."

"I don't have any trains to catch. You want some more coffee?"

"No, thanks." He breathed out heavily. "Okay. Louise Lewis, known as Weezie, was a client. I hadn't been able to get her off, but I did manage to win her a reduced sentence. She was a druggie, mostly a user, not a pusher, but she'd been in trouble since she was a kid. When Sissy got sent away, I remembered that Weezie was in the same facility." He sighed again. "I thought it might help my sister, to have someone who knew the ropes, you know?" His laugh held no humor. "Bad move, as it turns out."

I thought I had the connection then. Hub had talked to his sister about the land thing, she'd shared it all with her new best friend, now undoubtedly on the outside, and Weezie had sniffed a golden opportunity to cut herself in on the action.

In a few brief sentences, Hub confirmed my supposition.

"But why didn't you blow the whistle on her the moment you found out she was impersonating your sister? You never batted an eye when I told you I'd met her."

"She'd already told me about attacking Uncle Malcolm by then. She said she'd swear I'd put her up to it, that it had all been part of my plan to steal the property."

"But why would she do that? You needed the old man alive, didn't you?"

"Absolutely. Waiting for everything to clear probate would have been my ruin. Even if Uncle Malcolm had a will, who knows who he's left everything to? It could be some charity or church or even his next-door neighbor. I could never get him to talk seriously about his own death, even when he was mostly in his right mind. There was no way I wanted to take a chance on that. No, I needed to be appointed his guardian. Then it would all have been so easy. Cyn stood ready to buy the land the second I had title. And Uncle Malcolm would have been taken care of for the rest of his life. I swear it."

The pain I saw in his eyes convinced me of his sincerity, even if his scheme had ultimately been for his own benefit.

"So who killed your ex-wife?"

"I don't know! As God is my witness, I don't know!"

"If you had to lay money on it?"

For the first time, he looked directly into my eyes. "Weezie," he said softly and burst into tears.

It took two more cups of coffee and another hour for everything to fall into place, but I finally felt as if I understood most of what had happened. Hub Danforth slumped in the corner of the sofa while I put in a call to Mike Raleigh. I knew he wouldn't be on duty at well past midnight, but I hoped the dispatcher would forward my message with enough details to roust him out of his warm bed on a blustery autumn night. I gave serious thought to just calling out the cavalry, reporting the old man's abduction, and getting the entire sheriff's office scouring the island for him. But that had its own risks, not the least of which was Weezie Lewis's apparent lack of concern for anyone's health and welfare except her own. No, I argued with myself, it was better to come up with some way to get her to reveal their whereabouts. I trusted Mike

Raleigh to see it my way, to work with us. I hoped my belief in him didn't turn out to be misplaced.

One of the many things I marveled at while Hub and I sat silently in the soft glow of the lamps in my great room was his unwavering faith in his sister Clarista. He had to know that she'd been the instigator of this nightmare, even though she was orchestrating everything from a woman's prison in upstate Georgia. She hadn't believed he'd take care of her, had enlisted her old jailhouse crony to run interference for her on the outside, and had, perhaps unintentionally, unleashed all the misery that had followed. Whether she had suggested the encounter that had led to Cynthia Merrill's death or whether her cohort had acted on her own didn't really matter at that point. And while Hub had been adamant in his assertions that he fully intended to hold his sister's share until she came out of prison, Sissy had apparently not trusted him as far as she could pitch a piano.

As we waited for Mike Raleigh to call or show up, I wondered if she'd planned all along to cut her brother out of the whole deal. Maybe that was what had sent Weezie Lewis to her confrontation with Hub's ex-wife. Clubbing people over the head seemed to be her reaction to any attempt to thwart their plans, so it wasn't a big stretch to see her as Malcolm's attacker and the agent of Cynthia's death. Murder might not have been her intention in either case, but we wouldn't know that until we had her.

And that was priority number one. We needed to find them. Fast.

It was nearly one when Mike Raleigh rang the front doorbell and well past two when he'd heard Danforth's full story. Somewhere after my umpteenth cup of Earl Grey I'd gotten my second wind, and I could feel the electricity dancing along my nerve endings.

"So now what?" I asked from my post next to the French doors.

I don't know how many times I'd twitched aside the drapes to stare out into the darkness that lay around the house. The wind had dropped, and the stillness was complete. I wondered what the place must look like to any passing ships. Lit up like a Christmas tree, it could have seemed like a tiny beacon in an otherwise endless sea of black.

240 KATHRYN R. WALL

I turned to face the men, neither of whom had offered an answer to my question.

"Mike? What's our next move? We can't just leave Malcolm—"

"Slow down, Bay." He spoke from his post in the wing chair opposite the one I'd been occupying, the ever-present notebook resting on one knee. "We need to think this through."

I could feel myself bouncing on my toes, a surge of energy coursing through my body. "What's to think about? We have to find him. This Weezie person has already hurt him once. And you know as well as I do that she probably killed Cynthia Merrill. Are we just going to hang around here talking about it all night, or are we going to get our asses in gear and find him? Jesus, Mike, I didn't call you so we could *talk* ourselves to death!"

To his credit, Detective Raleigh didn't fire back. He regarded me thoughtfully for a moment before saying, "I understand your impatience. But let's look at the facts. First, we don't know where he is."

"But—"

He held up a hand to forestall my interruption. "Second, even if we did, we can't just swoop in and start something. If this woman is as dangerous as you believe, we'd put the old man right in the middle of things. He could get hurt. Is that what you want?"

"Of course not! But how do we know she isn't hurting him right now? She wants him to sign his rights away. It seems to me she's proved she isn't squeamish about how she goes about getting what she wants."

"Hold up a minute, Bay. The detective is right." Danforth spoke for the first time since he'd answered the last of Raleigh's questions. "And Weezie doesn't have any papers for Malcolm to sign. It's true I drew up something that would make me his power of attorney, but she doesn't have access to that."

"So what do you think she wants, then? Could she be holding him for ransom?"

Mike Raleigh answered for Hub. "What would be the point? She knows Danforth here is in financial difficulties, and his sister is in jail. Who does she think is going to pay?"

They both studied me, waiting for my reaction, and I could feel the moment we all hit on the same answer. Into the silence, I dropped the only name that made sense.

"Me."

CHAPTER
THIRTY-SIX

I woke up around seven thirty, disoriented and feeling as if I'd been run over by a bus. After the men had left, around three in the morning, I'd dropped, fully clothed, onto the sofa in the great room.

I forced myself up into a sitting position, working my neck around on my shoulders to get the kinks out. I stretched, my cramped muscles protesting the abuse I'd just subjected them to, and tried to clear my head.

Through a slit in the drapes, bright sunshine rippled across the carpet, and a few dust motes danced in the air. I plodded to the French doors and flung them open. Immediately, raucous birdsong attacked my aching head, and from the beach I could hear a few faint shouts and the answering yelps from dogs enjoying their morning romp.

I blinked against the brightness and shivered a little in the chill wind off the ocean. It was enough to bring me fully awake and once again back to the horrible images I'd done my best to banish during the short night of restless sleep. I closed the doors and made for my bathroom, peeling sticky clothes off as I went.

"'Sufficient unto the day is the evil thereof,'" I muttered to myself as I stuffed my discarded things into the hamper. "Saint Matthew. Two points. Amen," I added as I stepped under the pounding spray.

The shower felt like a gift from the gods.

Refreshed and dressed in clean slacks and sweater, I forced myself to wolf an English muffin and peanut butter. I took a slug of orange juice right out of the carton to wash it down, and ten minutes later I was pulling into the parking lot in front of the office.

I let myself in and powered up my computer. For the next half hour, I entered everything I could remember from the events of the previous night, including as much verbatim dialogue as I could pull out of my fuzzy head. I'd never rival Nero Wolfe's sidekick, Archie Goodwin, but I did the best I could. Halfway through, I took a break to crack open a Diet Coke and down three aspirin. By the time I heard Erik's key in the lock, I had pretty much recorded every important detail along with my own speculations. I added the plan, reluctantly and tentatively agreed to by Mike Raleigh, that Hub Danforth and I had worked out. Although we might never put it into action, I thought it was important to have some record of it.

In case things went wrong.

"Aren't you the early bird," my partner said. He must have read something on my face then, because his next words came out in a rush. "What happened?"

I almost didn't know where to start. And, truth to tell, I didn't feel like hashing it all over again. "I just wrote it all up. You should be able to access it from Danforth's file, right?"

"Right. But why can't—?"

I cut him off. "Just read it okay?" I saw Stephanie standing behind her fiancé. "Both of you. Then we'll talk."

I leaned back in my chair and closed my eyes, effectively forestalling any further discussion. When they popped back open, I glanced quickly at my watch, relieved to find I'd only been out for about fifteen minutes. I chugged down the now-flat Coke and rubbed my hands over my face a moment before the tentative knock on my partially closed door.

I blinked a few times. "Come on in," I said, squaring my shoulders for the battle I knew would be forthcoming.

And they didn't disappoint me. Stunned by everything that had gone on while they'd been tucked up in bed, Erik railed at me for shutting him out. I apologized, genuinely, but insisted that things had happened too fast. Perhaps not entirely true, but close e-nough. Stephanie was appalled that we had not mounted a countywide search for Malcolm St. John the moment Hub Danforth had revealed his part in the deception. I did my best to reassure both of them that Mike Raleigh knew what we had in mind and that he believed our plan had a good chance of success.

"But what if Danforth doesn't—or can't—hold up his end of the deal?" Erik leaned forward, his elbows resting on his knees. "A lot of this depends on him holding onto his nerve. Are you sure he's up for it?"

I shrugged. "He swears he can pull it off. I guess we just have to trust him."

"Well, I don't!" Stephanie was displaying as much emotion as I'd ever seen from her. "I told you right from the start that there was something . . . just not right about him. You only have his word for it that he hasn't been in on the whole thing from the beginning!"

"You're right. And all I can say is that I believe him when he says he wasn't. You didn't see the way he broke down when he talked about his ex-wife's death. I don't think a person can successfully fake that."

"What does Red think?"

I'd been waiting for Erik to ask the question almost from the first moment of our discussion, so I was prepared.

"He's still in Beaufort. And he has enough on his plate right now, so I made the decision not to involve him." I stared straight at my partner. "It was my call, and I made it. I hope you can live with that."

I watched him struggle to keep from firing back at me. I would have deserved it, I supposed, but I was eternally grateful when Erik simply said, "Understood."

"So now what?" Stephanie's voice had dropped a couple of levels.

"Now we wait. As you said, it's all up to Hub. If he can convince the Lewis woman to deal directly with me, I'll make sure she leads me to Malcolm."

"Why would she do that?"

"Come on, Erik, you've watched enough crime stuff on TV. I'll have to make a drop with the money, and she'll have to come and get it. She may have some street smarts, but she's not the sharpest knife in the drawer. She's pretty much made a hash of this whole thing, and I think she knows it. Her only hope now is to grab some cash and get the hell out of Dodge."

"So you think she'll just take the money and run?"

"I do. Don't forget she's probably got a murder charge hang-

ing over her head. Not to mention the attack on Malcolm. But if
Hub can't find out where she's holding him, then following her
back there is our best chance. Erik, you'll be able to wire me up
somehow, right?"

While Mike Raleigh had offered the tech services of the
sheriff's office, I had more faith in my partner when it came to
gadgetry.

I watched some of the gloom lift from his face.

"I'll need equipment. Are we buying it, or are we going to use
theirs?"

"Your call. But it needs to happen fast. Hub is supposed to
contact Lewis . . ." I glanced down at my watch. ". . . in about half
an hour. He wants her to think he's calling from Atlanta, and he'll
spin some yarn about stepping out of the courtroom."

"You mean we only have half an hour?" He rose from his
chair as he spoke, and I waved him back down.

"No, no. He's going to tell her that he wants in on the game,
that they'll split the money or he'll turn her in. And she'll think he
has to drive down from Atlanta. Either she'll wait for him to make
the move on me, or she'll crank up her timetable. No matter
which route she goes, I'm going to try to stall her off until tonight.
I have no idea how much she's going to ask me for, but she'll have
to believe that I'll need time to get it together. As far as she
knows, this is coming straight out of the blue, and I'll have to
convince her that I'm hearing the whole scheme for the first time.
If she won't tell Hub straight out where she is, then Plan B is for
the sheriff's guys to follow once I make the payoff."

"It sounds like something out of a movie," Stephanie said
softly.

I laughed, but with a decided lack of humor. "I know. I've
seen this scenario a dozen times on *Law and Order* reruns." I
leaned back in my chair and passed a hand over my eyes. "Most of
the time it works."

"And some of the time it doesn't," she said, even more faint-
ly.

I had no comeback for that.

CHAPTER
THIRTY-SEVEN

The next hour seemed to last a lifetime.

When the call finally came, I had to swallow hard before I picked up.

"Hub? How did it go?"

He sounded more than tired. His voice seemed to have aged at least a decade since the night before.

"She won't tell me where she's holding Uncle Malcolm, but she's agreed to let me in. I told her I have the best chance of convincing you to come up with the money. I sort of improvised because at first she didn't want me anywhere near her scheme. But I told her you had no vested interest in Malcolm, even if you did give her the impression that you cared about him. I said that I'd tell you I couldn't get the ransom together, and I'd ask you for help."

He paused then, and I had a feeling he didn't want to tell me what came next.

"Go on," I urged him.

"Well, I said that you and I sort of had a . . . thing going, and—"

"A *thing?* What the hell does that mean?"

"You know exactly what it means! You can't have been unaware that I find you a very attractive woman, and Weezie had already picked up on it. She made some crack about it." He swallowed. "But none of that matters. I said I had the best chance of getting you to 'loan' me the money, and she bought it. She's waiting for me to drive down from Atlanta before she makes the demand. At least that's what she said."

I lifted my head at the ringing of the phone on Stephanie's desk. I held my breath and craned my neck around so that I could see her out in the reception area. A moment later she shook her head, and I relaxed back into my chair.

"Bay? Is that her?"

"No," I said, my heart slowing back to its normal rhythm. "Did you get to talk to Malcolm?"

"Yes, I insisted. He was rambling about the old days again, the poor old man. He asked me if I'd talked to Miss Lily lately and if I knew when she was coming to see him again."

I spoke around the lump that had risen in my throat. "But otherwise he sounded okay?"

"Yes. I asked him where he was, and he just said that it was a dump, and he didn't like the food."

"No hint of where it might be? Did you hear any noise in the background? Traffic or anything like that?"

"Nothing. There was a television or radio going, but it was too muted to make out any specifics." He hesitated. "He did say the place stunk. I wonder if it might be fish. Maybe she's holed up by the water."

"Could be, but it's not much help. There are about a million places around here, not to mention up and down the coast, where you could smell dead fish, if that's what it was." I paused. "What did he say, exactly?"

It took Danforth a moment. "I think he said, 'It smells like something Ol' Blue dug out of a burrow.' I thought he was probably talking about a dog dragging in some sort of animal it had killed. It probably has to do with that hunt club he worked at when he was a boy."

I couldn't make any better sense out of it than Danforth had. Yet, it seemed an odd thing for the old man to say. Did he have enough of his senses left to try and drop a clue? I wouldn't have thought so, but then there was so much I didn't understand about the effects of Alzheimer's on the human brain. I'd witnessed his moments of lucidity before, and they seemed to come out of nowhere. I wrote the strange sentence down on my desk pad to ponder on later.

"So have you spoken to Detective Raleigh?" I asked.

"Before I called you. He said to tell you that your partner is down there right now getting checked out on the equipment, and that you're to call him the minute you hear from Weezie."

"Understood. Why don't you come on over here to the office? That way we can both be on hand if she calls."

"*If?* Why would you think she won't?"

"Because this isn't a movie or a TV show. Because people, especially criminals, usually screw things up, one way or another." I sighed. "And because . . ." I found I couldn't put my worst fears into words. "Just get over here, okay? We'll just have to play the cards we're dealt and hope for the best."

Hub Danforth didn't answer, mostly because there wasn't anything to say.

By one o'clock it looked as if we'd decided to throw a party in the reception area of the office, except that the mood was decidedly somber. Stephanie had made a lunch run to Subway, and the detritus of our various sandwiches and drinks still littered every available surface. None of us had had the energy to clean up.

Erik and I had been over the details of the wire I would be wearing, a tiny thing that would have taken a full body frisk to locate. I didn't think Weezie Lewis was ready for that, but we'd managed to hide it as best we could. I left the paraphernalia on so I could get used to it. During a brief phone conversation, Mike Raleigh had regaled me with his efforts to convince the sheriff to let him run the operation alone, with half a dozen deputies on call to back us up if we managed to make contact. It was still under discussion. I'd been on the line to my banker, arranging for an un-specified amount of cash to be made available to me at a mo-ment's notice, although I had no idea how much she'd ask for. Stephanie had purchased a duffel bag at Walmart on her way back from picking up lunch, just in case I needed one.

And so we waited. I took the rest of my bag of chips with me and retreated into my office. I sipped from my cardboard cup of iced tea and found myself studying on Malcolm St. John's strange words, the ones I'd jotted on the desk pad. On impulse, I re-trieved my briefcase from the floor and pulled out the book I'd bought at the Coastal Discovery Museum. I opened it to the page with the picture of the boy Malcolm standing next to the horse that dwarfed him. Miss Lily Armstrong smiled demurely at the camera, and in the background I could make out what must have been the main house that now housed the museum.

Idly, I flipped back a few pages and began reading at random, my eyes darting to my watch every few minutes. What the hell was taking the damned woman so long? Hub had called her to say he was almost to the island, but she hadn't answered. There was no voice mail—probably a prepaid cell, I guessed—so he'd just kept trying every fifteen minutes. So far, no luck. The longer we were out of communication with Lewis, the more worried I became. What if she'd just decided to cut her losses and run? Maybe she didn't trust Danforth any more than his sister did. What would she do with Malcolm if she decided to bolt? If she just left him, would we be able to locate him? There didn't seem to be any up side for her to kill him. The poor old thing probably wouldn't remember anything about her that would prove helpful to law enforcement.

The more I thought about that scenario, the better I liked it. Malcolm on his own might find a way out and make himself known. Even if he just wandered around, surely someone would come across him. I found myself hoping that Lewis had gotten spooked and just taken off. Maybe the longer we waited for a call, the better it would be for Malcolm.

I found myself reading the same sentence over and over and jerked myself back to the page spread open in front of me. I flipped to the next photo and stopped in amazement. An older black man stood in an open field, a pack of dogs spread out around him. Some sat at his feet, while a couple of others seemed caught by the scent of something on the air, their noses raised, ears high and alert. But it was the caption that sent me flying out of my chair:

"Sammy Reeves and his pack of hunters, including the legendary Old Blue, at Otter Hole near Honey Horn Plantation."

I suddenly understood Malcolm St. John's bizarre message.

And I was pretty damned sure I knew where he was.

CHAPTER
THIRTY-EIGHT

It took some convincing, but Hub Danforth eventually saw things my way. Erik couldn't have been more thrilled that he was finally in the middle of the action.

"She knows me by sight, and she's seen the Jag," I said as we hustled around getting organized. "It's probably one of the things that led her to believe I was an easy touch for the ransom money." I'd slipped into the restroom to remove the wire. "And she sure as hell seems to be avoiding you. She won't recognize either Erik or the SUV."

"I still think this is something that might be better left to the sheriff," the attorney said, running a hand through his close-cropped hair.

"You don't think someone who's been in trouble with the law most of her life won't recognize an unmarked cop car the minute she sees one?" I looked away from both of them before adding, "Besides, I'm going along."

I could hear Erik's sharp intake of breath.

"Look, I could be completely wrong about Malcolm's message. If we don't find anything, then no harm, no foul. If we do . . ." I patted the right pocket of my slacks where the Seecamp nestled almost invisibly.

"I don't like the idea of you waving a gun around. That's how things go wrong. I'll try talking my way in first, and if that doesn't work, we step back and let the pros handle it. Agreed?"

He said it so earnestly I almost thought he expected me to cross my heart.

"Agreed." I turned to Hub Danforth. "Try her one more time."

He pulled out his cell and punched in the number from memory. We all stared at the phone pressed against his ear. Finally, he shook his head.

"Nothing."

"Okay then. Erik, you all set? You know what her car looks like?"

"A rusted-out Taurus, right?"

"Right. I'll stay hunkered down in the back seat unless you need me. And if things get hairy, I can call for backup." I grabbed my bag, comforted by the heft of the Seecamp. Just in case things got *really* hairy. "Let's go."

I had one foot out the door when the phone rang. I froze almost in midstride.

Stephanie lunged for the desk. "Simpson and Tanner, Inquiry Agents," she gulped out, her hand shaking more than a little. "Oh, hey, Red." She darted a glance at me, and I shook my head. "She's, uh, sort of tied up right now. Do you want her to call you back?"

I watched her face for some sign of trouble, but she nodded once, said, "Okay," and hung up.

"What?"

"He said he might be a couple more days, and he wanted to see if you could come over for dinner tonight. He'll catch up with you later."

"How thoughtful of him," I said and bolted out the door.

Otter Hole Road slides into Pembroke Drive right at the back entrance to Walmart. I knew there was a small business park, but in all my years on the island I'd never driven back there. Even in the glare of a bright, cloudless autumn afternoon it looked sad, a short stretch of pavement lined with trailers and doublewides that had mostly seen better days.

From my perch on the floor of the back seat, my head raised only far enough for me to see out the wide window, I watched the sagging homes creep by as Erik drove at a snail's pace toward the obvious dead end just ahead of us.

"I don't see it," he said, his head swiveling from side to side once we were past the short row of commercial buildings.

"She might have pulled it around back."

I strained for a glimpse of the old beater Weezie Lewis had undoubtedly used to transport Malcolm St. John, but I, too, was coming up empty. The adrenaline of decoding the old man's strange message was fading, and I could feel a knot of fear and frustration growing in the center of my chest.

"Damn it!"

I shifted my weight as Erik backed around at the end of the road and began the slow passage back the way we had come. I had just about decided to have him stop and let me jump in the front seat when his voice sent me scurrying back under cover.

"Here she comes!"

"Are you sure?"

"It has to be the car. It's just like you said. One woman driving. No one else I can see. What do you want me to do?"

"Keep going." I crawled up onto the back seat. Keeping my head as low as I could, I stared out the back window. "It's her. She's turning into one of the drives." I whirled toward Erik. "Pull up in front of those businesses. Park facing out."

I swayed as the big SUV made the turn, my attention back on the rusted-out Taurus. Weezie Lewis eased around to the side of one of the trailers, hiding as much of the car as she could between an old pickup raised up on blocks and a cluster of shrubbery gone wild. A moment later I watched her heft a Wendy's bag and an old, battered backpack and head toward the rear of the house.

The second she disappeared I was out the door. "Come on!"

"Wait!"

I whirled at my partner's voice. "What?"

"The plan is that I just walk up to the door and knock. I'm selling insurance, I'm lost, whatever. Remember?"

"That was before I knew what this road really looks like. We can head down through some back yards and take her by surprise. She'll never see us coming."

"No! We're not going to charge in there. You wait here."

Before I could open my mouth, he'd stepped out into the street and was striding away from me.

"Damn, damn, damn!" I muttered to myself. I crawled back into the SUV, pretty sure I'd have a better view of things from its height.

I watched Erik take a quick look around before he mounted the two rickety wooden steps. Both the screen door and the interior one were closed, and he rapped on the outside one first. When he got no response, he pulled open the flaking metal door to a loud screech. I could hear the echoes of his knock in the quiet of the dead-end street. Still nothing. Without thinking about it, I pulled the Seecamp out of my pocket and set it beside me on the seat.

The sounds of another series of raps floated to me, and I swiped at a rivulet of sweat running down the side of my face. I fidgeted as Erik stood, unsure now what to do, before he finally turned and made his way down the steps. I shoved the pistol back into my slacks.

"I can hear someone in there," he said a moment later as he slid into the driver's seat.

"Real voices or just the TV?"

"The TV for sure, but I could also make out someone moving around. I can't tell if she's in there alone or not. The blinds were closed."

I detected a slight tremble in the hand that reached to wipe his own sheen of sweat from his forehead.

"Now what?" he asked in a low voice.

"Help you?"

The booming voice next to my right ear sent a stab of fear through me like a jolt of electricity. I clamped my hand around the gun just as Erik lowered my window.

"You folks lookin' for someone?"

He was tall, rail thin, and looked to be about sixty. His once brown hair was streaked with gray, as was the stubble on his chin. But his blue polo shirt and shabby jeans looked clean, and his smile let me relax a little, although I maintained my grip on the Seecamp.

"Hey," I said, stalling while I scrambled for what would make Mr. Helpful go away. "We're, uh, looking for a friend of ours. We heard he was staying with his niece over this way, but we aren't sure which house."

"Well, that there place you was callin' on b'longs to Bobby Turner. He ain't to home, but his sister's using his place. He tol' me 'bout it 'fore he left. Said it was okay if'n she was there." He paused and favored me with another wide smile. "We sort of look out for one another down here."

"That's wonderful," I said, "to have such caring neighbors. Is Bobby's sister there alone, or maybe she has an older man with her? That would be her uncle."

I could see the denial forming on his lips before I'd even finished the question.

"No, ma'am, ain't nobody there but her, far as I can tell. Course, she come late last night, so I'm not rightly sure she's by herself."

"Okay, well, we must be mistaken. Thanks so much for your help."

I grabbed the shoulder harness and made a production of fastening it around me, hoping our informant would take the hint. He didn't.

"I b'lieve she's there. Leastways, that's her car. Maybe she didn't hear you knock."

I knew the next offer would be for him to *mosey* on over and check it out himself, so I gave Erik a pointed look. He took the hint and cranked up the car.

"Thanks so much for your help," I repeated. "We'll just check back later."

Erik didn't run over the old man's feet in an effort to make our escape, but it was a near thing.

"Where to?" my partner asked as I checked the sideview mirror to see Mr. Neighborhood Watch following our progress down the road. His image finally faded when we turned onto Pembroke Drive.

"Pull into Walmart."

Erik complied and swung into a parking space with empty ones on both sides. He shoved the gearshift into Park and turned to face me.

"You're not going back there," he said, and I smiled.

"You know me too well."

"I'm serious, Bay. With that old coot standing guard, you won't be able to take a step without him noticing. I say we call Mike Raleigh. We know Lewis is in there. If Malcolm's not, then . . ."

"I know, Erik. You're absolutely right. But you have to believe we've spooked her now. I want to make sure she doesn't shove the old man in the car and take off." I swallowed hard. "Or something worse. Come on. Let's get back over there. I'll call Mike on the way."

The Expedition was already moving before I'd finished my spiel. In a few seconds we were at the back entrance, once again facing Otter Hole Road. As Erik eased across Pembroke, I strained to see down to the trailer where I knew in my gut I'd finally find Malcolm St. John.

"I don't like this," Erik said, slowing to such a crawl that I could have walked faster.

"Okay, I get that. But our Mr. Helpful isn't anywhere in sight. Stop and let me out." Before he could argue, I had my fingers wrapped around the door handle. "And you call Mike. I'm just going to make sure she doesn't make a run for it."

I grabbed my cell and flicked off the shoulder harness. The huge Expedition was actually still moving when I slipped out onto the pavement.

"Stay here. And call Mike!"

I raced down the short stretch of blacktop and tucked myself up against the side of the trailer where Weezie Lewis had parked her old car. Just as Erik had said, I could hear muffled voices inside. I glanced back up the street where the Expedition sat idling, hoping that Mike Raleigh and his deputies were even then scrambling into their cruisers.

Suddenly, I heard a high-pitched screech from inside the house. I didn't wait to find out if it had come from the TV. In two seconds I was out and up the steps of the sagging trailer. I wrenched open the screen door and pounded with my fist on the flimsy wooden one.

"Malcolm! Mr. St. John! Are you in there?"

Nothing. I banged harder.

"Malcolm? It's Miss Lily. It's okay to open the door. I've come to take you home."

I raised my head at the distant sound of sirens. Help would be here soon. I shook the knob, hard, and the old door rattled in its frame. I kicked it once, just to be sure, then jumped off the narrow porch and raced around to the back. That door was locked as well, and the windows were too high up for me to see into.

"Malcolm!" I shouted again, kicking at the door, just as I had out front, when it suddenly flew open.

The impact knocked me backward off the short stoop, and I landed on my butt on the hard-packed dirt. Weezie Lewis was on me before I could react, but she wasn't interested in a protracted battle. The first kick landed squarely on my chest and drove every ounce of breath from my body. The shock of it immobilized me, and I fell onto my back. But I could see that the next one was aimed at my head. I tried a feeble roll, my lungs bursting for lack of air, but it was enough that she caught me in my bad shoulder instead. If I'd had breath, I would have screamed in agony, but all I could muster was a pitiful whimper. My arms refused to obey commands as she took aim again at my forehead.

The nearness of the sirens probably saved me from a concussion—or worse. Her head whipped around, and she turned and bolted. Through a fog of pain I saw her disappear around the side of the trailer, and a moment later I heard the old Ford wheeze to life. I had one brief glimpse of the car wheeling out into the road before the haze descended.

I didn't actually pass out, at least I don't think so. But I had no concept of how much time had passed before I blinked up into the face of Mike Raleigh.

"Bay? Can you hear me?"

I tried to sit up, and the pain in my shoulder made me gasp.

"She's . . ." I began, but I couldn't seem to get the words to form in my head, let alone make it out of my mouth. "Malcolm . . ."

"I know. She got past Erik, but we're on it. Lie still, now. Paramedics are on the way."

"Malcolm," I managed again. I squirmed to sit up, and this time Mike Raleigh supported me. "Did you find him?"

I heard a jangling noise and wondered if it was coming from inside my head.

"Hold on." He whipped his phone from its holder on his belt and grunted a couple of times in response to whatever he was hearing. "Good. Good work." He returned the cell and grinned up at me. "We got her."

"Already?"

He shrugged. "One good thing about policing this island is that there's only one way off. We blocked the intersection at Moss Creek. She didn't have a chance." He half-smiled. "She didn't put up much of a fight, either. A good outcome all the way around."

I felt a lot of the fuzziness pass as I managed to sit up completely. "He wasn't with her?"

The smile faded. "No. You think he's in here?"

"I sure as hell hope so," I said.

CHAPTER
THIRTY-NINE

He was unconscious, but alive. Barely.

Over the next few days, I beat myself to a pulp with what-ifs and might-have-beens. No one, not even Red, who graced us with his presence for a quick debriefing, could convince me that nothing I did—or *didn't* do—would have changed the outcome.

I spent a lot of time at the hospital, just sitting beside the old man, the book from the museum often open on my lap. At first, the nursing staff gave me a little grief because I wasn't a relative, but eventually they relented. After all, Malcolm St. John's only living family were in jail: Sissy for at least another few years once her part in Weezie Lewis's scheme got unraveled, and Hub Danforth until his trial date or until he could manage to make bail. I'd offered to put it up, but Hub had refused. I thought he probably felt he deserved to be punished for his sins, and I admired him for it. How far the county solicitor wanted to take the charges of attempted fraud, collusion, and who knew what else remained to be seen. I couldn't help hoping they went a little easy on Hub, although I seemed to be a cheering section of one.

I eased my shoulder around, wincing a little with the residual pain, but the worst of it was behind me. The bruise in the center of my chest had begun to yellow and had stopped resembling the bottom of Weezie Lewis's size eight shoe.

Malcolm St. John stirred every once in a while, mumbling, mostly incoherently. The second blow to his head, probably meant to silence him while Lewis made her getaway, had only compounded the complications of his previous injury and his already diminished mental faculties. He'd had a couple of other visitors, including Sheila Mahony and the kind woman who drove him on his errands once a week. And Marshall Miller, who flew down just to check in on his friend. All of them offered to spell me, but I was adamant. I felt responsible for the old man in some gut way I couldn't explain, and I was more than content to let the hours slide by as I watched the gentle rise and fall of his sunken chest.

It was on the fourth day of his hospitalization that Malcolm finally opened his eyes. I'd been reading about the old hunt club days, of visits to the undeveloped island by heads of state and other dignitaries, including some of the wealthiest and most powerful men in the nation. I wondered what it must have been like back then when the only access was by ferry boat, and wild game flourished where mansions and developments and businesses now stood. I remember I had closed my eyes, envisioning Jarvis and Broad Creeks teeming with fish; deer and wild boar roaming the old-growth forest; hundreds of waterfowl rising in unison against a cloudless sky. And not a square inch of concrete to be seen in any direction. Malcolm's voice jerked me awake.

"Miss Lily?" he said, so softly I almost missed it.

"Yes, Little Mal. I'm here." His hand moved restlessly on the sheet, and I reached over to take it. "How are you feeling?"

His eyes remained clouded, and I could see the confusion on his face. "I don't rightly know what's happened."

"You got hurt, and you're in the hospital. But you're going to be okay now."

I squeezed the thin, bony hand clasped in mine, hoping I was telling him the truth.

"I ain't been out to see to the horses for a long time, have I? They be okay?"

"They're fine. They're being well looked after, don't you worry."

He nodded once and dropped back into a doze. A few minutes later his eyes popped open again.

"Where's my Sadie?"

It puzzled me for just a moment before I remembered the phony Clarista Gaines saying Malcolm had been calling her that, a reference to his long-dead wife.

"Sadie? Honey? How come you ain't come to see me? Sadie?"

His agitation level rose with each mention of his late wife's name, and I had no idea what to do. As I rose to look for a nurse, his thin fingers clasped my wrist and held me fast.

"I think she just stepped out for a minute." I fumbled for the right words—if there were any that would calm the poor man's muddled mind.

"Liar!" He flung my hand away in disgust. "My Sadie's been gone a long time. Too long. Ain't right for a man to be alone so long." His voice dropped to a whisper. "Ain't right, is it?"

I thought about all the years my father had spent without my mother, even though he had the love of Lavinia Smalls to ease his way. I thought about my own husbands, one gone in an explosion of metal and death, and the other . . . Was Red gone, too? He'd scurried back to Beaufort, back to his ex-wife and children, after only a few short hours on the island. Maybe his loss would be slower, more subtle . . .

"No," I said, forcing myself to speak softly. "It ain't right at all."

I took a break at dinnertime on that fourth day of what I hoped would be Malcolm's recovery. I'd been existing on cafeteria food, grabbed hastily when I couldn't ignore my growling stomach any longer. And the truth was I needed a breather, some time away from the agony of watching the old man drift in and out of consciousness. And lucidity.

I stopped at the office, one of the many things I'd woefully neglected over the past few days. I closed the door behind me, welcoming the silence. I knew from hurried phone consultations with Erik that we had taken on a couple of new clients, but I couldn't bring myself to give a damn. My whole energy was focused on willing Malcolm St. John to recover, to be ready for the place I'd found for him thanks to suggestions from the amazing people at Memory Matters. They'd proved to be an inexhaustible resource for every question I had relating to Malcolm's dementia, and I felt confident he'd be well cared for in the facility I'd chosen. I'd had a chance for a quick tour in between my vigils at the hospital, and I'd made all the financial arrangements. I'd get my attorney to draw up whatever paperwork was necessary, and it only required the old man to recover sufficiently to put everything into motion.

I sat down at Stephanie's desk, glancing through the appointment book I insisted she keep, mostly for my benefit. She and Erik, of course, had it all on their smart phones and iPads and whatever other gadgets they carted around with them. I smiled, wondering if my aversion to all the newest technology was simply a kneejerk reaction to getting older. I didn't like change. Never had. And yet, there seemed to be endless variations of it in my personal life, almost on a daily basis.

I banished thoughts of my errant husband and opened Stephanie's supply drawer. I'd pull up the new clients' info and take some notes, try to make at least some small contribution to the operation of my business. I couldn't find a legal pad, and I'd just about decided to give it up and use my own desk when my hand closed around the box of notecards with the Harbour Town Lighthouse. Something about the size of them suddenly clicked in my head, and I lifted out the cardboard box with the clear plastic cover.

No, I told myself, *no way*.

I stared at the small box for a long time before turning it over and dumping everything out onto Stephanie's desk. For a moment, I refused to believe what I was seeing: Tucked underneath the cards were three envelopes, one white and two blue.

The exact shape and size my stalker had used to leave the ridiculous notes under my windshield wipers. And Red's.

"Stephanie?" I said aloud, unable to wrap my head around what was staring me in the face.

I don't know how long I sat there, memories and possibilities swirling around in my head before I found myself at last able to look at it rationally. The facts were ugly, but nearly inescapable.

One. I had been, if only obliquely, responsible for her father's death. No matter how often she seemed to have absolved me, the stark truth remained: If not for me, Ben Wyler would still be alive.

Two. She had access to my car, my schedule, my house. I gasped when I recalled Erik's tale of the book club that didn't meet. The same night the intruder had tormented me with the branches scratching against my window. The flowers? I'd bet if I checked, I'd find she'd been out that night, too.

And then the last clue clicked into place. She had access to her father's notes and case files. Hell, I'd even had her and Erik rifling through them back during our investigation of the suicide out on Jericho Cay. Maybe that's what had given her the idea. If Ben had had his own record of the case Mike Raleigh recalled from his course at Quantico, she could have replicated the notes with no problem whatsoever.

It all made sense. And yet it didn't. Could she possibly hate me that much and still be able to be pleasant to my face every damn day of the week? Could she share meals and make friends with Red's kids and love my partner with that much—

"No!" I shouted into the empty office. There had to be another explanation.

And then I remembered the last note with the single word: *Sorry.*

Without thinking about it, I picked up the phone and stabbed in Erik's number. I would never believe that he'd been a party to this in any way, shape, or form. He'd been betrayed just as I had. His cell rolled over to voicemail, and I hung up. My shaking fingers managed three digits of Stephanie's number before I slammed the receiver back in its cradle.

Face to face was the only way this could be resolved. I had just shoved the notecards and the damning envelopes into my bag when I heard a key in the lock. I whirled, my hand reaching for the Seecamp when I heard Erik's voice.

"Bay? It's me." He stepped inside, his face a mask of misery.

"What's the matter?" My mind flew to the frail old man in the hospital bed.

"What're you doing here?" He closed the door gently behind him.

"What are you?"

We stood staring at each other for a long moment before he dropped his eyes, and I suddenly noticed the papers clutched in his hand.

"Erik?"

"It's Steph," he said, his voice choked with emotion as he lifted the crumpled sheets.

For a second, I thought he might have somehow stumbled on his fiancée's deception, her unbelievable treachery. But his words, filled with anguish, told me his pain was something deeper, more visceral.

"Did something happen?"

"She's gone," he said simply.

"What do you mean, gone?" I found my hand grasping at my chest as if I couldn't breathe.

My partner shook his head and handed me the papers, damp with his own sweat.

I glanced quickly down the two pages of neat handwriting, so different from the plain block letters of my tormentor, and yet so familiar from the many messages and notes she'd produced in the office.

It was a confession of sorts, short on details, but heavy with remorse. Bottom line, I'd been right. I found no comfort in that, none whatsoever. Looking up into Erik's eyes, I knew there would be no satisfaction in having solved the mystery. For either of us.

"Do you want to talk about it?" I asked.

He didn't answer me right away. "She's gone to Arizona. To stay with her mother and stepfather."

"I know." I set the two pages on the desk and smoothed them out with my hands. "She says so in here."

"Did you have any idea?"

I reached into my bag and pulled out the notecards and envelopes. "Not until about five minutes ago. I'm still having a hard time believing she hated me that much."

Erik paced back and forth across the carpet, his hands shoved in his pockets as if he didn't know what else to do with them. "I don't think she hated you, Bay, I really don't. Maybe she *did* blame you—us—for what happened to her father, and it messed her up, you know?" The misery in his eyes nearly broke my heart. "I thought she loved me. How could I have been so goddamned stupid?"

I stood then and laid a hand on his shoulder. "Give it time, Erik. You're right, she's messed up, about a lot of things. Maybe getting away is the best thing for her and all of us right now." I reached for Stephanie's letter and held it out to him. "But don't give up on her just yet."

He didn't reply, simply crushed the papers in his trembling hands and tossed them into the wastebasket.

"Look," I said, trying for a return to normality, "I'm starving. You want to grab a bite?" I forced a smile. "I'm buying."

He shook his head. "Another time, okay? I have to figure out what to do about my stuff that's at her place, and we need to find someone to take over here."

"All that can wait. I'll be back in the morning, and we'll manage." I wanted to say that we'd done just fine, the two of us, before Stephanie came on the scene.

"How about Red?"

The question stabbed me in the heart, but Erik deserved the

truth. "I don't know. I don't see him coming back any time soon."

He raised his eyebrows in question, and I waved it away.

"Let's just take Scarlett's advice and worry about it tomorrow, okay?"

Erik managed a weak smile. "Okay."

CHAPTER
FORTY

I ended up just going home.

As I trudged up the steps from the garage and reset the alarm, I kept trying to recall a quotation from a poem, something about home and being taken in, but I couldn't wrap my tired mind a-round it. Carl Sandburg, maybe? I dropped my bag on the console table, admitting defeat.

Anyway, there wasn't anyone *at* my home to worry about. I checked the machine for messages, found none, and stood for a while in front of the open refrigerator door, pondering on food to keep from thinking about any of the staggering problems that seemed to have lined up like a phalanx of soldiers waiting to ambush me every couple of days.

Thank God for Dolores, who had left some sort of casserole on her last cleaning visit. A sticky note attached to the clear lid instructed me to heat it in the oven for twenty minutes. I didn't even bother to check to see what it was, just thrust it into the microwave, did a rough time conversion, and pressed the button.

I jumped when the phone rang, breaking my usual protocol by checking the caller ID. Lavinia.

"Dear God," I whispered, "don't let this be trouble."

I cleared my throat and picked up. "Hey, how's it going?"

"Just fine, honey, how about you?"

She sounded chipper and in better spirits than the last time we'd spoken. I tried to recall how long ago it had been and could-n't. My days sitting by the bedside of Malcolm St. John had slid into each other to the extent that I wasn't sure if it was Saturday or Sunday. Not that it mattered much. The weekend had been barren of the squabbling and giggling of Scotty and Elinor, just as the last one had been. I thought briefly of the half-finished redecorating of Elinor's room and wondered if there would ever be an opportunity—or a need—to finish the job.

"Bay? You there, honey?"

"Yes, sorry." I forced my voice into something resembling normality. "How's Julia?"

"Oh, we're just fine. We've been having the best time rooting through the attics. She has such an interest in this old place, and all the history that goes with it." She laughed. "Puts me in mind of you when you were a little girl. Always wanting to hear stories about the old days."

I didn't remember ever having the slightest interest in the past, especially, I supposed, because my mother seemed so obsessed with it. But memory is an uncertain thing, and if it gave Lavinia pleasure to believe I had shared my half-sister's passion, so be it.

"Find anything interesting?"

"Well, yes, that's why I'm calling. Remember those old journals you took out of here right after the hurricane? Didn't you say the girl's name was Madeleine or something like that?"

It seemed a thousand years since I'd looked up from one of the leather-bound diaries to find Julia staring at me from the open door of the attic. I shook off the feeling of dread, so well-remembered, and pushed it into a dark recess of my mind.

"Yes, Madeleine Baynard. Why?"

"Well, we found a portrait of her! Not a real portrait, mind you. Not like the ones hanging in the hallway and the front parlor. More of a sketch, I guess you'd call it. Julia and I thought you might like to have it."

"I'd love it," I said, not needing to feign my enthusiasm. Suddenly, I wanted to drag those musty books from the floor of the closet and lose myself in the story of someone who couldn't hurt me or disappoint me or betray me. "Yes, please do save it for me."

"You can pick it up next time you stop by." She paused. "How's Redmond?"

Another step into the minefield of my life. "Fine. He's been spending time with the kids. He loves Mrs. Burton, and we're so grateful to you for finding her for us."

Please, just let it go, I thought with a fervor that surprised me.

The bell on the microwave *dinged.*

"Listen, my dinner's ready. I'll talk to you soon, okay?"

"You heatin' up one of those awful frozen things? Why did I

spend all that time teaching you how to cook if you're just gonna—"

"No, no, it's something Dolores left for me . . . us. Give my best to Julia."

I had a moment of clarity so strong it nearly took my breath away.

"And be careful on those stairs, hear?"

"Don't fuss," Lavinia said sharply and hung up.

The single lamp next to the sofa cast a soft glow over the piles of journals I'd hauled into the great room from the closet. I'd polished off two bowls of the chicken and broccoli, and my empty plate sat congealing on the coffee table. Deciphering the handwriting was proving to be more of a problem than I'd anticipated, and the faded ink didn't help any. I was wondering if maybe I should try transcribing them onto the computer when the phone rang.

I gave thought to letting it go, but I managed to drag myself up and reach it before the answering machine clicked on.

"Bay Tanner."

"Bay, it's Marshall Miller."

My heart dropped into my feet.

"Malcolm?"

He cleared his throat. "I'm afraid so. I was here, just wanted to pop in for a few minutes, and he went into arrest. They did their best, but I guess it was pretty hopeless, what with his injuries and his age and all. I figured they probably wouldn't notify you since you aren't family, but I felt certain you'd want to know."

I could barely speak around the tears clogging my throat. "Thank you for calling, Marshall. I really appreciate it."

"It's for the best," he said, "hard as that is for us to grasp sometimes. He didn't have much of a life in front of him."

I thought of the caring people I'd encountered at Memory Matters and the residential facility I'd arranged for Malcolm. Maybe it wouldn't have been much of one, but it would have been a *life*. And again the image of my father, refusing the surgery that might have given him a few more years, flashed into my mind. Who was I to judge?

"I suppose you're right. Thanks again."

I hung up and slid down onto the floor, my arms hugging my sides, the pain and fear and betrayal welling up until I thought I might fly into pieces.

And the sobs came then, unchecked.

I wept for Malcolm, for Stephanie, for my father. And for myself.

I wept until there was not a tear left to shed. And then, right there on my kitchen floor, I laid my head down and slept.

Which is where Red found me, who knows how many hours later.

I felt his hand on my shoulder.

"Oh, sweetheart," he said, scooping me into his arms and pulling me close. "Oh, honey, what's the matter?"

My cheeks were caked with dried tears, and my eyelids seemed glued together. I forced them open to find his face creased in worry.

"Red?"

"Yes, Bay, it's me." He buried his face in my tangled hair. "I'm home. If you'll have me."

"'Home is the place where, when you have to go there, they have to take you in.' Robert Frost." I sighed and let my battered mind and body settle into the comfort of my husband's arms.

"Two points," I whispered into the enfolding silence.

ABOUT THE AUTHOR

Kathryn R. Wall wrote her first story at the age of six, then decided to take a few decades off. She grew up in a small town in northeastern Ohio and attended college both there and in Pennsylvania. For twenty-five years she practiced her profession as an accountant in both public and private practice. In 1994, she and her husband, Norman, settled on Hilton Head Island.

Wall has been a mentor in the local schools and has served on the boards of Literacy Volunteers of the Lowcountry, Mystery Writers of America, and Sisters in Crime. She is also a founding member of the Island Writers Network on Hilton Head.

Wall is the author of the Bay Tanner mysteries:
IN FOR A PENNY
AND NOT A PENNY MORE
PERDITION HOUSE
JUDAS ISLAND
RESURRECTION ROAD
BISHOP'S REACH
SANCTUARY HILL
THE MERCY OAK
COVENANT HALL
CANAAN'S GATE
JERICHO CAY
ST. JOHN'S FOLLY

All the novels are set on Hilton Head Island and in the surrounding South Carolina Lowcountry.

visit Kathryn online at: www.kathrynwall.com

CPSIA information can be obtained at www.ICGtesting.com
Printed in the USA
BVOW07s0930061113

335602BV00001B/69/P

9 781622 680412